Watching

Copyright © 2006 J A Pettitt
All rights reserved.
ISBN: 1-4196-3476-3
Library of Congress Control Number : 2006903174

To order additional copies, please contact us.
BookSurge, LLC
www.booksurge.com
1-866-308-6235
orders@booksurge.com

J A
PETTITT

WATCHING

2006

Watching

PROLOGUE

I AM an Angel!

Or do I mean a spirit, or a ghost even?

Well anyhow, it doesn't really matter who or what I am, as much as WHY I'm here!

Aye, and there's the crux of it all, because I know what I have to do, But I don't yet know WHY!

Other than to say that I know someone must be hurting real bad and it MUST stop!

All very "La De Da" I know, but it does happen. In fact, it happens quite often. For those of you who believe in something (anything) after death, and are not conceited enough to dismiss it all out of hand, then you will understand what follows, as for anyone else, well they've stopped reading already!

You see, although I have been here before many times, I have only been a "Watcher." I have never used this format before. In fact I am feeling a bit smug, bugger it, I am feeling "Cock A Hoop[1]" with myself. You see, the person writing this really believes that this is their idea!

NOT SO! There has never been an original thought....
Well not for a very long time anyway...

TRUST ME!

I am back here in Durham City. My Home! Durham is a

small university city, ranked alongside Oxford and Cambridge and is located in the North East of England. It is steeped in history and was once home to the Prince Bishops of England, answering only to the sovereign. Still called "The Land of the Prince Bishops," Durham is surrounded by the River Wear which forms the natural moat for the Castle and Cathedral on the hill. The Cathedral is the resting place for Saint Bede, The Venerable Dean. Durham Cathedral was once classed as the eighth wonder of the world. Finally completed in the twelvth century, it stands as imposing and grand today as ever. Throughout the centuries this almost impregnable city on the border of England and Scotland has played a major strategic role for the Monarchy.

In later years the County of Durham was renowned world wide for its shipbuilding, steel and railway engines. It was indeed home to George Stephenson, inventor of the "Rocket," the first steam railway engine. A few miles to the north lies the City of Newcastle Upon Tyne, original home of the "Geordie," but everyone in the North East is now called such. These inhabitants are renowned throughout the world for their friendliness, generousity and sense of humour. A blessing indeed, in the close-knit mining villages dotted around the County, as circumstances and history have often made this part of the country the poorest in England. However, through hardship comes resilience, and WE Geordies have a saying: "The Lord only gives yer what yer can cope with." IT IS HERE WE BEGIN!

CHAPTER 1

She didn't really want them here, but she knew it had to be because that was what was done! Soon someone would come and take her to bed to rest because that was what was done as well (when they didn't know what to do with you). She couldn't say who was there, because all their voices just made a humming sound in her head, and she couldn't look up because that would let them in!

"AW RAY. RAY. RAY...MY RAY........."

❧

They were waiting for her to cry, to make those loud choking sobbing sounds, to heave and jerk and rock with a wet face, and the "snots tripping you up" that was what usually happened. They could understand that!

She wouldn't do it. What was in her she couldn't share with anybody. Oh she was crying, but not that soft, showy crying they all wanted. NO, all of her was crying, with ANGER, and JEALOUSY and HATE...for all the world. Her belly was crying, her bones were crying, her head was crying...and she knew that if she looked up just once, it would all come out! If she looked at their faces, at their eyes, it would all come out! She couldn't share it, it was all she had left of him. She had to remember, she needed to, but she also needed to be greedy and do it by herself. After all whose bairn[2] was he?

"MINE...MINE. MY BAIRN, MY RAY, AW RAY RAY RAY..."

Hetty and Jean were helping her out of the seat now, to take her upstairs because the doctor had come to give her something to make her sleep, and she wanted to sleep. Oh she wanted to sleep forever, because then she could dream! And in her dreams Jessy knew he would NEVER be gone. Dreams had always been Jessy's escape over the years, the only thing that sometimes kept her going, and she was anxious to get back to them now because she needed to see his face again, and hear him call her "MA!" To see his bonny hair and to smell the soap and tobacco smell of him...

Wait! she told herself, NOT YET. Soon, best to do it by yourself, lass, because then he'll be all yours

Again!!!!!

So Jessy looked and nodded at the feet she passed, allowing them to offer their condolences in phrases like, "Such a shame, lass" and "Lovely service though wasn't it?" The lasses were thanking them for coming, and she could see the doctor's shiny shoes at the bottom of the stairs.

Not long now, no not long now...but why was everything happening so slowly and so muffled like in a big snow fall, when everything was hushed and heavy? Then Jessy had a thought, Oh wouldn't it be lovely if THIS was a dream, but she knew, real deep down, that she was not going to wake up from this one!!!! The feeling in her was SO very BAD, she knew it had to be real, and with this realisation her head started again to say, "Aw Ray, Aw Ray AW RAY"...over and over again. She would never stop saying his name, she loved his name, it WAS HIM. He had been her Ray, her Ray of comfort, a Ray of love but more than anything her Ray of hope!!!!!!!!

Ray was born in 1926, then there was two more about every three years, then a five year gap to the last one. She loved them all, Freddy, Hetty, and Jean, but mebbie because Ray was the first she had always loved him a bit more. Or mebbie it was because of Bullum, because the more she loved Ray the more Bullum seemed to hate him. From being a bairn he'd always took the brunt of Bullum's temper at first only to protect her and then later for the others too.

She'd married Bullum because she had to. No she wasn't pregnant, but she was no catch and getting a bit long in the tooth. She was past twenty when she had married him, skinny and plain and from a "poor as piss" (as Bullum used to put it) family. Her Ma had told her to marry him or get out. After all, who else was going to ask her? So she had. There was no love in the union, and Bullum was aptly named, he was a Bully. A one-legged, loud-mouthed, tight-fisted bully. He only wanted someone to cook, clean and service his needs. He had some kind of war pension, (she never knew how much) and he was a money lender (a bad one, always charging too much interest for people to afford to pay him back, and never having enough clout or bottle to collect when they didn't). Still he always seemed to have money, not that she had seen much of it over the years.

But she really knew why she had loved Ray the most, in the beginning he had needed her most. He was born a sickly child, skinny, scrawny and weak, nothing particularly wrong with him, just weak. The advice from the doctors was "to try her best, but not to expect more than a few months, he would be prone to every and all infection and was probably not strong enough to cope." So she had bound his little body with cotton wool, padding him up in the winter and nipping bits of in the summer, rubbed him with goose grease once a week, saved coppers from the housekeeping to buy medicine and mainly kept him away from Bullum. He thrived, aye he was always catching something, coughs and colds and the like, but it never stayed with him long. For some reason Ray liked life, no more, he loved it, seemed to gobble it up. Things never seemed to get Ray down for long. She remembered he had even been a smiling baby, always quiet and content, as if he knew Bullum would take it out on Jessy if he cried during the night. The others hadn't been as considerate, many the times she had a hiding over the years.

So her Ray had grown to be a man. He still had to take his salt tablets to help with the boils and carbuncles. He never got them on his face, but for a lot of years he was never without one or the other on his chest or his back or sometimes on his neck. He always wore a scarf, no matter what the weather, when he had one on his neck. That's how Jessy often knew because when he got older, Ray wouldn't tell her. He was too proud, and he was always a bit ashamed, believing that people would think he was dirty. Him dirty, never, never in this world. He was always messing over what he looked like, always had, from being a bairn. Why, Ray bathed or washed two, sometimes three times a week! Bye they must have been sore, especially those carbuncles. She remembered seeing one on his back with four big "mattery" heads the size of tanners. He had asked her to help him with that one, because he couldn't get at it. It took some doing, that one, but she managed to get rid of the stinking yellow puss, the poison, and rub some salt into the puncture marks from the needle to stop it getting infected. He never said a word, and it must have hurt like buggery, but he just sat grinding his teeth.

She remembered how he had told them all a funny story about his salt tablets. He had been to the pictures with Big Gloria (not called because she was that big, but only because Freddy was also courting a lass called Gloria and she was really little, so she was called Little Gloria, to stop any mix up). Wasn't it funny that the lads were to both marry Glorias and that they would always be known as Big and Little Gloria. Anyway, they were sitting in the pictures in the dark, and Ray now and again had one of his salt tablets. He hadn't told Gloria about his problem, in case it put her off, but Gloria thought Ray was sneakily eating sweets, and was too greedy to give her one, so she sat in a huff for the whole of the film. Every time Ray went to put his arm around her she pushed him away. In the end she said to him that he was eating "bullets" and was too greedy to share, so our Ray had just put two of the salt tablets in her hand and sat and watched as she gobbled them down, and then brought them and all of her tea back up as she was running up the aisle to get to the lavvy[3]. Oh they had laughed, even Gloria had laughed in the end.

"OH GOD, WHY, WHY, WHY?WHY TAKE HIM BEFORE ME?"

When it had been Bullum, if she dared, she would have sung and danced when he died. Whaaat a feeeeling! She was FREE. Free of his hidings and his swearing and shouting but most of all free of his filthy dirty cruel ways. The relief of never having to hear him shout, "Ower here Cunt" while he lay on the couch unbuttoning his trousers. She knew what she had to do, take off her drawers and sit on "it" and bring him off. It had to be done this way because of him only having the one leg. It was off from right up the top as well, so it made it hard for him to balance. He had tried in the beginning to be on top, but he kept rolling away. She remembered she had found it funny and smiled at him and told him it didn't matter. She had thought his fist was going to smash right through her face, she heard her nose crack and her head was like a firecracker. She nearly fainted, she remembered wanting to faint, then he had yanked her over him and was shoving it in. He wouldn't let her pass out, he shouted for her to "Fuck it, ya Cunt. Fuck it" and as he shouted, he nipped at her, then worse he was biting her, biting her hard. She knew she was bleeding in places, he was biting at her breasts and she still couldn't move, it had all been so quick!

She knew he had come because the biting stopped and when he knocked her off the couch onto the floor she was wet, but she was wet in a lot of places. When she looked she was bleeding all over, her nose was pouring, but what shocked her more was the number of bites there were over her arms, shoulders and breasts. One nipple was hanging off, and she remembered being surprised that there was some even on her belly. She didn't know what to do, so she just crawled out of the room as he snarled at her to get out and let him sleep.

That was the first time she had gone to see Wilmy Moyes. Wilmy fixed everybody up, everybody like her. There was a good few, it wasn't out of the ordinary for wives to get a backhander now and again, especially on a weekend when the men had been for a drink. She was good, they all said she was good, even the men who slipped her a bob or two now and again for keeping her mouth shut.

Wilmy had been "doing" for as long as she could remember. She started helping her mam and carried on from there. Now she was the main "fixer" for the whole of the estate, aye, and it was still growing. They were still building, mind you, they only put the dregs here, the "skivers" "dole wallers" "bad detters" and sometimes just the unemployed, but it was all good business for her because nothing was as sure as poverty makes folk sad and then angry. Wilmy could see herself maybe having to take on a "young un." Well, if she kept on doing the laying out and the fixing and what about the unwanted "buns in the oven" aye, she would mebbie need somebody.

Wilmy thought she had seen it all, but she hadn't seen anything like this before on any woman, not even the sluts. Eeh the viciousness of it, the pure viciousness!

"Sit down, Hinny, come on through and sit yersel down. Awe divna be crying now, we'll soon have ya fixed."

When the lass had come to the door, she hadn't known what the damage was, but when she got the coat off her and saw her standing there in her slip she felt sick. Oh aye her face was a mess, but that was normal damage; the rest she had never seen the like of. Why the lass had more bites than Auld Nick himself, and they were deep annuall. She could tell now that she was going to have some sewing to do. Better get her on the couch, and give her the gin, and plenty of it, she could see this was gonna be a long job!

Jessy couldn't remember a lot about the rest of the night. It seemed that Wilmy had been sewing forever, she had managed to stitch her up and even to put her nipple back, but none of it looked very pretty. Well so what? As Wilmy said, she hadn't been a raving beauty before, and who would want to look bonny for a cruel bastard like that? She could see the sense in that, and the thought that he might leave her alone gave her some comfort.

Jessy had gone home to her Ma only the once, after the

first time. She never bothered again. It wasn't that her mam didn't care, but as her mam told her, "It happens all the time, lass, and anyway you'd do better to keep out of his bloody way, surely you can do that. Why he's only got the one bleeding leg!" It was only later, after another hiding, when she had got far enough away from Bullum, (the doorway) and she felt brave enough to shout that she was going to leave, that she found out that her Da and him had an "agreement."

Oh he liked telling her about that, about how her Da had owed him money, and about how it would be forgotten when he married her. "But that wouldn't count if you fucked off, so get in here and shut the fucking door, you stupid twat!!!! And I'm hungry annaull[4]" Bullum looked at her as he shouted, knowing he'd won, and turned away and gave a low laugh!

Jessy did as she was told! She slowly walked through to the scullery[5]. She needed to think, she'd pretend to be making him something to eat, but she knew within a few minutes he'd be asleep anyway. He wasn't really hungry, and he'd a belly full of beer. He just wanted to show her who was boss!

As Jessy dropped wearily into a chair she realised he'd done just that! She thought of the few times that she went to visit her Ma and Da, how her Da couldn't look her in the eye and always went out for a walk or to see to a bit of business! She wasn't angry, she accepted that the both of them had never loved her like she loved Ray, or even any of the others. It had been enough to them to provide for her and her Da had done that over the years, in a fashion anyway.

He was a miner and worked hard, but he played hard, and there was never much left after his playing. Her Ma had done mending and cleaning to eeke it out, so her Ma hadn't had it easy either! Jessy remembered feeling that she had always been a bother rather than a comfort, even when she tried. Ruthie, her sister (younger by 18 months) had a better time of it, mainly because Ruthie was bonny, or mebbie because she knew that she was able to get round her Da, and to get more out of him. She remembered even her Ma had sometimes stroked and brushed Ruthie's hair. Black, shiny and wavy. Aye, Ruthie was bonnie!!! Life had taught Jessy that bonnie lasses had an easier time of it, like when they had both been in service together, Jessy got the hard dirty jobs, so that Ruthie could stay nice and clean to wait table. Nevertheless, she loved Ruthie, and she knew Ruthie had always loved her too. Over the years Ruthie had told her she was "not that bad" and even tried to convince her that her hair would change (from lank and greasy brown) to something different later, sometimes even trying to "rag" it into ringlets for her. It always dropped and went poker straight, but Ruthie had bothered.

She remembered Thomas, her older brother. He'd been lovely had Thomas. Always happy and laughing and full of love. Jessy had never thought of Thomas once in her life without thinking of his smile. He'd died when he was seven and she was five. Now there was the real favorite, all her Ma and Da's love for her seemed to die when he did. They had both got measles. Ruthie had been lucky and was sent away to stay with a neighbour (everybody wanted to look after Ruthie). Her Ma said "Tommy just wasted away" and then the pneumonia killed him. The warmth was gone from the house, and Jessy, many a time wished she could be with her brother, wherever he was! There had been others, one died after a couple of months (Benjamen), one was stillborn and then there had been miscarriages. There must have been lots of miscarriages because it seemed her Ma was pregnant for a lot of years!!!

Now, lying here in bed, hearing the "Tar rahs" of the last few stragglers, a feeling of total regret came over Jessy, not for

Ray but for her Ma and Da, because if she had lost Ray in the same way, mebbie she would have treated the others different as well! Mebbie? She never got close to her Ma and Da, never got the chance to say she understood, or to even try to make up to them, but she couldn't think of that anymore, not right now. The stuff the Doctor had given her was taking her somewhere else and she wanted to go, she wanted to go so much. She knew that if she was ever to get through this, she had to dream. Dreams and memories had served her well always, they were her comfort!!!!!!!!!!! So she slept.

"Ma, Ma, I'm back. Is there owt[6] to eat? I could eat a scabby horse!"

Ray could always eat a scabby horse, he was always hungry. Nowt[7] filled him for long, but that was because he was never still, always doing sommit. Today he'd done the washing at the public baths for her, Jessy knew she was too far gone with the fourth un, to go herself. No wonder the bairn was hungry. Why it was a good 2 miles to the baths, pushing that old pram. Not so bad going, all downhill, but eeh, coming back with wet washing was a heavy haul, specially on those skinny pins of his. She wished Bullum would give her a bit more, just so she wouldn't have to take in washing! But every time she mentioned being short he made her pay in other ways. So she'd do the washing!

He was out now, probably collecting money. Aye he could get around on them crutches when he wanted to! Dragging that big fat body door to door, then to the pub to spend what he had collected. Oh but when he was in the house he never moved off that bloody couch, lying there and reeking of sweat and stale beer. He was even too bone idle to use the lavvy out back, and had a "piss pot" beside the couch. She really hated the smell of that room when he was in. Everything was sour!!!!! But he wasn't due back for a while yet, so she could get on with her work. First of all though, feed Ray. He was already in the pantry trying to find the bread and dripping!

"Ray, Ray, out of there. I've got broth, and I'll dish it out now."

"Aw, mam, not broth again!!!!" then he stopped and looked at her. "Aw well at least it's filling with the bread, eh Ma?" He put his head down and sat at the scullery table.

She never had to say much to Ray, it was as if he knew what she was feeling. She hated making broth, but she did it twice a week anyway. She knew if there was nowt else in, that they could still eat!!

Jessy sat down with Ray. She treasured these times when she watched her family eat. Aye it was only broth, but today it did have a few bones thrown in, to give a bit of taste, instead of the usual carrots, turnip and barley. She soothed herself by thinking At least it's a hot meal. A lot more than some get, and there's always plenty of hot "stotty cake[8]" to go with it!

When Bullum was out, the house was a different place, the smell of the washing drying on the lines, strung from wall to wall, and over the fireguard. The laughter in the house, from the bairns, (mostly Freddy and Ray) "tom fooling and fighting." Eeh, they were like chalk and cheese," thought Jessy, There was only a couple of years between them, but Freddy was already bigger than Ray. He looked like a twelve-year old, rather than seven, that was all the Stotty cake he rammed into him. He was even the same shape as a stotty, round and dimply. That wasn't the only difference though. Freddy was a greedy lad, always wanting more, and making a fuss, and it never seemed to bother him if he was taking somebody else's share. Freddy had to have it all! It wasn't that he was a bad lad, he just seemed to have no give in him. Hetty the bairn of four years was a good lass, she just seemed to find Ray and Freddy funny and she loved being around them. She didn't seem to smile much, but her eyes would follow them all over the place. Well that was mebbie her way, we're all different. Jessy rose, and started the tidying and the making of His tea.

It was all done! The house was tidy, the tatties and turnips in the pan, to go with the haslet, table set, and the bairns were fed and washed. Jessy had put her clean pinny on and combed her hair (a habit she'd got from being in service). He was due any minute. Even Bullum couldn't moan tonight, thought Jessy. Aye but it depended on how much he'd had to drink. Sometimes he'd just eat and then sleep it off on the couch, other times he was bad-tempered and foul-mouthed, giving her a quick punch or slap, then making her go upstairs with him to satisfy his filth. They never knew his moods, so they had all, Jessy and the bairns, taken to looking out of the window when he was due, to try to see the mood he was in. Ray said he could always tell by the way he walked, but Jessy always waited to look at his face, and when he was close enough, his eyes. Bullum had hard eyes that never softened, or if they did, Jessy had never seen it, Eyes with cold blue middles, small and squinting eyes. Jessy knew that when they squinted like they were nearly shut, and if he was grinding his teeth between muttering to himself as he walked, then she was in for it.

He was coming round the top corner now. "It's alright, Ma, he's going real slow, he must have had a skinful. We'll be alright the night," said Ray. They all came away from the window and sat down except Freddy, who went to the door to wait for him. Jessy never knew why, his only reward was either a cuff round the ear, or on good nights, a stroke on the head. Tonight he got the stroke. Everything was going to be all right!

The bairns had gone out to play, Ray had taken Hetty in the old pram, and even Freddy had gone! Normally he stayed to see if Bullum left any of his tea, so he could gobble it up in the scullery. It was better that they were out, because Bullum liked his tea in peace, and the bairns couldn't make any noise or play when he was in anyway. Let's not ruin a good mood, thought Jessy. She was looking forward to the night. If Bullum slept she could pop next door to Ellen's for a cup of tea and a natter.

What happened next she was to REMEMBER FOREVER, with a FEAR SHE WOULD NEVER RID HERSELF OF!!!!!!!!!!!!!!!!!!!

CHAPTER TWO

He was eating his bread and butter now, while she was mashing the "tatties" and turnips together. She went to the pantry for the haslet to go with it. AW NO, MY GOD NO! There had been four slices, four big fat slices, now there was ONE. He'd kill her, what could she do? He was already waiting, no money to get more, and no time even if she had the money. She tried to slice it in half, so it would look like two. He was shouting for his dinner now. There, done! Not very neat, but if I turn them over and pile his plate with the mash, mebbie he wouldn't notice.

She thought she'd got away with it, he was eating and saying nowt. Just as she was starting to relax she heard a low growl, and knew no more until she was knocked off the settle[9] by the range when the plate with the dinner on it hit her on the side of the head. She must have been slow because she would have normally got out of the way after the first blow, but when she turned her head the first thing she saw was Bullum above her. One of his crutches crashed down onto her arm and shoulder, he hadn't caught her properly and she knew there was more to come. She was crying for him to stop, that she would get him something else. She knew he couldn't hear her, he was enjoying what he was doing too much, and the look on his face told her he was not done. He was calling her filthy names, and bringing the crutch down on her with almost every swear word. She knew she had to protect her head, so she rolled into a ball by the side of the fire. As she did she saw the poker sticking out of the coals. She had to stop him, he might kill her this time, but she had to be quick because if she left her head bare she knew he would cave it in. She grabbed for it, but her fingers wouldn't work, they were all bashed and bleeding, and she couldn't get a proper hold. Out of pure desperation she tried again, managing to grasp it with her thumb and palm, she pulled it out and with every last bit of strength she had, she poked the red-hot end into his good leg. She remembered wishing she could swing it and really hurt the bastard, but it did the trick. Bullum suddenly stopped and dropped, first onto his one knee and then onto his side, the sounds coming from him were horrible. He had his head down when he lunged for her, that's why it was so unexpected, now he was holding her head by the hair and when she looked at his face she knew she was as good as dead. She tried to get away but he was not weak now! They were both on the floor, and by god, he was strong. There was nothing she could do, she was dazed, hurting and bleeding and very tired of it all.

"Try to burn me, ya lazy cunt, would you? Would you eh? Now it's your turn you twat!!!!!"

Then he had her head above the fire, and he was pushing down harder so that her face and head got nearer the burning orange coals. She put her hands on the fender to stop him pushing, she could feel them burning, but the fear of her head burning made her keep them on and push back, but he was winning, she WAS burning. She closed her eyes as she smelt her head burning, but the heat was still burning her eyes. Her face was burning now, really burning, she could feel her skin going tight. She thought of pork crackling because she knew she was cooking.

Her head was free. She could hear shouting and she had just enough sense and strength to push herself away from the coals before she collapsed into them. She passed out for a couple of minutes, then she kept coming in and out of consciousness. She knew it was Ray who had stopped him because just before she went out again, she saw Bullum lunge for her bairn, she heard the others screaming and crying and then she was gone again!!!

"Aw Ma, Ma. Please be alright, PLEASE MA.

"Bring some more water, Freddy and some butter annaull"

Ray was putting her hands in bowls of water and sprinkling some on her face with his hands when she came round.

If her throat had worked she would have screamed with the pain that tore through her body but she couldn't speak, never mind scream. In the same instant she thought of Bullum. Where was he? She needed to know where he was, she needed to know if they were safe, at least for the time being.

Ray caught her looking around the room through eyes that were barely open and he knew immediately what was in her mind. "He's gone to the pub for a pie. It's alright, he's not here, Ma."

As the relief came, so did the pain again. I must think, must stay with them, she thought and as she looked down at Ray tending her, she wondered why he was wearing a balaclava in the house. She tried to concentrate and as she looked at his face she said to herself, Not too bad, he didn't look too bad at all. A split lip and a few bruises, nowt that he didn't get most weeks from Bullum. She was so relieved, she'd thought in his temper he would kill the bairn annaull. He must have burnt out, thought Jessy.

In the background she could hear Hetty sobbing, and she turned her head a little and there was Freddy, just sitting quietly looking at her. He was trembling, but he couldn't say anything to her, he just kept staring at her. She tried to smile to show them everything was alright, but her face wouldn't let her. Her eyes wouldn't open properly and she knew with a great suddenness that she was really hurt this time.

"Ray, go get Wilmy," her lips cracked as she tried to form the words and nothing came out.

Ray bent his head to hers, "What, Ma? What? What do you want Ma? I cannot tell what you're saying. I'm gannin for Wilmy, Ma...alright?"

She nodded slightly, then he was gone.

He'd meant to kill her. Oh aye, as sure as god made little apples he'd meant to kill her. When Wilmy looked at what lay in front of her, by the side of the range, she knew that if the bairns hadn't come in when they did, she would be "laying this lass out the night." Bye he was a cruel fat bastard and no mistake, she was going to have a word with this one, no doubt about that, and she'd hit him in his pocket annaull. That might make the bastard smart a bit, she thought.

As Wilmy looked down she saw that the older lad was kneeling beside the poor lass, he was rocking back and forth with his hands folded into his chest, just saying, "Ma, Ma, Oh Ma!!!!" over and over again. He'd had a go at him annaull, by the look of his face, but she'd see to that later. She lowered the littlest bairn, the lassie from her hip to the floor and asked the other lad to keep an eye on her. She didn't know if he had heard, he hadn't said owt since she'd got here. She couldn't worry about that now because by the look of things she had a hell of a lot of work ahead of her, "needs must."

She slowly rolled Jessy over. Dear God what a mess. The lad beside her looked at Wilmy with wet frightened eyes. "It looks worse than it is lad, we'll soon have her fixed up and back to normal." But Wilmy knew that Jessy would never look normal again. Most of her face was burnt, less at the bottom and gradually getting worse to her brow and her forehead. It dawned on Wilmy then that he had tried to push her head into the fire, and she couldn't stop herself from saying out loud, "The cruel bastard, the cowardly cruel bastard." She looked back at Jessy and thought that luckily most of the burns weren't too deep and would heal, except her forehead where she had lost most of her hair. What was left was just charred friz, and she knew from experience that this would never grow back properly, nor would her eyebrows and lashes. Thank God for small mercies, although it would hurt like buggery for a while, her face would eventually heal. Well, in a fashion. It was her hands Wilmy was really worried about. "Eeh, she must have been as frightened as fuck," she said to herself, "to hold onto that range that long."

The lad was holding a pot of dripping and was just about to smear it onto Jessy, Wilmy bent down and took the pot out of his hands. "I'll do it soft-like," he said to her between sobs.

"I know you will, hinny."

She said, "It's just that we've got to get them burns clean first, so we'd best get her to mine, where I can look at her properly."

As the younger lad started to cry the older one looked at Wilmy and said, "What about us? We can't stay here. Please don't take me ma away!"

She looked down and her heart softened, she sighed and then cheerfully said, "Oh dinna worry, ya can all come. I need to look at your face anyway, and even if it's a bit knocked about, I'm sure yer ma will be pleased to see it when she comes round."

Bullum would pay for this, for the keep of all of them. Who knows, it could be for a full week or mebbie even more. Wilmy tried to ease her conscience a bit by thinking, Oh she'd get the lass fixed up all right, but she wasn't a charity. After all she had to live as well!

They managed to get Jessy into the old pram, she was still out for the count. Best thing for her, and the bairns, thought Wilmy. Slowly, because the pram had no tyres only the outer wheels, they trudged back to Wilmy's house in Elk Avenue. Introductions had been made on the way, so now Wilmy knew all their names. She thought that Ray, the oldest lad, must have felt every bump of the journey, probably more than Jessy did at any rate, because as she was pushing, he was pulling. Every time they got to a hump or a kerb he physically lifted the whole of the front wheels over the offending obstacle.

Wilmy lived in the corner house of a cul de sac, so everybody knew her comings and goings, but the neighbours, instead of just standing on the doorstep, or peering out from behind grimy net curtains as was usual, the sight of this pityful group brought them out into the street.

"Eeh, what a shame," said Joannie Mowlem. "You've got your work cut out this time, mind you have, Wilmy." Others nodded in agreement and came closer to look at the mess of a woman lying over the pram.

Joannie's husband, John said, "You'll be lucky if you pull that one round." At this Joannie elbowed him in the guts, and pointed to the bairns. John doubled over and said nowt, just gasped and kept quiet. Joannie's claim to fame on the estate was that John had never raised a hand to her. This was regarded as quite a claim until you realised that Joannie frightened the shit out of John. She was three times his size and had a temper to go with it. More than once she laid into him in the street because he'd had a drink out of his dole money before coming home with it. In fact, when Joannie bragged to the other women about this, her stock phrase was, "He might be the laziest twat on God's earth but he has never laid a finger on me." This brought howls of laughter, as everyone knew John's only job in life was finding ways of doing as little as possible. In later years he became a much sought after advisor and expert on "How To Fiddle The Social." More people were gathering now, someone said, "That fat bastard wants some of his own medicine." Murmers and nods followed, then the usual "Eeh what a shame" and "nobody deserves that."

Wilmy was enjoying this attention. After all it might do her a bit of good, there was still some of them on the estate who didn't use her, those who saved up, or borrowed for a Doctor's visit. If she could pull Jessy round she would definitely be thought of differently, but that depended on her pulling the lass round. With this in mind she turned and said to the crowd, "Well I'll be getting her in now. Who'll give us a hand getting her out of the pram?"

People were stepping forward when the laddie, Ray, came and stood in front of the pram and said, "No, we don't need your help, thanks but we can manage," and looked at Wilmy with tears still in his eyes. The look on his face of pure desperation and of wanting to protect his Mam touched Wilmy. She'd had seventeen bairns, eleven of them lads, and never had she seen a look like that on any of their faces.

"Aye, lad, you're right. Your Ma wouldn't want anybody

else seeing her like this would she?" Wilmy turned and said, "It's alright, we can manage." The neighbours must have seen the look of the lad too, because nobody argued or said anything, they just turned to go to their homes. She watched the lad walk ahead, opening the gate and then lifting the front of the pram up the steps. She knew from how he was holding his head that he was hurting from his own good hiding, but he never thought that he couldn't do it. In fact, thought Wilmy, he could probably lift it himself if he needed to. He just gritted his teeth together and got on with it. Even when his nose started bleeding, he didn't stop to wipe it on his sleeve, she didn't think he even noticed. Oh he was special. Wilmy knew this. He was different, she searched for words in her head. HE WAS A "GOOD UN!"

Jessy was sleeping at last, she hadn't slept much in the two days they'd been here. Wilmy had changed the dressings every six hours and kept the burns clean, but that was all she could really do. The rest was up to the lass. She'd also checked on the "bun in the oven." Until now everything seemed to be alright down there, which was a miracle in itself. The lass had tossed and turned for the two days she had been there before falling asleep knackered. Her face would heal, in a fashion, but her hands were a different matter. Wilmy knew that at least two of her fingers were broken and had set them before bandaging them, but the burns were real deep and without a doubt they would never straighten out properly. "Eeh, well thank God for small mercies. It could have been worse, not much mind you," she said aloud.

Jessy didn't know about Ray yet, and by the time she needed to, he would look a lot better. Anyway he'd been lucky, thought Wilmy, one more clout on the head would have definitely killed him. She hadn't know the extent of his injuries until after she'd seen to his Mam, and that had taken a good few hours. She'd fed them all and got the other two settled down to sleep. The worst of it was trying to get the lad's balaclava off. When she went to pull it off he let out a hell of a yelp, there must be something wrong, this lad didn't shout for nothing. It was this noise that brought Freddy, the younger lad out of bed to investigate.

"How about if I just bathe your face for the time being eh?" asked Wilmy, "then we'll look at yer head a bit later."

She hadnt got the words out of her mouth when Freddy said, "His head hurts. He hit me Da with his crutch so me Da gave him a lathering. He didn't half lather him annaull, but I stopped him, Wilmy, didn't I Ray? I shouted at him to stop and he did, didn't he Ray? Didn't he, when I telled him to?" Freddy had blurted all this out with pride and was now sitting on the floor next to Ray. Ray put his hand on his shoulder and said, "Aye, that's right, Freddy, you did that."

Although Wilmy couldn't bring herself to like this lad, Freddy, she could see that there was something between the two brothers. They were very different lads, yet there was a definite bond there, mebbie it was born out of the hardship in their lives. She shrugged, who knows, but it was warming to see. She didn't believe Freddy's story, knowing Bullum of old, she could easily picture the scene: the lad, Ray, had seen what was happening to his Mam and just picked up the first thing that came to hand, anything to stop what was happening. Bye he was brave though because he must have known what would happen to him. Mebbie Freddy shouting and Hetty crying had stopped Bullum, but Wilmy would lay a pound to a penny it was the grog wearing off a bit, that had made him come to his senses. He'd have known that if he went any further he'd be up for murder. Bullum was frightened of the "Polliss," he knew if they turned on yer they could always find something to get yer for.

"You're gonna have to let me have a look at that head of yours sooner or later, lad. Best make it sooner, eh?"

Ray looked at Wilmy and nodded, then he said, "Can we go somewhere else, just in case me Ma sees?"

She took him through to the parlour, which was part of the front room divided by two screens, the part that she kept polished for when she was seeing folks for an appointment. Wilmy sat him gently on one of the high back chairs and turned and told Freddy to go back to bed. Ray seemed relieved that there would only be the two of them to do what had to be done.

It was a sod to get off, the blood had dried underneath it. At first Wilmy thought that some blood had just run underneath, from the cuts on his face and lip, but there was too much of it. The whole of the balaclava was full of it, some still damp and sticky but most of it dry and hard. "I'll have to use the scissors, son, this bugger won't budge." Ray looked at her and nodded, there was so much trust in those eyes. Wilmy was extra gentle. First she cut a bit then she pulled a bit. "Eeh, where had it all come from? This thing is stiff with blood." As she got to the top of his head he winced, but still said nowt. She pulled a bit and the last of it came away.

The whole of his head and neck were a reddy brown colour, in the same shape as his balaclava. His hair was stuck to his head flat, but at the very top near the crown was a spot where the blood was still slowly oozing out. She tried to part his hair to see what was underneath, it was nigh on impossible because of the matted blood and hair. "Sit a while, lad, while I get a dish of water, then we'll be able to see what we can see. Do you want to tell me what happened? It might help to know so I can fix yer."

As Ray sat bowed over the dish he told his story in a calm and matter-of-fact way, almost as if he was talking about somebody else. "I heard him from along the street, so I got the others and went home. When I saw me Ma I just wanted him to stop, but I think he was too far gone. I hit him with his crutch, it was the only way to get him off her, but I musn't have hit him hard enough because he was on the floor and he grabbed me leg and pulled us down." Ray stopped for a second and thought, then said, "If I'd hit him hard enough I might have killed him. Anyway he started laying into me with both fists, but I was wriggling and kicking so not many punches caught me full on. I got loose, but when I was getting away, he threw his crutch at me. It hit us full on the head and me head started to bleed, so I put me balaclava on so me Ma wouldn't see." Ray paused then, "That's all that happened. The crutches weren't near him now so I knew he couldn't get us again. I told Freddy to lock him and Hetty in the scullery. I knew I could keep out of his way because he's not fast, he's too fat. Then he went to the pub."

While Ray talked Wilmy had a chance to see the damage to his head and face, and there was a fair bit. To say he hadn't caught him full on, one eye was nearly closed, two top teeth had gone through his lip, he was bleeding from inside his ear, but the worst of it was his head. There was swelling and bruising from where he must have pummelled the lad with his fists, but the cut that was caused by the crutch had laid bare some of his skull. Wilmy could actually see his skull, it was that deep. She looked. It wasn't a straight cut either, more like a flap, this would take some stiching, even if the lad was able to take a drop of gin without puking, it would still hurt like the Devil. "I'm gonna have to shave your head and get this stitched before it gets 'fected,'" said Wilmy. "It's gonna hurt. Will ya take a drop of gin, lad? It might help a bit with the pain!"

"Do ya have to shave me hair off? Can ya not do it with it on?" The tears spilled over Ray's eyes for the first time, and she knew why. His hair was drying around his face now, and it was lovely. At first, when she had been washing it, she thought that the blood had coloured it because it was orange when it was wet. Now she could see it was a yellowy gold, wavy and thick. The bonniest hair she'd ever seen. Wilmy couldn't help thinking of Bullum, who was bald, and Jessy with her ordinary lank brown hair. She wondered if there was mebbie another story to all of this. Anyhow, she'd think of that later, for now the lad needed her to ease his suffering a bit, and she didn't mean just the pain of his wounds.

"Oh, lad, never worry. I know what you're thinking, you think everybody will say that the 'nit nurse' shaved your head cause you had lice. Well the way they gossip on this estate, I have only to tell them it was me who shaved yer, and by the morrow the whole world will know." Wilmy had tried to make a joke of it, she knew the lad was really bothered about this. He'd had nowt in his life, but he had his hair! If it was her hair, she wouldn't want to lose it either. "Anyway it'll grow back in no time at all."

"How long?" asked Ray. "How long till it grows back?"

"Oh a month or two," said Wilmy, knowing that a month or two to a bairn was a lifetime.

He looked at her and took the gin that she had poured for him, and drank it down in one. She could tell it hurt his throat, but by now this lad was used to pain, and to hiding it.

He never coughed or wretched, just ground his teeth then said, "Best get on with it then eh?"

Wilmy nearly broke down herself when she was cutting and shaving him. "Eeh it was truly lovely," she thought. It curled into perfect rounds when it hit the floor and it was so thick and healthy. She hoped it would grow back the same, but ya never can tell. Sometimes shock does funny things to folks.

The gin was taking effect now, the lad's eyes kept closing. They would soon open, when she started stiching, but for now she would be gentle and give him a break from the pain.

Seventeen stitches, that's how many it took, and it was difficult. He'd sat there and never made a sound, only the constant grinding of his teeth. The other two were both up and in the room by the time she had finished, so she'd given them a slice of bread and marge and now they were playing with Madge's kids across the road. She wanted this lad to sleep now, he deserved it. It didn't even matter that he was on her couch with his dirty plimsoles, because for some reason Wilmy felt for this bairn. As much as she felt for her own, mebbie more when she thought of the life ahead of him. Well mebbie I can do something about that annaull, we'll see, she thought, we'll just have to see.

Wilmy had just checked on Jessy, there was nowt more she could do for the lass. The pain and the tossing and turning would keep her worn out and she would sleep again. She'd asked about the bairns, Wilmy had said they were safe and this seemed to sooth her. Ray had asked her not to say owt yet to his Mam. She hadn't, but she would know soon enough. He was right though, let her rest in a bit of peace for now. Wilmy sat down on the couch next to Ray. She was knackered, it had been a long day and she too needed to sleep. On her lap was the folded bit of old newspaper that she'd taken from the lavvy. She unwrapped it and touched the golden curl, then she quietly wept!

Jessy had been at Wilmy's over a week now. She was out of bed but still in a good deal of pain and sometimes her head went fuzzy and she had to sit down. That usually happened when she thought back to what had happened. She wasn't one for crying, but that's just what happened on these occassions. Jessy would apologise to Wilmy but Wilmy dismissed it with, "There's nowt wrong with that, it'll do you good to get it out of your system, instead of bottling it all up, anyway. It's natural after what you've been through."

Nevertheless she didn't want to cry, she wanted to feel hate and anger. She wanted to curse him and she wanted to imagine him suffering. The crying stopped that from happening. Looking down at her hands, even under the bandages, she knew they would never be right, but she thanked God that she would still be able to use them. How they looked didn't really matter, after all, Who cares what your hands look like? You're not a lady ya know. Her face was a different matter, she'd looked at it two days ago, and not since. Her heart ached for her old face, she could hardly recognise the one in the mirror, not because it was all tight and shiny with red patches, not even because she had no hair at the front. It was the eyebrows and eyelashes she missed most because without them, her face looked big and strange, and sort of stupid. A bit like those poor bairns that hadn't been born "quite right." This saddened Jessy more than anything else, she didn't claim to be clever, but she was definitely not stupid. Stupid people wouldn't know that the way yer looked would alter the way people treat yer. "Aw, dear me, dear me, what a palaver," she said and then she swallowed hard, and got up from the chair to go to the back window.

The lads were playing in the cornfield out back with the other bairns from the estate. Wilmy had taken Hetty on a bit of business so she was in the house by herself. She touched her belly, the bairn inside her was alright. Wilmy had checked her over and said, "It's a bloody miracle, but yer still carrying it well." She hadn't wanted this one, it only made life harder and she'd even thought of seeing Wilmy about it in the beginning. She hadn't made her mind up, weeks passed and then this happened. Well the decision had been taken away from her because as she gently rubbed her small roundness, she said to her belly, "Ya really want to be in this world, don't ya hinny? You've shown us all that alright. Aye you're a fighter alright, and you'll need to be, but I reckon you'll do good." Jessy gave three light pats to say goodbye, and went back to the window. "Eeh it was lovely here." She could see right over the fields to Durham, and there was the castle and the cathedral on the hill it was a Sunday so the bells were chiming. There just might be something to like life for again, thought Jessy.

Ray was in the field, the corn was high, and Jessy just caught a glimpse of his new balaclava, the one Wilmy had bought him to hide his bald and bandaged head. He wouldn't go out before that, saying he just wanted to stay with her.

Now the hate for Bullum was there, she hoped he'd burn in Hell. What kind of a man laces into a lad like that? She knew the answer, a coward, nowt but a coward.

She wrapped her arms around her stomach and said out loud, "I'll see my day with you, Bullum, as God is my witness, I swear I'll see my day, and I'll show you the same mercy that you've shown us. The Lord says, 'an eye for an eye and a tooth for a tooth' and waiting for that day'll make us strong. Naw you'll not grind us down anymore, we're here to stay, all four, eeh no five, all five of us. We're here to live." Her tirade had left her exhausted, she dropped into the chair and dozed.

When she woke the house was still quite, she supposed they were all out playing. She'd wanted to keep Ray in, but as soon as he'd got his new balaclava he was away. She worried that he'd hurt his head, but ya just couldn't stop bairns from playing. She reckoned that he'd heal a lot faster if he was happy and forgetting things for a while. With time on her hands she'd thought about what she could do. There was nowt else for it, but to go back. If she went elsewhere, she knew the bairns would be taken away and put in a Home. Why did they call them "Homes" when they were just workhouses. No point in trying her Ma and Da, she knew they wouldn't have them all, they couldn't afford to feed them! Which reminded her, she must find out how much she owed Wilmy. She knew the lads were eating her out of house and home, especially Freddy. He was a greedy bugger that one. She knew it was him who'd took the haslet from the plate. Sometimes it was hard to love Freddy. She'd decided that she would have to pay Wilmy back a bit at a time, out of the housekeeping, although it would be a bit because there was never really enough to go round. Nevertheless she'd find a way. She patted her stomach, when this one was born mebbie she'd get a little job or take more washing in. Ray was old enough to look after them for a few hours a day. But what about his school? He loved school, he hadn't been much lately because his plimsoles had worn through and he had no proper boots. He was always worried about how he looked. She'd tried telling him that some kids didn't even have plimsoles to wear, all he said was, "Aye but that's not me though is it Ma?" No that was not her Ray. It never bothered Freddy. Freddy was just the opposite, you had to catch hold of that lad to make him get a wash. Sometimes yer could plant tatties in his neck, and he was never tidy. As soon as she stitched a button on, it was off again, he just didn't care.

Now that Jessy thought about it she hadn't seen Freddy get a wash all week. She knew Wilmy wouldn't make him. Wilmy wasn't exactly "nippin clean" herself. Aye but she had a good heart, people said she did nowt for nowt, but Jessy knew that Wilmy had gone out of her way for them all. Especially Ray, aye Wilmy had a soft spot for Ray alright.

Wilmy had never really talked about her own kids, the lasses popped in sometimes with bits of food and had a cuppa, but they didn't stay long. They were all grown up, and had their own lives she supposed, but she felt that there was no love lost between them and their Mam. Rather they came because they should or because Wilmy would give them a bollicking if they didn't. The lads only came when there was owt heavy to do. While she'd been there she'd seen a few of them. In the main the lads were handsome and the lasses were bonny. That was Wilmy's gift to her kids she supposed, good looks. Rumour had it that Wilmy had been a looker herself in her day. Well she must have been to have had all those kids, and not to the one fella either. Jessy smiled as she remembered that she had been told that the Vicar had refused to christen the last two, until Wilmy got married. "They'd wait a long time for that coming." She must have been a strong woman, thought Jessy, not to care what people thought, especially in them days. Her Ma had said that they used to call her a Witch, Wilmy the Witch, because she was known far and wide. She only used to have bairns with Well to do Men in order that they could pay for the upkeep of them. That being the case, thought Jessy, she was a lot cleverer than all of the women she knew, including herself. Wilmy had her head screwed on alright!

Wilmy had been knocking for a good while now. Shame if the bastard's not in, she thought. She'd rehearsed what she was going to say all night, and she'd pulled herself together enough to face him. She was determined not to let him bully her out of what she had to say. Hetty was with her, but kept pulling away and saying she wanted her Mam. Little wonder the bairn didn't want to go in, but she would have to get over it, and the sooner the better. Suddenly the door opened.

"What, the fuck, do you want witch? Pissoff my doorstep." Bullum knew where Jessy had got to, buying a few drinks always loosened somebody's tongue. He'd been relieved really to hear that there was almost no permanent damage to the lad. There was no way of avoiding the "Polliss" if there had have been.

"I want me money, Bullum, for the mending and keeping of your wife and bairns."

Bullum came forward with one crutch lifted.

"Don't even think about it, ya yella bastard. I'm not Jessy, and if I don't lay you out meself my lads will do it for me. Aye and take fucking pleasure in it annaull"

Bullum stopped. Wilmy knew he was thinking, he still looked crazy but his crutch was back on the ground. She took the opportunity and continued, "I can talk to you out here about it, or we can go in. I'm not bothered, I've got nowt to be ashamed of, but I don't think you want the world to know exactly what ya did to that family of yours."

Hetty had been clinging to Wilmy's leg under her coat

through all this. Bullum just turned around and went in, but left the door open. Wilmy hoisted Hetty up and they both followed him. The bairn didn't cry, she just hid her head and clung tight, it was as if she knew she daren't.

She left the door open, just in case. He hadn't been at the grog, she knew it was too early, she'd planned that, but he had a helluva temper anyway, and she was taking no chances.

He sat on the couch and ground out from between his teeth, "Well how much?"

"Two pounds," said Wilmy.

"How fucking much?" He spat as he shouted, "You dirty thieving whore, if ya think I'm givin you two pounds yer fucking daft! I'll give yer ten bob, and I'm being generous at that. That fucking hovel that yer live in is no hotel, and I'll bet me balls they've had nowt but bread and drippin to eat. Ya can fuck right off. Two pounds, my arse. Why I'll see you in Hell first, yer dirty bitch. Why I wouldn't have paid a proper Doctor that much, not half that fucking much. I'll come over there and..."

Bullum went to get up, and Wilmy looked him straight in the eye and with a slow deliberate voice said, "Just you try it. Come on, ya coward, just you try. I've already told yer once what'll happen, and I meant it annaull. There's nowt I'd like better than to lay one on ya, and as God is my witness, I won't stop there, I swear I won't."

She put Hetty down and told her to wait outside. She was ready for this big sack of stinking pus, she knew she'd give as good as she got. She was no soft touch like he was used to, she pulled the stone rolling pin from under her coat. Aye she was going to enjoy this!

When Bullum looked at Wilmy he knew she meant it.

No woman had ever spoken to him like that. If you could call her a woman, thought Bullum, she was built like a navvy, and he knew she was strong, she had to be, to have shed more kids than anyone could count. Naw, this might take a bit of handling, he thought, cause when he looked into Wilmy's face and saw all that hate and determination, he knew she'd knock the living daylights out of him.

He sat back and said lightly, "Now no need for all this, lass. I was just a bit taken aback that's all. To tell the truth I haven't got that kind of money." He was looking at Wilmy all the time to see if she was swallowing it. She was saying nowt so he went on, "I could mebbie let you have half a crown a week, even that would leave us short, but I'll give ya me word. Ya know yer'll get it sooner or later."

There was quiet. Wilmy was still looking at him, then she just shook her head and quietly said, "Well let me tell you this, you'll give me it all now, cause I wouldn't trust ya as far as I can throw ya. I knew you were yella and now I know you're a lying bastard as well."

Bullum started to say something, but Wilmy went on, still slowly and calmly.

"Cause if ya don't, I'm gonna leave here and tell my lads that you threatened their Ma, and they'll be round here quicker than spit, to give you the biggest hiding of your life."

Bullum jumped in and said, "I'll get the Polliss to yer, as soon as yer go. Your lads will be able to do nowt at all then."

Wilmy looked at him, the boot was on the other foot now, and by the looks of him he didn't like it one bit. Now for the big guns, she thought.

"You do that, you just do that ya fat bastard. I really hope yer do," She paused, "Cause you were right yer know, about the whore bit. Two of my lads were born to the fella who is now the Chief Constable of Durham Police! I don't think the Polliss is going to interfere much do you? Specially when I tell them what you did first. They might even think you're worth locking away. I hear not many men like fellas that beat their bairns up."

He was silent now, and Wilmy was nearly worn out. It had taken a lot out of her, she knew he would love to land her one, but she had the upper hand and he knew it. She could tell by his face that he was holding his temper as best he could, he was grinding his teeth and muttering under his breath. He got up slowly and said through his teeth, "Wait here while I get the money."

He went past her, towards the stairs. The look he had given her would have frightened the shit out of a lesser woman. He was evil, thought Wilmy, real evil, because even with all that she'd said, she knew she would try to keep out of his way in future. He wouldn't forget this, not by a long chalk, and she definitely wouldn't like to meet him on a dark night because she knew he would "do for her" as sure as God made little apples he would.

She heard him going upstairs. He was a long time getting up there. Not so nimble with the stairs eh, thought Wilmy, that's where the lass could run in the future!

He threw the money at her, then said, "You've got your money, now get out, ya blood-sucking twat."

Wilmy picked it up and turned to go, then thought, well in for a penny in for a pound. She said, "Remember, Bullum, I can tell the Polliss anytime, so if you lay one finger on any one of them bairns again, that's exactly what I'll do! Nobody likes men who bash bairns!"

Bullum turned on her now, his face bright red with anger, but before he could say anything she went on.

"I'm not one for interfering with what happens atween man and wife. God knows I've seen enough of it, but I'll tell you this: if your lass ever comes to me again with anything more than a cut or a bruise, my charges will be more than you can imagine. I'll make two pounds seem like chicken feed, cause I'm sick to death of stitching up and cleaning up your mess. Aye and that goes for bites annaull, yer filthy pig. Mind what I'm saying, Bullum. Yer know I mean it."

Wilmy thought she had gone too far, he looked like he was fit to burst. When she looked into his hard cold eyes she knew he would never let it go. Then he blew, "What I fucking do with my fucking wife in my fucking house, is my fucking business. You mind your own fucking business. Now get out yer interfering slut."

"Ay I'll go," said Wilmy. "But think on what I said, Bullum. You made your business my business when you nearly killed your wife and son, and I'll not let that happen again, cause I'll turn ya in first."

His face was inches away from her now. She could smell him, he smelt sour, like kiddy's sick. There was another smell, the kind of smell yer gets in an undertakers, the kind that makes yer sad right inside. She had to get out and quick, or she knew she would cave in. She turned her head away slowly so he couldn't see the fear in her eyes.

"Get Out. Get fucking out!" His stinking breath was hot on her face as he shouted.

She turned to go, and pulled all the stops out now. She used everything she had left to turn back and steadily say, "Ya know I mean what I say, Bullum."

"I'll have to put ya down a minute hinny," said Wilmy, as

she stood Hetty next to her. The bairn was ashen and clung to her. She must be scared shitless, she thought, I know how that feels. Ya bugger a hell I do.

Wilmy had got to the end of the street before stopping, she was pleased about that because at least now she was out of sight of him. If he had seen how she was shaking that would have truly given the game away. He'd be a monkey on her back alright if he thought she was the least bit scared. She just needed her knees to stop now. She willed it to happen, holding on to a fence and pressing down through her body to her feet. She thought about what had just happened and the money in her pocket. Hugging Hetty to her, she smiled and bent down to the littlun's face and said, "Aye we did alright there. You were very brave. Aye we both did alright."

She stood upright and took a deep breath, her head was asking her if it was worth it? Worth making an enemy out of him. She remembered his face close to hers and the real black hate in it. She shuddered because she knew if ever he could get even, he would. Oh aye he would alright, and there was murder in that man, he wouldn't think twice about it. She looked at the lass who was still silent. She just looked up at Wilmy and waited, as if she knew what was going through Wilmy's mind. There was the same fear mirrored in the bairn's eyes as she knew must be in her own. As she looked at the bairn some of the shock went. Wilmy knew then if she had helped Jessy and the bairns, even in a small way, it had been worth it! Picking the bairn up again she gave her a loud smacking kiss and said in a cheery voice, "It's alright, hinny, it's all alright now. Let's go and spend some of that money eh? How about I buy ya some taffee and mebbie some bullets annaull?

CHAPTER THREE

It was time to go back, more than time. Jessy had been here nearly three weeks now. It had flown by, she couldn't ever remember being happier. The bairns had been happy too, they were different when he wasn't about. They played like normal kids, even Freddy seemed a nicer lad. She had started to like Freddy a bit more over the last few weeks, he'd lost some of his sneakiness. He just seemed like an ordinary lad now. Jessy knew she had dragged out staying here, they could have gone back a week ago, but she had been loath to spoil it all. Wilmy didn't seem to mind, not now that she was well enough to help around the house and look after the bairns herself, while Wilmy did a bit of business.

Eeh, she'd been good had Wilmy, not that she was soft with them. Many's the night she clouted one of the lads for giving her a bit of lip. It was funny that she was strict like that, even with her own, who were grown now. You'd think she wouldn't have any standards, what with what she'd seen and done in her life. Aye there was nowt like people for surprising ya, thought Jessy.

She didn't know what sort of welcome she'd get, but Wilmy had told her about the money, so she was hoping he'd keep his hands off her for a while, cause nothing hurt Bullum as bad as parting with money. "Ya nivver know, he might think twice about lifting his hands again." Saying it out loud comforted her, otherwise she didn't think she could make herself face the pure fear of walking into that house again. "Anyway that's not till the morrow, and today Ruthie's coming." Jessy stood up and went to the window to look for her sister, she was at last looking forward to something. Ruthie always made Jessy feel happier, mebbie it was because she knew Ruthie loved her, or mebbie it was because she was proud of Ruthie, who always seemed to be happy. And why wouldn't she? thought Jessy. Their lives were as different as chalk and cheese. Ruthie semed to sail through life, always being lucky. That's what being bonny did for yer, thought Jessy, then she felt awful for thinking like this, and chastised herself by saying, "Fancy thinking them things! Shame on ya, Jessy. Ruthie's a good person, and kind to you and them bairns. Shame on you."

Ruthie had visited Jessy a couple of days after the event, as soon as word had got to her. She'd heard about it at the undertakers where she worked. It was a great place for gossip, undertakers always knew what was happening to who. Ralphy, her fella, who was the son of the owner, said "It was a way of looking out for business" and that she should always keep her ears open. That's how she found out about Jessy and the bairns. Somebody had said that, "If Bullum the moneylender wasn't lucky, he'd be putting a good bit business their way," then they went on to tell what had happened. She'd hoped they were exaggerating as people do when relaying gossip. Ruthie thought, funny how bad tidings seem to give pleasure to the bringer as much as good.

She hadn't known what to expect. She was over the moon when she'd seen Ray out playing as she walked down the street. When he ran up to her, shouting to the other kids, "It's me Aunty Ruthie, it's me Aunty Ruthie," and got close enough to say, "bye you're the dog's dinner the day, Aunty Ruthie," she knew he would be alright. She had heard he was on death's door. As she looked at him she could tell he'd been through the mill, but he was a fighter, this one. He'd have to be, she thought, cause there wasn't a picking on him, he was built like a whippet. Whereas Freddy, who was walking slowly towards them, was the opposite, plump and chubby-faced, but when he smiled, like now, he had the look of an angel off one of them cards, thought Ruthie. Ray grasped her hand and said, "Bye yer look grand. Me Mam will be real pleased to see yer." Freddy took her other hand and looking up at her, asked, "What have ya brought us? Have ya brought us owt?"

"I have," said Ruthie, "but let's get in the door first, or else you'll have to share your bullets with the whole street." She knew that would quiten him. Freddy wasn't one for sharing.

Jessy was still in bed on Ruthie's first visit, so she gave the bairns the sweets and told them to go and play. She'd nearly had to push Freddy out of the door because he'd wanted to stay in to "be with Aunty Ruthie," but she knew he was only thinking on what she'd said about sharing. As she hurried them to the door she asked, "Where's Hetty? Is she with our Jessy?"

The door had been on the latch so Ruthie supposed Wilmy wasn't in. "Naw she's out somewhere with Wilmy," said Ray. "Wilmy says to tell yer 'it's not as bad as it looks' and she says me Mam is going to get better." He turned back now and tears filled his eyes, he asked, "She will won't she, Ruthie? She will get better?"

"Oh I wouldn't doubt it," was her reply, "if that's what Wilmy says, lad, that's what'll happen. Now go an play and stop fussin. I'll see ya both later." As she closed the door she wondered what had happened to the "Aunty" when he'd asked the question, then shrugged and took the latch off, so as not to be disturbed and went to find Jessy.

Ruthie wasn't shocked when she looked at Jessy. She'd seen some sights, training to be a Mortician. It was a job she was really proud of, because to Ruthie's way of thinking, it was nigh on a Profession. It didn't matter that she'd only got the job cause she was dating Ralphy, the undertaker's son. She loved it! She knew she would be good at it from the very beginning. Her favourite bit was doing the make-up for the laying out, and she was always real happy when the family commented on how well the deceased looked. Ay, I'm lucky, she thought, I love me life and I even love Ralphy a bit annaull, If ya could give luck away, I'd give you a shit load, our Jessy.

No she wasn't shocked when she looked at Jessy that first time, but she was so very sad for her. She knew that her Jessy must have been scared out of her mind. She imagined the smell of her own hair and skin burning, and thought, aw God, how do ya cope with that? It's enough to turn yer mad. Dear God help her, and she took Jessy's hand. When Jessy looked at Ruthie and smiled, there was no change in her, she was still the old Jessy. Her eyes were still kind, and Ruthie knew she was going to be alright. "Bye you look lovely, Ruthie," Jessy said as she pushed herself up in the bed with her elbows. "Come on then, tell us all the gossip. How's that fella of yours? Is it still the same one?" They had nattered and they had laughed, and Ruthie watched Jessy's shiny red face smile while it hurt, but they never mentioned what had happened on that visit, it was too soon.

"Aw, Jessy, you're looking loads better and you're up and about," said Ruthie, as she held her sister for a cuddle and gave her an extra kiss on the cheek.

"Aye, I'm a real pin up aren't I, you daft get!" Jessy was smiling as she said it "But you, now you do look nice. Dealing with dead bodies must suit yer, Ruthie, cause yer thriving." They both laughed.

Ruthie took off her hat and said, "Why don't yer make us a cup of tea and I'll tell yer about my surprise."

"Yer not up the stick are yer?" said Jessy lightly. "I can't see you in them fancy togs of yours with a belly the size of this." She pointed to the now ever-growing bump on her front. "Cause if you are, it's been a long time coming. How the hell it hasn't happened before now beats me." Jessy was joking, and she didn't know why she felt relieved when Ruthie said, "Naw, nowt like that. Anyway, have you forgotten surprises are supposed to be good news!" Jessy looked at Ruthie, took a long deep breath and swallowed hard to stop the tears. "Aw I'm sorry lass," said Ruthie, "I'm real sorry. I just wasn't thinking. I know that you've not had much good news in your life, lass. I'm real sorry," and she went to hug Jessy.

"Its alright, hinny, don't worry. It's not you, it's me. Lately I don't know what's the matter with us. I'm a real watery-eyed bugger. I fill up at the drop of a hat. Now don't worry, gan on, give us your news."

The sisters looked at each other and an understanding took place. Jessy didn't want sympathy and Ruthie wouldn't give it. She knew Jessy had to be strong and sympathy wouldn't help.

"I'm getting MARRIED."

"Oh Ruthie, that's grand. I'm real happy for you, lass. I suppose it's Ralphy? Well I hope it is, otherwise you've been a bit of a dark horse, our Ruthie," Jessy was laughing.

"Aye it's Ralphy alright. Who else would it be? He's quite a catch you know. And he's a lovely fella Jessy, He's spotless clean and tidy and never messy Jessy. Eeh that rymes!"

They were both laughing again. It was good to feel good, thought Jessy, and as she looked at Ruthie in her dark brown coat, with matching gloves, she knew that it was Ralphy who was the lucky one. Yes, she was bonny, but when Ruthie smiled, she could catch everybody up in her mood. That must be like a breath of fresh air, thought Jessy. She was smiling to herself when she finished the thought with "specially in an undertakers."

"Oh I know he hasn't got that much upstairs mind you," continued Ruthie, "but he's really kind, Jessy, and he thinks the world of us. He's worth a bob or two annaull." Then as if trying to convince herself she finished with, "No, Ralphy will do for me."

"There's no need to tell me, lass, it's you who's got to be sure, but I'm happy if you're happy. You are, aren't you?"

"Oh, aye, happy enough. I mean he doesn't take me breath away, but he's pleasant enough. Anyway there's more to life than a good fu......seeing to," said Ruthie quickly.

Jessy watched Ruthie giggle. She was glad Ruthie was thinking like this because in the past she hadn't, by God she hadn't. Ruthie had HAD a good few blokes, (the master's son at the Hall included) and every time she was In Love. Her looks had always attracted a lot of attention, and she'd taken advantage of that fact. Presents from this one and that one, she was always two-timing one or the other. How she'd kept up with names and times of dates amazed Jessy. But she was older now, and she'd known this lad Ralphy going on two years, so she must know what she was about. It would be nice, thought Jessy, if she could have been In Love this time annaull, but well yer couldn't have everything could ya? And the lad did have a future, even if it was a bit of an odd one. I know one thing, thought Jessy, I'd settle for her life any day of the week.

"So when's it to be?"

"Soon," said Ruthie, "Ralphy's buying the ring this weekend, and telling his dad, so we thought in six month's time. Ralphy says it'll take us that long to arrange everything and that summer's the best time for the business anyway. It's less busy, yer know. Bad weather brings on coughs and colds and stuff that turns to pnuemonia in the old uns, and we're all rushed off our feet."

Bye she was already thinking like a member of the family, thought Jessy. Eeh, she did love Ruthie, she could even make marrying an undertaker when business was bad sound exiting!!

Ruthie was blabbing on about a big do, at a church with a white dress, bridesmaids and pageboys. Suddenly Jessy had a picture in her head of Ruthie arriving at the church in a hearse, the horses all black with little posies in their bridles. The bridesmaids were the pallbearers in black, walking slowly behind, carrying bouquets and there was Ralphy waiting in the church in his black bowler. It was hilarious, this vision, then Jessy couldn't keep it in any longer, she started to giggle, slowly at first, then it all came out in a great roaring laugh. It hurt her face but she didn't care. She was laughing a real belly laugh and it felt so good.

Ruthie watched her, at first a bit frightened, then she was laughing as well. They held each other and laughed hard together. Ruthie didn't know why, but it was so good to see and hear it from Jessy that she was completely caught up. She didn't really care about the reason.

"Why yer bugger," said Ruthie, when it was over. "What brought that on, our Jessy?"

"Aw it was nowt, lass, nowt. I'm just pleased for yer that's all," said Jessy wiping her face on her sleeve.

"Here let's see ya," Ruthie took a clean white handkerchief out of her sleeve and gently wiped Jessy's eyes. "Well I hope everybody doesn't do the same thing when I tell them, cause I'll feel a real laughing stock." Ruthie looked at Jessy and smiled. "Eeh, it's really good to see you laugh, Jessy after what you've been through," and she put her hanky back in her sleeve. She gave her a quick peck on the cheek, before turning to pick up her cup of tea.

"Cheers," said Ruthie, holding her cup of tea up.

"Aye, cheers, and congratulations annaull said Jessy.

They sat silent for a few minutes, drinking the tea and getting their breath back. Then Ruthie turned to Jessy and blurted out, "Will ya be me bridesmaid, Jessy? Me chief bridesmaid?"

The change that came over Jessy was immediate and unexpected. At first she looked as if she was going to burst into tears, then all of a sudden, she was angry and shouting, "What the fuck are you on about, our Ruthie? Are ya mad? Why I can't even come to the wedding, never mind parade myself like a freak show. Is that what you want? To look extra good, standing next to yer FREAK OF A SISTER!"

Jessy was standing over Ruthie now, angry tears raging down her face. Ruthie tried to say something.

"But, our Jessy, I know..."

"Shut it! Just shut It, Ruthie, will yer I can't believe you! Are yer that dense? What are ya thinking?" Jessy was shouting as loud as she could, her voice kept breaking, turning it into a shriek. "YOU STUPID CUNT. YOU STUPID, STUPID CUNT!"

Ruthie was frightened now, not because Jessy was shouting at her, but because she'd called her a C.U.N.T. Ruthie couldn't say the word in her head, other than to spell it out: see,yew,en,tee. It was a bad word, she couldn't believe Jessy was saying the "c" word at her, her own sister. Aye, they swore, everybody swore, but only real bad men ever used the "c" word. She didn't know what to do, she didn't know how to stop her.

She was marching and swearing all round the room, using every swear word she could think of, calling Ruthie some really terrible names. Ruthie kept her head down, she didn't want to see Jessy like this. Then, suddenly it stopped. Ruthie looked up just as Jessy dropped into the chair.

She'd never seen Jessy cry like this, she didn't think she'd ever seen anybody cry like this. Big barking noises, hacking their way up out of Jessy's throat, her body was doubled and jerking. Ruthie was frightened for her, she was frightened for the bairn in her belly as well because the noises seemed to come from that far down, but there were no tears. Ruthie very slowly knelt next to Jessy and slowly and gently put her arms around her. Jessy eventually quieted, and then just as gently put her own arms around Ruthie. It was with pure relief that Ruthie felt Jessy's tears on her face. Just as they had laughed and hugged together, now they cried and hugged. Both of their faces and hair were sodden with tears. Both of them believed they were comforting the other.

"I'm sorry, Jessy. I'm really sorry. I didn't mean it like that, honest I didn't." Ruthie was stroking Jessy's back and saying "Ssshhhh ssshhhh there now. Sssshhh, hinny. Sssshhhh."

"I'm sorry," Jessy spoke into Ruthie's shoulder, and hugged her a little tighter. It came out deep and quiet because her throat was hurting. She was feeling calmer now but also guilty. "I didn't mean it, our Ruthie, the things I said. I didn't mean them, ya know that don't yer?" Jessy sat up, looked at her sister and waited for her to answer.

"Why I Man, I know that." Ruthie put her hands on the side of Jessy's face and looked straight into her eyes. She had to make Jessy understand that it didn't matter what she had said. It just didn't matter. Jessy had enough to worry about already, she didn't need anymore. Ruthie got her handkerchief out of her sleeve again and wiped her eyes. Then she handed it to Jessy, smiling and said, "Here, ya snotty-nosed git, take a blow. Then you'll have the pleasure of knowing that me whole arm'll be wet and soggy all the way home." Then she laughed and turned and said, "Suppose it's my turn to make the cuppa now, is it? I don't know. Ya come visiting and yer end up skivvying as well."

Jessy joined in this light banter, "Oh aye, that'll be the day, you skivvying? God forbid, why yer might get yer clothes grubby."

"You'll not be so bloody mean when ya see what I'v brought ya, ya watery-eyed cow," shouted Ruthie jokingly from the kitchen. "Aye you'll be falling all ower yersell to be me friend then, I know that much."

Jessy didn't say anything, she just smiled. Everything was back to normal. She didn't care what Ruthie had for her. It was probably a "cardi" or a dress. Over the years Ruthie had taken to bringing her something nice now and again. She said it was important to have nice things. Jessy was grateful because it saved money, but having something nice, as Ruthie had put it, meant very little to Jessy. After all, who did she have to look nice for? Nobody ever noticed anyway. Except the lad, he noticed. Ray always noticed everything, she'd forgotten about that. Aye, she'd wear what Ruthie had brought her, she'd put it on tonight, if only to cheer Ray up!

"Right are ya ready then, for me other surprise?" said Ruthie coming back with two cups of tea. She gave one to Jessy and put the other on the sideboard and went over to her bag:

"Taadaaa."

Ruthie was holding what looked like a black animal, she was shaking it in front of Jessy. It took a few seconds for it to dawn on Jessy what it was.

"It's a wig," said Ruthie. "It's a good un annaull. Why it's just the job, our Jessy, didn't I always tell yer you'd have bonny hair one day? Eh didn't I?"

Ruthie had her hairbrush now and was brushing the black animal. Jessy could see she was excited, she looked like a magician who'd just pulled a rabbit out of a hat. Now that Jessy looked at it she could see that it was bonny, aye and it did shine, but where had Ruthie got the money for it? It must have cost a fortune unless...... Jessy didn't want to go any further with the thought that was in her head. She shrugged and told herself, anyway what does it matter? Her need was greater.

"Aye and that's not all," said Ruthie, delving into her bag again. "Look...Make-up. I'm gonna make yer up Jessy, and then I'll teach yer how to do it yerself."

Jessy looked at her and smiled. She knew Ruthie was trying to fix things and she wasn't doing a bad job. She was quite looking forward to it now, mebbie Ruthie could make her look bonny? Now that was a helluva task! Mebbie she could make me look more normal though, thought Jessy and this pleased her.

Ruthie was still nattering, "There's really nowt to it, once you've seen how it's done, you'll be able to do it yerself. Now don't look like that. I got taught, so I know how easy it is. Why Ralphy says that I can 'Make a silk purse out of a sows ear' with me talent."

Jessy laughed, "Aye alright, but gan steady. I don't want the bairns to be taking me pulse, to see if I'm alive all the time."

"Aw, our Jessy, you are a case." Ruthie was laughing too now. "Why, here I am trying to save yer some money in the future, by teaching yer how to 'lay yerself out' and you're still grumblin. Now stop all that giggling and let's get on. I'm used to faces being a lot stiller than this!"

With the last remark they both burst out laughing again. It was a full ten minutes before Ruthie could start her task, and even then she had to keep stopping so she could turn away and giggle, so she wouldn't start Jessy off again.

It was done!

The wig was on (how she was gonna keep it on, Jessy didn't know, but Ruthie had said, "just put a headscarf over it in the wind, and the rest of the time gan careful"), her face was made up and Ruthie was standing back admiring her handiwork.

"Why, it's not me best work," she said, "But this is me first time with a LIVE UN." She was smiling, not only because of the joke she had made, but because Ruthie knew it probably WAS her best work, to say what she had to work with! The shiny face had gone, she'd powdered and rouged some colour into it, drawn eyebrows that were softly arching, added some rouge to Jessy's lips and combed the soft curls of the wig over her forehead. Ruthie could hardly believe the transformation. Jessy had lost that 'simple look,' she looked completely different. Naw, she wasn't bonny, thought Ruthie, but there was something about her. Her bones were good, that was it! The make-up had softened the boney look of her face, yet it had highlighted them annaull, even her nose didn't look so big. Her eyes without eyelashes looked big and wide, and the colour was lovely. She hadn't realised that Jessy had them green eyes before. Yes, she was real pleased, then she got it. Our Jessy looks like a Lady! She really does. Eeh, she'll be pleased, thought Ruthie with pride.

Jessy was waiting, looking at Ruthie to see if it was going to be alright. She didn't expect her to work miracles so she hadn't got her hopes up, but now that it was done, she wanted it to be alright as much for Ruthie's sake as her own. She started to feel a bit impatient, but also excited because Ruthie was looking at her and saying, "Aw, our Jessy. Eeh, our Jessy, wait till yer see, just wait till yer see!"

"I am waiting, ya daft git, I've been waiting ages while you pranced around," said Jessy lightly. "Well let's get this over with." Jessy got out of the chair to walk to the mirror.

"Wait, wait a minute," said Ruthie. "Close yer eyes and I'll take yer!"

Ruthie linked her arm in Jessy's then said to Jessy, "Now don't look til I tell yer! Promise?"

"Promise," said Jessy, "but let's get on with it, or the bugger will have have worn off."

"Stop! Turn! There now, are yer ready? LOOK!"

Jessy opened her eyes, never imagining what would look back from the mirror at her. At first she thought she was standing in the wrong place and it was Ruthie's face, then it dawned on her!

"MY GOD, RUTHIE! AW, MY GOD...I'M NOT UGLY!"

She was awake. It had been the door closing, even gently, that had brought her from her dreams. The lasses had probably been checking on her. She knew they meant it kindly, but she wished they would leave her alone. All she wanted to do was to sleep, the pain stopped when she slept. She was still tired, so very tired. She focused her mind on getting back, to remembering where the dream had ended. She slept again.

She dreamt of that day, the "Make-Up" day. It was one of the happiest days in her life. She remembered Ray's face when he had seen her, he couldn't say much, he was that shocked. Only thing he kept saying was his stock phrase, "Aw Ma. Aw Ma," as he looked at her in disbelief. Even after a good hour of sitting on the floor next to her chair, he was still looking up at her and grinning. Jessy had never been looked at like this before, she really liked it. It makes yer feel important, she thought. "You're quiet, our Freddy, what do yer think of yer Ma now?" asked Jessy. Freddy hadn't said a word since he saw her, nor had he hugged her or even looked happy for her.

"Yer look different. Ya don't even look like me Ma," was his reply. Jessy went over and cuddled him in to her, she stroked his head and then kissed the top of it. He never relaxed in her arms, he stayed completely stiff and when she pulled away from him, he still looked sullen.

"Don't fret Freddy, I'm just the same underneath. Why it's only a bit of make up." She was just thinking how change affected people in different ways when she heard the front door open. Jessy rushed to the mirror and tweaked the curls of the wig around her face (just like Ruthie had shown her) then smoothed down her pinny. When Wilmy walked in and laughingly curtsied saying, "What can I get you, Me Lady?" her day was complete, they were all so happy.

They had been home for two weeks now and Jessy and the bairns had settled into a routine, which mainly consisted of keeping out of Bullum's way. Funny enough, it hadn't been difficult. The first day when they had got home, he'd had a good laugh at her, saying "She looked like a fucking circus clown," then he shuffled out, went to the pub and stayed out all day and night. Since then he'd been out most days and nights and when he did come home, he was always dead drunk and slept on the couch.

After the first few days she asked, "Should I make yer any dinner the night?" not that it was going to waste cause the bairns could always eat more.

"Please yer fucking self," was all he'd said as he went out the door. So Jessy continued making it, and the bairns continued eating it. If this was the way it was going to be, then that's grand, thought Jessy, cause the last few nights they hadn't even gone to the window to look out for him, and the house had been a happy place to be in. Just the relief of not having him around made a difference.

She was sitting by the fire sewing, or trying to. It took a lot longer now because her fingers were all still bent and wouldn't move in the same way that they used to but she'd learn! Aye it'll take a bit of time, thought Jessy, but I'll get the hang of it. She certainly wasn't going to let it get her down, not when things were going so well. Why, HE'D even left her alone about the "Other Thing" annaull, so no, she wasn't going to tempt fate by asking for more. My God, that would be ungrateful that would!

"Penny for yer thoughts, Ma," said Ray.

"Oh I'm just counting my blessings, son."

And he nodded as if in agreement, Jessy knew he knew what she meant.

He was sitting next to her, her in the chair and him on the floor. Freddy was out playing somewhere(probably running errands for money), thought Jessy. Hetty was playing with an old rag doll that Ruthie had brought her a couple of years ago, nursing it and rocking it to sleep as she quietly sung to it and it was warm and peaceful in the room. She was startled at first when she felt the babby in her belly kick. It's about time, thought Jessy, I didn't think I was gonna hear from you at all.

"Ray, Hetty come and feel this." They both came over and she placed their hands gently on her belly.

"Is that the babby coming out Ma?" asked Hetty, backing off a bit. "No, she's only letting us know that she's alright, she's not coming for a while yet, hinny!"

As Jessy finished speaking, Ray cottoned on to what Jessy had said. "How do ya know it's a girl Ma?" he asked. "Why its not even born yet."

"Oh I know, lad, I just feel different when it's a girl. Like I felt different with our Hetty after you and Freddy. Why, don't ya want another baby sister?" she asked.

"Oh I don't mind. It makes no odds to me, cause we'll all love it anyway, well nearly all of us. As long as yer both alright is the main thing," said Ray.

He was growing up fast, it was shame, thought Jessy, cause he was still a young un. Eleven next birthday, but he talked as if he was the man of the house already. He sat back down on the floor next to her and started polishing his new boots. Before they had left, Wilmy had bought new boots and shoes for all the bairns, and a coat for the lads. "To help keep them warm when it was nippy," was all she'd said, then she'd gone through to the scullery before they could thank her or make a fuss. Mind you, they weren't new, but they were still good, and would give a good few years wear because they were certainly big enough. Wilmy had said that she got them a bit big so they wouldn't grow out of them that quick. The boots had pleased Ray, he put them on as soon as he got them and was running around shouting, "I'm gannin to school. I'm gannin to school summer AND winter!"

Freddy had looked at his and put them down after a minute and followed Wilmy. Jessy knew it wasn't to say thanks, rather to see what was in the other bags. After all, some of it had looked like food! Jessy had looked at the little booties for Hetty, they were lovely, shiny black with a gold buckle. She had put them on her little feet, and Hetty had tried to dance. She was trying to do a jig, she said, "it was like what the Morris Dancers did in the Market Place." Oh she had looked funny, with her real skinny little legs kicking this way and that, and her falling over. Jessy, Ray and Hetty had all been laughing.

Aye, that had been a fine night, even Freddy was happy. Probably because of the dinner Wilmy had put on the table. There was pies and stotty cake sandwiches and even a bought cake, and they all had "bullits" for afters. Freddy had stuffed himself so much that he went to sleep straight after he had finished eating and slept through to the morning. It was the one time Wilmy hadn't bollocked him for being greedy. She would always say, "That little fat git, he's not hungry, just plain greedy." Jessy didn't say nowt cause she knew that what she had said was right, but sometimes it hurt her. She knew that grub was Freddy's way of coping and that it gave him comfort. So Jessy only ever replied with, "Aye, I know but he'll grow out of it." Wilmy always replied back, "Yer better hope he does."

It was that night, their last night at Wilmy's, that Wilmy had given Ray a small tin box. He hadn't known what it was, so he had brought it over to Jessy to show her. Wilmy stood and waited this time, keen to see his reaction.

"Look, Ma. Wilmy says this is for me annaull What is it?" he asked.

"Well, read the top of the tin," said Jessy.

Ray looked at the lid and started to spell out the words, "Sss h sh o oo shoooe…"

"Aw, for God's sake," said Wilmy, "it says 'Shoe Polishes' and ya cannot get back to school soon enough if ya ask me!"

They both watched as Ray opened the tin. Jessy saw that Wilmy was nearly as excited as Ray, she felt a small pang of jealousy because she knew that this was a Good present for Ray, and that Wilmy must have thought long and hard about it. The fleeting feeling of jealousy passed and was replaced with pride, pride in her son who could even make a hard heart like Wilmy love him.

Her thoughts were interupted by Ray running between them both and saying, "Aw, look. Look at this and this, and this." He was taking out of the tin, one at a time, two small brushes, a soft yellow cloth and two small tins. "Aren't they grand!" he turned to Wilmy as he said it. "Why, they've never hardly been used. Aw, ta Wilmy. Thanks a lot." He grabbed her around the hips to hug her, and amazingly she let him, her voice softened almost to a whisper as she stroked his head and said, "You're welcome, lad." Jessy and Wilmy's eyes met, each of them gave a gentle nod to the other, each respecting the part they had played in this lad's happiness. Ray looked up and asked, "I don't have to share it do I? with our Freddy and Hetty I mean?"

Wilmy's reply was still gentle as she said, "Naw lad, that's for you from me," and then more lightly, "if ya can stop clinging to us for a minute, I'll show yer how to use it, cause it's an art ya know, getting a good shine. Quite an art."

Jessy's thoughts were interupted by the sound of Ray spitting.

"Have yer got to do that, our Ray? It nearly makes me heave every time I hear it."

"Sorry Ma, but it's the only way to do it properly. Wilmy said so, and anyway it saves on the boot polish. I don't want it to run out."

Jessy was a bit short with him when she replied, "That's all well and good, but Wilmy doesn't have to sit here and listen to your 'hockling' night after night, and anyway them boots can hardly need polishing all the time. Yer don't wear them enough to get dirty. You're still gannin to school in your 'sandshoes' most of the time."

"Oh but I'll wear them when the weather turns, mam, and anyway, polishing helps to keep the water out. Wilmy says it'll make them last longer as well"

"Wilmy this, Wilmy that," muttered Jessy as she got on with her sewing. "Why there'll be no boots left for the bad weather gannin on like that."

Ray didn't hear her, he was so absorbed in his task, and Jessy wasn't really angry with him. She was just a bit "cockly" what with being pregnant and everything.

She was to often think that she never saw him in a pair of unpolished shoes ever again. This one small gift had been the starting point of Ray being different to the rest of them on Shilbon Road Estate because he not only looked different, she knew he felt different too.

CHAPTER FOUR

Doctor McFarlan had been concerned about Jessy. He didn't know if she would get over the shock. It had all happened so suddenly. He had been the one who had attended her son Ray and until that day had never seen him before. He presumed because he would have appeared healthy enough.

He'd been a doctor here for almost eleven months and he could still count the times on one hand that the men came to surgery, apart from the ones wanting a sick note signed. He was also treating Ray's wife, and in his opinion both women needed the same!!!!! Total rest.

He'd left sleeping tablets with both sets of daughters, there wasn't a great deal more he could do at present. The only true healer was Time. "This family would need time," he said out loud. Jessy's son had died so suddenly, one minute sitting with his family, the next having a huge stroke, in what he could only perceive to be an entirely healthy body. And at Forty Nine? He was curious as to the cause and had asked the family if there had been any signs like headaches or dizziness leading up to the stroke. When it appeared that there was nothing to indicate any illness, he was perturbed enough to return home on the evening of the death, and take down one of his medical journals. He seemed to remember reading that past accidents involving head injuries could in some unique cases have an effect in later life. He found nothing that he didn't already know, and certainly nothing to quell his feelings of uneasiness.

As he sat in his office after returning to see Jessy, he thought of the stories he'd heard of this family, stories of the late husband, and his cruelty. He hadn't believed them, until now. He could see that this woman had suffered, the scars as old as they were, were still obvious, and her hands were totally deformed, but that was not what was worrying him. It was as if she had lost the will to live. He had become used to dealing with grieving families, but in all of his years as a doctor he had never seen grieving like this. The look of total emptiness in that woman's eyes was chilling to him. It was as if she was bereft of all hope, and without some kind of miracle Doctor Mcfarlan knew he would be lucky to bring her through this.

He pulled out her medical notes. There was very little on them, he understood that in previous years not many people had been able to afford the doctor, but Jessy's notes didn't even contain details of the birth of her children. He wondered who had tended to her, seen to the burns and such like. Well, whoever it was, they hadn't done a bad job, the fact that she'd lived proved that. She wasn't the only one, there had been quite a few inconsistancies regarding medical details when he took over from his predecessor, something he was still coming to terms with and having to correct. He would concern himself with that later. At present he had found what he was looking for, Jessy's age. She's in her seventies, he thought to himself. Well, she didn't look that old, sixties perhaps, she was still a trim women, and even with the scars, she had a certain elegance. She dressed well and kept a good clean home. She must have been active until this recent event now she seemed to have had all the life sapped out of her.

The last visit had confirmed his worst fears, she didn't

want to eat, nor drink, and she wouldn't speak to anyone, not a soul. Not even himself. He had explained to her how difficult it is to treat someone when they won't tell you how they are feeling. She had merely raised her head and looked right at him, her eyes had seemed to widen and as he looked into them he shivered. For a brief moment he had seen into her world, had seen the years of suffering, and as those green eyes had softened he understood.

He knew that all of those years of pain and indignity had meant nothing compared to what she was feeling now. He had stood in that room and felt abjectly humbled, and it was with some ache in his chest that he took a step nearer the bed and took her hand and said, "I'm sorry. I understand now, you need to be left alone. You need to do what you need to do." He was whispering, so that only she could hear, and there was an understanding between them now, he felt it. It was confirmed by the ever-so-slight increase in pressure from the hand that he was holding. Then she closed her eyes and slept. When he took that one last look at the doorway as he was leaving, he was relieved. She seemed to be breathing easier and her face had taken on a peaceful and content look. There was even a slight smile, not on her lips, but silly as it seemed, around her eyes.

The medication and instructions had been left with the girls. At least with tablets instead of a drought she would take some liquids to get them down. That would do no harm, but in the meantime, until someone sends for me, I'll stay away. Deep inside David McFarlan knew this was for the best, so why could he not accept it in his mind? He thought it was perhaps due to the losses he had endured in his own life. He was no stranger to bereavement.

David lost his Mam when he was only seven, and he'd been brought up by his Grandmother. Although she was a strange woman the love that she had showered on him had been his only mainstay in life. He smiled as he thought of his late Gran. She'd worked all her life to put him where he was now, if you could call reading tea leaves and palms working. Still, he thought to himself, she had used the proceeds from her so called Gift, to provide him with the education to get him to where he was today. At the age of twenty seven, he was, so the newspapers had made out, the youngest G.P. in the country, and that was entirely down to his Gran, and her belief in him.

From a young age she had noticed a difference in him, saw that he had a quicker and greater grasp of things factual than anyone his age, and she had pursued this belief with diligence. It was due to her that he had sat exams early, entered medical school when he was not yet twenty, passed every exam he sat with ease.

He could have gone anywhere at that point. He had thought about research or surgery, but he had wanted all his life to be a doctor, to help people. David believed this was best achieved at a grass roots level and had stood his ground, insisting that he wanted to be a G.P. He had even chosen to work within the poorer areas, knowing that since the introduction of the National Health Service he would still be able to support himself. He smiled as he remembered his Gran's face as he told her of his offer as a Locum in this area, the worst part of Durham, some would say the worst part of the north east. She hadn't been disappointed, in fact, just the opposite, she had hugged him and stated calmly that he must go where his gift took him!

Talk of the gift being passed down to him was commonplace from his Gran, she had been saying it since he was a lad. David's agile mind wanted to dismiss it as non scientific and just silly superstition, but over the years, he had feelings that he couldn't explain. They came as sorts of warnings or sometimes answers to his problems, just like a feeling of knowing what to do. Whether or not they were getting stronger as he grew older, or he was just learning to cope with them, he didn't truly know. However, they were certainly more frequent than they had ever been, especially so since he had moved to his new position.

He sighed loudly, blowing the breath out of his body and inhaling deeply. He thought again of Jessy and her son, he once again remembered the total devastation he felt at the loss of his mother and then the repeat of the pain when his last link, his Gran, had left him. He saw Jessy's face again in front of him, his body ached with sadness for her, he knew that he could not give her what she neded! Only her family could help her now!

The Doctor's thought process was interupted by the buzzer from the receptionist, indicating that there was a patient waiting. "Well, no point crying over spilt milk," he said out loud, trying to shake off the lethargy that had come over him. Then in a quieter tone, "Good luck Mrs Ste…Jessy, and pleasant dreams.

The bed was all soft and clean. Jessy liked clean, clean had been her friend over the years because "if yer had nowt, yer could still be clean." She'd often said this to herself and tried to live by it, not just because of the obviouse reasons, but because it had given her a small degree of dignity and perhaps even a slight superior attitude. It was something to hang on to when yer had very little else.

She was lying in bed, dreaming, or was she remembering? Then it came, that swift sharp ache in her, right down deep, like no pain she'd ever felt. She wanted her head to stop her from realising he was gone, she wanted to deny it. The words came out on a sob, "Not Ray! Not MY Ray!" Jessy had no sooner whispered the words when the thought came into her head, she thought it! She actually thought it! WHY NOT ONE OF THE OTHERS, GOD? WHY RAY?

Jessy felt sick with guilt, she was dizzy, overwhelmed with disgust for herself, but she still kept thinking it!

She remembered reading a book where the woman in it had got to choose which one of her two children could live, as they were being separated at a concentration camp. When she was reading it she'd thought, that's impossible. How can a mother choose between her bairns? Now Jessy knew how, how yer could choose because given the choice, she knew she would have chosen Ray. "Aye, within the blink of an eye I would have!"

This outburst had been very quiet, but it had tired her. She was holding her stomach and slightly rocking to and fro on her side, telling herself she was wicked and may god forgive her. The others would be a comfort to her because after all they were still her bairns." Throughout all this murmuring her head was still shouting, "Oh God, why MY Ray?"

She'd dozed and when she woke she could still hear voices

downstairs. Probably Hetty and Jean, she thought to herself. Freddy and Little Gloria and their lot had left a while ago, she'd heard them saying their goodbyes. Big Gloria hadn't come back after the funeral, her lasses had taken her straight home. The doctor had kept her medicated, and she was in no fit state.

Jessy wished for a moment that they had come back because the oldest lass was the double of our Ray, not only in looks but in ways as well. It might have been nice just to look at her. "That's selfish Jessy," she said to herself. "Yer know that Gloria needs them now cause if anybody is hurting like what you are, Jessy, yer know that Gloria will be. Oh by God she loved our Ray," Jessy continued talking out loud. "Gloria worshipped him, she'd been a damn good wife," and she added, "a good mother annaull." She paused, "But she never loved those bairns like she loved our Ray. Aw, poor Gloria, poor lass."

For the first time since this had all started Jessy felt pain for someone else. As she thought about her, she could't imagine how Gloria would live without Ray, any more than she would. Jessy thought about how they had been over the years. Aye, she had loved our Ray alright. Ray had grown to love Gloria, but Gloria had been swept off her feet by Ray from the first. Somebody had told Jessy that there was one who did the loving and one who was loved. Who was that? thought Jessy, Aw well never mind and her mind moved on. Ray and Gloria had always had their ups and downs, mind you! By God they had. Jessy couldn't remember a week going by when they hadn't been arguing and fighting about something (mainly money), both of them giving as good as they got. At the beginning she wondered why Ray had stayed with her because Gloria could test his patience like no other person on God's planet, but he had! And when the bairns came along, she knew Ray would never leave, not only because he thought the sun shone out of them, especially the oldest, but because she knew that in his own way he needed Gloria. He needed to be loved and believed in like she did!

Jessy had never known love like that, either given or received. It had taken her many a long year to come to terms with the physical side of marriage, and even now she didn't like to think of her bairns actually liking and taking part in this bit of life.

"I know it happens, so let's leave it at that," she said to herself.

But for some reason, she couldn't get these thoughts out of her head as she drifted back off, and she found herself thinking thoughts that she had long since pushed deep down inside of her.

Eeh, fancy having them feelings, fancy having them for a man. She'd gone through the whole of her married life dreading and wanting to escape Bullum's attentions. It must be lovely to be held and touched, and to not even mind the other. She wanted to drop off, but she couldn't get there, there was something at the back of her mind!!!!!!

She fleetingly felt something, It felt like a gentle kiss on her cheek. She knew she had definitely felt something, because something was happening, something inside her. She felt it again on her face. Am I crying? Was it a tear? As Jessy touched her face the memory that had eluded her suddenly surfaced. She felt at peace, as if she were about to go on a journey that would take her somewhere wonderful, with someone wonderful. As she dreamed, she did remember, she remembered that ONE TIME.

Although these memories were over thirty years old, Jessy was seeing them as if it was all happening again now. She could finally face them! Thoughts and feelings that had been too painful then, would help her now. All the guilt and fear of discovery of past deeds vanished. This was a greater loss, she needed these dreams!!!!

CHAPTER FIVE

After the period of The Burning Jessy had a fairly peaceful time. Bullum did give her a backhander now and again, but he never went at her like he used to. Mind you, she did stay out of his way as much as possible as did Ray. The looks he used to give Ray would have killed a cat. Aye, the hate was still in him alright, but Jessy reckoned he was never sober enough these days to do owt about it! He was drinking more and more, that was mebbie why he hadn't bothered Jessy for a 'bit of the other', or mebbie it was because of her face (well ya couldn't have a face full of make-up on all the time). After a while she realised there was more to it than that. Hell's bells, thought Jessy, when had he ever looked at her face anyway? Aye, there was definitely more to it than met Jessy's eye, but who was she to question her luck? Best leave well alone.

So in her own way she was happy!!

Jessy had another baby girl, she called her Jean. She only weighed just over five pounds. Jessy was relieved she was healthy after what the both of them had gone through. She was delivered by Wilmy of course, and although the labour had been short, it had been bloody painful with Wilmy needing to cut her to get the bairn out in the end. Afterwards Wilmy told her that the bairn was nearly breach. Jessy didn't ask what "nearly breach" meant, it was enough to know that the bairn was alright. As Wilmy tidied her up, and had a drop of gin herself, Jessy held the bairn to her breast and wondered what kind of life she'd given this one!

Ruthie had been married and Jessy had gone to the wedding. No, she hadn't been Matron of Honour or even a bridesmaid, but she'd had a good time. She didn't stay long because Jean was only a few weeks old and needed the breast, so she came away early and left the rest of them with Ruthie and Ralph. They all looked grand. Ruthie had kitted out every single one of them, she'd even bought a new Matinee Coat for the babby. Eeh, she was kind like that our Ruthie, thought Jessy, but so was he, Ralphy, cause after all it was his money that Ruthie was using. She was genuinely happy that Ruthie had got herself a nice lad. Oh, he was no looker, except for when he looked at their Ruthie, then a change came over him, sort of like a pride in his face and a gentleness in his ways. It changed his features, thought Jessy.

So time had passed, Ray had left school. He started working for a fella who bred dogs, not ordinary dogs but dogs that were worth a lot of money. He'd done well at school, hadn't left till he was twelve. Even then his teacher had said that he should stay on and sit some tests, but the way things were at home, he knew he had to bring a bit into the house for grub. Aye, Bullum was leaving them all alone, but he was meaner than ever with money, and Ray knew many's the time that his ma didn't eat. So he'd taken the job that was on offer, he was lucky to get it. There wasn't many jobs going, other than going down the pit, and Ray didn't want to have to gan down underground. He didn't think he could stand being shut up in the dark. There were plenty of them did it though, thought Ray, and good on them, but he dinna think he could. So Ray counted his blessings and got on with the job. He could always go back to The Learning later on. Well that's what the Teacher had said.

The first year in the new job was rough on him, all he did was muck out and clean and scrub the outhouses where the dogs were kept. It was bitter in the winter and because of the tin roofs, red hot and stinking in the summer. Yet he never missed a day. He loved the dogs, he would often pet them and snuggle up to them for warmth, thinking, the poor buggers were only used to breed to make money for the Gaffer. Naw they they didn't have much love in their lives neither. Ray would come home excited when the puppies were born and tell Jessy all about them, about how sweet they smelt and of how he used to lie down in the straw with them and let them lick him and chew at him. Those nights were lovely, thought Jessy.

So, all in all, life wasn't bad. They certainly all seemed to laugh a lot more, and although money was real tight and they were often hungry, by God they all counted their blessings.

Jessy stirred. She was finding it easier now to stay asleep. She needed to! No, she had to!

Freddy had left school annaull, (he hadn't ever been keen and missed more lessons than he went to). He didn't really have a job, but he used to run Bullum's messages which meant he went to doors, knocking for money. It seemed to work because Bullum was happy with the results. Whether or not it was because a bairn was asking, or because he was a vicious sod, breaking windows or throwing waste and rubbish at the doors, as Jessy suspected. It seemed to work and pleased them both. Freddy was the only one that Bullum could stand having around him. Jessy didn't like it, but it was the lesser of two evils. Truth be told, thought Jessy, the very fact that our Freddy wants to be around him makes it hard for me to get close to him. She recognized that left to his own devices and with his greedy ways, he could be another Bullum.

Well, not if I have my way. Naw yer won't get the better of me, my lad. Even as she was saying this to herself, she knew that she could do nothing about the cruel streak that was in Freddy, nothing but watch out for it! Like the times he would give Hetty a slap when he thought no one was looking. When he was thirteen she'd caught him pouring a cup of cold water over Jean when she was sleeping. He just stood and smiled when the bairn started crying.

Bye, she'd given him a real good hiding that day, and not with just her hands. She couldn't hurt him with them anymore. She'd used anything she get a hold of to pummell him. Eeh, she'd been mad with him.

Ray told her later that night that Freddy had seen Bullum looking at the bairn, and then he'd tucked the blanket in around her. "It's jealousy, Ma. Why me Da's never shown a bit of kindness to any living thing," said Ray, "and yer know how hard he tries to get him ter notice him, Ma. Anyway I've had a word and he's really sorry Ma. Honest he is. I've told him that if he ever touches one of the lasses again, I'll kick the shi...I'll give him a right good hiding."

Ray was waiting for Jessy's reply. She didn't know why he bothered, cause it was a thankless task, being Freddy's friend. It still wouldn't mean that he would share anything with anybody, Jessy knew that much. She also knew that Ray liked peace, and he needed to be happy with them all. He deserved that much, thought Jessy.

"Aw, our Ray, man, I don't know why yer bother. Yer know as well as I do he's only worried he'll get no supper the night." She paused and then said, "Well on your head be it, tell him he can eat when he's brought a bucket of coal in and after he apologises to us. I'm warning yer, and yer can tell him this from me. If I ever even think that he's been up to no good, or that he has laid a finger on any of those lasses, then he'll never get another morsel of grub in his gob again! And you tell him I mean it, our Ray. Cause I DO this time!"

It was a good ten minutes later that they both came into the room. She knew they had been talking about the apology. Freddy wouldn't want to apologise, she knew that, so it was a sullen, mumbling affair of, "I'm sorry" when it did come out. She let it go, for the sake of the others and for the sake of her own peace!

So Jessy and Freddy now understood each other, and even though Jessy was wary of him, she knew that as long as he wanted food in his belly, she would have the upper hand.

The girls thrived. Hetty finally had a playmate, someone to love and look after. It was funny to watch them. Whereas the lads had light hair and eyes, the lasses were dark. Miniature Ruthies, thought Jessy. Well good for them, at least they don't look like me or Bullum. They have my build though, long and skinny. Ray calls them "Pond Life" and when they laugh, he says it's cause they've got frog's legs. Our Ray has the same build though, and she smiled. It was a bit like the kettle calling the frypan "Grimeyarse."

"Eeh, that's a Wilmy saying," said Jessy out loud to herself. She hadn't seen much of Wilmy in a good while, in a good long while, thought Jessy. I miss her, I'll try and call more often, but everytime I've been, she hasn't been there.

She knew that if anything was wrong with her she'd know

about it, there were no secrets on The Estate, and anyway, Ray called in on her now and again. It had been a lot less often since he started work, but he still called. Jessy reminded herself to ask about her as soon as she saw Ray. Jessy looked back at the lasses playing together on the floor: They were bonny girls, already when she had them out they were turning heads, even strangers told her they were 'lovely'.

Sometimes they even offered a bullit to them. Jessy always felt happy when this happened, and in her own way felt a little more attractive. She would say to herself, "I made these little beauties."

As the years passed Jessy learnt to come to terms with the way she looked. The scars had healed and faded, but she never grew eyebrows or lashes again. What had made it more bearable had been the wig Ruthie had got for her. She didn't wear it in the house, but she never crossed the doors without it! She didn't bother putting the make-up on much, it took too long. Now and again, if she was seeing Ruthie, she'd make an extra effort and put some rouge on her cheeks and lips, just as Ruthie had shown her.

She was into her second wig now, she liked this one better. It was real hair, not the horse hair normally used. Not that Jessy cared about what it was made of, she just liked the style of this one better. It was just like what they wore in the films. She knew this because once a month she and Ruthie would go to the Majestic film house (Ruthie's treat). She tried over the years to thank Ruthie for what she'd done for her, but Ruthie just brushed it off. Jessy needed to say it, needed to tell her how much she meant to her because in a lot of ways it had been Ruthie who had kept them all going.

It was on one of these nights that Jessy remembered turning to Ruthie and saying, "Eeh, our Ruthie, what would we all do without yer, me and the bairns? If there's ever owt I can do for yer, yer know you've only got to ask."

"Don't be daft, lass, and if yer talking about that bugger on yer head, well there's always gonna be more where that came from. Let's face it, the last owner doesn't need it now, and I'm sure the Lord's got no room up there for anything other than souls, never mind owt else."

Jessy didn't want to laugh, she wanted to tell Ruthie that what she said was terrible, that it was sinful, but she couldn't hold it in. Her eyes started to water with the effort of trying to keep a straight face, but it all burst out when Ruthie piped up with, "Here, yer don't think the Lord wants them for himself do yer? Yer don't think God's pinching everybody's wig when they get there cause he's bald?" Ruthie pretended shock and as she turned to Jessy she said, "Bugger me, Jessy we're doomed. St Peter's not ganna let us in the Pearly Gates now."

Jessy hadn't had a 'belly laugh' like this for ages. She was doubled over, it took her all her time to pull herself together. It wasn't till they got to Ruthie's house that she calmed down. Ruthie lived over the undertakers, Naw, it wouldn't do to burst in on Ralphy and his family laughing their heads off, thought Jessy, She needn't have worried, there was no one in the house above the shop. She knew that Ralphy and his Dad often worked late when there was a rush on, and she supposed his Ma was in bed. Jessy was just starting to feel sensible again when Ruthie pranced across the room, saying in posh voice, "Peter, my man, I've decided to go blonde tonight."

The silence was broken, they were screaming together laughing, one setting the other one off. Jessy was laughing so much that she was leaking down below. She started pointing to the offending area, Ruthie knew what she trying to tell her, but it just set her off again. Jessy was laughing so much that she didn't care what else was happening, she couldn't have stopped anyway!

After they both calmed down, had both visited the lavvy and Jessy had borrowed a dry pair of knickers, they had their usual cups of tea and sat down for a natter. They both nearly started off again when Jessy said, "We're lucky we didn't wake Ralphy's Mam." Ruthie replied with, "I wouldn't worry, she sleeps like the dead!"

'Eeh, wasn't it funny,' thought Jessy. Ruthie could work in a place like this and still laugh. Mebbie that's how she coped?

"I'll bring yer knickers back the next time I come, our Ruthie," said Jessy, "but yer better give me mine back at the same time. I've only got the two pairs and those ones are me best."

"I'll rinse them through for yer. In the meantime keep them ones of mine," was Ruthie's reply, and she made a mental note to try to get their Jessy some new knickers.

Jessy was still chatting, "I think it must be when yer have bairns. Everything seems to go a bit slack down there," said Jessy as she pointed to her nether regions.

"Well, I don't think that I'll ever know about that because nowt seems to be happening in that area." Ruthie looked away so that Jessy wouldn't see the tears in her eyes. "Me and Ralphy have been trying for a good few years now and nowt's come of it. Mebbie it's just not meant to be!"

Jessy knew she was upset and trying not to show it, she always tried to be happy when they were together, but Jessy knew it must be hard for her sometimes, what with her talking about her brood all the time. She didn't mean to, but they were her life. After all there was only so much yer could say about taking washing in. Now that she thought about it, she realised why Ruthie made such a fuss of her lot, specially the lasses and most specially Jean, the little un. Why the times, thought Jessy, that Ruthie had offered to have them stay over on a weekend, and Jessy had said "No," thinking that she was putting on Ruthie. "Well I got that bugger wrong," said Jessy to herself. She'd listen a bit more in the future when Hetty said, "But me Auntie Ruthie loves us to go, she says we're not any trouble."

As she looked at Ruthie, a married, childless Ruthie, Jessy's heart went out to her. Jessy felt real love for this sister of hers. Her Ruthie, with her own problems, always tried to make her happy! Aw she always loved Ruthie but sometimes, like now, Jessy felt it so much. She went over and sat on the arm of the chair next to her sister, she put her arms around her and said, "Yer DO make me happy, our Ruthie, yer really do!" Jessy held her little sister and let her sob. Nothing was said, she just stroked her back and kissed her head and let her sob!

Although Ruthie died childless, she did know the very real love of Jessy's bairns. Jessy never laughed with anyone like she had laughed with Ruthie.

Jessy moaned in her sleep with the pain of remembering, but she had to keep going, she had to getto the next bit of her life. Even in her dreams she knew it was important.

CHAPTER SIX

It was 1943, everyone said that the war was almost over, but they'd been saying that for years. Jessy's life had changed very little, she still kept out of the way of Bullum because she was still frightened of him and his moods. It had been nearly five years that she'd managed to keep out of his way, but things came to a head and took a turn for the worse towards the end of the year for Jessy.

The money Bullum had been giving her for housekeeping had steadily got less and less and Jessy was often pennyless halfway through the week. All she had was what Bullum deemed to give her, the coppers she got from the washing and the bit Ray earned. Ray always tipped up the lot, but she wouldn't have that! Jessy would give him a bit back for himself. He would save it up until he could buy something to wear (always second hand). he was getting older now, seventeen next birthday, and he took a real pride in his dress.

Even that helped a bit, thought Jessy, cause when Ray got something new, he passed something down to Freddy. It didn't matter that it was a bit tight or a bit long, Freddy didn't really care. It was just another layer to keep the cold out to Freddy. Just as well, thought Jessy, there's no money left after feeding them to put clothes on their backs annaull. The lasses fared better, Ruthie always came up trumps for them, but Jessy didn't like to say owt about the lads because it looked like begging, and although she knew that Ruthie would help, Jessy got sick of relying on her and Ralphy to dig them out of holes. So she kept the way things were with the money to herself.

It was October and bitter, there had been snow already. The fire was on, but there was little enough coal left in the coal house for the morning. Never mind, I can nip out later to the coal yard, thought Jessy, It was Thursday and Bullum usually left the housekeeping on the mantlepiece as he went out. Ray was out already, probably looking for lasses, not that he ever had a problem there. Jessy was sick of answering the door to them, asking if Ray was coming out for a walk.

A walk my arse, thought Jessy, I know what's going on. But she didn't have the time to worry about that as well.

The lasses were already in bed, snuggled up together for warmth in one of the two bedrooms. The lads had the other room. Bullum had taken to sleeping on the couch full time now, so Jessy slept with the lasses. They weren't asleep, she could hear them giggling on together. She didn't mind, she just wished they'd wait until He went out.

Freddy was watching Bullum having a shave in front of the fire. He was balancing on the mantle with one hand, shaving with the other. "Aye, his face was clean alright," said Jessy under her breath, "But I cannot remember the last time I filled the tin bath for him to wash the rest of his body." As she looked at him she felt sick Yer dirty Sod, she thought, I bet yer could plant tatties in the muck on the rest of his body. He was putting his coat and scarf on now and Freddy was following him around, she knew what for, she wasn't supposed to see.

But she knew Bullum would give Freddy a few coppers on the sly. Freddy always grabbed it and hid it straight away. No, that lad wasn't gonna share, she knew he would leave with Bullum and spent it on bullits straight away. He would never come in the house and eat them, he would rather stand out in the freezing cold than share. Well, he'll be bloody cold tonight, thought Jessy, And I'll bloody let him be, by God. He can stand round the side of the coalhouse tonight till he's finished the lot! The greedy fat get!'

The door slammed hard, it was Bullum's way of saying he was still the Boss. Now that they were both gone Jessy started to clear away the dirty shaving things from the mantelpiece. "Where's the money then?" she said to herself. Often Bullum would put it under something, just to frighten her. She lifted the shaving mug, the bowl and the cheap vase. She moved the rent book and the coalman's book, nothing!! Could it have fallen off? Surely she would have heard it! Now Jessy was on the hearth, looking amongst the ashes, her face inches from the grate. She screamed and threw herself backwards, she was shaking and sweating, her stomach was turning till she thought she would be sick. Just for a moment she had imagined Bullum was behind her, she had even thought she had felt his hand on her head, pushing it forward towards the flames. Jessy sat for a while, trembling, the tears streaming down her face with relief.

Bullum turned away from the window, smiling, and shoved a sixpence in Freddy's hand.

A whole tanner this time, thought Freddy. Eeh, it had been worth having a laugh at his Mam. A whole tanner.

They parted company at the gate, neither of them saying a word. Freddy headed for the corner shop and Bullum for the pub.

I'm still the fucking boss around here. STILL THE BOSS, was all Bullum could think to himself as he hobbled along.

"Jessy, Jessy, pull yerself together lass. Nowt's happened,

come on pull yerself together," she was saying it out loud to herself, softly at first, then louder and with more determination. She gradually pushed herself up from the floor and leaned on the back of the chair to steady her legs. She said to herself, "It's your magination, yer soft lump, nowt but yer magination. Why ya could have had the bairns down here with all yer palaver. Come on, pull yerself together and let's get that money found!"

She'd searched everywhere, but she knew deep down that if it wasn't on the mantlepiece it wasn't going to be anywhere. Nevertheless she checked the windowsill, the top of the old burea (He always kept it locked), on and under the tablecloth. She even checked down the side of the couch. By this time she was just hoping something might have come out of his pockets while he was asleep. But no...nothing.

It dawned on her that he must have meant to leave nowt. She wanted to believe that mebbie he'd forgot, that he'd been in a hurry and just forgot. I'll have to have a word with him when he gets back, thought Jessy. Aye, best to tackle it as if he'd just forgotten. But she knew, oh she knew alright, that he'd done it on purpose, that he wanted her to ask for it. He wouldn't make it easy either, he'd draw it out, making her suffer. She knew Bullum well enough to know that he would enjoy seeing her beg.

"So what!" she said to herself, "So bloody what, all it's gonna cost yer is a bit of pride." She slumped down in the chair, put her hands over her face and cried. Quietly.

It wasn't that she was that frightened of the violence anymore, she knew how to keep away from him now. Since he'd been staying out most nights, and sleeping on the couch when he did bother coming home, it had been a lot easier. Ray had put a bolt on her and the bairns' bedroom door. "Just in case," he said. At least now she could get away from him because she could always get up the stairs a hell of a lot quicker than he could. No, it was talking to Bullum that was petrifying her.

They had never talked, other than her to answer him when he shouted for his dinner, or to fetch him a clean collar for his shirt, or more often than not, to tell her to empty his piss pot. Jessy couldn't remember EVER talking to him, not in all the years they had been married. Oh she talked to the bairns in front of him, but now that she came to think about it, she had never talked to Bullum.

Jessy's belly was empty, but the dread that she felt made her feel sick. She looked at Bullum's razor on the table next to her. She picked it up, felt the edge of it and then closed it. She wasn't thinking of taking her own life. She had, in the past, thought about it once or twice, very briefly, but the thought of leaving the bairns with Bullum had put paid to any such escape. But she had often thought about doing him in, about how it would feel to be rid of him and not to have him around them anymore. But what then? She'd be jailed or even killed, then what would happen to the bairns?

Hope stirred when she thought of Ruthie, after all, the lasses were at Ruthie's house most weekends now. Ruthie adored them and spoilt them rotten, especially the little un, Jean. Jean had called Ruthie "Mudder" since she was able to talk. She hadn't been able to pronounce "Mother." Jessy didn't mind, in fact it had been her doing. When Ruthie used to be constantly picking Jean up and out of her sleep as a baby Jessy would say, "Well yer can bloody mother her when she cries annaull" Ruthie smiled and said she didn't mind one bit. Since then, every time Jean cried when Ruthie was around, Jessy would simply pass her to Ruthie saying, "Here, gan to yer "Cuddle Mother." She knew this pleased Ruthie and it was a bit like giving something back to her. Jessy didn't want to be called "Mother" anyway, she liked "Ma" or "Mam," so to Jessy's mind, no harm was being done. Aye, Ruthie might take the girls, but what about Ralphy? He mightn't want that, although he was lovely with them, they still weren't his!

She knew Ray would be alright, he would always find work, and mebbie Ruthie and Ralphy would take the girls, but what about Freddy? Jessy knew that nobody would take Freddy. People didn't 'take to' Freddy, it was his sly sullenness that was the problem. "But he's still my bairn," said Jessy out loud now. She sighed, pushed the razor away, wiped her eyes and straightened her pinny. "Best go and get the greedy git in. He's probably half frozen to death by now. I wouldn't care but he'll not have got many bullits with the rationing, he's probably sucking on liquorice sticks." As she opened the back door, she shouted, "Get yersel in here, our Freddy. They're all asleep, yer can gan and hide what yer've got left. By God, yer'd cut yer nose off to spite yer face, wouldn't yer?" Jessy sat back down in the chair. She'd left the back door on the latch. After a couple of minutes Freddy was warming his hands by the dying embers of the fire. He doesn't even look guilty, thought Jessy, but when he turned and kissed her on the top of the head and said, "Nigh Night," he dropped a stick of liquorice onto her pinny in her lap. She watched him leave the room then replied gently, "Nigh night, son......and thanks." There was no answer.

Jessy sat in the darkness. She knew what she had to do, and accepted it. There was no room in her life for foolish pride. Aye, she'd wait up for Bullum tonight and have a word!!!!

The queues outside the butcher's was worse than she'd

thought. Ray had given her the nod last night that the butchers would mebbie have some meat today. He'd been to call on a lass whose Dad had told him. "The gob shite must have told every bugger else annaull" said Jessy under her breath. Would this queue ever end? She was already along the street and round the corner. At last the end, and it's already starting again behind us and it's only half past six! She'd finished having her 'bit of a moan' to herself and turned to the lass in front of her. "Eeh, but it's bitter this morning." In return, the girl nodded and smiled, pulling the youngest of three bairns further under her coat. All four of them stood in a huddle together trying to keep warm. As Jessy looked along the queue she noticed that most of the women had bairns with them. Why yer cannot leave them I suppose, not with the men away. Jessy recognised some of them whose men hadn't even been called up, for one reason or another, and they still had their bairns with them. Now it dawned on her, they were trying to soften the butcher up a bit. Yer know, the look of hunger on the bairns' faces, mebbie he'd put in a bit of sausage or a bone extra in the rations.

"Wish I'd bloody well thought of it," said Jessy to herself. Getting the bairns up out of the warm bed hadn't occurred to her, and as she stood with the bitter wind nipping at her, she was pleased it hadn't!

Ray was home with them today, he'd keep them away from Bullum. Ray was working in The Factory now, had been since not long after the start of the war because as he said, "We're all needed." He never complained about the twelve, sometimes fourteen-hour shifts, not even when he'd been put on nights. He would be seventeen in another few months, but he'd been the man of the house in Jessy's eyes for a good few years. He was earning a bit more now and he'd tried to give more to Jessy, but the more she got from Ray, the less she'd had from Bullum. It was as if he sensed, even knew, when Ray gave her more. She knew it was Freddy, but she didn't say anything to Ray. Ray loved Freddy, and she couldn't take that love away from him. Aye, Ray knew what Freddy was about, but it didn't seem to matter to him. He would defend him to the end, even to her.

Jessy couldn't count how many times Ray had looked at her when she'd lost her temper with him and said "Don't give a dog a bad name, Mam." Jessy knew what he meant, but it was hard with Freddy, hard to think the best of him. It was one area that Jessy and Ray would always disagree about. Mind you, thought Jessy, Freddy is different when he's with Ray. If only he didn't hang about Bullum so much, then mebbie he'd change.

As Jessy waited in the cold, she counted her blessings. Her bairns had been too young to go to war, that was when it started anyway, and with any luck it would be over soon. A matter of weeks, that's what folks were saying (but that had been said for over four years now), and yet lads were still being called up and killed. Jessy wouldn't let herself worry about that today, she had enough on her plate just trying to keep them fed!

She noticed the queue hadn't moved. He mustn't have opened the doors yet. Fancy keeping them waiting in this weather! He was a rotten sod, that butcher, had been since rationing come in. They were up and out of bed alright because she had noticed that the curtains were drawn open as she passed.

Yer think he'd open up and let some of the bairns take a bit of shelter from the wind. As she was thinking this, she looked at the others in the queue. Kids hopped from one foot to the other, then stamped and swung their arms around their bodies to try to keep warm. Young lasses in thin threadbare clothes, the clever ones who'd brought an old grey blanket. She felt lucky. Jessy's coat was thick and warm (a castoff from Ruthie) and the wig was like having a hat on. Not so lucky with the food though. No sooner had she sorted out the money with Bullum than the rationing got worse. Not that Bullum gave her much, and she did earn it, but she managed!

Jessy remembered the night of the Money Talk. What a night that was, she could still feel the panic in her.

She had been sitting in the dark, the bairns were asleep. Ray had come in a couple of hours ago, and asked her "not to be long getting to bed, as she'd freeze down here when the fire went out." The fire was out now, which meant that not only was there no heat, but she couldn't make a warm drink neither, and it wasn't gonna get any better unless she asked him for the money.

"No, there's nothing for it but to ask him," she said out loud. "He could have just forgot, everybody forgets something now and again."

She said these things out loud to make her feel stronger, to make it all seem a little more reasonable, because every bone in her body knew he'd done it on purpose, to hurt her and to show her he still had the upper hand. It didn't seem to matter to him if the kids were hungry. He could always buy something. He could afford to!

God knows she wasn't bothered about her own belly but she wouldn't let the others hunger!

So she had it planned, she'd wait until he was on the couch, make sure the door to the stairs was open. That way if he tried to get her, she could be up the stairs into the room and bolt the door before he could lay a finger on her!!!!

That's more or less the way it happened. In the beginning...

He'd had a bellyfull, so nearly collapsed onto the couch. She knew she had to say something before he went to sleep because once he was out, there would be no way of waking him. She took a deep breath.

"Bullum." It came out strong. He hadn't known she was there and she'd made him jump!

GOOD! Bloody good, see how you like having the shit frightened out of you! she thought.

"Bullum," she said it again, just as firm but followed up with, "It's me, Jessy." After all, she didn't want to aggravate him too much. "Yer didn't leave any money tonight and I need it for coal and food the morrow, and the rent's due annaull" there she'd said it!

Silence.

"So where is it?" she was shaking inside.

He didn't say a word. She lit a candle, she could see the outline of his head, but she needed to see where his crutches were. The candle illuminated them on the floor. He could still reach them but she would see him if he tried and be off like lightning.

He still hadn't said anything, he was looking at her in a funny way, not with his usual hate, but a different look. She couldn't fathom it, but his silence made her go on.

"Mebbie yer just forgot it earlier on, but I'm reminding yer now, cause I need it first thing."

Still nothing. He was wide awake now, saying nowt. Not even when she spoke to him like that? He was frightening her and she wanted to make her escape, but she had to stay determined!

"Just leave it on the mantlepiece then, tonight, and I'll sort out the coal and the rest first thing!"

She waited...NOTHING. She couldn't stand this

"Are ya deaf, man? Are ya ganna leave me money or not?"

Before she had finished speaking, he was grinning, then there was a deep rasping hollow sound!!!!!!!

By God, he was laughing, not nice laughing, but a bitter black laugh, like a river of black nastiness coming out of him.

Jessy turned to go to bed. She was frightened of not getting the money, but she was petrified of what she was seeing.

"Why should I?"

Jessy turned as Bullum spoke, yes spoke, he hadn't shouted.

"Why should I give yer the money? What do yer do for me?"

She didn't understand. He wasn't shouting, he was calm and menacing.

"I cook and clean for yer. I do all yer washing and look after the bairns," replied Jessy, she was confused.

"I coooook an cleeeeen for yer," he was mimicking her now.

He'd sat forward. She saw his eyes in the light from the candle. In all her days Jessy had never seen eyes as cold and cruel, there was no soul in those eyes, no warmth. If bitterness could come out of him, it would come out his eyes, thought Jessy. They're dead, just like him inside. He might be breathing, but he's dead!!!!!!!!!!

She felt herself shiver, she was chilled to the bone, but she couldn't leave. She knew he wasn't finished yet.

"The ginger whore in the Rising Moon's been more of a

wife to me than you have. Aye, that's where your money's been gannin to, and well worth it annaull"

Bullum was grinning now as he spoke. Before he'd said the words she knew what he wanted!

"Yer can always earn it back," he ground out. "But mind you, yer'll have to be good if yer getting paid for it. It'll be grand. I won't have to cross the doors to see a whore, I'll have one right here in me own house."

He grinned wider. "But mind, like I said, if yer want paying yer better be fucking good at it."

Jessy wanted to laugh at the words he'd used. In her mind they seemed funny "Yer'd better be fucking good." The funny side of it was fleeting and she felt the fear of the situation.

"So whats it to be? Are yer ganna be a proper wife or are yer ganna go hungry? Don't go thinking that yer blessed Ray can sort this one out, cause he might be able to help with the food and odds and ends, but he won't be able to pay the rent annaul, Yer know that if I stop paying that, yer right up shit creek."

Bullum paused and watched Jessy. He knew she was looking for a way out, he also knew that he'd left her none! "If yer think that yer posh sister'll help ya, think again. Her man's family won't want any trouble, and I can make trouble, yer know I can! Trouble that can make that business of theirs gan downhill in a flash!!"

He could sense he had her beat. In the near darkness he watched her outline, he noticed her shoulders slump forward slightly. Bullum felt no regret or pity. It wasn't in him to feel these things. He lived on anger and anger could be passed on, he had been this way for so long now that he truly didn't know any different. There was no softening of Bullum's heart, instead he was able to justify his actions by constantly quoting from the bible the phrase that had kept him going since his leg had been taken: "an eye for an eye and a tooth for a tooth."

He sat silent, waiting for her submission. Aye, he could afford to give her housekeeping, but why the fuck should he? He'd been cutting it down over the years but she'd always seemed to manage. He knew she went hungry cause there wasn't a picking on her, but he liked that. He didn't like fat on women, not like the ginger whore he'd been using. He hadn't paid her much, she didn't deserve it. She was a fat ugly cunt and none too clean neither. He could have got better, but yer had to pay for better, and some of them wouldn't give him a fuck anyway because of his leg and also because of the way he was with them. He didn't want to be friendly with them, he found it hard to be even civil to them!!

As he sat thinking and waiting for Jessy's reply, he tried to see her face in the darkness. Her face isn't up to much, he thought, even before it was messed up with the fire, but give her her dues, she kept herself alright, especially when she put a bit of that make-up on and that wig her posh sister had given her. Now there was one he'd like to give a good fucking to, but Jessy would do. Next best thing anyway, wasn't it?

So Bullum sat patiently and waited. He could afford to take his time, he knew what the answer would be. It had been a good few years since he'd felt this much control. "I'm boss of me own house again," he said to himself. "Aye, my time has come and nobody can do owt about it this time, not even that fucking witch, Wilmy. She'd had the upper hand for a while, threatening to call the Pollis on him, the Twat, but I've fixed her. Oh aye, I've fixed her good and proper.

He knew that Wilmy was keeping away, that she'd got the message because he had people looking out for her. He'd had to pay for that annaull, but it was worth it. It had taken a while but now it was Bullum's time, things would be different now because over the years, he'd learnt that yer couldn't always use yer fists. Sometimes when yer thought things out yer could hurt a lot more! Like now, thought Bullum, just like now.

If only he'd tried to hit her, or shouted and swore, if he'd called her all the filthy names he could muster, she'd have understood better, been more able to cope. But not this, NO NOT THIS!!!!! Jessy couldn't think, she'd got used to not having him interfering with her. Eeh, it had been years. Naw, aw no, she couldn't. She couldn't go back to that.

He was still quiet, quiet and smiling and waiting. She hated this man so much it made her head ache and her stomach churn. If she'd had owt in her belly she would have thrown it up, instead she tasted the dry burning acrid sick in her throat and mouth. Then came the realisation that he'd WON!!!!

As Jessy stood there, she knew this night would change her life. Any peace or bits of happiness she'd had in this house were gone.

"Alright," that was all Jessy said. She waited, she knew he wasn't finished yet!

"Right then," he grinned even wider as he spoke. "I have a fuck twice a week. Wednesdays and Sundays I think'll do. Ya do anything I ask, and on a Sunday afternoon I want the bed. I'll have a nap afterwards."

He was talking like he was arranging business, or like he was talking to a whore, thought Jessy, but that's what I'll be. After all I'll be letting him at me for money, that's really what I am. A WHORE.

He'd continued talking. Jessy hadn't heard it all, but she'd caught the bit where he said he'd give her the housekeeping back. Something in her awakened!

"Alright," she paused, "but I want a bit more. If yer want

it twice a week I want a bit more. Specially if yer want to use the bed, cause that makes more work for me."

There was no way on God's earth that she was gonna let the bairns sleep in the same bed as he'd been in, without washing the bedding.

"I want half a crown a time, and if I'm gonna be your whore, I want the money before any hanky panky starts."

This speech cost Jessy, but she'd told herself he wasn't the only one who could talk business. She'd also needed to keep a bit of her pride. Just a little pocket of it somewhere, thought Jessy.

Bullum threw a half crown down on the foor in front of her feet. As she bent down to pick it up, she could see he was unbuttoning himself. she watched as he started pulling and playing with himself, then he said, "May as well start now then. Get your mangy fucking mouth round this!!!!!!"

And she did!!!!!!!!

CHAPTER SEVEN

Jessy could feel herself waking up.

NO!!!! Not yet! her mind screamed at her. Please not yet!

She knew she had to get back to the dream, to the butcher's queue.

"Please, please let me back," she moaned the words in a half sleep.

She refused to waken, and whether or not it was her determination or just the drugs the doctor had given still doing their job, she drifted back again. Even in her sleep she sighed with relief because Jessy knew she was back, back still waiting for meat...still waiting for love.

"Bye this queue's slow." She'd been standing in the bitter cold over an hour now, they all had. It was a mistake to bring the bairns to stand like this, specially the little ones. A few of the bairns were crying with the cold. Eeh, it's a shame, thought Jessy.

The queue was moving a bit now. Bout time, she said to herself. Everybody shuffled forward together, it was tightly packed, and everybody huddled together for warmth. She could see the butchers shop's doorway, and the people leaving it with small paper parcels of some form of meat. "Bugger me if those parcels aren't getting smaller with every person that comes out," she said to the lass in front.

A tall gangly fella was talking to the people in the front of the queue, then he was coming further back and starting again. People weren't happy, one woman pushed him away. Jessy strained to hear what was being said against the noise of the crying bairns. Then the butcher came out of the shop, walked to the front of the queue, looked along, then stood and shouted, "NOWT BUT BONES LEFT! I'VE GOT ENOUGH FOR TEN OF YER." He turned to the tall fella and said, "Georgie, count out ten." Then to the queue, "THE REST OF YER BETTER GAN HOME."

Silence, and then moans and groans of disappointment, one or two even took to crying as they turned away. Then somebody shouted, "The butcher and his family would eat well tonight though, while their bairns starved!" Then the fella, Georgie, walked up to them and spoke in a voice that was calm but loud enough for a good few of them to hear. "I'm sorry that there's nowt for yer, but you're wrong. I won't be eating meat tonight and nor will me Ma and Da. Cause when me Da says it's all gone, it's All Gone!! And that's FINAL."

Oh, he had a lovely way about him, he was firm but gentle as well, and when he said he was sorry, yer knew he really meant it! Jessy looked at him properly for the first time, as he walked towards her, counting. She thought, he must be in his middle twenties, mebbie a bit older. He had scarring down one side of his face that dragged his eye down a bit and when he got nearer, she saw that his left ear was all but missing. Aw, but he'd been bonny, she thought, no more, he'd been...... handsome!

Jessy had heard of this lad, the butcher's son, he'd been sent back wounded, got some shrapnel in him. Even though he looked as if he was on the mend now, his face still looked raw and red.

Of all places, why his face? thought Jessy. It must hurt so much to have been bonny and then have yer face ruined.

Jessy had been lost in her thoughts when he caught her looking at him. He knew she was looking at the scars and she knew he was looking at her face. Jessy couldn't look away, but he could, and did!

He'd counted to ten, two lots in front of Jessy. The lassie in front of her, with the bairns clinging to her, was asking him to just give them a bit of something. He looked at the shivering freezing family and let them through. Jessy was turning to go

"You're with this lot aren't you missis?"

Jessy looked at him and was about to speak

"Come on then, it's not getting warmer for anybody out here. Get on in to the shop with the rest of them!"

He was still looking at her when he gently touched her elbow, as if to usher her along, but also to make sure that she got his full meaning. Then he was walking slowly behind her, making sure nobody else joined the queue and shepherding the rest of them along.

Jessy couldn't speak to thank him, she couldn't think. In fact, she could barely walk. Everything was fuzzy, a bit like being in a tunnel, she thought. She felt so safe with him behind her, safe and protected-like, but more, when he had touched her elbow, something had happened to her belly, like a big ball burstin in it.

He was being kind, a man was being *kind* to her, Jessy? He'd touched her in a *gentle way* and *no* man had ever done that to her. It was as if he cared, because Jessy knew that for the little time that they had looked at each other's faces, they had an understanding. She had seen it in his eyes. She knew that he knew the *pain*!

"Pull yerself together," she said to herself. "It was nowt but the butcher's lad being a bit generous."

She straightened her shoulders and waited for bones. While she waited, she felt strange, she felt a bit sick and dizzy. She wanted a wee and her head was aching a bit.

"I must be coming down with something, not surprising in this bloody weather," she said to herself.

Most of all, Jessy wanted to hide her face, but then she thought of him, and the way he had looked at her. She stood tall. He wasn't hiding his, then I'll not hide mine, and she felt stronger.

In the background she could hear his Dad moaning about how many he'd let in, then Jessy heard his voice, clear and firm replying to his Dad. "Well, we'll just have to try to eeke them out a bit further, Dad."

Jessy knew she would have something to put in the stock pan, cause he was looking at her when he said it!

She was the last to leave, the parcel was very small but she'd seen that some of the bones still had a bit of meat on them. When he'd rolled them up in the paper she hadn't spoken, not even to say "thanks." She'd looked at him at the same time he had looked up at her! She knew there was no need! He understood!...

Jessy couldn't sleep that night. Must have a bit of acid belly. After all, she hadn't eaten much, she couldn't face it. So after she'd fed the others, she'd gone to lie on the bed. Ray had followed her up and he looked worried when he asked, "Is there owt I can get yer, Mam? It's not like you to want to lie down this early. Have yer got a temperature or summit?"

By the "summit" Jessy knew he meant her monthly. Bye he didn't half look uncomfortable standing there, trying to talk normally about things that he wasn't at all comfortable with. As he'd been talking, he'd sat on the edge of the bed. He was feeling her brow now, she saw some of the worried look leave his face when he felt her cool head.

"Why, yer haven't got a temperature, Ma, so it must be the other thing." He was talking quicker now. "There's not a lot ar can do for yer about that, but I'll gan down and make yer a cupppa if yer like? How would that be?"

As he was talking, Hetty came into the room, followed by Jean. They all wanted to see what was wrong with their Mam. Jessy knew Freddy was out, he'd gone as soon as he'd finished eating. He was either up to no good or had money to spend, she thought.

"Look, all of yer. I'm alright, there's nowt to worry about. Can a woman not have a bit of a break now and again without all this pallaver?" Jessy was smiling as she spoke. "Now come on, all of you, get yersels downstairs so I can have a bit of peace. I'll just have an hour or so then everything will be back to normal."

Ray looked at the lasses and put his arms up to steer them towards the door. Jessy heard him say to Hetty in a whisper, "I think it's her monthly." It occurred to Jessy that Ray always whispered when he was embarrassed about something, but he'd no sooner got the words out of his mouth when Hetty turned back and shouted, "Oh, it's the curse is it? Why that'll count for it, she must have the cramps real bad this time!"

She could still remember the colour of his face as he turned and gave her an embarrassed smile. He closed the door gently.

Time had flown by, before she knew it, the lasses had come to bed too. They all snuggled in together. Normally Jessy loved these times, the times that she could hold and cuddle her babies, but tonight she didn't want to sing to them or even with them. She didn't want to tell stories, she just wanted quiet. Ray had been out and got her some milk and warmed it for her. Where the hell he'd been able to get that was a mystery to Jessy. He must have paid over the odds for it, she thought. So she'd drank it even though she didn't want it really, but she wouldn't hurt his feelings, he was only thinking of her!

All Jessy wanted to do was to be able to think of HIS face...of his eyes...

She could remember every detail, almost as if she were looking at him again. She smiled when she thought of how it was slightly twisted because it sort of suited him, she didn't think he would have looked half as nice if he'd been perfect because then she wouldn't have noticed his eyes as much. Aw, he had lovely, lovely, lovely eyes. They were deep and brown and gentle and caring. And just soo lovely...

It was like nothing she'd ever seen in a man. "Mind you, yer daft get, how many men's eyes have you ever looked into?" Jessy chided herself. But she knew she would remember HIM all of her life. Yes, a man had really looked at her and was not 'put off'. He hadn't turned away and pulled a face to others, hadn't smiled or even laughed at her!

"Aye, but it was only kindness," she kept telling herself, "even so, kindness or not, it was lovely of him. Lovely actions from a lovely man! Now sleep yer daft bugger" she told herself.

She hadn't slept, and her belly still wasn't right. It wasn't hurting, but it kept sort of jumping and popping, a bit like when she...

OH MY GOD NO!

She grabbed her belly at the same time as the thought occurred, and she sat back on the bed to steady herself.

"Think, lass, THINK."

She'd been extra careful, she'd always had a wee straight after Bullum had been at her, like Wilmy had said, and she had religiously squeezed water from a rag inside herself afterwards. It had worked. Jessy was trying to keep calm enough to remember her periods cause even the thought of another one to feed and keep petrified her. As much as she loved her bairns, she wanted no more.

"I couldn't be. I've been regular an I've got no signs, no feelings of carrying owt." She was starting to feel better. "Anyway this is a different feeling...like a good feeling in a way! Just a belly ache with some nerves. Then it dawned on her, she had a belly ache because of somebody being nice, not just somebody, but him...*Georgie*. Jessy even liked the name, it suited him, sort of royal-like.

By God that's a relief, she thought, and as she looked out of the window on another day of bitterly cold weather, and thought of another day of washing and scrubbing, she actually felt happy.

She was lighting the fire downstairs, she hadn't realised she was humming, she couldn't help it. But she'd better keep it quiet cause Bullum was still sleeping on the couch. She was still humming quietly while giving the bairns their breakfast. The lasses smiled and Ray and Freddy whisperingly 'skitted' her. They asked her if she'd found some money, or had she been left some in a will? She didn't care, as long as they were quiet. She liked seeing them smile, so the only thing she said was, "Life could be worse and I've got a lot to be thankful for!" When they both chimed in with "What?" even Jessy laughed.

This seemed to please them and even Freddy left for work smiling. As she was clearing away she was talking to herself, "I'll get you two sorted out" she was looking at the lasses as she spoke, "Afore I wake him for his grub, then I'll go see Wilmy afore the washing. I'll drop you two off at your Auntie Ruthie's if yer like, don't worry about school, one day's not ganna make much difference and anyway yer know Ruthie, she'll be over the moon to see yer, Uncle Ralphy annaull. So go on, eat yer bread up and let's get sorted."

Jessy hadn't had a good "chin wag" with Wilmy for ages! When she thought about it she couldn't remember the last time she'd had a natter with her. Time had passed and she'd seen her out and about, they always had a word or two, but Wilmy was always in a hurry, always busy doing something. On the odd times she'd called at Wilmy's house, she'd either been on her way out to a job or not in at all. Jessy knew she was alright because Ray always called at least once a week and came back and told Jessy what was happening: who had died, who was having a bairn and other tit bits. We'll have a nice cuppa, thought Jessy, cause if I go early she's bound to be still in. Jessy knew from the time that she had stayed with Wilmy that she didn't surface sometimes till eight o'clock. Mind you, she often had late nights, what with folk dying and others birthing. She was a little excited, she would tell Wilmy about the butcher's lad and his kindness, mebbie Wilmy would be able to give her something for her belly, cause it was still churning over.

Wilmy watched from behind a corner of curtain as Jessy walked back up the street. She wished she'd stop calling, not because she didn't want to see her, but cause she daren't.

"Aw, hinnie, I feel for ya! But I daren't, I just daren't let yer in. But I miss yer lass," and the tears poured down her face. Not just because she liked, no more, she loved Jessy, but because she knew that Bullum had won!!!!! "Oh aye he'd won alright," she said as she wiped her face on her sleeve and took a deep breath. With the breath came the anger, not just at that fat bastard, but at herself for not getting the measure of him. Not taking him seriously enough.

"I'll take him serious now though," she said. "Oh by God I will, cause if I don't I'll be jailed or worse, dead."

She now knew the depths of Bullum and the true evilness that was in him.

At first she'd not caught on to what was happening, when she looked back she realised things had been going on for some good while, at least a couple of years. In the beginning she'd put it down to kids messing about, it had started with leaving rubbish on the step, bins being emptied on the path. Then it had got worse, dead mice and rats and even a cat once. She'd even taken to asking some of her kids to call in on her at night and have a look around. On these nights nothing ever HAPPENED!

There was the other thing too. Wilmy often felt she was being watched, she'd got in the habit of keeping the curtains closed when she was by herself, but it didn't help. She still had the feeling that someone was out there. She'd mentioned it to a couple of her older lads, and give them their due, they'd taken turns in coming down and looking around during the night, but after a while she knew they thought she was imagining things. And they stopped coming.

Lately the feelings had been stronger, she even felt she

was being followed a few times, but she could prove nothing! There were times when Wilmy herself thought she must be imagining things, but Wilmy had always trusted her sense, it had never failed her. She'd seen and known things all her life with her Gift, just like her mother before her, and it had never let either of them down!!!!!!

Even Wilmy, who knew who her enemy was, wasn't prepared for the recent happening.

She'd been out most of the morning trying to get the food. When she got home she was nithered, and rationing or not, she was going to put a shovel of coal on the dying embers of the fire and make a cuppa. The coal scuttle was empty, so she trudged out to the coalhouse in the back yard. She was on her way back when she saw the cat, outside the lavvy, scratting at a bundle of rags. As Wilmy went over to the animal it turned on her and started hissing and spitting, and trying to pull the bundle of rags backwards and away with it! But the cat was skinny and scrawny and didn't manage to pull the bundle very far. Wilmy gave it a good sound kick, it squeeled and spat then ran, but not before she had seen the red around it's ginger starving mouth. At first she thought that mebbie somebody had left her a bit of meat, as a sort of thank you present what with everything being rationed. But why not leave it in a bit of paper and why leave it in the yard? As she bent down to it she asked herself how long it could have been there? The last time she had been in the yard was yesterday, late afternoon for coal. It hadn't been there then!

As she reached for it she got the smell. "Bugger me," she gasped as she gagged at the stench. It must have been off already, cause nowt would rot in this bloody weather. It was cold enough to freeze it bloody solid.

With that thought Wilmy had another, mebbie it was

just the outside that had gone, if she cut away into it till the middle, she still might get a bit of something that was fresh enough to eat. Wilmy pulled the rags away to look, thinking that she'd gan indoors for the cleaver to cut it outdoors, rather than take the stench inside. Anyway she'd leave the rest for that stinking cat. It made her feel better for kicking it!

Wilmy didn't think that there was anything left in this world that would shock her. But as she untied the dirty torn cloth roll she got a feeling. As she unraveled, she noticed it was a torn sheet. It's been wrapped well, that's before the bloody cat got it, she thought, like I wrap things, done with a bit of care. The bundle rolled out of the rags, at the same time it dawned on Wilmy what was in it, and why she knew!

"OH MY LORD! NO! NO! NO!!!!!!!!!"

She fell backwards off her haunches and sat looking at the contents. She was gasping for air, it was hard to breathe! She didn't want to look, to think! But she couldn't tear her eyes away from the tiny rotted black frame that was lying there. So she sat and she stared! She started trembling, then shaking and finally heaving. Heaving involuntary sobs.

It was the cold getting through that brought her round, she didn't know how long she'd been sitting on the yard floor, but she was starting to go numb. It hurt to move, and her aching bones creaked as she eventually rose from her bottom to her knees and then slowly to her feet. She felt old, and she felt tired. As she folded the rags around the bundle and picked it up she felt like she had never felt before: total uselessness.

The fire was forgot, she gently carried the little girl wrapped in rags indoors. She closed the back door gently, as if she had to be quiet to show some respect, and put the bundle on the old wooden block table in the sculllery.

The tears came now, and as she looked at the babby through her tears, the little face seemed to soften and gain some peace. It took on a kind of haze, as if its little spirit was only now being allowed to leave its body!!!!!!!!

"STOP IT! PULL YERSELF TOGETHER WOMAN."

Wilmy wiped her eyes, looked down at the table and knew what she had to do, and as she filled a tin basin with the bitterly cold water, she thought about her life.

For many a year Wilmy had hated her life and what she did! She accepted it with bitterness cause she knew there was very little alternative now. After all she'd been "round the houses" with men in her younger days, and certainly no one was going to look at her now so she had to look after herself, and more often than not her brood. She remembered, she'd been a looker in her day, and probably got more attention than most lasses, but Wilmy listened to her Ma, and gained enough knowledge to judge how men's minds work. Though they thought she was giving it away (cause it eased their conscience if they thought they weren't seeing a prossy[10]), she always made them pay in some way after the event! Oh, they had thought she was stupid and desperate but they had learnt the hard way.

As Wilmy had been thinking, she'd taken the dish of water and was now holding the babby on one of her arms in the dish and bathing the water over the little body with her other hand.

"Not full-term, but big and well-formed nevertheless." Wilmy started to sing gently, and paid special attention to the hole in the side of the tiny body where the bloody cat had got at her, and washed it clean. The babby had been in the ground less than a week.

Aye, thought Wilmy, I know this one! "I know you, my little lass. I saw yer just a few days ago," she bent her head and whispered.

"I'm sorry, hinny, but yer better off where yer are. Aye, yer better off than living with that lot yer were gonna be with. Specially with you being a girl and that family of yours." Wilmy sighed.

"Your Ma couldn't have helped yer, she's past helpin herself. Oh not exactly simple, just given in sort of. I reckon she doesn't speak now cause nobody ever listened when she did. Oh and if she WAS ever heard, it was only to earn her a slap. But never mind that now, we'll clean yer up and wrap yer again. We'll put yer to rest where nobody knows this time and yer can start yer journey afresh!"

It was half past four in the, morning when she let herself out the back door with the newly-wrapped parcel. Wilmy had rocked the babby on her knee all night, humming to her and then dozing with her in her arms. As she picked up the spade from the yard, she knew she'd given love that night, and if the Lord be willing she'd get some back. Sometime.

But for now, Wilmy had the final bit to do, then they could both rest!

Bullum wouldn't find this one again, naw not this one anyway.

It would be a very long time till Jessy and Wilmy had another nip and a natter!!!!!!!!!

Freddy didn't know why his Da hated Wilmy like he

did, but it didn't matter, cause he knew what he'd done would please him. For years now, he'd been taking tales to Bullum, about the goings on at Wilmy's. He'd learnt stuff from his mates, from his Ma when she was talking to Ellen next door, from Ray after his weekly visits. He would listen in when Ray was telling his Ma all the gossip. Wilmy fascinated Freddy and it was this fascination that had led him to spy on her. He often climbed the back gate on a night, stood in the dark, hiding and listening to the goings on. He would spend hours trying to get a glimpse of something through the scullery window (the only one without curtains), just waiting and watching, and then reporting back!

Freddy had found his niche in life, it proved very profitable, not only with his Da, but with the other blokes from The Estate who didn't know what was going on in their families. It was as if what his Da had started had now become a way of life for him. Freddy was known to often say, "Knowing things makes yer strong!"

AYE, FREDDY WAS ON HIS WAY!!!!!!!!!!!!

Hetty watched her Mam turn in her sleep. It was time for her tablets, she sat gently on the side of the bed and lifted her head. First the tablets. She put two of them in her mouth and then held the cup of water to her lips. Jessy drank and swallowed, she wasn't fully awake but Hetty knew that she would welcome the medication.

"Sleep now, Ma, get some peace. The doctor's stuff's good, he says yer'll be out for hours with it." A slight smile came to Jessy's face and she seemed to relax and sink deeper into the matress. Hetty looked at her painfully thin body and her shrunken face. She wanted to touch her face, or even her hand to try to give her some sense of comfort. But she didn't, something in her knew that she was best left alone. Instead she sat and looked at her mam, the woman that Hetty could and had always relied upon to make life seem a little better. She knew that she'd always loved her ma, but she'd never known how much till now. This little, old now, woman, whom everybody had depended upon to keep going.

Hetty sighed with pain. "It looks as if that's all over now, Mam," she whispered, "I cannot see yer getting over this one Ma, but yer know Mam I miss him annaull, we all do. Even our Freddy, he's felt it really deep, mam, for some reason. I think he blames himself. I know that's daft but I think he wishes it was him instead!! Just a bit of him mebbie."

As Hetty stood, she wished she could lie down and sleep beside her Ma, she was tired. She too kept asking herself, what would they all do without our Ray? Who would protect her and Jean? Who would stand up to Jean's man and tell him that if he ever laid a finger on her again he wouldn't live to see another day? Aw, Ray had always looked out for them, and not just when Bullum was alive. Even after they were married and had kids of their own, he was always there for them. He'd got a reputation on The Estate of being a hard man, but anybody who knew him also knew that he was fair and kind, he just didn't like cowards and those who picked on the underdog. Certainly when he was home and with his family there was no one more gentle and loving and kind and...

Hetty was crying softly now, she had an empty, waiting-for-something-to-happen feeling.

"Aw, our Ray...I miss yer, I miss yer already." She asked herself, how will we get by without him? She sat a while. How will we EVER laugh again?

After a few minutes her mind answered her: keep busy, that's the best thing to do.

So Hetty breathed deep, patted her hair and prepared to go downstairs, to get rid of the last few hangers on, the ones that would drink yer dry before they left. "They'll get short shrift from me now," she said to herself, "it's about time they were on their way. I'll definitely see them OUT."

Hetty thought that once that was done she would pay a visit to Big Gloria, to let her know how it all went and how her Mam was. Cause if anybody was hurtin as much as her, it was Big Gloria.

"No woman ever loved a man more."

Hetty, Jean and sometimes even Freddy would say this many times in the years ahead, and it would always be a source of comfort to them: RAY WAS LOVED!!!

CHAPTER EIGHT

Jessy had been disappointed at not being able to see Wilmy, she knew she was in, she saw the curtains move. Jessy thought she was probably busy. "Nevertheless, she could have come to the door and had a word," she said to herself as she walked back up the street.

She had decided to go back to Ruthie's and get the lasses, she felt as if she wanted company. When she got to Ruthie's door at the back of the shop she heard singing, not just from Ruthie and the lasses, but she could hear a man's voice as well. She knew the door would be on the latch, as she opened it she could hear howls of laughter in with the singing. "What a difference to our house, no wonder the bairns like coming round here!" It was Ralphy who saw Jessy first, he straightened up, cleared his throat and became the sensible Ralphy that Jessy knew in a matter of seconds.

"Come on in, lass, rest yer legs. Bye that was a short visit, yer haven't been gone an hour. Have yer come to pick them up already?" Ralphy looked sad as he asked.

They were all looking at her now, waiting for her reply, and although Jessy felt like she would have liked a bit of company today, she couldn't do that to them. Ralphy loved having the lasses around but Ruthie loved it even more.

"Naw," said Jessy. "Something's come up, and I just wanted a word with our Ruthie. Now don't go looking like that all of yer, it's nowt bad. I've just got a few wimmen's problems."

Jessy knew this would get rid of Ralphy quick enough, and sure enough he was fast to reply, "Well I'll take the lasses with me, and we'll gan and see the horses. How would that be, you'se two? Do yer fancy it?"

They couldn't wait to get out the door. Ralphy and Ruthie coated and booted them, and then with a quick peck for her they were gone. Ralphy put his head back round the door. "I'll drop them off later, so don't go worrying about coming out again if yer not well," then turning to Ruthie, "I'll be about a couple of hours, alright?"

"That'll be long enough, thanks Ralphy. I'll have to get some work done today, so don't go staying out on my account," Jessy had answered for Ruthie. Ruthie smiled and blew him a kiss, then they were gone!

"Well, what brings yer round twice in one day, our Jessy? He's not been acting up again has he? Because if he has, Ralphy's told our Ray afore that he'll gan with him and sort the fat get out!"

Ruthy was concerned for her, but Jessy didn't know how to tell her what she was feeling, she'd have much preferred to talk to Wilmy. She wouldn't have felt so daft talking to her, cause although Jessy felt properly sick, she knew it was her head, and her thoughts that were making her feel this way. She decided to make light of it!

"I just felt like a bit of company. I called on Wilmy but she didn't answer the door and it's left me feeling a bit at a loose end." She went on, "And I'm a bit worried about our Ray, he hasn't been as talkative as normal. It's like he's keeping something from us, you don't know nowt do yer?"

Ruthie looked at her, was silent for a while, then replied, "Aye, alright we'll deal with our Ray first, if that's what yer want, then we'll tackle what's really bothering yer, but first I'll put the kettle on."

Jessy had been telling the truth about Ray, he had been keeping to himself lately, and that wasn't like him. It couldn't be a lass cause he always told her about the lasses. Not in any great detail, but usually enough to put her mind at ease. Funny, it had gone right out of her mind since she'd seen Geor...the butcher's lad. Jessy couldn't bring herself to say his name in her head, it made her belly worse!

"Won't be a minute now," Ruthie was shouting from the scullery. "I wouldn't worry about our Ray, he's old enough to look after himself now, and he's got a good sensible head on his shoulders." Ruthie brought the cups of tea and carried on, "He'll tell yer in his own good time, and anyway if it was owt serious, you'd have heard about it by now, cause nobody can keep their gob shut for long around here." She paused to take a sip of the tea. "So what else is on yer mind, our Jessy, and don't go saying "nowt" cause I can tell from looking at yer something's bothering yer."

Ruthie was speaking the truth, when she looked at Jessy she could see that there was a change. She looked different, sort of flushed, and there was something else that she couldn't put her finger on. Naw, not happy, she didn't look happy exactly, more a bit sparkly! Naw, not that even that...That's it! She looks excited, like she's got more life in her!!!!!!!!!!!

"Aw, come on, our Jessy, spit it out. After all, it cannot be that bad if it makes yer look this well."

"There's nowt to tell really, nowt out of the ordinary anyway, and I'm probably just under the weather."

Jessy knew this wasn't going to satisfy her, that Ruthie wouldn't let it drop. She could tell by looking at her that she felt the "bit between her teeth" and she wasn't going to let it go. "Well alright, to cut a long story short..." began Jessy.

Jessy told Ruthie about the queue at the butcher's, she

concentrated on stressing how cold it was, and how many folks had bairns, but when she got to the part where she saw Georgie for the first time, unbeknown to her, her voice softened and she lingered overly long on the description of him.

"That's it," Jessy had finished relating the events of that day. "That's all that happened, I just thought what a shame it was that he'd been injured, cause he seemed quite a nice bloke! Apart from that, the only other thing is this bleeding belly of mine! It won't stop aching. I wonder if I'm ganning through the change early."

Ruthie was smiling, "I can tell yer now that yer not going through any change and that there's nowt wrong with yer belly, that is nowt physical! Yer've got a CRUSH! Aye, yer've got a crush on this fella." She could see the confusion on Jessy's face. "It's like being in love, our Jessy, he's touched yer and ye…"

The cup fell to the floor as Jessy jumped up. "He did not, naw he didn't, our Ruthie, why only on the elbow and not like you think!!!"

Ruthie was laughing as she came over and gently pushed Jessy back down on the chair.

"Now don't go getting on yer high horse, I didn't mean touch yer like that! I meant that he's sort of touched yer soul, got inside of yer. Now don't look at me like that, yer getting the wrong meaning again."

As she'd been talking, Ruthie had got nothing but blank looks from Jessy. She really doesn't know what I mean at all, she thought, how can yer describe love to someone who's never felt it before? Why, not for a man anyway!

"It's natural, lass, nothing to be upsetting yer. All that's happened is that yer've seen someone that yer like the look of, someone that's making yer feel like a woman, making yer come alive inside." She was kneeling and holding Jessy's hands,

"Surely yer've felt this before, our Jessy, at least sommit like it, before yer met Bullum mebbie?"

It occurred to Ruthie as she waited for some kind of recognition to happen on Jessy's face, She hasn't, she really hasn't and she was filled with a deep feeling of guilt. Guilt for not realising just how empty and unhappy Jessy's life had been. Ruthie had thought that if she helped with other things it would make things better for Jessy, and mebbie it had, but she could have done more, she could have talked more and listened more and been more interested in Jessy! Not Jessy and the kids, not Jessy and Bullum. Just Jessy, the woman.

Jessy still hadn't said anything, she was thinking, asking herself if what Ruthie was saying could be true! She knew she hadn't felt like this ever before, and it wasn't such a bad feeling, but surely she couldn't be in love with him. She didn't know HIM! Then Jessy remembered how he had looked at her! How she had known that he knew how she felt, like there was an understanding between them, and more than that, like sympathy. She'd wanted to hold him, to take some of his sadness, and since then, during the night she'd even imagined him holding her!!!!!!

She whispered, "Surely not, Ruthie, it can't happen that quick?" She wrapped her arms around her belly, it was playing up again.

"Yer've got yer answer right there, our Jessy, if every time yer think about him yer belly flips." She squeezed Jessy's hands a little tighter. "Enjoy it, Jessy, think about him, dream about him if yer want, and God willing, if yer get the opportunity, do something about it annaull, cause nobody would blame you, yer know, not after what yer've been through with Bullum." Ruthie's tone changed, she was serious now. "Let yerself be happy, lass, it might come to nowt, but yer've still got yer thoughts!"

"There's no "might" about it, course it'll come to nowt. I mean, he was just being kind, wasn't he, our Ruthie?" asked Jessy.

"You know the answer to that better than I do, lass. But I don't think yer'd be in this state if yer truly thought it was just kindness. Mind you, yer better make yer mind up, cause if this is ganna take the road that I think it is, we'll need a plan!!"

Jessy had come to her senses with Ruthie's last statement."Yer getting ahead of yerself, Ruthie, have yer forgot that I'm married with bairns? Even if Geo...this lad has any feelings for me, why I'm a lot older than him, he can only be in his twenties, late twenties I'll give yer that, but even so I'm coming up forty three next birthday. So NO, I don't want a plan. I'll do as yer say and try to enjoy these feelings, cause now that yer've explained it all, and I know that it's natural I think I could do that!!!! But as far as thinking anything else, never mind owt else happening, then I've got to say "No." Apart from anything else, expecting more would only probably lead to disappointment, and I want to think well of HIM...Always."

She knew if she pushed her, Jessy would only close up completely. So instead of trying, she lighly said, "Alright, our Jessy, have it your own way, but promise me something now: yer won't go out that house in future without putting a bit of make-up on, just in case!!!!! Yer never know who yer can bump into yer know."

Jessy promised. Ruthie needn't have asked, cause there was no way Jessy would ever want to bump into HIM looking a mess. Even if there was nowt in it, she would never want HIM to see her a mess.

Ruthie took the cups away, as Jessy put on her coat to go. You mighten't want a plan, our Jessy, she thought, But there's nowt to say I can't have one of me own!!!!! Ruthie knew that

Ralphy knew everybody who had a business in the area. Surely there was something she could do!

"Yer don't half suit that coat, our Jessy, yer look real smart in it! Yer could do with a hat to match though." Ruthie was looking at Jessy with new eyes now. Our Jessy's kept her figure alright, she thought, even after having bairns. Ruthie had filled out over the years, it didn't bother her cause Ralphy said he liked a "bit of flesh on her, more to cuddle and keep yer warm."

The compliment really pleased Jessy. If Ruthie said she looked nice, she must. Ruthie was always as smart as a "new pin" and so coming from Ruthie it was a real compliment.

As she opened the door to go, Jessy turned to her sister, "Thanks, our Ruthie, for everything, the coat, the bairns' things, the chat and everything else." She was laughing by the time she got to the last phrase, then became more serious as she said, "Especially the chat." She pecked her on the cheek and was on her way home. Ruthie's parting words as she got to the gate were, "Let us know what happens, mind you." Jessy turned back smiling and said, "Well don't hold yer breath and remember 'no news is good news.'"

Both sisters would have been a great deal happier had they known that the turmoil being felt by Jessy was being duplicated by Georgie!!!!!!!!

There was a change in his Ma lately, it had been going on this past week now. She was different somehow. Aye, she's definitely happier, thought Ray, but it's not just that, she'd been acting different but she looked different too. She was spending more time on putting make-up on, even when she wasn't going anywhere, she went around the house singing (when Bullum wasn't in) and Ruthie had sent some clothes down for her and she was wearing them around the house!!!! Bullum didn't even seem to get her down, not even the times she had to disappear upstairs with him. Ray hated these times, he knew what was going on, and he knew his Ma hated it (why did she do it?). But he couldn't interfere with it, naw not with that part of their lives. If his Ma had ever said owt, he would have. But she never did.

Ray watched his Ma combing her wig. His Da was out already, Freddy had gone with him, and the lasses were copying his Ma, combing each other's hair.

Well now's as good a time as any, thought Ray!

"You're in a good mood again the night, Ma. Do yer want to hear some more good news?" he asked and then went on quickly, "I'll soon be able to give yer a bit more help with housekeeping. there might be no need for yer to take washin in and yer won't have ter suffer Ma cause I've arranged things with our Freddy. He's gonna........."

Jessy stood still with her back to him, he was still talking. She felt as if an icy hand had thrust itself into her chest and was pulling her heart out. Oh don't say it, our Ray, please God don't let him say it. I'll do anything. I'll go to......

"I'VE JOINED UP!!!!!!!!!!!!"

She'd heard the words, but her head was still crying "No!" She wouldn't listen. She bent to pick the coal scuttle up, she still had her back to him. "We need coal for the fire, or it'll go out." She was talking to herself as much as to anyone else. "We don't want the fire to go out, in this weather specially."

Ray came and took the coal scuttle out of her hands, looked at her bent head and said, "Will yer sit down for a minute, just so as I can talk to yer? I'll get the coal in for yer."

It took all of her strength but she pushed him away. She peeled his hand off her arm with a strength she didn't know she possesed, and now she was looking at him. She wasn't crying, she couldn't.

"Naw, Naw yer won't, our Ray, I'll get me own coal thank you very much!! Cause I'd better get used to it hadn't I? And don't stand there pretending to care, cause if yer really cared, yer wouldn't have done what yer've done. So much for all this concern but when push comes to shove, yer all alike, only concerned with what you want, with what you want to do and bugger everybody else!!!!!"

Jessy's voice had risen to a high pitch now, the lasses had stopped playing and were staring at their Mam. They didn't say anything, they knew better because neither of them had ever seen their Mam like this, this angry, talking to Ray like this, shouting the way she was.

Ray went over to them and bent down. "Hetty, can yer take Jean and gan and play upstairs for a while? It's alright divna look so worried, everything will be alright. Now come on, yer know when I say it's gonna be alright it always is! Isn't it?" Ray stroked both of them on the head as they passed and said, "I'll come and get yer in a little while and everything will be alright."

"Started lying to them now, have yer?" Jessy sounded bitter. Ray didn't recognise her and the way she was talking. "Cause you are lying, yer know yer are. It won't be alright," she flopped down into the chair and said quietly, "It'll never be alright again!!!!"

Ray crouched down beside her chair. She turned her head away from him, she wouldn't or couldn't look at him. As he went to take one of her hands, she snatched it away saying, "No, don't. Don't you touch me. Yer not getting off as easy as that. Yer think you can butter me up with all yer "soft soap" talk. Well yer can't. Do yer hear me, YER CAN'T!"

She'd been shouting at the top of her voice at him, he didn't know what to do. He stood and stepped back. Give her some time to calm down, he thought. He went and sat on the couch.

It was silent. Jessy stared at the fire, she had no fear of it anymore, it could only give her physical pain and that was nowt compared with this!!!!!

The ungrateful sod, the selfish pig, Jessy kept saying these things to herself. "He's only thinking of himself and what he wants. Aye, well I've got your measure, me lad. Oh I have alright, yer just the same as the rest, selfish through and through!!!!!!"

Jessy couldn't keep it up, she couldn't hate him, CAUSE, DEAR LORD, I LOVE HIM SO!

Her head dropped forward, she saw her tears falling onto her clean pinny, but she was making no sound. If only time would stop, if only she could just stay like this. He was at least near her, in the room with her and SAFE.

Ray didn't know she was crying. It wouldn't have changed his mind if he had. He knew he had to get away from this house, for a while at least. It seemed his Ma could cope much better with his Da than ever Ray could, especially since he had got older. Ray knew he needed to get rid of some of this pent up frustration before something bad happened. The anger he felt inside sometimes was terrible, it often frightened him, and of late, had been becoming more and more frequent. Ray knew if he didn't get away soon he was capable of violence! Especially to his Da.

"Yer can't go anyway. Yer not old enough. I won't sign anything, I'll not let yer!" Jessy's voice was tired. This was her last chance. She didn't want to hurt him, but she couldn't let him go to WAR!

"It's too late, Mam, me Da's already signed the forms. Please try and understand, Ma. I've got to go, I nee..."

Jessy got up from the chair and put her coat on. Ray watched her, he didn't know what to say, didn't know what to do. He presumed she was gonna talk to Ruthie. "I'll look after the lasses, Ma, you take yer time. Ruthie will make yer see that it's not that bad, you'll see, Ma!!!"

Jessy slammed the door so hard that it opened again. She turned back to Ray and said, "Yer've got it wrong this time, Ray, this is one time when the family can't help."

Jessy walked. She walked without purpose. She didn't know how long she'd been walking when she ended up at the race course, sitting inside the bandstand by the river.

"It's a bit less windy in here," she was talking to herself, "I'll stay here for a while, just till I've thought things out." She felt the need to talk out loud to herself. It semed to have more effect and calmed her. She looked around her. It was a lovely star-filled night, it was clear and quiet. "Hard to believe that there's a war on at all. Aye, but we've been lucky. Haven't seen many bombs. Not like them poor buggers down south. People said that they were being bombed every day poor sods. Mind you, there was that one that hit Durham Cathedral and didn't go off. That was lucky l......" Jessy talked out loud about this and many other things, it was a little too soon still to think about Ray.

She had no idea how long she'd been there, but she was chilled to the bone. Jessy wasn't angry anymore, well not with Ray anyhow. But Bullum, well that was a different matter. She knew exactly why Bullum had said "yes" to Ray. It wasn't because he was trying to be fair or reasonable, he wanted Ray out of the way!!!

She kept going round in circles. "What can I do? There must be something I can do. Please, God, there must be somebody who can help me. This can't be right, why he's not old enough surely. Surely they don't take them in that young? RALPHY. I'll ask Ralphy." She almost left the warm bit of the seat. "Yer silly sod, Jessy, how the hell would Ralphy know? He'd been excused, due to his lungs. The chemicals they use in the undertakers had something to do with it. So no, Ralphy won't know!!!"

Jessy had never felt so desperate, her usual way was to give in for an easy life but this time she couldn't, she just couldn't. "But I've racked me brains, and I still don't know what to do. Oh there must be something, some way I can stop him. They can't take them that young, they just can't."

This last tirade was all she had left. She lay on the bench in the bandstand, pulled her knees up to her chest and cried. As the tears froze on her face she drifted off to sleep!!!

"She's been gone for hours, Ruthie." Ray was worried, he felt sure she would make her way to Ruthie's. "She's not at Wilmy's either, and I've called on anybody else that she could likely have gone to. There's no sign of her."

Ralphy took charge. "Right, I'll gan with yer, we'll get some of the men together and gan look for her. Ruthie, stay here with the bairns in case she comes back here."

Ruthie nodded and bustled the bairns into the scullery to give them a treat.

Georgie had volunteered for Blackout Duty. He needed to get out of the house now and again, he wasn't one for going to the pub. He knew he made the regulars feel uncomfortable. Besides that he got sick of having to tell everyone over and over again about how he got his injuries. Oh they meant well, even made out that he was some kind of hero, but he didn't even want to think about it, never mind talk. He enjoyed these nights, everything was quiet and he was able to think. After he'd done the rounds, Georgie always walked, generally down to the river. When there was a full moon he could see Durham Castle and the Cathedral silhouetted against the sky. He'd sit on the tree stump, eat the bit of "bait" his Ma had packed up for him and forget about the War for a short time.

He was on his way home now, he'd had a good walk. The weather was nippy and yer had to keep moving to keep warm. He'd not ate much of his "bait," it was too cold to sit for long. He'd walked the length of the river and was crossing one of Durham's bridges up by the bandstand when he caught a glimpse of something on the bench.

When Georgie first saw Jessy lying there, he thought she was dead! He'd remembered her straight away. He'd seen her face every night before he went to sleep since that day in the queue. Georgie's heart went out to her. Despite her age, she looked like a bairn lying there, curled up in a ball. As he touched her face to see if there was any life left in her, she moved!

"Missus, can yer hear us Missus?"

Jessy didn't want to hear him. She wanted to sleep, she didn't feel cold anymore!

"Come on, Missus, let's get yer out of this cold. Can yer stand? Can yer stand up for us Missus?"

Georgie got his reply when he hauled Jessy to her feet and she collapsed into him.

"Nowt for it but I'll have to carry yer then. Up yer come!"

She was still out for the count when Georgie picked her up in his arms. She's not heavy, he thought, but it's a fair treck back to the Estate. I'll be better off cutting through the graveyard and taking her to our house, it's the nearest. Me Ma can look after her and warm her through while I gan and tell her lot where she is. Georgie shifted Jessy's weight in his arms a bit and as her head turned, he caught sight of her face. He couldn't see her clearly, he didn't need to, he'd seen her poor face already. Georgie knew she couldn't hear him, but still he spoke to her.

"I'll tell yer what, Missus, I thought I'd been through the wringer till I saw you. Aye, I know what happened to yer, you were the talk of the street for a good while. Do yer know me Da stopped serving pies to your man, when he heard what he'd done? Aye, he did. Mind you, he got a brick through the window a few nights later for his trouble, but he still wouldn't serve him! Me Da's like that, so's me Ma. They're fair-minded, both of them. Yer'll like me Ma, and I know she'll like you!"

He stopped walking, and shifted her weight again. As he hoisted her further up his body, her head fell into his neck. He bent and kissed the top of her head and said gently, "Not far now, lass, nearly there."

The door had been on the latch, he'd carried her through to the parlour and laid her on the couch. Then he stripped all the blankets from his bed and put them over her. He'd explained as best he could, or as much as he wanted to his Ma when he'd woke her, and left it to her to tell his Da, who was a sounder sleeper than his Ma and was just now waking. Georgie didn't want to leave her by herself too long, in case she woke and wondered where she was. He was lighting the fire in the parlour when she murmered.

"Ma, get a move on with that cup of tea will yer? She's coming round."

Georgie's Mam came in with a tray, "Alright lad, I'm gannin as fast as I can. It is the middle of the night yer know, the fire in the kitchen needed to be built up afore I could boil the kettle."

His Dad walked into the room now, pulling on his braces. "Is this the lass then? We'd best let her family know where she is afore they get the Polliss out looking for her, which they might already have done! I don't know why yer brought her back here, lad. This'll cause nowt but trouble and I can te......"

His Ma interupted his Da. "I've already told yer this once, here was the nearest. And as far as trouble goes, when have you ever shied away from doing the right thing Mr William Gregg?"

Aw, his Mam knew how to put things right with his Da, thought Georgie. His Da was still mumbling something about, "That's as may be, but you mark my words, there'll be......" as he left the room to get more coal.

His Ma sat on the edge of the couch and lifted Jessy's head and shoulders up, then she sat next to her and rested Jessy against her. She pointed to the cup of tea and Georgie passed it to her. She put it to Jessy's lips and said, "Come on, lass, try to take a warm drink. That's it. Come on, a bit more. It'll do yer good."

She was coming round now. Georgie's Mam was relieved cause when she'd first seen her, she thought she mightn't come out of it. She'd known she'd been crying cause all of that thick make-up was all streaky.

Poor Bugger, she thought, having to wear that all the time. She was watching Georgie bending down and talking to Jessy now. He was telling her what had happened and where she was. Not that the lass was taking a lot of it in, but that was not what was bothering Georgie's Mam at the moment. She was watching her Georgie, how gentle he was talking, and not just that, how he was looking at this lass!

She said, "I think yer better go and tell her family where she is now. They must be worried to death." She could tell he was reluctant to go. "She'll be alright with me, she'll probably just go back to sleep anyway, she looks worn out."

He looked at Jessy as she closed her eyes. His Ma eased herself from beside her and laid her gently back down. His Da was stoking the fire. Aye, she would be alright!

He'd put his coat on and was heading for the back door when his Mam stopped him.

"What's going on, our Georgie? Do you know this lass? I mean afore tonight?"

"Well, no more than you do, Ma. I'd heard about her afore, and I've seen her in the queue, but that's it." Georgie avoided his Ma's eyes.

She replied with, "Aye, well if that's the case, why are yer the way yer are with her? Don't look as if yer don't know what I mean, our Georgie." She waited and when nothing was said, "I can understand yer feeling sorry for the poor bugger, but I need yer to promise me that's all it is. Say that's all it is, our Georgie?"

"Yer want me to say that I pity her, that all I feel for her is pity. Well I do, I DO PITY HER!...... But I cannot say that's ALL I feel, cause it isn't. It isn't all I feel for her. But I don't know what I do feel! I mean, I don't even know her, yet I don't want anybody to hurt her, not more than she's been hurt already."

He stopped and thought. "I don't want people to look at her as if she's some kind of freak. I don't want her to be frightened or ashamed anymore. I don't want people to talk about her as if she's some simpleton...And if yer must know, now that I think about it, I DON'T WANT A LIFE WITHOUT HER IN IT!

Aye that's right, yer heard me right. I'll tell yer something, since the day I saw her in that queue in the freezing cold, I've felt more alive than I ever thought I could be. I've watched out for her every day, and I've seen her, seen her pushing that old pram with the washing in it up them banks to and from the baths. I've seen the kids taking the piss out of her cause of her scars. Aw, I've seen her getting on with her life and never feeling sorry for herself! Believe me, she could teach me a thing or two. So when yer ask me if all I feel for her is pity, I can definitely say "no." No it's not. Who am I to pity her? Why, my God, Mother it's a privilege to be around her, and if I get my way, that's where I'll be!!!! Around her and protecting her and mebbie if I'm lucky, loving her annaull."

He stopped and took a deep breath, looked at his Ma and said gently, "Im sorry, Ma. I know it's not what yer were wanting to hear, and I know what yer gonna say: 'She's a married woman' and I know yer think it's not right. But Ma, there's a war on, and if it's taught me owt, it's that yer can only live for now!! After all, how can something be wrong if it makes two unhappy people happy?"

He'd finished. His Mam hadn't heard him talk this much...ever! She knew she couldn't win this battle. Oh she wanted him to be happy, and if this lass could do that, she'd have to accept it because otherwise she'd lose him, but she didn't think he'd thought it through. What about her age?

There'd be no bairns for him! Had he thought about that? What about her other bairns? Was he gonna take them on annaull?

"Will she have yer lad?" was all she asked.

"I don't know, Ma." It had only just dawned on him that he didn't know how she felt. "She doesn't know about any of this. I didn't even know how I felt meself till now. I don't even know if she knows I exist. All I do know is that I've got to try! If she doesn't want to know, I'll at least know that I did try." He was thinking, then said out loud, "Don't go thinking that this is a physical thing, Mam, cause I don't know if I want her at all in that way. It's hard for me to explain, but the nearest I can get to it is to tell yer that I know that we can both be comfortable with each other, and give each other comfort. I've known that since the first day I saw her!!!!"

"Well then, it's early days yet," was her reply. "In the meantime, yer best be on yer way and tell her lot where she is."

She watched him close the back door, and when he was out of hearing distance she said, "It's a rocky road yer gonna tread, son, and me and yer Da won't be able to help yer much on this one, but we'll do what we can. Aye, if it makes yer happy we'll help all we can!"

Georgie's Dad had gone sraight to sleep in the chair once he'd built the fire up. But Jessy had been awake the whole time.

When she'd first woke, she was groggy with sleep, but as she warmed through, she had gradually come to her senses. She could only remember slight bits of the journey back here, she had been aware of who it was that was carrying her. At first she'd thought she was dreaming, but the heat of his body next to her kept bringing her back from her sleep. She didn't remember getting here, nor how long she'd been here, but she knew these were Georgie's blankets around her, she could smell him on them.

Jessy had heard his mother asking her to drink and she'd heard her tell Georgie to go to tell her lot where she was. She was just dozing off again when the voices from the back started. At first she couldn't make out what was being said, but after listening for a while it got clearer.

She was frightened! Frightened that she'd heard it wrong, frightened that he was talking about someone else! But what about the queue, and the pram with the washing? she thought, there's only me, that wheels all that washing in a pram. It's me, he had to be talking about me! Oh, this bleeding belly of mine, it's jumpin fifteen to the dozen.

If Georgie's Dad had woken he would have seen Jessy sitting up, smiling, looking not only a lot healthier but smiling like a cat who'd got the cream. She went over in her head all the things he'd said about her. Eeh, for a man to think that deep! And to think all those nice things about HER. Jessy was confused but thrilled, until Georgie's Mam came back into the room.

"By the look on yer face I suppose yer heard what was being said," she was talking to Jessy in a nice way, so Jessy thought everything must be alright. His mam sat on the couch next to her and looked at Jessy kindly, then said, "Yer know what yer've got to do, don't yer?"

Jessy looked at her, she didn't know what she meant. His mam carried on, "Be his friend if yer want to be. I think yer both need a friend, but that's all it can ever be, lass! He hasn't thought this through, so what I'm saying to you has nowt to do

with whether I like yer or not. I want yer to know that, lass."
As she was talking, she had taken Jessy's hand, and when she
looked down at it, at the miss-shapeness of it, it stopped her
in her tracks.

Her eyes were full as she lifted her head and looked into
Jessy's face. Now Jessy knew, now she knew what she was
gonna say!

"I want yer to think, lass, I want yer to think of what
the person who did this to you is capable of! Not just what he
could do to our Georgie, but think about what he would do
to YOU. Oh I have no doubts that our Georgie could "knock
him into a cocked hat" but yer know yer husband. He wouldn't
let it go at that, would he? We all know about him, and his
viciousness. I want you to imagine your son in our Georgie's
place and tell me what you'd do if you were me?"

Jessy liked this woman. She hadn't said a word about her
face or the age difference, or even anything about Jessy having
a family already. She didn't need to tell Jessy about what could
happen with Bullum, she was ahead of her there! To Jessy,
everything was moving very quickly, she had never imagined
that she would have anything to do with ANY man, not even
one as good as Georgie. Oh aye, he affected her, made her feel
like she'd never felt before, but Jessy was very frightened of men
and her mind had never got any futher than imagining talking
to him. This in itself was a lovely thought, and knowing the
way he felt about her was the icing on the cake. This would do
her!!!!!! It was more than she'd ever imagined anyway.

"What do yer want me to do?" asked Jessy.

"I'm sorry, lass, but I need yer to promise me that yer'll
not have owt to do with our Georgie, romantically-like. I've
said already that it's alright for yer to be friends, and I stick
by that. I'm gonna trust yer, lass, with me only son. I'm gonna

trust that yer'll never put him in a position where he can be hurt. And I'm asking you now, please don't let him be hurt anymore. Yer know what hurt is, so if yer think anything of him at all, help me!!! Help me protect him."

Jessy gathered this little woman to her and when her head was next to hers, she hugged her a little tighter and said, "I promise you that I will never hurt your son. I will speak to him and be civil to him, and think of him as a friend, if just for what he did for me tonight. And there'll be no more!"

The body that Jessy was holding relaxed and bent in to her a little more. They both sat like that for a few minutes, then they heard voices.

She could hear Ruthie. She was saying, "Yer a daft get, Ralphy, somebody should have been back at the house, even just in case she went back there. I don't know what we'd have done if this lad hadn't used his brains. Why we'd have been out all nig... Aw, our Jessy, yer had us all worried to death. Why, when our Ray told us what had gone on..." she stopped mid-sentence. "Ralphy, don't get comfortable, gan and find our Ray. He's still out looking. Well, what are yer waiting for? Get a move on, he'll be worried to death." Ralphy wearily put his coat back on, he'd only just took it off at the back door. They'd all just got to the parlour doorway when Ruthie gave him his task. As Ralphy backed out with one sleeve in his coat, Ruthie shouted, "Bring him back here, just in case his Ma's not strong enough to walk home. Yer can carry her atween yer."

Jessy looked on as Georgie introduced his Ma and Da. He'd had to waken his Da, not even the shouting of Ruthie had dented his dreams.

While this was happening and Georgie was telling Ruthie where he'd found her, his Ma came to plump up Jessy's cushions and while she did, she whispered, "Our Georgie doesn't know you were awake. He doesn't know yer heard anything and please don't tell him about our chat."

Now that the formalities were over, Ruthie sat down beside Jessy, "What possessed yer, lass? Yer had us all out of our minds. Why, I've had yer dead and buried a thousand times over this night." Ruthie paused for breath.

"Where's the lasses, Ruthie, are they alright?" Jessy felt funny talking in front of Georgie. She'd never said a word to him before, but there were things she needed to sort out.

"Oh we left them at your house with our Freddy. We managed to find him a couple of hours ago, he was out looking for yer with Ralphy. Eeh, yer've caused a bit of a palaver, there's been a good few out looking for you tonight!! We only just missed our Ray. Him and that lot went in the opposite direction."

Jessy was calm as she said, "Well there's no need to worry any more is there? As yer can see I'm alright and thanks to the butcher's lad." She was interrupted.

"It's Georgie! Me name's Georgie."

There was silence. He'd been very definite that she should use his name. No one spoke for a full minute, but it seemed longer to Jessy.

Georgie's Mam finally said, "Aye, that's right. Let's be on first name terms. After all, after tonight we're all friends here!"

She had looked at Jessy when she had said it, and Jessy got her meaning.

"Well now that that's all sorted, I'm away back to me bed. I'm sure you lot can get yerselves sorted out. I've got an early start so I'll say goodnight to yer all." Georgie's dad looked confused as he left the room, but he knew he'd find out what the story was later on!

With the mention of Ray's name, Jessy had remembered what had started this whole thing. The panic was back. The feeling of dread, the desperate need of not allowing it to happen blocked out all the joy she'd felt at hearing Georgie's words.

'GEORGIE,' she thought, 'Mebbie Georgie could help? He would know about these things, mebbie he'd know of a way around it to stop Ray going.' She knew she had to ask him now, before Ray arrived cause Ray wouldn't like her talking to anybody else about it!

"Could I have a word with yer, Georgie, about sommit that yer'll know about?" Jessy knew she had coloured' as she spoke to him. She could feel her face grow hot.

He looked across to her from the chair that his Dad had recently occupied and Jessy felt another flush finding its way up her body to her head as she looked into his eyes.

"Why, lass, if there's owt I can help yer with I will." He'd spoke so gently to her, and his eyes had never left hers. He was still looking at her when his Mam said, "Well I suppose I'd better put the kettle on again. Do yer want to give us a hand, lass?" She was speaking to Ruthie now. As Ruthie started to get up Jessy said, "No need for that, it's nowt private. Our Ruthie probably knows about it all anyway. I'm sure our Ray gave her the story when he was along there, so yer may as well sit yerselves back down."

She could see the relief on Georgie's Ma's face as she turned to Georgie.

"It's about our Ray, me son, the eldest!" Jessy took a deep breath. "He's joined up! And he's not yet seventeen and I don't know what to do. He's still only a lad and I've got to find a way to st......" Jessy was gabbling now, she'd started to cry halfway through the explanation, now she felt ashamed, cause of all the good things he'd said about her, and now she looked weak. She wiped her eyes, looked at him as Ruthie put her arm around her and continued. "I need yer to tell me how I can put a stop to it, Georgie!"

She'd said his name! It had been easy, natural-like!

To the two onlookers, Ruthie and Georgie's Mam, there was a strange scene taking place here! Ruthie didn't know what had happened so she didn't know what was going on, but she knew enough to see that there was more going on here than a conversation! Why, he can't take his eyes of her, and the WAY he looks at her. Naw there's a "rabbit away here" somehow, she thought. Georgie's Mam was also noticing the same things. She too saw how he looked and spoke to the lass. Yer can cut the air with a knife when they're in the same room together. For weeks now she'd prayed that her Georgie would get better. It wasn't just his face, she knew that there was more hurting him than that! It was as if he'd been robbed of life, like all his happiness had gone. She'd seen a change come over him this last week, she knew it was all down to this Jessy. But she trusted her, she liked her and she knew that she wouldn't hurt her lad. As she got up to go to the scullery, she asked again if Ruthie wanted to give her a hand?

It was alright to leave them alone cause Jessy had made her a promise and she knew she would keep it!

Georgie threw his cigarette into the fireplace and moved the chair closer to the couch where Jessy was sitting. As he sat down he leaned forward towards her to talk, Jessy moved sharply backwards and put her head down.

She doesn't want me to see her face. Georgie knew how she was feeling, he shuffled the chair back a little and she seemed to relax a bit

Jessy quickly told Georgie about Ray, and waited with baited breath for his reply.

"I've not got good news for yer, Jessy, they'll take him as long as one of his parents has signed the form!" He waited, she still had her head down. "It's happening all the time, all over the country, and he won't be the youngest, I can tell yer that! Yer can mebbie make him stay yerself after all that's happened, but yer've got to ask yerself if that's what yer want?" Still nothing from her, he went on, "Anyway he'll probably get called up not long from now, and there'll be nowt yer can do about it then! How long has he got to go till he's seventeen anyhow?"

Jessy couldn't look at him, she wouldn't be able to control her feelings if she saw sympathy in his eyes. He spoke so nicely, and was talking to her in such a soft gentle way, but what he was saying was tearing her heart out. The pleasure she'd felt when she heard him say her name soon disappeared as she took in what he'd said. But he doesn't understand, she thought, he doesn't understand about her Ray. He's special. He can't go to war, to where people are being killed and maimed, to where he could be hurt himself! No, not her Ray, he was too gentle, his soul was too soft. He can't go...I can't let him.... What'll I do without him? He's my life!!!! I can't live without him, YER KNOW I CAN'T, GOD!!!!!!

"Just over two months," Jessy said brokenly in answer to Georgie's question, "but yer don't understand, he's still a bairn.... Still just a lad. I canna let him go." She was openly crying now, "I have to stop him, I've got to find a way. Please help me, help us find a way, Georgie...PLEASE!!!!"

Jessy had her hands over her face and was gently rocking herself. Ruthie had come to the doorway and watched him take a handkerchief out of his pocket and place it behind one of

Jessy's hands over her face, then she returned to the scullery to get the rest of the story out of Georgie's Ma, cause what she'd seen so far was a bloody miracle.

He'd wanted to put his arms around her, but it would have been too soon. He knew that she was wary of him and he didn't want to do anything to give her any more pain than he was witnessing. He almost reached out to take one of her hands down from her face, to hold it, to give her some form of comfort but instead he had merely placed the handkerchief behind her open palms. He stood up and walked over to the fireplace and lit a cigarette.

"Do yer smoke? Do yer want one of these?" he asked.

Jessy had never really smoked, she'd had the odd one when she was having a cuppa with Ellen next door, but she'd never had money left over to buy tabs with. But she could do with one now!

So she replied, "Aye, please. Thanks," and wiped her eyes.

He passed her the one he had lit for himself saying "It's alright I haven't had it in me mouth" and went back to get another.

"Look Jessy," he was speaking quietly to her, "it sounds to me that your lad has made his mind up about all this, from what I've heard about him he won't have done it lightly." When she looked quizically at him he said, "Oh aye, a butcher's shop's the ideal place to get to know anything," and then jokingly, "Why yer family is almost famous around here! Now don't look like that, I didn't mean it in a bad way, it's just that gossip spreads like wildfire in these parts." He took a drag of his cigarette. "Anyhow, if yer ask me, and yer are, aren't yer?" Jessy nodded. "Yer could keep him here with you, if yer make enough fuss about it, for a couple of months that is. But after that he'd be on his way, and there'll be nowt ya can do about it.

In the meantime you'll be stopping him from doing something that he feels he needs to do, and that could end up driving a wedge atween the two of yer."

She was listening, so Georgie continued, "It's up to you!!! But I think yer should ask yerself why yer stopping him? Is it really for his own good or is it for you Jessy? Could it be because you don't want him to leave YOU? That yer want to keep him here for your own sake, to comfort and look after you?"

Jessy was shocked that he would talk to her like this. She couldn't speak, she didn't know what to say to him, she felt betrayed by him, that he could think those things of her. Why, he didn't know her, didn't know her at all, and yet he'd said the things he had. She was still angry with him when he strode over to her and took one of her hands in both of his and held it tight.

He said, "Don't look like that, lass. I wouldn't hurt yer for the world, you've had enough of that, but it had to be said. Sometimes yer've got to let them go to keep them. Ask me Mam."

Jessy was about to reply when she heard Ray at the back door. She snatched her hand away, and prepared to meet her lad.

It wasn't like she expected. He didn't rush in and cuddle her and tell her he was sorry. Instead, he stood in the doorway until he was introduced to Georgie by his Mam. He looked at her and simply said, "Well you've led us all a merry dance the night mind you, Mam."

"Will yer sit and get warmed through?" asked Georgie.

"Well, if me Mam's feeling alright I think it's time we got home." Ray looked at her and waited.

"Aw, don't be inhospitable, our Ray." It was Ruthie talking.

"Anyway there's a fresh brew going and I know our Ralphy wouldn't mind a cup, isn't that right Ralphy?"

Ralphy was standing at the back of the room, near the door. He too could feel the tension in the room, but he knew better than to turn Ruthie down so he said, "Aye that'll be lovely."

"A cup of tea would be very welcome," Ray said as he sat.

Georgie's Mam came from the scullery to say, "There's not enough milk for everybody, so I thought I'd just put it in the women's cups, if that's alright with yer all."

Jessy watched as they all murmured, "Aye" and "That's fine" then she looked over at Ray. He looked worn out. She realised she must have worried him to death and she was sorry. Jessy had realised that some of what Georgie said had been true! She did want Ray to stay with her. She wanted to have him near her and to know that he was safe, cause that would make her happy. So yes, mebbie she was being selfish. But he had no right to tell her that!!!!!

Ray caught his Mam looking at him. Just ten minutes ago he'd wanted to cry with relief when he found out that she was alright, then he'd felt anger towards her for doing what she'd done. But now, looking at her, all the bad feelings vanished and he couldn't stop himself from asking, "Are yer alright now, Ma? Are yer feeling alright?"

The whole room seemed to relax.

Jessy smiled at him and said, "Don't worry, lad, I'm fine. The other thing's sorted out annaull. I've talked it through with one or two people, and thought it out and..." she stopped. She wouldn't allow her voice to waver, she didn't want to upset him anymore today. "I'll accept yer decision!"

"Are yer sure, Ma? Cause I won't go if yer that set against

it. I wouldn't cause yer know I'm not doing this to hurt yer, don't ya?"

"Aye, I'm sure Ray." She'd said it with a lot more conviction than she felt. As she looked towards Georgie, he winked and nodded at her.

Ray's eyes followed his Mam's. He saw the wink from Georgie to his Mam and thought, so that's who she's been talking to eh! Well at least he knows what he's talking about, having seen it all. He quelled the thoughts he was having by saying to himself, "Nowt more natural than asking him for advice after all he'd been in the War." Ray was relieved enough to start a conversation. "It probably won't be for long anyway, Ma. Knowing my luck it'll be over afore I get there. What do you say Georgie?"

He knew the lad was trying to cheer her up, so he went along with it, said, "Aye" and nodded, but from his experience there was a way to go yet before Hitler was done!

"I'll send yer letters and yer can write back to me, and I'll be home on me leaves. Why, it'll fly over mam!"

Ruthie interupted Ray with, "Well I hope yer'll send me a letter or two annaull, Ralphy can read them to me." She bent down, smiling to Ray, but it was a forced smile, and her tone although remaining pleasant took on a firmer note, "Cause as you well know, our Ray, I never learned to read and write, so somebody will have to do that for us, won't they?" The "won't they" was said as she looked at Jessy. She was trying to let her know that Ralphy would help with the reading and writing, cause Jessy had never learned either. Ruthie couldn't believe he could have forgotten and babbled on as much as he had. But he'd got her meaning now because he said, "I'll do that, Auntie Ruthie."

Georgie had been watching this play acting and although

Jessy had not looked at him during the exchange, he knew what it was all about. He knew Jessy couldn't read, and he also knew that she would feel terribly ashamed of it. So Georgie would have to think of a way to help her, a way that wouldn't frighten her away like a scalded cat!!!!!

Ruthie took charge again, "Well, best be making tracks. Ray, you gan back to your house and look after the bairns with Freddy. Tell HIM that yer Mam's collapsed with a bad belly, and that she was brought to the butcher's shop, and that she's gannin home with me for the night. My house is nearer. He'll be alright if yer tell him that if she needs the doctor Ralphy will pay. That should shut him up alright, for the night anyway!"

Ray didn't argue, but Jessy did. "I need to go home, Ruthie. It's very kind of yer both, but I need to see to the lasses. They'll be wondering what's happening. And I've missed them."

"Alright," said Ruthie. "Ray bring the lasses to my house, bring Freddy annaull, if yer must. Yer can even stay yersel if yer want, but tell yer Dad the story I told yer to tell him. Is that better, our Jessy?"

Jessy nodded and looked at poor Ralphy. She asked, "Is that alright with you, Ralphy?" He smiled when he said, "Oh if Ruthie's arranged it, it'll have to be, but I'm pleased somebody remembered to think to ask ME."

He was joking at and with Ruthie. As she linked his arm to leave, she turned to Georgie and said, "Thanks for bringing her home, and thanks for the tea and sympathy." He knew what she meant. Her parting words as she was leaving the room were, "Call round in the morning if yer like. Yer can see how our Jessy's feeling and I'll repay yer cups of tea."

Jessy could kill her, the match-making little minx. And

in front of his Ma. Fortunately Ray had said his goodbyes and only just left, she felt herself going red yet again! But when she looked at Georgie he was smiling. She'd lingered back a bit, she wanted to say a quick thank you to him herself. Georgie watched her embarrassment at Ruthies invitation and helped by coming over. Taking her hand he said, "No need to say owt, Jessy, and certainly no need for thanks. I think yer made the right decision tonight, but I do know that it'll hurt yer. So if yer don't mind I'll take Ruthie up on her invitation and call on yer all tomorrow as I've got a couple of things I need to talk about with you and Ray. Now go and try to rest. In some ways you're lucky yer know, there's a good few people who think a lot of YOU!"

This had been a night to remember, and it wasn't over yet. Georgie's Mam knew Georgie was wanting to talk to her, but she didn't think she could cope with any more tonight.

"I'll away to bed then, son. Don't be long yerself, time's getting on."

She thought she'd made her escape when Georgie said, "Can yer hang on a bit, Mam? I need to ask yer something." He looked at her and felt sorry for her, she looked worn out, so he added softly, "It won't take but a minute."

"I don't think Jessy can read, and I want to teach her. I feel as if I'm a bit responsible for her lad going now, and I think it would help her if she had something to look forward to, what with letters and stuff. It might give her something to take her mind off things as well!" He stopped and looked at his Ma. She'd sat down and was silently looking at him. "The thing is Ma, she's gonna need somewhere to come to learn. I thought that mebbie she could come here of an evening, when everybody's in, so you've got no fears that way about gossip, and it would be a bit of company for you. Yer do like her don't yer?"

She knew he had his heart set on this, and when he got something into his head, she knew from the past that he wouldn't let go. The alternative to her was that they would meet somewhere else, be alone together, and no matter what he said, she knew without a doubt where that could lead! At least this way she could keep an eye on things. Aye, it's mebbie the lesser of two evils, she thought.

"I like her well enough, lad, but my liking her or not doesn't change the situation. She's a married woman and there'll be gossip anyway. If yer determined to do this, I'd better put it about that she's coming to do a bit of cleaning for me, once or twice a week. But I want yer word, our Georgie, that that's all it is, you wanting to learn her to read, cause I'm having no part in coming atween man and wife. No matter how much of a pig *HE* is! So if you can tell me honestly that's all there is to it, then I'll square it with yer Dad."

"Aye, alright Ma, I get yer drift. I can tell yer this, all I want to do is to help her, and I think this is the best way to do it at present. I'll not lie to yer, I will be pleased to see her. But I swear to yer that the only thing I'm thinking of right now is getting her through her lad leaving, and I really think this'll help. So naw, yer've no worries on owt else. Anyway when I gan and see her the morrow she might put a flea in my ear and not want to bother. She might be too ashamed to want to try." He stood up saying, "Well I think we've all had enough for tonight. Let's get yer off to bed, Mother, afore yer asleep on yer feet."

She smiled as he used the term, "Mother." He only ever used it when he was happy with her, and she let him take her arm and lead her to the stairs. She knew Jessy would come to learn to read and write, cause she knew her Georgie would make sure she did! She was thinking this as she kissed him on the cheek and said, "Goodnight, lad."

CHAPTER NINE

There was somebody in the room with her, Jessy was sure of it. She'd thought she'd opened her eyes, but she must have still been dreaming because in her dream, the room looked different, somehow warmer. It felt like that too. It was filled with a kind of hazy light, like when the sun shines very brightly through lace curtains, with lots of shadows dancing about. I thought it was still nighttime? Well, never mind, she thought, whoever it is, is being quite enough. Just let me get back to me dream! She sighed with contentment. It was easier this time, somehow she knew she could get back. AND THEN SHE WAS!

Ray had been gone seven weeks and three days, Jessy lived for his letters. She could almost read them all by herself now, but she still needed help with writing back to him. They'd all been right, Georgie and Ruthie and Ralphy, the learning had took her mind off him being away, a bit anyway! At first she hadn't thought she could do it, let him go, but as they'd all said, "What was her choices?" He'd left on a Sunday morning when the sun was shining, they'd all been there to see him off, even Georgie's Mam had come along. The only one missing was Bullum, but Jessy hadn't wanted him there anyway! Since then, she worked hard at her reading and writing, never missing the allocated twice–a–week lessons with Georgie and his Mam.

The writing was the only thing that eased her mind from the constant worry and the feeling of waiting for something to happen. It gave her a link with him, without which she knew she would have given up on her life. Yes, he had meant that much to her!

The girls were a comfort, and even Freddy had tried to help. It was as if now that Ray was gone, he took on the role of protector. Jessy knew that Ray had probably had a word with him before he went, but nevertheless, she thought. He had spent time with the lasses, keeping them out of the way of Bullum and even minding them when she went to the "butcher's to do the cleaning." She hadn't told Freddy of her real reason for going. She didn't trust him enough yet, he was still running round after Bullum too much, and as she often thought when she looked at him, a leopard can't change its spots. So the only people who knew of Jessy's secret were those who were present the night Georgie had taken Jessy home.

Although her life was desperately saddened by him going, even Jessy thought he had probably done the right thing. He was away from Bullum, and though she worried for his life and safety, she knew that he needed to get away. After all, she had still worried for his safety when he was at home, but more than that, Ray needed to find himself, not always worrying about her and the others. It wasn't his role yet to have all that responsibility thrust upon him. "Aye, when one door closes another one opens." Georgie had been Jessy's "opening door" "Well that and the reading and writing," she said to herself. "And if yer remember, yer weren't too keen on the idea at all to begin with! Yer mighten't have known it at the time, but that night changed yer life, lass, it did that!"

"Come on in, Georgie. As yer can see we're all at sixes and sevens this morning. I'll put the kettle on, you go on through." Ruthie had pointed to the parlour door, and as Georgie passed her, she noticed he'd had a shave and put on his best togs. He must have been up at the crack of dawn, she thought. So much for our Jessy saying there's nowt in it! She was feeling a bit put out, she'd expected Jessy to tell her everything about what had happened, but instead Jessy was very hush hush. By the time they got back last night it was very late, and even later still by the time they had got the lasses off to bed (neither Ray not Freddy had stayed, she didn't encourage them. They would be sleeping in the same room as where she had made the couch up for Jessy, and she wanted to have a talk with her). So when the lads had decided to go home she'd been relieved, cause there were a good few things that had happened that Ruthie needed explaining. But Jessy had not been that eager to tell Ruthie much, or so it seemed to Ruthie, just saying that she was tired and that she would see her in the morning about it all!

Now Georgie had arrived, and she would have no time to sit down and have a natter with Jessy. Aw well, at least he's keen, and he's made an effort, thought Ruthie as she resigned herself to having to wait until later to hear the full story. Best keep the bairns out of the way though, cause they'll want a bit of privacy. I hope! She smiled as she filled the dish to wash the lasses' faces.

Jessy was washed and dressed already. She hadn't slept well, the events of the previous night kept going through her mind. The decision to let her Ray go had been the hardest thing she had ever done. The bile rose in her throat when she thought about it. "What am I doing?" she asked herself, "letting him go where he can be killed. Surely that can't be right. She knew she wasn't alone, that there were lots of Mothers out there thinking and feeling the same thing, but that didn't help her. They didn't have Ray, they couldn't love their bairns like she loved her Ray, cause if they did, they would have stopped their bairns going too. Then there wouldn't be any BLOODY WAR! These thoughts were interrupted by the arrival of Georgie.

Georgie sat on the edge of the chair nearest Jessy and leaned forward. "How are yer doing today, lass?"

Jessy noticed that he always sat with the side of his face that was scarred away from her, he had last night as well! She hadn't felt like she wanted to see him today, she wanted to be left alone. Her feelings had come and gone and changed so many times in the space of a few hours. At first, hearing what he had said about her and how he felt made her feel excited and special, then after the conversation with his Mam, she had felt the uselessness of the situation. The disappointment of hearing the truth from his Mam was nothing to the way she felt when, after asking for his help with her Ray, he had gone against her! Jessy wasn't angry with him, she just felt let down. Oh I know he's telling the truth, and he knows what he's talking about, so why do I feel as if I've lost something already? She wasn't only thinking about Ray.

"As yer can see, I'm up and about, feeling better and stronger all the time. Ruthie wants to have me stay here for a day or so, but I think I'll be getting back. After all, I've got a husband and family to look after!"

Jessy couldn't help herself, she'd wanted to hurt him! She justified it to herself by saying, "Why, if he's so fond of the truth, that's the truth annaull." The effect it had on him made her want to rip out her own tongue. His head had snapped round so that he was facing her full on, and she saw the hurt that she had caused him in his eyes. She was stunned and as she continued to look at him she saw him remember his face. He bent his head and then slowly, as if not to attract attention, he turned it once again to one side.

It was this one simple action that brought Jessy back to herself, and she was filled with guilt. She cried out in her head, I'm sorry, lad, I'm so sorry. I didn't mean it, I didn't mean to hurt yer!!! She would have said it aloud but for the fact that Georgie didn't know that Jessy had heard his conversation with his Mam. Instead she leaned toward him and smiled as she said, "But I'll always have some time for you, Georgie," then qualified it with, "After all yer nigh on saved me life, yer know."

"I've come to offer to teach yer to read and write, yer know, so that yer can keep in touch with your lad while he's away. It'll be a comfort to yer of some sorts. I know it was for me Mam!"

Georgie had been determined to be business like with her, and her coldness towards him at first re-inforced this intention. But when he saw the shame and embarrassment on her face, all such thoughts left him, and he found himself wanting to pick her up in his arms again to keep her safe. What is it about this woman? That she can make me feel like this toward her, by God, I swear I can feel her pain way more than I can feel me own. I CAN! I swear I can."

"Who said I cou..."

Georgie cut her off and replied, "Oh nobody did, lass, I just supposed. I mean, there's very few around here who can. In fact, the only reason I can is cause me Grandma taught me." He gabbled on, "In a way it's been passed down the family cause she taught me Mam and then me Mam taught me Dad."

They both knew this wasn't true, but the white lie had served its purpose. Jessy had relaxed a little and Georgie could tell she was considering it.

Jessy had another letter from Ray, she had read most of it but there were one or two bits she couldn't make out. She would take it along to Georgie's house tonight and him and his Mam could read it with her. She didn't mind sharing it with them, she thought that Georgie's Mam enjoyed hearing from him too. After all, she'd been through this all before with her son. Things had worked out alright, thought Jessy. Well as best as they could. Georgie's Mam had spread the rumour about her doing a bit of extra cleaning, and so far nobody had asked any questions about the arrangement.

At first Jessy had been nervous of his Mam, cause she knew how she felt, but she (Molly was her name) had been very kind to her. She had welcomed her from the first, and sat in and helped since then. Jessy knew that she was probably sitting with them on purpose, so that they weren't alone, but she didn't mind cause as time had gone by, she felt that Molly had started to trust her, and that she actually liked and looked forward to Jessy's visits.

The door was on the latch, it always was when she was due. Georgie's Mam was making a fresh pot of tea ready for her coming. "I must think of her as Molly," Jessy said to herself, but it wasn't easy for her, after all she was "Georgie's Mam."

"Sit down, lass. He's just having a word with his Da. They'll be discussin the war again, they gan through that newspaper with a fine tooth comb every night, debatin this, debatin that. Why yer'd think they were running the country not Mr Churchill."

Jessy smiled and did as she was bid. "Is there any more news of when it's ganna be over? Or is just the same as always all that popa...pop...all that bull?"

"Propaganda's what yer mean, Jessy." Georgie's Mam spoke kindly, she did correct Jessy on occasion. Both her and Georgie had explained to her that they would do this, not to be nit-picking but so that it would help with her reading, to know the proper words and how to use them! So Jessy wasn't offended by this. In fact, she often tried to use a new word in front of them so that they could see that she was taking their help serious-like.

"When our Georgie comes through, ask him to bring the

newspaper with him, lass. Yer can mebbie try to read a bit of it yerself now. It'll do yer good to stretch yerself a bit, and just think, it won't be long now till yer'll be able to read the whole of it. Won't that be grand?"

Jessy got the gist of what Molly was meaning It wouldn't be long before she didn't need Georgie to help her. Her heart sank. He had been her lifeline, when Ray had gone she'd felt so lonely and so empty. She still did, but the learning had filled some of the void, and seeing Georgie and hearing him speak kindly to her had eased some of the terrible ache that she felt. She realized that she had started to rely on him, not just for the learning but for easing her mind when she was worried. He had kept her spirits up when she was worried about Ray's safety by saying things like, "Aw, he's only young, the other fella's will look after him," and "He's got good men around him, who know what they're doing." She could tell that he believed this and it had helped her! "What will I do when he's not there?" As she asked herself this, the look on her face betrayed her thoughts and was noticed by Molly.

Molly felt for the lass, and give her credit, she'd kept her word. There had been nothing but friendship and kindness between her and Georgie. Oh I hope I'm doing the right thing, Lord, cause I don't know anymore. She's been good for him. In the few weeks she's been coming he's definitely changed, and for the better. Molly thought about what he'd been like when he had first come home. Why, he wouldn't come out of his room for weeks, never mind venture outside. It wasn't just that he'd been disfigured, he'd been affected in other ways. Like when he heard a loud noise or somebody slammed a door, he would drop to the floor, shaking and mumbling. Molly and his Da couldn't get him up when this happened, so they had to let him be, until he came to his senses, which often took hours.

It had broken Molly's heart at first, then it had frightened her, cause the words he used to say when he was down there on the floor were filthy and cruel. It wasn't like her lad, no this creature on the floor on all fours, mumbling those words to himself was not her Georgie. "Shell shock, that's all, quite normal really. It will pass but it could take a while." The doctor's words hadn't really helped her because she knew that he was suffering and there was nothing she or anyone could do to help.

But that was then! He hadn't had one of his turns for weeks now, well not like he used to get. He was still wary of loud noise, but instead of hitting the floor, he jumped and trembled and was able to pull himself together better than he used to. Molly was thinking this as she watched Jessy. She repeated her prayer to herself, "Please Lord let me be right" She knew if she wasn't, she was definitely ruining two good lives.

Georgie had heard Jessy arrive. He'd wanted to have a wash and comb his hair before she got here, but as usual when his Da got talking, he couldn't shut him up. He didn't mind really. It felt good to have a bit of banter with the old fella again, he knew it made both him and his Ma happy. All the while his dad had been talking to him he'd been thinking of the time, saying to himself, "Not long now, not long now till I see her."

To Georgie these nights were very important. He got to see her and talk to her. He knew that she had no idea of the depth of his feelings for her. He'd had no idea himself until he'd started to teach her to read and write. At first he'd had to be very careful with her cause she was skittish and she felt ashamed. With time and encouragement she had come out of herself, enough to even sometimes joke back to him. He had been amazed by her diligence and determination, indeed she had proved to him that she was not the dummy that many around here supposed she was by looking at her. Georgie had had girlfriends in the past, nothing serious, but he liked one or two of them well enough to write to them when he was away from home. That had stopped when he got injured, and after being sent home, he had looked at himself and dismissed the idea of ever wanting to look at or to be looked at by a woman. The feelings with Jessy were different. Aye, it probably did have something to do with the way she looked. After all, they had that in common, neither of them were bloody oil paintings. But what he felt went a good deal deeper than that, he admired her, he knew what kind of life she'd had, not from her, cause she never talked about anything other than Ray or the other bairns. He thought his life had been hard but compared with the stories he'd heard about hers, it seemed like a walk in the park. Yet, she never said owt, she never complained or seemed sorry for herself. The only time Georgie had seen her upset was the night he'd found her, since then she'd managed to cope with her hardships, even when her lad went away. God knows how she's carried on. I couldn't."

"See yer in a bit then Dad." Georgie had made his escape when his Dad paused mid-sentence to sneeze.

"Are we ready to make a start then?" he asked as he entered the scullery where his Mam and Jessy were sitting.

"Well, we are. We've been ready for ages. It's you who's been doing the gabbin," said his Mam.

He sat down at the wooden table next to Jessy, the chairs had been arranged so as to offer a good distance between them. 'His mother's doing, no doubt, he thought.

"I've got a letter from our Ray, can we start with that first?" Jessy's excited voice brought a smile to both Georgie and his Mam's faces. Molly watched her son smile and say gently,

"Why aye lass, do you want to read it? Or do yer want me to?"

"Well I've tried to already and I got most of the words, but the ones I got wrong or couldn't get, make all the letter seem a bit mixed up!" Jessy took the folded piece of paper from her pocket and with real tenderness opened it and smoothed out the creases, so that it lay flat on the table for them all to see.

"Do yer think you could read it out first? I'm dying to know everything he says, then yer can show us the words and mebbie we can do them together. That way I'll be able to show yer what I get stuck with."

He reached over and took the letter and laid it in front of him. Jessy could still see it, but his Mam couldn't. He looked at his Mam, but she pre- empted him by saying, "Don't worry, lad, I'm just as happy to hear it without having to see it."

"Dear Mam," Georgie began. He was pointing to each word as he read it out and Jessy had her head down and was, he presumed, following his finger.

Jessy listened to his voice. She hung on every word that Ray said, which wasn't much, other than he was safe (so far), that there wasn't much food, and that he even missed her broth. He'd met a lad the same age nearly as him and they got on like a house on fire. He did say that all of the older blokes were fond of him. This made Jessy feel better because wasn't that just what Georgie had said would happen?

"Please read it again to us, then I'll go over it with yer, Georgie. Please!" Jessy asked as soon as he'd finished.

"Aye, alright but then I want you to try it yerself, alright?"

Jessy could recite the letter off now, she'd almost been able to read all of it anyway. Her real reason for getting him to read it to her again was so she could listen to his voice and lean herself towards him a little so she could smell him again.

He'd started again. As he was reading, something was happening to her, the sound of his voice was making her feel all funny but in a lovely way. She looked out of the side of her eyes at his face. It was the good side she was looking at, he still always sat with his good side to her. Oh, he's lovely," she thought. His skin's so clean and he smells of soap and another smell, like sweat but not sweat. It smells nice! She could see a light shadow of stubble from his chin to his hair line at the side. He had long eyelashes that were very dark. But his hair is fair, funny that! She noticed that his hair had grown lately and it fell over his forehead towards his eye. She went down his face again, she watched his lips say the words in the letter.

"Eeh, there's not a flaw on his face, not this side anyway," she said to herself. "His lips are lovely annaull, all pink and full and soft, not like other fella's lips, all hard and dry." She watched as he licked his bottom lip as he was speaking. She suddenly shuddered. It made her jump and both George and Molly noticed.

"Are yer cold? Are you cold, Mam? Shall I build the fire up a bit for us all."

"Naw, I'm alright," said Jessy. "I'll put me coat back on. Dinnit bother putting a load of coal on at this time of night on my account."

Funny, she thought, I didn't feel cold but I must have been if I shivered.

"I'm not cold at all," said Molly, as she looked at Jessy.

Georgie smiled at them both then said, "Well now that that's settled, I think it's your turn to read for us, Jessy," and he slid the letter over to her. As she reached for it, his hand touched hers.

"It's happened again," Jessy couldn't understand it. "I shivered again, well not exactly a shiver more like a shock. I must be coming down with something!"

"Well that settles it," he stood up, "I'll put more coal on and you make a fresh pot up, Mam. Jessy, you put yer coat on till I get this room warmed through."

"It's alright, don't worry. I'll be going soon anyway," she was putting her coat on as she said it.

"No, my lass, yer won't. Yer won't get out of it that easy. We're gonna practice yer writing tonight or yer'll never be able to write to that lad of yours, and I'll tell yer, when yer away from home, them letters keep yer going, so yer may as well settle yerself for a while yet. Right then, that's done. How's that tea coming, Mam?"

They might not know what's happening, but I DO, thought Molly. So much for him not thinking of her like that, well the lass hadn't been the only one who'd 'jumped when they'd accidently touched. I cannot think he would have lied to me though, he never has! Molly stood thinking with her back to them messing with the tea cups. She came to her original conclusion! I was right, the daft buggers have no idea what's happening. This didn't help her, it made her feel worse, cause although she trusted them both, she knew that there was definitely something between them. It made the promise she'd gained from Jessy seem all the more cruel. If only yer weren't married, lass. I don't care about yer age or yer looks, I don't even care that yer'll never give us grandchildren, but I cannot condone the mess yer gonna put my lad's life in, with that husband of yours. I just cannot!" Molly had said these things to herself to try to take away some of the guilt that she felt. It hadn't worked. Well, all I can hope is that the lass keeps her word, and that she's strong because from what I've seen when he's around her, our Georgie's daft about her."

She'd read her letter out, and Georgie had said it was "nearly word perfect." She wanted to get on with the writing bit so she could send a letter to Ray as soon as she could. It would be lovely when she could write properly and say all of the things that was happening to her, a really long letter. The writing bit was proving difficult for Jessy. She found it hard to grasp the pencil properly in her twisted fingers and even harder to get it to perform the task of circles, swirls and straight lines, which is what Georgie had told her make up all words.

The same thing was happening tonight as always happened, but tonight Jessy felt she couldn't cope with the pencil slipping, not being able to hold it tight enough to use it, and all the while Georgie sitting next to her, watching her misshaped hands. They look like bloody bird's claws, and he's looking at them close up. She could hardly hold the tears in. Aw, don't go crying as well, yer soft sod. Often when Jessy talked to herself or told herself off, it worked. Not tonight. It wasn't working at all, she knew she had to get out of his house or she would show herself up.

"I have to go, I'm not feeling well, must be coming down with something." She already had her coat on, she picked Ray's letter up and thrust it into her pocket, and she was out the door before either Georgie or Molly could say a word.

For a brief second Molly saw the look of absolute desolation on her poor Georgie's face, then he was up out of the chair. She just had time to put the scarf around his neck over his coat before he was out the door. As he went through the yard he shouted back to his Ma standing in the doorway. "If I let her go tonight she'll not be back." He turned at the gate for a second to look at her and then said, "Try to understand Ma, she just won't come back if I don't catch her!" and he was gone.

"I understand, lad," Molly muttered to herself as she resignedly closed the door.

Jessy hadn't gone home by the main paths, instead she turned down the back of the houses, between the back-to-back yards. She didn't want to see anybody, she wanted the quiet of the night so she could think. It wasn't that she felt ill, but she did feel a bit funny. Now that she was out of his house and in the fresh air she also felt stupid! "Well that was a bloody silly thing to do, wasn't it, lass? It would serve yer right if he never taught yer another thing. What's the matter with yer? Don't yer want to be able to write to Ray and have him write back to yer?" She leaned against the wall of one of the outside lavvies at the bottom of the yards. "Yer a stupid sod, Jessy, that's all yer are," she said it out loud. She no sooner got the words out of her mouth when she heard a mans voice, "Who's that? Who's out there? The lavvies' busy so yer'll have to wait."

Jessy put her hands over her mouth to keep the laughter in, and hurried on.

It seemed he'd been waiting at the bottom of the cut for ages, he'd ran along the front paths to almost her house and he hadn't seen her. "She can't have got that far ahead of me, she must have gone a different way." Georgie knew that from where he was standing, she would either have to pass him or he would see her coming from the opposite direction. Either way he would wait to have a word with her, no matter how long it took.

Jessy was thinking about collecting the lasses and going

along to Ruthie's, she needed to talk and Ruthie was always the one for that. She'd avoided answering a good deal of Ruthie's questions lately, not because she was trying to hide anything, but because she truly didn't know what was happeniung to her. She was confused about everything it seemed, what to think, what to feel and what to do!

"Aye, but Ruthie won't mind that, she'll understand. Yer can always count on our Ruthie for a bit of a natter, no doubt about that."

As Jessy turned the corner to the cut that was a path between the left and right hand parts of The Estate, she was feeling a little better. The thought of seeing her sister and talking things through with her always made Jessy feel better. "Eeh, what would I do without ya Ruthie?" she sighed and put her head down against the cold wind and went about her way.

She reached the bottom of the pathway and turned in the opposite direction. Georgie had seen her and started walking behind her. He didn't want to shout her name because he knew it would scare her, instead he walked faster. He was only a couple of steps behind her, Jessy was so lost in her thoughts that she didn't hear anything until a voice called in a whisper, "Jessy, Jessy wait on a minute."

She had stopped, but she didn't turn round. She didn't need to, she would know his voice, even in a whisper, anywhere. Jessy felt light-headed and foolish at the same time. She was excited at the thought of seeing him but she also dreaded the thought of explainimg herself to him. You're a silly cow, Jessy, she told herself. How the hell are yer gonna be able to tell him what was wrong?

He was behind her now, she could see his breath over her shoulder, she could feel the warmth of his body through her coat. She felt warm, warm all the way down to her feet.

She didn't care if he never said a word, just feeling him this close to her was more comfort than she had ever known, more excitement than she had ever felt. If only the world could stand still and time would stop, if I could just stay like this forever, feel like this, then I wouldn't ask for anything else, Lord, I swear I wouldn't! Jessy had never been alone with Georgie since the night she was brought home, and then she hadn't been conscious for most of that journey. Standing here with him behind her was a totally unfamiliar feeling, and one that she couldn't explain other than to wish deep down inside that it would never end.

Georgie touched Jessy's arm, he felt the tremor run through her. He mistook it for fear and pulled away from her.

"Please turn round, Jessy. I cannot talk to yer back all night!" he waited.

Jessy had to regain some of her composure before she could do as he asked, she took deep gulps of air, trying to do so quietly so that Georgie wouldn't think that he had upset her. She would hate him to think that he had done anything, anything at all to make her feel sad.

He was still waiting, she had started to move now. She slowly turned to face him, but her head was down.

Jessy couldn't look at him, not yet, what she was feeling had taken her by surprise. Just the nearness of him was making her head all swirly, like cloudy. It doesn't feel like a head cold, but I'm probably coming down with sommit. She was trying to think everyday thoughts, to rationalize her feelings, this was Jessy's way of coping. To Jessy's mind, everything could be explained away by commen sense! Funny how this feels so different though, she thought.

When Georgie looked at her he felt like a knife was cutting through his heart, he didn't know why she was this sad, but he did know that he couldn't bear to see her like this. All he wanted to do was put his arms around her and keep her safe and free from any harm, just hold her forever and stop the whole world from hurting her anymore! He understood why she kept her head bowed, he'd had the same feelings for a long time, but as he stood with her, he realized that for a while now he had stopped seeing her burns, stopped noticing anything about her face other than her eyes. When she smiled or was happy within herself her whole face changed to that of a little lass. Aye, a lass, who felt the newness and the joy of doing and learning, and hadn't been touched by the horrors that she must have gone through in the past.

"Don't run away from me. Please, Jessy." He didn't know if he should carry on, he had waited for some kind of answer, but she hadn't even let on that she'd heard him. She stood stock still in the silence.

"I don't know what happened back there, but if I did owt to upset yer, I want yer to know I didn't mean it! Will yer not tell us lass what happened? What went wrong? Was it me Mam? Something she said to yer afore I was there? Did she upset yer in some way? Cause if she did, I'll sort it out, yer know I will. I just cannot imagine her doing that, I mean, she always speaks well of yer and I kn..."

"It wasn't you or yer Mam, honest," Jessy had interrupted him because she could see that he was suffering, trying to work out what he'd done wrong. Watching the look of concern on his face had overcome any feelings of shyness and fear that she had.

"Well, what then? What was it Jessy? Is the learning going to fast for yer? I know I've been pushing yer, but only because I thought yer wanted to learn as fast as yer could, in order to keep in touch with your Ray. But we can slow it down, yer can even have a break from it for a couple of weeks if yer want."

I'm saying it but I don't mean it, Georgie thought to himself. He wanted to tell her out loud that he lived for the two nights a week that she came to his house for those couple of hours. How every other minute spent doing something else could only be borne because of the sweetness of having her visits to look forward to.

At the mention of Ray, Jessy came out of her void and to her senses. She realized now that not only had she been stupid to run away like she had, over something as daft as scarred hands, but she could have ruined any chances she had of keeping her Ray close to her. "That's what this whole thing is about after all, Jessy me lass," she spoke seriously to herself. "The only way is to tell the truth, that's right, gan on tell him the truth, come clean and at least put him out of his misery. That's the only way lass."

The conversations that Jessy had in her head with herself had saved her sanity over the years and had also given her the inner strength she needed to carry on.

"If I tell yer will yer not be angry? And will yer not laugh at me neither," she was looking directly at him now. He knew that she had had to dig deep to face him, so it was with a hushed gentleness, much like approaching a frightened animal that he had replied.

"I promise you that I will never be angry with you, Jessy, no matter what you do! As for laughing at yer, I cannot make the same promise, but I can tell yer I'll never laugh to hurt yer either."

"Aw, it's nowt really. I just didn't want yer to keep on looking at me hands," Jessy paused, she hadn't explained it right. He deserved to know the whole lot. "It wasn't just the way they looked, it was how they can't do owt! Yer know, like write and hold the pencil even, how I keep dropping it and it doesn't lay right in me hands like it does yours. Oh it just made us feel stupid and ugly." When she said the word "ugly" she remembered his hands, and how clean and beautiful and gentle they looked. She had a funny feeling, deep down below her belly button. She wished he would take them out of his pockets so she could look at them again while he was talking to her.

"Show me them!"

Jessy looked at him in silence.

"Show me your hands, Jessy."

"Aw, I can't. Not now, Georgie, not now I've made such a fuss. I just can't. Please don't ask me to."

He was standing close to her, he took his hands from his coat pockets and held them out to her, palms upwards. He was still looking at her when he leaned forward and extended his hands even closer.

She couldn't take her eyes away from his, she could feel her own heart beating, all she was capable of was returning his gaze. Jessy didn't feel her hands go forward towards him, didn't realize she was holding them out to him, inches away from his own. She did feel the surge of joy that raced from her hands through the whole of her body the very moment he held her hands in his own. She had to close her eyes, then she had to open them again because everything was swaying. "Please, God, don't let me pass out. Please don't let me miss this, not one bit of it!! PLEASE PLEASE PLEASE." She kept saying this to herself, to keep from what she thought was fainting! He was speaking, she could see his mouth moving, she knew he was talking quietly because it wasn't moving very much, but she couldn't hear him. The sounds in her head were filling her ears, it really was like the waves at the sea, like what she'd seen at the pictures.

He had turned her hands over in his own, he was stroking them and then gently running his thumbs over the backs of them. Georgie had no idea of the effect that this was having upon Jessy, but she hadn't pulled away from him and so he held on and stroked, believing he was soothing her. At least that's what he thought at first, then like an infection, some of what Jessy was feeling was passing to him. His hands tightened over hers, he could feel the warmth of the fast little breaths she was taking on his neck, where his scarf had fallen away. His body tensed and he could feel a heat inside of him, then an ache, a sweet ache in his groin, making him harden. He wanted to pull her close to him, to show her, make her see what was happening to him, what SHE was doing to him. He HAD to feel her next to him! He slid his hands up her own, onto her arms, he watched as she closed her eyes. They were both feeling it now, lost in the moment, the small act of Jessy closing her eyes had made Georgie even harder!

She nearly lost her balance, he'd let go that quick.

"There's somebody over there, Jessy. I caught a sight of him when the moon was out. Stay here!"

Georgie walked a few steps and then paused, he was looking back up the cut that Jessy had come down. He was going to walk further but both of them heard footsteps running away. As he returned to where Jessy was standing, Georgie was already speaking, "Well whoever it was, they're gone now, probably just a kid, having a nose around." He was standing in front of her again, his voice softened when he said, "Let's get you home, lass, yer must be freezing."

Jessy turned and as she started walking, he fell in step beside her. "May as well see yer all the way now that we've come this far, anyway."

"There's no need, I'm alright now and it's not far. Anyway what would people say if they saw us walking along the road together?"

"Why, for me own sake, they can say what they want, but as far as anybody's concerned I can't see owt wrong with the son of the woman yer working for walking alongside yer if yer both heading the same way. Can you?"

Jessy could definitly see what folks would say, she knew how they gossiped, but he was right in one way, they could only say they had seen them walking together. At that moment Jessy didn't care, she was happy that he wanted to be with her, and when he asked her if she would be carrying on with the learning she had nodded and then they had walked in silence to the end of Jessy's street.

"I'll leave yer here then," he said. "And I'll see yer at the next session then?"

"I'll see yer," was all she could say. She was still feeling nonplussed from what had happened to her only a few minutes before. She turned first to go. As she entered the gate she looked back and he hadn't moved. She raised her hand to wave, and then on an impulse she raised the other as well and waved them both at him.

He lifted one arm to return her wave, then he copied her and raised both also. It was such an innocent thing to do on her behalf, but it made him smile because he knew what she meant, she was showing him that her hands were still good enough to do some things with. He watched till she disappeared into the house, still waving to the very last second. As Georgie turned to go he thought, the world hasn't ruined yer spirit, lass, there's a lot could learn from you, meself included!"

Freddy had just made it back before Jessy. The nights that she went cleaning he was supposed to stay in with Hetty and Jean. There had been times when he'd had to go out and he'd told her about these times, but he had only left them for an hour or so. So Jessy was alright about it, as long as he did his Dad's messages before it was too late and got back to sit with the lasses straight afterwards. Anyway Hetty was old enough to look after Jean now, but not on a night was all his Ma had said.

Tonight Freddy didn't tell his Ma that he'd been out, there wasn't much time anyway, cause as soon as she came in, she bundled the lasses into their coats saying they were going to see Ruthie. She said he could come if he wanted to, but that they would mebbie stay over. No, he wouldn't go, Freddy needed time to think. To think about what he'd seen whilst he was in the cut!

Jessy was dying to see their Ruthie, she had so many questions for her, things she needed to ask her and things she needed to tell her. As she got the girls ready it passed through her mind that Freddy was very quiet. She couldn't think about him now, anyway there was always something up with Freddy, she'd tackle him tomorrow. It wasn't Bullum's night for "thingy" and Jessy knew that he probably wouldn't even miss her. By the time he got in from the pub he would be so drunk that he would be nigh on unconcious anyway. Other than the night when they had an arrangement he never made it up the stairs to bed. He went off on the couch and was dead to the world.

Jessy looked at herself in the mirror as she was straightening her wig, she looked different! She knew she felt different too, alive-like, sort of buzzing and there was another feeling annaull but she didn't care to think about that!

The lasses were only too happy to go to see Auntie Ruthie, it meant that they would get to stay there and be real spoilt. Hetty thought that is was unusual for them to be going on a week night, but she didn't ask why, she was just pleased. The speed that her Mam was taking them along the road brought questions from both Hetty and Jean. "What's the hurry?" and "Slow down, Ma we can't keep up. We're running already." Jessy hadn't realized she was walking that fast, but she couldn't help it! She needed to get to Ruthie's to tell her what she was feeling before it wore off.

Molly was sitting beside the range in the kitchen when Georgie got back. The room was only lit by the flames from the fire and it felt warm and snug when Georgie had entered.

"You've took yer time haven't you?" Although she had been sitting waiting for what seemed like ages, Molly spoke softly. "Do yer want a hot drink? I'll have one with yer if yer do!"

Georgie knew what was coming, his Mam wanted to talk. He knew that there was no getting away from it, because in her own determined quiet way she would hang on for what she wanted like a "ferret on yer neck." He didn't mind, he was in too good a mood, he knew that nothing or no-one could change what he felt. But the devil was in Georgie that night, not evil, just mischief, and he thought it would be funny to keep his Mam hanging on a bit longer. So, whilst he was hanging up his coat and scarf, when he still had his back to her (so she couldn't see his smile) he casually said, "Naw, no thanks, Ma. I think I'll be going straight up."

"Why, the kettle's been boiling it's arse out for the last half hour, our Georgie. I only waited up to see yer in safe and make a hot drink for yer. I could have been abed hours ago!" Molly looked at Georgie and smiled, she lifted herself from the chair with a low sigh and a slight groan and placed her hands on her lower back as she stood. "Surely yer can spare ME a couple of minutes of yer precious time. Anyway it looks as if yer might have to help me up the stairs tonight, me back's that stiff with sitting for so long!"

Georgie nearly laughed out loud, she was a wiley one alright. The guilt thing might work with me Da, but I know yer too well, Ma. These were his thoughts as he turned to her with total resignation, not because she had won, but just because he loved her enough to let her think she had!

"Gan on then, I'll have a cuppa with yer," he paused. "Then mebbie we can talk, I've been wanting to have a word with yer, and tonight's as good a time as any." He still wasn't prepared to let her have it ALL her own way.

Molly was taken aback, it was she who wanted to have a word with him. It was with some trepidation that she softly said, "I was wanting to have a little word with you annaull our Georgie."

"Why, you gan first then, Ma. I'm happy to sit here toasting me toes, so carry on."

She didn't know how to start. He was behaving oddly, he wasn't in a bad mood or nowt, it was just that Molly felt he was the one in control and that he was allowing her to speak. This is not how it's supposed to go, not at all. Why, I know your game, our Georgie, that nice-as-ninepence smile that yer giving me won't wash. I'll say my piece.

"It's about Jessy!" She saw the look come over his face, the look where he just shut down. She went on quickly, "Well about you and Jessy really. I know yer don't want us to go on, but there's things that I've noticed lately and I'm not happy about them. So. I've got to tell yer, our Georgie. Well I have to speak me mind don't I? Yer wouldn't want it any other way would yer?"

It had stopped being a game to Georgie now, he knew she was right. She was entitled to speak her mind, and he did respect her for it. But, he still didn't want to hear what she had to say.

"Aye, Mam, yer right, say what's on yer mind. But mind you, when yer've done, I'll be doing the same and I'll want you to give me a hearing too."

Molly looked at this son of hers, the one child she'd been able to have. She loved him with all her heart and she wished that she didn't have to say what was on her mind, but she knew that if she didn't, she wouldn't be able to rest. She took a deep breath.

"Right then, yer know mebbie what I'm gonna say, yer must have thought about it yourself. Georgie, the lass is married, she's got family, and from what I've heard, the second eldest lad is a bad bugger. She's got a husband that's as evil as they come, and he'll not let this go lightly, lad. And there's the other bairns as well. Do yer really want to take on all that trouble? Have yer thought about it lad? I mean really thought?"

Georgie hadn't spoke. Molly took this as a good sign and carried on. "I know yer told us a while ago that yer just thought yer wanted to be her friend, and I'm not saying yer were lying, lad, naw I'm not saying that at all, but I've noticed changes in the past weeks, atween the both of yer."

Still not a word from him. "I know yer meant well when you came up with the idea of teaching her to read and write, but, even if you can control your feelings lad, I'm not so sure about her. That's why she rushed out of here tonight, she was hurting, cause she doesn't know what's happening to her. I think it's time for yer to put a stop to all this, our Georgie, afore one of you get's hurt. And I'll finish up by saying this: Don't go thinking that I've got owt against the lass, that couldn't be further from the truth. In fact I like her a lot. I like her company and so I thought if she's not yet had enough of the reading and writing, then I could take over from you, our Georgie, and I could continue her teaching. That means yer wouldn't really have to see her again, other than in the butcher's that is, and there's nowt I can do about that." Molly had given him his tea, now she sat down and sipped her own and waited. When he didn't say anything she thought he'd fallen asleep! She walked the few steps over to the fireplace. He was awake. He looked at her and she knew he'd been listening, she could see when she looked at him that he'd been thinking about what she'd said. It was there in his eyes, the utter sadness of his eyes. Molly gasped on a sob, "Aw lad, I'd rather cut me own arm off than hurt yer." Her heart was truly breaking, she laid a hand on his head and stroked down the back of his head to his neck, like she used to do when he was a lad. "Please say something, lad. Yer not angry with us are yer?"

He got up out of his seat and went over to the sink with his cup.

"I'm not angry with yer, Ma. I always knew yer would have something to say, that's yer job. You're me Ma."

Molly went over to him and circled her arms around him. He responded by holding her close to him and putting his chin on the top of her head as he said, "But I cannot do as yer ask, Ma."

She pulled away and looked up at him quizzically. "What do yer mean? I thought it was all sorted, I thought yer'd seen sense, our Georgie. I mean, I know yer've got to think of a way of not hurting the lass but surely we ca…"

"NO, MA, I CAN'T!"

He surprised her, he hadn't really shouted loudly, but he was such a gentle talker most of the time that when he raised his voice it was a shock.

"Everything yer saying to me makes sense, Mam, aye it does, yer right about that. But yer just don't understand what yer asking me to do. Yer right things have developed, not in the way your thinking of. It's not that coarse, Mam. I don't know how to put it to yer, but I can tell yer this: nowt's happened atween us like you're thinking of!"

"Well, if that's the case, lad, then wouldn't this be the ideal time to end it?"

"What's time got to do with it? Is there a good time or a bad time, Ma? Well go on, answer me! Cause you must think of time a lot bloody different to me."

Georgie was pacing as he talked, he felt so full of things he wanted to say, but he just couldn't get them all out. His head felt like it would burst. If he could alter things, so that he didn't feel the way he did, he would!

"Yer asking us to change something that I've got no control over, Mam. It's not like I planned it, all I know is that I've never felt like this afore, never thought I would feel anything for another human being like I feel for Jessy. Yer know what

Mam? Until I met her I never thought that anybody else's hurting would be more important to me than me own. Aye that's it, she takes away me own feelings of self pity, cause that's what was happening to us, Ma. I was wallowing in me own pity."

He put his clenched hands up to his head and thumped them against his temples.

"Yer frightening us now, our Georgie." Molly could see the frustration in him. "Don't take on like this lad, there's no need for it!"

He turned to face her and took his hands from his head, clenched his fists and with all the strength he had, brought them down on the kitchen table.

"THAT'S WHERE YER WRONG! I HAVE TO MAKE YER SEE, MAKE YER UNDERSTAND. I CANNOT GIVE HER UP. SHE IS LIFE! SHE MAKES ME WANT TO... LIVE!"

He could see the look of confusion on his Ma's face, he turned away and walked to the wall near the door, turned again and leaned his back against it. As Molly watched in horror he slid down the wall to the floor and sat with his hands over his face, sobbing.

"Tell me, lad, talk to me please. Please, son, don't do this to yerself, just talk to me!"

Molly sat next to him. At first she didn't touch him for fear of him rejecting her, but after a while, when his sobs became softer, she put her arm round his shoulder and pulled him towards her. He fell gently against her, his head resting on her shoulder and she waited, waited for him to calm.

It was some minutes later that she heard him say, in a near normal voice, "How can I tell yer, Mam? How can I explain to yer what it is to lose hope, and then find somebody who's doing nowt special, just living their own life in their own way, but being braver than me or anybody I've ever known? Cause she is, Mam, she's braver than me! Thing is, she doesn't know it, she doesn't question the world or even her part in it. She gets on with her life, she lives from one day to the next, and even with what she copes with, she still has the spirit to go on!"

Molly sat quietly, she knew he didn't want her to say anything. She wanted him to talk, to get it all off his chest, to start a healing process that had been slow in coming.

"When I was 'Over There' yer saw death every day, saw things that would make yer belly wrench, heard dying men moaning and crying like babies with pain. Yer lived among it in the trenches." He paused and took a deep breath, "I can still smell the stench of it: DEATH. Yer can even taste it in the back of yer throat, the air is filled with it, and when yer swallow and eat, or even breathe, yer know that yer swallowing death, that it's going down deep inside yer and you'll never be rid of it again! It isn't only them that loses a leg or an arm that leaves bits of themselves over there. If the stretcher bearers picked up 'sanity' out there then they would realize how many casualties there really was. But that's alright, cause what keeps yer going is that yer there for a purpose, yer at war. There to keep yer country free, to keep England safe. And anyway it can't last forever. So yer keep on going, till yer no use any more or yer get yer realease papers from the 'lad upstairs'. Georgie had been sarcastic about the justifications for what he considered was mass slaughter. But he wouldn't expect his Mam to understand that! Naw she couldn't understand what was going through Georgie's mind's eye at that moment, how he re-lived many of the horrors he'd seen on a daily, sometimes hourly basis and that he'd never had a good sleep till the night he brought Jessy home. It still wasn't a full night, but he was getting sometimes three to four hours at a time without the nightmares.

"It's true though, Mam, most of us in the war are doing our bit cause we know that it's got to end sometime, and there's a reason for it. Can yer imagine what it feels like to live every day knowing there's no end to it, that there is no reason, that somebody can hurt yer as much as they like and there's nowt yer can do about it? THAT'S JESSY'S LIFE, MAM."

Georgie stood up and took his Mam's hands to help her up too. She put her feet on his, as he had done as a lad to her, and he pulled her up.

"I CANNOT GIVE HER UP, MAM! I need her, funny that isn't it? Yer'd think it would be the other way round, but it isn't. And if there's a chance that I can make her life a bit easier in the process, well then I'll be right proud of meself. All I know is that my life would be a good deal poorer without her, without being able to see her scarred face now and again light up when she smiles." He turned to Molly and looked at her full on.

"Please try to understand this, Mam. Jessy is NOT using me, it's more the other way round, cause without her, without her spirit and soul to teach me that there must be something still to live for, that there is really some good in this world, then I don't know how I would have got through the past weeks and months. From the first time I saw her, I thought, 'dear God, if she can still smile then so bloody well can I'. If yer can't live with this then you'd be within yer rights to ask us to leave this house, Ma! So it's up to you!"

"Now, lad, don't go saying things like that, why yer know that I'd never ask yer to gan and leave yer home. I just don't know what future there is for yer with her!"

"I know, Ma, probably none, cause it'll not be easy for us, and it might never happen, but one thing I do know, is that if it goes no further than this, then that's alright annaull. I'll not ask for no more as long as she is still in me life, and one thing that I think we both know, me and her, is that yer can only live for today. Tomorrow, if it comes, will bring it's own problems with it."

William Gregg rose from sitting on the stairs, he was stiff from sitting and tried not to groan as he stretched his arms and back before going back up. He'd rather they didn't know that he'd been woken by the bangs and noises that were coming from the kitchen. Over the years he'd held his tongue with respect to Georgie where Molly was concerned, it seemed the best way. He had no regrets, the lad had grown up to be a fine respectful man, and he was proud of his lad, never more so than tonight. He knew in his heart that Molly had lost this one and that she would need comforting by him, it was a side of her that he loved, the part of her that only he knew. Over time he would try to explain to her, or even remind her, how they had felt about each other, how no one could have parted them neither!

"But that's for another time, not tonight!" he whispered to himself at the top of the stairs. "She'll give her blessing one day, lad, you'll see" and he quietly closed the bedroom door.

It was no more than a few minutes later he was listening to Molly's stifled sobs, he turned over, took her in his arms and held her close to his chest. He soothed her until she slept. His last thought before sleep took him was, I know how yer feel, Georgie!

At the other end of The Estate Jessy was helping Ruthie make up the couch, the lasses had settled down to sleep in the spare room and Ralphy had gone to bed, albeit on Ruthie's instructions. He was alright about it though, he knew that the sisters wanted to natter and he had to be up early anyway. There was a good day's work ahead of them all tomorrow, it didn't seem to matter to Ruthie how late she got to bed, she was still up bright and early the next morning. He often wondered where she got her energy from, she rarely even caught a cold. Ruthie would say to him, "It's being happy with you, our Ralph, that does it, happiness is still the best medicine!" Aye, all she ever ailed was a headache now and again, but that was just women's ways! Ralphy fell asleep to the sound of giggles.

"He kissed yer didn't he? Please say yer kissed."

Ruthie was tucking one end of a sheet into the cushions on the couch, when there was no reply from Jessy she stopped what she was doing and looked up, waiting.

"Aw come on, our Jessy, yer can't come round here like this and expect us to just accept that yer looking like yer are because yer had a TALK with him?"

"Weeeellllll, we did talk. No we didn't kiss," Jessy was searching for the words. In the meantime Ruthie must have sensed there was more to the story because even the fact that they hadn't kissed didn't stop her from quitting what she was doing and coming and grabbing Jessy's hands before saying, "There must be more to it than you're letting on. I can tell by your face. If I didn't know better I'd say that yer'd been in the bushes with Erroll Flynn." Ruthie laughed at her own joke, then continued. "I'm not joking, our Jessy, something more must have happened, yer can't fool me with that 'I've just popped along to tell yer about our Ray's letter' and it must have something to do with the butcher's lad, or else how would you know what was in the bloody letter?"

Jessy was serious now when she looked at her sister.

"I need you to be sensible, Ruthie, I want to talk to you, that's why I came, but I need yer to be straight with me. So that I can understand a few things, cause all I'm feeling at the moment is messed up in me head. So before I tell yer anything at all, I want yer to promise me that yer won't make a joke of it and that yer won't make fun of me."

Jessy sighed.

"I really don't know what happened tonight, Ruthie, and if I don't talk to somebody about it, I know that I'll never be able to look him in the eye again. So do yer promise Ruthie?"

Jessy's tone had subdued Ruthie, she could see that her sister was confused and worried, she wouldn't make light of her situation anyway, but she made the promise to ease her sister's mind.

"I promise, Jessy, and I'll go further than that. I also promise not to say a word until yer've finished telling us what yer've got to tell!"

Jessy smiled. That was Ruthie, always going one step further. Well this was going to be an experience, her Ruthie not saying owt or interrupting a conversation. "I'll believe that when I see it!" was her reply.

Jessy told Ruthie of the night's happenings, she confided in her how she felt about her hands when he was looking at them, and why she felt she had to get away. How he had come looking for her in the cold, how he'd gone one way and her another and that he had been waiting for her. These were the facts, what Jessy didn't know was how to describe to Ruthie her feelings.

Ruthie could see her discomfort, Jessy had stopped talking and appeared to be unsure of what to say next.

"Did he say something to yer, Jessy?"

Jessy looked at her and could only whisper, "It wasn't what he said." She was remembering the way he had looked at her, how he had stroked and held her hands, how she had felt when she looked into his eyes.

"Well what then? There must have been something to get yer into this much of a state!" Ruthie was trying to be gentle with her, but bugger me, she thought, it's like trying to get blood out of a stone!

"He held me hands."

"Is that it? All this carry on over a bit of hand holding?" Ruthie was about to carry on when she looked at Jessy's face. It was lovely! For the first time in her life Ruthie could honestly say, Jessy looked LOVELY.

"No think, Ruthie, just think." Jessy held out her hands to Ruthie. She turned them over and then back again. "He held THESE. He held and stroked them." Jessy was now reliving every second of his touch. "When he touched me, it was like a feeling that I've never had. Aw, I can't describe it to yer, our Ruthie, but when he stroked them, and kept on stroking them and then he was looking at me, I felt as if I was swaying around and that I might fall! Other feelings were coming over me annaull" Jessy stopped and leaned a little closer to Ruthie, then said in a hushed voice, "I was getting very warm in some bits, yer know, down below-like."

As Ruthie looked at Jessy, the humour of the situation completely disappeared, and was replaced with a feeling of such intense anger that it made Ruthie say out loud, "That lousy bastard Bullum. Are you telling me that you've never in all your married years COME?"

Jessy didn't understand what had just happened. One

minute she was telling the story, the next Ruthie was like this.

"What are yer up in arms about? What's all this got to do with Bullum?"

Jessy was frightened now, not only had she rarely seen Ruthie this angry but the mention of Bullum's name sapped all the joy she was feeling out of her and replaced it with dread.

Ruthie saw it all now, not that Jessy had ever said much to her about that side of things with Bullum. She knew he was a cruel violent git, but because Jessy had had the bairns, she had thought that mebbie, in that area of things, there had been a bit of tenderness from him. She should have known better, he didn't have a good bone in his body. Aw, my poor Jessy. All those years. She looked at Jessy's frightened face, and went over to hold her. As she put her arms around her, she buried her face in her wig, and said, "I'm so sorry, our Jessy, we should have had this conversation a long time ago, lass. Now don't worry, there's nowt wrong, yer haven't done owt or said owt that isn't NORMAL. And what's more, the feelings that yer getting down below are normal annaull."

She had whispered the words "down below," much the same way that Jessy had whispered them to her.

Jessy looked at her and whispered back, "We're starting to sound like seafaring men."

This was how it always was between them both. When they were together, neither one could be sad for very long. At this remark Ruthie buried her head into Jessy's shoulder to stop the laughter, after all, she had promised to take this seriously. Jessy could feel her laughing against her. What made it more funny was Ruthie trying to hold it in, pretending like it wasn't happening. Now Jessy was trying not to laugh, but no good! She let a little giggle out. That was it! Ruthie fell onto the floor with the guffaw that came out of her, she was rolling around, holding her belly. Jessy was crying with laughter, watching her.

By the time they were done, both of them had jaws that were aching and eyes that were red!

Jessy had never imagined that such things as Ruthie was telling her really happened. She obviously knew about the act itself, and she knew that sometimes yer had to do a bit more than the normal to make things happen. But the idea that the woman got something out of it as well as men, well that was a nigh on impossible idea to Jessy.

"You're telling me, our Ruthie, that women come just the same as men do?"

"Aye, that's right, and it can be just as good for a woman as it is for a man, in some cases better, cause women don't have to wait as long as a man to do it again!"

Jessy was looking at Ruthie to make sure she wasn't joking with her, but she looked serious enough.

"But how, how can a woman do THAT? Yer know, SQUIRT?"

Ruthie would normally have a good laugh at this, but the look of total confusion on Jessy's face stopped that from happening. She knew that she had to try to explain this in words that Jessy understood, make it seem commonplace and ordinary because the last thing that she wanted was for her to be scared off.

"Naw, yer don't squirt, well not really," Ruthie stopped

and thought for a moment. "Yer just get a bit wetter down below, and IT tingles, so like yer want to rub IT."

She was struggling to explain, she could tell by looking at Jessy that what she was saying was not making sense to her. She tried again.

"Yer know the feelings of dizziness yer were getting and the warm feelings in yer knickers?" Jessy nodded. "Well that was part of it, like the build up to it. After that, it happens sort of natural. You get wetter, that's so he, the man, can get his willy inside of yer. There's ways of making that happen annaull, yer know!"

Jessy was still looking at Ruthie in a totally disbelieving way!

"Aw, come on, our Jessy, yer must know what I mean, or else how would that fat git have got inside yer?"

Jessy looked as if she was thinking about what Ruthie had said.

"Well, sometimes he doesn't! Yer know, if he's been drinking-like, I just hold me legs together and sometimes he can't tell. Other times, especially when he was younger, it was a bit tight, and it used to make us a bit sore, but I hated it anyway so it didn't matter!"

Ruthie couldn't hardly believe that her sister, a woman of her age, could be this innocent.

"Have yer ever been KISSED, Jessy?" Ruthie waited. "I mean, really kissed by a man, not the hugs and kisses yer get from the bairns and me?"

"Afore Bullum, I was kissed a couple of times by a lad from the stables up at the hall, but that was a long time ago. Why I must have only been about fifteen. I didn't think much of it, I can remember that much!"

Jessy was still thinking about this episode when Ruthie

said, "And nowt since then?" She knew the answer before she asked. "Well, if that's the case, then that's where we need to start! With the kissing, and work our way, so to speak, up from there! Eeh, our Jessy, I can't believe yer've never asked us afore now about this stuff. Did yer never wonder at all?"

Jessy was silent for a good while. She was thinking of when she was first married, she hadn't known what to expect, but in the first few months, she remembered thinking that there should be a bit more loving atween a man and wife. But after that, and as time went on, those feelings left her, and with the arrival of the bairns she soon forgot about any expectations she'd had. She had got used to "thingy being only to satisfy the Man, or to make babies." She could honestly say that she looked at it with dread and something to avoid if at all possible. What Ruthie was telling Jessy was unbelievable, but she wanted to know more!

For the next half hour, Ruthie told Jessy about the woman's part in sex, or "thingy" as they both called it. Jessy said very little, the disbelief and sometimes shock, then outright humour that she was feeling showed on her face. All Jessy could find to say all the way through this lesson was, "Never" or "Get away" and on one or two occasions pull a face and say, "EEUACK!"

Ruthie had finished. She was worn out, she tried to make it sound as nice as she could, but even as she was telling it she thought some of the things she'd explained, when they were just said, sounded a bit awful. She thought mebbie she'd gone too far, cause from the look on Jessy's face she could tell that it was a lot for her to take in all at once.

At last she spoke.

"Well I can tell yer, our Ruthie, not only has none of that stuff ever happened to me, I can state for a fact it never will! Why most of it sounds terrible. Apart from anything else it all seems a bit messy!"

Ruthie smiled and was about to speak when Jessy continued.

"Aye I might like him, our Ruthie, and I do feel different around him, but there's definitely nowt like what you've been talking about gannin on, and nor will it! No, we're just friends, and I probably felt like I did because he was being nice to me, and as yer know, I'm not used to that kind of thing from a man. Anyway I could still be coming down with something, I mean, I haven't been feeling meself yer know!"

Ruthie nearly laughed, she hadn't told Jessy about that bit of things. Best leave well alone, she thought, I think she's got enough to think about for present.

"Don't take on so much, Jessy, things that happen atween a man and a woman when they love each other is lovely, and it doesn't feel bad or messy and dirty like what you're thinking. It's just something that happens, sometimes whether yer want it to or not."

"Get away with yer, our Ruthie, I don't believe that for a minute. Yer can always help how yer feel, we're not dogs in the street yer know."

Then Jessy remembered how she'd swayed and gone dizzy when he was near her, how she'd felt when he'd just touched her hands, the smell of him when he was next to her, the feeling she got when she looked into his eyes! She was feeling it AGAIN, now, here in front of Ruthie!

"Are you by any chance thinking of Georgie at the minute our Jessy?"

Ruthie's question had brought her out of her imaginings. She was a bit huffed that her thoughts were interrupted. It showed in her voice when she replied.

"I don't know what makes yer think that, can I not be quiet for even a minute without yer thinking dirty thoughts? I was thinking of reading you our Ray's letter as a matter of fact. At least then yer'll see how much better I am at reading, and forget about all your silly thoughts about Georgie and me."

"Aye, alright Jessy. But afore yer start can I just say that if yer going to wear a liberty bodice and not a brassiere then yer should wear a thicker top."

Jessy looked down at her front. Aw, my Lord, she thought.

Ruthie saw the look, and couldn't resist. "Aye they're like 'Chapel Hat Pegs', but we'll say no more about it the night eeh?"

Ruthie listened to Ray's letter, stood, kissed her sister and said, "nigh night." She wasn't worried, she knew that things would take their course, and no matter what Jessy said, Ruthie knew that things had a way of progressing. She was happy for her sister, because although Jessy didn't know it herself yet, Ruthie knew that she was in love.

God willing, she thought, things will work themselves out, and she'll have some happiness. But we'll all have to help, cause there'll be hell to pay if that bastard finds out! She was thinking about the lasses as she tucked them in. They're getting older now, old enough to understand. Anyway who's to say that they couldn't come to stay with me and Ralphy for a while? She smiled because she liked that idea and she knew that her Ralphy would take to it annaull. Anyway he'd have to, her mind was set!

Jessy tried to read Ray's letter again before going to sleep, she could see all the words but she couldn't concentrate. She had a feeling that she knew what Ruthie was thinking, and that it was only a matter of time before the bloody medler started planning. "Why yer can plan all yer like, lass, it'll do yer no good," she was thinking aloud. "I'm still a married woman, and Bullum is still a vicious git, and I'll not put anybody in the way of him and his temper. I've made me mind up, I'll finish me lessons, and I hope that we'll always be friends. GOOD FRIENDS," she sighed, "But I won't let owt else happen, yer can count on that!"

Jessy finally fell to sleep to the sound of her words to Molly in her head: "I promise that I will never hurt your son. I will be his friend. NOTHING MORE!"

I RETURN TO YOU.

The true narrator of this story. We still have some way to go, but already I have been joined by someone else.

The presence is there to aid us all in what will be an even more disturbing journey. I certainly appreciate the help, and so will Jessy. This new presence can offer her the comfort, the peace and the strength she needs in order to continue. It always has!

As I said at the beginning, I am here to stop "A Hurt," but I shall need help. I now know that I shall be joined by others along the way and that my role is purely that of facilitator. In other words I needed to be here to allow the others to COME. I am the DOOR OPENER.

Unfortunately for you, the reader, the love that is now surrounding Jessy cannot be seen or felt by you, you will have to use your imagination. I hope that it is enough to bring you some comfort along the way.

We. must continue now. Jessy is stirring in her sleep and the need to resume is strong within her. I feel the presence beside me urging me on! On and back. On and back!!!!

CHAPTER TEN

He was coming home!

Ray was coming home on leave, only forty eight hours, but it didn't matter. Jessy would make every minute of it count. She'd already been round the doors touting for extra rations from the neighbours. Everyone had been very generous, giving as much as they could in order to give the lad a good meal when he got home.

"I'll do some broth with the bones," she was telling Hetty and Jean. "We'll let him think that's all there is, just you watch his face when I tell him." They were all excited, even Freddy had said that he would be around. Jessy knew that he'd been torn cause Bullum had said he was, "Gannin out, out the way of all the simperin wimen," and had asked Freddy if he was coming But give the lad his dues, he had stood up to him in his own way, saying that he wanted to stay and see Ray. He had followed Bullum outside though, to explain that he would get to hear all the gossip, and that he would let Bullum know all about it later on.

Everything was set. Besides the broth there was a pork chop for him with tatties and carrots, and thought Jessy, some of his Ma's home-made gravy. Then to follow, a bread and butter pudding, with a bit of real butter and some currants that she'd robbed from the cake she'd made for them all. Aye, cake annaull, Oh he'd be pleased. Jessy looked at the lasses' faces and thought, he won't be the only one neither. She kissed them both on the head. They were standing at the window, had been for hours now. She wanted to stand with them, but she knew that it would be agony to her, every minute of it.

"A watched kettle never boils, yer know," she said cheerfully to them. "He'll come when he comes, and standing there fretting won't make it happen any sooner."

She turned away, they were still watching and waiting. She heard the back door, it was Freddy. My God, thought Jessy, 'he's had a hair cut and bugger me if he hasn't had a wash annaull'

"Yer looking smart, our Freddy, yer are that."

The lasses turned and started whispering and giggling to each other. Jessy saw him frown at them, and rather than get him in a bad mood she said, "If yer both gonna carry on like that yer can do it upstairs. Now sit yerselves down and play with yer dollies afore I send yer up."

She was amazed when Freddy defended them saying, "Aw, they're only excited, Mam, they're doing no harm!"

Jessy was even more flabbergasted when he gave each of them a bullit from his pocket, saying, "Here gan on, take these. They might keep yer both quiet for a minute or two."

Jessy was SO happy, Bullum was out and Freddy was in a good mood! Soon Ray would be home and to top it all, they would all go to their beds with full bellies tonight. She went to fill the coal bucket out the back. She couldn't remember ever being happier.

He stood and watched her, he'd come round the back way on purpose to surprise them all. Ray looked at his Mam and his heart went out to her. She was thinner than he remembered, almost skinny, but the way she was filling the coal bucket showed that she was just as much a grafter as ever, everything done at a speed and with more energy than some of the young uns he knew. She still didn't know he was there until, as she went to pick up the scuttle, she saw his hand around the handle, lifting it up for her.

"I'll take that for yer Mam." It was said as if he'd never been away.

Jessy thought she would burst with love and pride. He was there standing in front of her. HER RAY!

She couldn't move, she hadn't said anything to him. As she smiled at him she felt the tears come, slowly and quetly. He put the scuttle down, and held his arms open to her.

"AW, MA! Don't cry."

Then she was there, in his cuddle. He hugged her so hard that she thought she would stop breathing. He lifted her off her feet then put her down gently. She stayed where she was, and he too stood still, holding her.

"It's better this way, Ma. This way I get to see you first. Stay as long as yer like where yer are. I like it."

Everybody had said he'd change, that he would be different. Some had even said that she'd hardly recognize him when he came back....... THEY WERE WRONG!

He wasn't any different, still her Ray. THAT WOULD NEVER CHANGE.

Seven months, to the very day, that's how long it had been since she'd seen him. Jessy looked at him properly now for the first time since he'd arrived. He was telling his stories to the lasses and Freddy, everybody had ate, and ate well. Even Jessy felt full, everybody said that it was a grand meal.

She sat on the fender and listened to his voice. It was a bit deeper, she supposed, and he was a lot darker in colour than when he'd gone. According to his stories that was what the desert sun did to yer. Apart from that he looked the same, the same as the picture that Jessy always had in her mind's eye of him.

"Punkawaller, Punkawaller, Punkawaller, Punka…"

"Alright, Jean, for God's sake, Ray teach her another word. I'm fed up already of hearing that one." They all laughed, "But later on Eeh, because we'll have to be heading to our Ruthie's soon, she's expecting us all any minute now." Jessy came back with her coat and a new hat for the occasion, given by Ruthie, and as she put it on in front of the mirror, she mimicked Ruthie's fake posh voice, "Now come on, all of you, let's not be late for this par-tea."

It was a real celebration, Ruthie had beer for the men and Port for the women. God knows how she got a hold of it all, thought Jessy. Best not to ask, why there's even sherbet for the bairns. Hetty and Jean were dipping their wet fingers in paper cones filled with the sweet red-coloured sugar. That'll be a bugger to get off their hands later, but Jessy didn't mind. She looked around and caught Freddy drinking beer with Ray and Ralphy. It didn't bother her that he was having a drop, it was just the way he was guzzling it down that put her nerves on edge. Ray caught her looking and she saw him have a word with Freddy. Funny that Freddy would take on what Ray said to him, but Jessy knew from past experience if she'd said owt to him, he would have gone off in a huff and been sullen for days.

She went through to the kitchen to help Ruthie with the sandwiches, though why she'd bothered Jessy didn't know. She'd told her that they would all be having their dinner before they came and Jessy couldn't see them wanting anymore!

"Yer needn't have done all of this, our Ruthie, yer know

our Ray would have been just as happy to come along and have a cup of tea and a natter with yer."

"Aw, our Jessy, don't be such a 'kill joy', after all, it's not just for you lot yer know. Why me and Ralphy haven't had owt yet anyway, and besides that, half of the street has promised to call in to see Ray. So it'll not go to waste."

Jessy looked at her busying herself. She was never so happy as when she was doing for folks. She walked over, hugged her and said, "Well, ta then Ruthie. Ta very much!"

As Jessy let go, Ruthie pushed a knife into her hand. "Yer can help while yer here, spread that marge on the bread will yer? Only thin, mind, cause there's not much of it. I'll do the fish paste as yer pass it along."

She no sooner finished when she turned her head and shouted "Ralphy!" No answer. "Ralphy??"

"RALPHY? ARE YER DEAF?"

Ralphy came on the last call, he looked flushed. Jessy thought the beer was leaving it's mark, and smiled when she saw him trip up a bit at the doorway.

"Aye lass, what is it?" he asked.

"Why don't yer get the dominoes and draughts out? Open up a leaf of the table and set them up, yer never know who might want a game. Yer should ask our Ray if he wants to play, after all it is a party yer know."

Ralphy looked a bit confused, "We're alright man! Just having a natter, it's early yet and we can play later if we want."

Ruthie turned and gave Ralphy a look that would curdle butter. "It's not just you I'm thinking about, there might be other folks that want a game when they arrive. It's not just about getting a skinful the night, yer know!"

Ralphy sighed, "Aye, alright I'll set them up," then rebelled with, "But I bet no bugger wants to play" and left the room.

The back door opened. A lad that Ray used to knock about with stood staring at the food on the table.

"Get yersel away through the other room, Micky," said Jessy. "Our Ray's through there and there's some beer through there annaull, We'll bring the food through later on. Divn't worry, yer'll get yer share."

"It's a shame about him being a bit simple, cause he's a bonny lad, and do yer know, sometimes when yer see him, yer wouldn't know there was a thing wrong with him. He's really helpful, yer know helps with bags, doing odd jobs and that! Naw it's a real shame."

Jessy nodded at Ruthie's statement, but couldn't help thinking, At least he didn't have to go to war!

It seemed she had been buttering the bread for ages. "Bloody hell, our Ruthie, how many are yer feeding? Yer've got a ton already, fish paste, braun and now jam. Yes I know, spread the jam thin. Well I hope yer right and it doesn't go to waste." Jessy was silent for a moment. "Mind you I suppose if there's owt left our Bloody Freddy will finish it. I've never known him refuse owt!"

Jessy had just finished speaking when there was a knock on the back door. Ruthie quickly wiped her hands on her pinny, smoothed her hair and rushed to open it. Jessy was just about to say, "Who the hell would knock round here?" when Ruthie opened the door and in walked Georgie, followed by his Ma and Da.

Jessy watched as Ruthie took their coats and hats. "Come

on through to the parlour, Mr and Mrs Gregg and have a comfortable seat. I'll get yer both a drink. Georgie, you've been afore, make yerself at home and I'll tell our Ray yer've come."

Jessy stood in surprised silence, she swore she would kill their Ruthie! He was looking at her.

"How've yer been, Jessy? It's been a while, how are yer doing with the reading and writing?"

"I'm doing good, keeping it up like yer said. Yer know, reading a bit each day, and when I've got time I practice me writing, but that's mostly done when I write proper to our Ray. I write to him three times a week now!"

You could cut the air with a knife! Ruthie had popped her head round the door and then disappeared again.

They were both feeling very awkward, Jessy wished Ruthie would come back through to the kitchen.

"That's good then!" He paused, looking for words. "It was well worth doing then, don't yer think? I mean it wasn't time wasted."

Georgie looked at her and understood, she hadn't known he would be coming! He felt her discomfort, but he didn't really know what to say. Ruthie had painted an entirely different picture of the whole evening, even down to saying that the celebration wouldn't be complete without him, and to bring his Ma and Da along as well. After all, they had been there the night everything was decided, and that she was sure Ray would be glad to see him. If only to thank him for teaching his Ma to read and write.

"Thank God," Jessy nearly said it out loud as Ray burst into the kitchen and went over and shook Georgie's hand.

"Come on through and have a drink. We've all had a couple already, so yer've got time to make up!"

As Ray led him through, Georgie turned at the door and replied to Ray, but was looking at Jessy, "Yes I think I have."

Ruthie appeared at the doorway just as Jessy flopped down into a kitchen chair, she had the bottle of Port in her hand and was holding it up in front of her.

"Yer wouldn't hit a woman carrying a bottle during a war would yer?"

Jessy looked at her and shook her head.

Ruthie's smile vanished, she pulled the door nearly closed and came and sat beside Jessy.

Jessy had resigned herself in the past to Ruthie's interference. But she had gone too far this time.

"When are yer gonna stop poking yer nose into other people's business, Ruthie? Yer had no right. Yer know how important tonight was to me, and yet yer still had to play yer silly games…. Well it's backfired on yer, cause not only have yer spoilt it for me, but now I wouldn't be surprised if yer whole "par tea" is spoiled annaull. cause of all the awkwardness that they're all feeling."

Jessy had no sooner got the words out of her mouth than she heard someone start to play the piano and then there was singing.

All this did was to make Jessy feel even more frustrated, she was now beyond anger, but she didn't know what to do with her feelings. She wanted to run away, get out of the house. But she knew she would then be responsible for spoiling everything. So she was trapped, she could do nothing.

Ruthie saw now how much she was hurting, it wasn't a joke anymore. Jessy's eyes had filled up.

"I'm so sorry, lass. I didn't think that yer would mind this much, I even thought that yer might be pleased to see him. I was wrong!" She waited for Jessy to say something. When she didn't she continued, "I promise I'll never interfere again, lass. I do. I SWEAR! Look, cross me heart and hope to die."

Ruthie had drawn a cross with her finger on her front, then raised her open-palmed hand to head level. She sat like this waiting for Jessy to speak.

"Oh you will, Ruthie. You know you will. You can't help yourself."

Jessy had spoken properly to Ruthie. Ruthie knew she was serious, she had never seen their Jessy this serious or this distant.

Jessy had made her point, she knew Ruthie was sorry. There was no need to say any more to her, she could tell from her wide-eyed look that she knew it had been a mistake.

"Well, now that they're here hadn't yer better get this food finished, and get out there with them? It'll look rude otherwise." Jessy stood. "Come on let's make another start then!" She wiped a knob of marge off the table and smeared it onto Ruthie's nose.

Four lasses had come, four of them, to see Ray! And another couple of neighbours had called in. There was quite a house full. Jessy hadn't been through to the front room yet, but she could hear that it was going well through there. As Ruthie came back to carry more sandwiches through, Jessy saw Molly through the open door. She looked to be enjoying herself, she was singing along with the rest of them. That reminds me, thought Jessy.

"Ruthie, are me Ma and Da not coming then? I thought yer said yer'd asked them?"

Ruthie turned with a plate of sandwiches in her hand. "Well, yer know how me Da is, he won't go anywhere but the pub and me Ma says she's not been feeling too well lately! Whether or not she was making an excuse, I don't know, but she didn't look that well when I saw her." She stopped and looked at Jessy. "I don't think they can face yer lass, what with all that's gone on."

When Jessy didn't reply, she continued, "Anyway there's no love lost atween yer all now is there? I mean, it's been years since yer've seen them both. Don't get me wrong, I'm not saying yer not right, and I'd probably be the same if I was you! Why, I only call meself once or twice a year now, and then mainly just to see me Ma. Anyway let's not let it spoil the night eeh?"

"Aye alright, but I did think they'd mebbie come along to see our Ray. After all, I've never stopped the bairns from seeing them, he is their grandkid. There was a time when I thought me Ma was fond of him. What with losing our Thomas and all that!"

Jessy had been talking to herself, Ruthie had turned and gone through the door to the "par tea" before she had finished. She didn't know where to go or what to do now. The making of the food was finished and she'd done all the tidying up that she could for now. She didn't want to go through to the front room in case she had to explain to Georgie why she hadn't kept in touch like she'd promised to! So she poured herself a large Port and sat at the table listening to the singing.

Jessy knew that what Ruthie had told her that night had been right! But it didn't make her feel any easier. In fact she felt worse, knowing the effect he could have on her. She'd decided that she would work real hard on her lessons and then she would stop as soon as she could. That's just what happened over two weeks ago now. Since then she'd not been out much, in case she bumped into him. Freddy had been going to the butcher's for her, and she'd changed her times to do the washing, leaving it till very late or extra early. Jessy was frightened, not of Georgie as a man, but of the feelings that she had for him! Even when she was at home and just thought about him, she felt funny inside herself. She knew that if she'd carried on seeing him something would have happened. "Naw, best leave well alone, lass," she was talking to herself. "Cause yer know what trouble yer'd bring down on the pair of yer." She sipped her Port and with a broken voice said, "But I do miss yer, lad!"

Molly had noticed that Jessy had not joined them in the parlour, she also saw that Georgie had noticed it too. He kept looking around for her every time the door opened. Molly had come tonight in the main cause she knew that Georgie had wanted to, but also to see the lad Ray. She'd liked this lad from the moment she'd seen him, he reminded her of Georgie, in some ways. He was caring and gentle to his Ma, like her Georgie, and he wasn't the usual dirty mess yer get around here, he did take a pride in his appearance. Why look at them together at the piano, with all them lasses around them. From the back they could be brothers. Molly's thoughts were interrupted when she looked through the open door that Ruthie had left to the kitchen and saw Jessy. She felt dreadful sorry for her. But it's for the best, she thought, and I'll say this for her, she's been as good as her word. Aye she's been the one to put a stop to it, and thank God cause I know our Georgie couldn't have! Ruthie saw Molly looking at Jessy, she went into the kitchen and closed the door, Molly got on with joining in the singing.

Ruthie sat next to Jessy and poured herself a Port, she topped Jessy's glass up at the same time. She looked as if she needed it.

"Are yer not gannin through to join in the fun? Your Ray's having a hell of a time, the lasses are all over him! Yer should be in there and seeing how happy he is!"

"Naw, let them get on with it, our Ruthie, I think I'll..."

Jessy didn't get the chance to finish. Ray had rushed in, went round to the back of her seat and lifted her out of it.

"I want me best girl in there singing with me, so come on then, Ma, howay through and join in."

"Naw, naw, our Ray, I'm better off here with our Ruthie."

"Well yer don't think that I'm ganna leave her sitting here by herself, do yer? No, yer can both come through and have a bit of fun! As Georgie's just said it's not fair on yer both, doing nowt but the making and the tidying so come on then, the pair of you, and I'll not take "no" for an answer."

He was pushing her towards the door, she knew there was no point in arguing with him, she grabbed Ruthie's hand as she passed. Ruthie looked as if she understood, she got up and linked Jessy's arm, then said, "We're coming, our Ray, just give us a minute to straighten our pinnies will yer, then we'll be through."

He turned and looked at Ruthie, then back at his Mam. He's so happy, thought Jessy, I cannot spoil it for him.

He took hold of Jessy's hand and said gently, "Well you make sure yer do, cause I've little enough time to spend with yer. I don't expect yer to be in one room while I'm in the other! Alright?"

She smiled and sighed, "Aye, alright our Ray, now get yersel away back in, those lasses will be waiting for yer."

When he'd gone Ruthie stood and puffed up her hair, and smoothed down her pinny, then turning to Jessy, "Well you heard him, get yerself straight and let's go through."

Jessy took off her own pinny, she had a new woolen dress on, one of Ruthie's cast-offs of course, but it was new to Jessy. It was straight and grey. Ruthie said it was a bit plain for her, but Jessy liked it cause of its simple lines, and she thought that it was the colour of a pidgeon's breast. She'd put an old cameo brooch on the shoulder and it seemed to make it look a bit classy. She went over to the small mirror at the back door and checked her hair and her face.

Ruthie had been watching. "Eeh, our Jessy, I never realized that yer had that dress on under yer pinny, it looks lovely on yer, far better than it did on me." And she meant it, the cut of it really suited Jessy, it was long and straight, but it was darted in all the right places for Jessy, it made her look like a lady.

Jessy was glad that she had worn it now, she hadn't been sure, she'd thought it was a bit dressy for tonight. Now she was glad, something in her wanted them all to see her at her best.

She was standing between Ralphy and Ray, William Gregg was playing the piano, he played well. Freddy had been next to her a minute ago, she guessed that he had gone to see if there was any food left. Georgie was over the other side of the piano talking to one of the lasses, well she was talking to him at any rate. Jessy had been watching this lass flirt with him for the past half hour. Bye, she's trying hard, thought Jessy, if she pushes herself much closer to him he'll be against the wall, but he doesn't look too unhappy about it. He could always walk away! Jessy felt awful, she didn't like this girl. It didn't make sense, she didn't really know her, but at that minute she really disliked her.

Georgie's Dad stood saying, "Somebody else can have a go now, I'm going to get meself a drink and sit with my lovely wife"

He looked around the room waiting for volunteers. "What, nobody's going to give us a break?"

"Well, our Ralphy can only play Chopsticks and he does that badly," said Ruthie to a giggling audience.

"Why it looks like the onus is on you, Georgie." William Gregg continued, "Don't tell me all those lessons were for nowt." He smiled with pride as Georgie reluctantly sat at the piano. He patted his shoulder and turned to go as Georgie started to play.

Oh he plays lovely, thought Jessy, 'as good, if not better, than his Dad. She was nearer him now, he'd looked at her as he sat down. He was playing something soft and slow, she didn't know what it was but she knew he was playing it for her. She was getting the feeling again, that feeling of drowning. As he played he kept looking at her. Most of the others had drifted away, now that there was no singing. For a moment, Jessy felt as if there was only her and him in the room. She was brought out of this by Molly coming up behind her and saying to Georgie, "Not that stuff, our Georgie, play something we can ALL enjoy, like yer Dad, play something we can sing to."

He said nothing, he stopped and then started again on a more lively tune. She seemed satisfied and she turned to go. They caught each other's eyes, Jessy and Molly. Molly smiled and Jessy returned it. Both knew what the other was thinking, but it was left at that.

The young lass, that had been flirting with Georgie was back, she stood next to him, real close, and put her hand on his shoulder. She didn't let it just rest there, she began stroking him across the back. Jessy was hit by an intense desire to thump her. The little whore, she thought, and in a crowded room where everybody can see. Why it's as if she owns him! The lass bent forward and whispered something in Georgie's ear, they both laughed. Jessy had very rarely felt this much anger, she was trembling with temper. It was a relief when Freddy came over to her and said, "I'm ganning now, Mam. I'll go and look for me Dad, see if he wants owt doing. Anyway it'll keep him in a good mood. I've told our Ray, and he's alright about it, so I'll see yer later." He waited for her to reply. "Are yer alright, Ma? I'll not go if yer don't want us to, but there's nowt for me to do here. I mean the lasses are not ganna look at me when our Ray's around and all the foods gone annaull."

Jessy couldn't help but smile, it was good to know that some things never changed.

"You be on yer way then, lad, but don't be in too late if yer can help it. I'd like us all to sit and have a cuppa together, just us lot. There's not long till he gans back and I want us to spend as much time together as we can." But as Jessy watched Ralphy playing with the lasses she knew that in all probability they would be staying here tonight anyway!

Freddy was gone with, "Ta Rah" and she looked round for Ruthie. She wanted to get away from the piano now, she felt like an intruder.

Ruthie was busy with Molly and William and a couple of other people that, although Jessy had been introduced to them, she had forgot the names of. So she made her way out to the kitchen. She picked up the Port bottle, then thought about it. I'm feeling a bit tipsy already, she hesitated, then poured an extra large one. On the table was a packet of tab's and some matches. She took one out, she didn't think anyone would mind, after all it was a "par tea" and everything was shared. Jessy put on her coat, took her drink and the tab and matches and went out into the yard. She made sure the door was closed quickly, cause of the blackout and leaned against the lavvy wall and lit the cigarette.

Georgie had felt uncomfortable most of the night, this lass that was hanging onto him for grim death, was the cause.

Yer can tell there's not many men to choose from now, he thought, or else she wouldn't have been bothering me. He stopped playing not long after Jessy had disappeared, Ralphy was having his turn now, and despite him not being able to play much, he was proving very popular. Everyone was having a laugh at his efforts, and he was having a good time trying to understand what Georgie's Ma was telling him regarding how to play. Who, in turn, was often interrupted by his Da, saying just the oppissite. While this hilarity was going on, Georgie took the opportunity of going to look for Jessy.

Ruthie had noticed what was happening. She was determined to give them some time together. A few minutes at least. "Whoa betide anybody who tries to leave this room in the next ten minutes," she said to herself. "I'll just have to think of a way to keep them occupied!"

Georgie put a cigarette in his mouth, he'd been disappointed that Jessy hadn't been in the kitchen and was afraid that she may have gone home until he saw his matches were missing!

The back door opened and then closed quickly, she knew who it was without turning around. She heard him call her name and then wait for a reply. She was pleased that he had come to look for her, but was also scared to talk to him. It was pitch dark, if she stayed quiet would he see her? He called her name again, and asked where she was.

Georgie thought he must have been wrong and was turning to go back in, to scrounge a light from somebody, when she answered.

"I'm here Georgie," she had said it quietly, she didn't even know if she wanted him to hear her.

She heard him laugh. "Why do women do that?" he asked

"Answer yer without giving any information? Where's here? Jessy."

"I'm at the back of the yard, up side the lavvy, stay still and I'll come to you. I know me way around this yard better than you do."

He was already walking towards her voice, as they collided he reached out to stop her from falling.

His arms were around her, she wasn't pushing him away. They both stood like this. Emotions were going wild in both of them. It was just as well he was holding her cause Jessy knew that she would have collapsed if he hadn't. There was such silence, the noise from inside the house seemed miles away, she could see him now, the outline of him anyway. His face was level with hers, she could feel the warmth of him. He kissed her forehead and round her face. She had never felt like this, her head was swimming. When she closed her eyes it was in an effort to clear her head, she lifted her head and tilted it backwards to take a deep breath. He saw the movement and took his opportunity. He kissed her on the lips, soft at first, then when she didn't pull away, firmer. She smelt good, clean without the fake flowery sweet smell of stale perfume. He felt her lean into him, his body came alive, he could feel the blood surge through him. "Don't go too fast," he told himself. "Bring her along slowly, be patient, wait till she's where you're at now!"

Jessy was beyond thought, she was drifting, her body was saying and doing things to her that she couldn't control. She felt her arms go to his head, she wanted his kisses. She pulled his head and lips firmer onto her own, he responded by pulling her even closer to him. She could feel the hardness of him, she pushed herself into him to feel it more. She was driven by passion. She pushed herself even more into him, she could feel her breasts against him, she had an overwhelming feeling of wanting to rub her whole body up and down him. He broke away from her for a second, her world had ended! Then he was holding her face. He started kissing her again, but this time it was different. He kissed her lips softly, then she felt him lick them. All the way around he took his tongue and licked her mouth, first on the outside then when her lips parted in an ecstatic sigh he softly put his tongue inside her mouth. Just the tip at first, then when their lips met, and she was kissing him back, he thrust it all in. She didn't know why but she was sucking it, sucking his tongue. He was pushing it all in her mouth and then he started pulling it out, then back in. She loved it, she was a different person.

His hands had moved down her back, over her hips and he was holding her buttocks. He pulled her into him and ground himself against her. She answered by tightening her hold around his neck, pulling his mouth and his tongue further into her and at the same time pushing herself against his hardness and grinding with him. Every bit of her body was thrust into him, she couldn't stop, couldn't stop rubbing against him, and him her. She parted her legs a little, so that she could thrust her hips upward and more forward. He sensed her urgency, and lifted her into him. It seemed impossible not to put her legs around him, but when she did, the feeling of him rubbing her was wonderful. It was building up to something, she was rubbing harder. She had no fear of him, she battled for the inside of his mouth with her own tongue. When she was in, he too started sucking, long slow deep wet sucks, drawing all of her feelings out, then it got faster and harder, he was nibbling it, then sucking again. Please don't stop, her head begged it not to happen. Please not yet. Please, God, not yet. Something was building up inside her, and it was nearly there. Georgie felt her thrust into him, hard, and then she shuddered and gave a little cry of, "Ooooh." Her legs relaxed around him, he didn't want to let her go, but he knew what had just happened. He relaxed his grip on her and set her down on the floor. He moved his hands up her back, her arms dropped to her sides. He folded her into his chest, she was still trembling. He stroked her back, saying "Ssshhh Ssssshhhh. It's alright Sssshhhh." His hardness was subsiding, and his concern over her was increasing. He knew that this had been special to her, that she must have been starved for affection, in order for what had happened to happen!

"Are yer alright Jessy?" He was still holding her close, he felt her nod into his chest.

"Will yer not say anything, lass? Will yer not tell us that you're alright and that yer don't regret any of this?"

Jessy pulled away from him a little, he still had his arms around her. He was going to let them drop when she put her own arms behind her back and held his hands so that he couldn't take them away. Her voice was clear and strong when she said, "I'm really alright, Georgie." She paused as if looking for words, then sighed. "I'm really a lot better than alright!"

Jessy laid her head against his chest, and listened as his heart started to slow down. After a minute or so she heard him ask, "Yer still haven't said yer don't regret it, cause if yer don't, we're gonna have to find a way of seeing each other. But if yer do mind, then I promise you, I'll do as yer've been wantin us to do these last few weeks. I'll leave yer alone. That is, I'll try to keep out of yer way. If that's what yer really want?"

"I have no doubt that later, when I think about it, I'll feel a bit silly, but no I don't regret it, Georgie." She still loved saying his name. "As far as seeing each other, then I don't think I could help meself, and after tonight I'm not sure that I care about trying to!" She felt the sigh shudder through his body, she knew that he felt the same as she did.

They had been gone no more than ten minutes, but Ruthie didn't think that she could hold Molly at bay much longer. Ralphy's piano playing wasn't gonna entertain the crowd much more, and Molly had grown bored of trying to teach him. She looked around suspiciously and asked where Georgie had got to? Ruthie fobbed her off with, "Probably trying to find summit else to eat, yer know what lads are like." When she saw her looking around for Jessy, she said she would go and look for him.

"We'll both go," was Molly's reply. She followed Ruthie out of the room.

Before they got to the kitchen door Ruthie started shouting, "GEORGIE, GEORGIE, YER WANTED!"

"What the hell are yer shouting at, lass? If they were in here you'd deafen them, anyway where are they?"

"I haven't the faintest," said Ruthie. "Unless" and she looked to the corner of the room at the door leading to the hall of the shop.

"Where's that door lead to?" asked Molly.

"Only the shop, but he won't have gone through there. Why, it's too dark. I mean, why would he go through there where it's all quiet, when there's so much gannin on out here?"

"Well that's just it. HE wouldn't! Not by himself!"

Ruthie feigned ignorance and looked at Molly with wide innocent eyes. Then said, "I don't know what yer mean, I'm sure."

This was too much for Molly. That wide-eyed look's not

fooling anybody, she thought. It was with fake sincerity that she asked, "Can I take a look, lass? After all yer never know, he might have had one of his turns and be hurt?"

"Well," said Ruthie, "we don't usually let people go through to the shop." She paused as if thinking. "I know, I'll ask Ralphy. After all we don't want you getting hurt annaull."

Molly was getting riled now, but she kept up the act of pleasantness. "No need to bother him, lass." She was halfway through the door when she turned and said, "I'll be back out afore yer get him through here!"

As Molly departed Ruthie smiled and walked over to the back door, opened it and quickly said to the darkness, "Georgie, yer Mam's on the warpath. She'll be out there in a minute" and hurriedly closed the door.

Ruthie was sitting at the kitchen table when Molly eventually returned. She looked up and simply asked, "No luck?"

Molly was ashen and Ruthie could tell she was upset. She nearly weakened, but then she thought, that'll teach yer for trying to control other folk's lives. instead she said, "Sit down, lass, yer look as if yer've seen a ghost." She turned away to smile at the phrase. "I'll put the kettle on. Yer look as if yer need one, have yer had a bit too much stout to drink, eeh?" Ruthie's voice had been total sweetness as she made the statement, and when Molly replied gruffly that it had nothing to do with the stout, Ruthie continued her act and merely said, "I've managed to get me hands on a bit of sugar. Do yer want some in yer tea?"

Molly flopped down in the chair, "Aye yer had better, I've had the shock of me life out there." She shuddered, "Yer didn't say owt about there being a dead body out there, why I nearly died meself, and yer want to get a bit of light out there annaull, I'd bumped into it on the slab afore I knew it was there, that was after I'd put me hand on its face trying to feel me way around."

It was just as well that Ruthie had her back to her, she could hardly keep the laugh in, and if she'd had to look at Molly's face, she knew she would have broken down. She pretended to cough, to clear her throat and replied, "Eeh, well I'm sorry, Molly. I never thought. I mean I thought that yer would have known what would be out there, us being an undertaker's. That's why I couldn't understand yer thinking that your Georgie was through there. Oh by the way, he's out in the yard having a tab. I looked a minute ago, he says he wanted a bit of fresh air!" She took the tea over to Molly and in a conspirational whisper said, "He's mebbie the worse for wear, yer know how men are!"

At the news of where Georgie was, Molly pushed the cup aside and strode to the back door. She opened it and peered out into the darkness, she could see nothing, her eyes were not accustomed to the dark yet. She was still peering out when she heard him shout, "SHUT THAT BLOODY DOOR, WILL YER? THERE'S A BLOODY BLACKOUT!"

"Why there's no need to talk to us li..." Molly was angry that he had shouted at her, and was about to tell him so when she was interrupted with, "DON'T STAND THERE ARGUING. SHUT THE DOOR!"

She slammed it shut, she could hear Ruthie in the background tutting and mumbling something about the way kids spoke to their parents. Molly sat down wearily to drink her tea, she would wait. They would both come in soon, it was bitter outside.

He came in a few minutes later, he looked at his Ma, waiting for her to ask. She was still looking at the closed door. Georgie chose to ignore her for the moment. Instead he turned to Ruthie and asked, "Is there any more tea in that pot? I could do with a cuppa."

"Sit yerself down, lad," Ruthie rose. "I'll bring it over. Do you need another one, Molly, for the shock yer know?"

"Aw Mam," said Georgie, "I didn't mean to frighten yer with me shouting, but you know well enough to keep doors closed during a blackout." He paused and looked at her, she did look a bit worn out! "Anyway I'm sorry if I upset yer."

"It's not just that, our Georgie, though that didn't help the situation," Molly was still unsure as to whether or not Jessy was still waiting outside. "I was looking for yer. I was worried. I mean, I wasn't to know that yer were outside was I?" She didn't wait for him to reply, but carried on, speaking in a hurt tone. "That's all the thanks yer get for worrying yerself sick these days isn't it? I mean how was I supposed to know that yer'd gone for a little talk outside." She waited, Georgie said nothing. "Yer were gone some time, yer know, everybody was asking where yer were. They were asking about Jessy annaull"

Ruthie gave a slight shake of her head to Georgie.

"Well, I don't know where Jessy is at the moment. I thought she'd left some time ago. But as for meself, I was having a smoke and a bit of fresh air, but if yer don't believe me, yer can gan and take a look yerself. But mind yer close the door fast!"

"Aw, no, there's no need for that. It's just odd that she didn't say 'cheerio' to anybody, that's all." Molly thought that she had got one over on him when Ruthie piped up with, "Eeh, now that I think, she asked me to say 'tar rah' to yer all, it was so noisy through there, and she didn't want to stop Ray's fun. Aye, that's right she went home with a bad head. She knew that Ray would insist on taking her home if she made a fuss, and she didn't want to spoil his night." Ruthie finished speaking and brought the tea over.

Georgie was fed up of this now, fed up of his mother interfering. He was a man, not some child that had to explain his every move. "So that's what was on yer mind was it, Ma? I've told yer afore Ma, Don't go messing in my business. I thought we'd talked about this and got it sorted out, but no, you still have to carry on pushing yer nose in where it's not wanted." His voice was getting louder, Ruthie could see that this could turn into a full-scale row, so she interrupted him herself.

"I don't think yer Mam's herself at the moment, Georgie," she turned to Molly and said, "Yer haven't told him about yer fright. Yer got started and then yer didn't get it said." She turned back to Georgie saying, "Wait till yer hear her side of the story lad, cause she has been upset."

As Ruthie left the room to join the others she heard Molly say, "Aw, don't be angry at us, lad, not till yer hear what's happened to us, and the terrible shock I've had."

Ruthie knew that Jessy had gone home. Georgie wouldn't have left her out in the yard! Ruthie knew that much about him. Oh, I hope it was worth it, our Jessy, she thought. If the look on Georgie's face is owt to go by, then summit must have happened. "Surely they got something sorted out, or else I've been running around like a headless chicken all night for nowt, never mind arranging all this and having all this bloody mess!" She was talking to herself as she walked up the stairs to get the lasses' bed made up.

Freddy hadn't meant to be there, not this time. He had been doing as he said, going to see his Dad, but when the fresh air hit him, he felt sick. He knew that it was the beer, and that he needed to sit down till he felt a bit better. He opened the lavvy door, saw the bowl and puked. His belly felt better, but his head was still hurting, so he sat on the lavvy with his head in his hands, waiting for the "whirls" to stop. Somebody came out, he didn't want anybody to see him here in the lavvy, puking. He knew they would laugh at him, and Freddy didn't like people laughing at him. He decided to keep quiet till they were gone, and just hope that nobody wanted to use the lavvy. At first he couldn't make out who it was, the gap in the wood at one side of the lavvy wasn't very big, and it was that dark. When he did recognize who it was, he was on his way out. After all, his Ma wouldn't laugh at him, and at least she'd know what to do for him. His hand was on the handle when he heard Georgie call his Mam's name. He sat back down.

He'd heard it all, he hadn't been able to see much cause his Ma had moved out of the way of the crack in the wood, but he'd heard enough to know what had been going on. Or so he thought. He was still sitting there now, trying to decide what to do with all of this new-found knowledge. Not only had he seen what he thought he had seen, but he'd heard them discuss where and how they would meet. How Georgie would know to go to the old cottage in the park, where he had a key, cause it was where all the stuff like lamps and blankets were kept in case of emergency. How, when his Ma wore the brooch that she had on tonight it would mean that she would meet him there. How, if Georgie couldn't go, he would close his bedroom curtains during the day as a signal to her. He knew that they were to meet in four day's time, he might just gan along himself then annuall. After all what had his Da always said? "Knowledge is power" and whilst he would never use his power to hurt his Ma, he knew that Georgie couldn't be short of a bob or two!

His head suddenly felt better, so did his belly. He didn't want to go home and be with his Ma by themselves, not tonight. He would go back in and get Ray to go home with him. It wasn't that Freddy was shocked, he wasn't even really surprised, not after having seen the pair of them together that last time. Thank god I didn't say owt then, he thought, if I had, this mighten'd have happened, then it would have been a waste.

Ralphy was surprised to see him. "I thought you went ages ago." He was annoyed when the reply he got from Freddy was, "Well I'm back now aren't I?"

He walked over to Ray. Ray turned and patted him on the back when he saw him, and before Ray could ask, Freddy gave his explanation. "I couldn't find me Da, so I came back here. Where's me Ma? Has she gone home already?"

"Aye, Ruthie's just told us not so long ago. She had a bad head and went. I was gonna follow her but Ruthie said that the last thing she wanted was to spoil me night. But to tell yer the truth, I've had enough. I'd rather be home with her, and spend a bit of time with yer all afore me Da comes home."

Freddy watched as Ray said his goodbyes, he shook Ralphy's hand, then Georgie's, he thanked him for helping his Ma with the reading thing! Molly, Georgie's Ma kissed him on the cheek and his Da shook his hand too. All very lovey dovey, thought Freddy, not one of them had come over to say goodbye to me though. I bet they didn't even notice I'd gone.

Ray was saying goodbye to the lasses now, one of them was moaning that Ray had promised to walk her home. When he said he still would, that he and Freddy would walk her if she came now, she said it didn't matter. Freddy saw this and was pleased that Ray had chosen him over her. As he watched, he had to admit that Ray WAS handsome. He could understand the lasses liking him, but it still made him mad to feel left out.

Ruthie caught them in the kitchen and gave them big slobbery kisses on the cheek. Ray laughed, Freddy scowled and Ruthie thought some things don't change.

Freddy felt special walking home with Ray. Ray told him about the war, told him more things than he told his Ma, they stopped once or twice for a tab. Freddy knew that this time was precious, not many people chose to spend time with him, he had known that for a while. But he never seemed to get on Ray's nerves, nor Ray on his. If I could be somebody, he thought, I'd be our Ray. Freddy was lost in his own thoughts for a moment. THEN I'D BE DIFFERENT!

Jessy was pleased the house was empty. What had happened to her tonight took some thinking about. Why, even on the way home, when she thought about Georgie she felt a tingling inside her.

When she got indoors, she was at sixes and sevens, she went to put the kettle on before she took her coat off, then forgot about it. She wandered from one room to another, asking herself what she was going to do.

She would think about him and everything else went out of her head.

"Come on, lass, pull yerself together," she said it out loud, "all he did was kiss yer, yer daft git."

Then she thought of the kiss, she was back there in Georgie's arms, being held and kissed and licked.

"Naw, now come on." She had to sit down in the chair. She put her head in her hands and tried to stop the trembling.

As she sat there she saw his face and the way he looked at her, she remembered how good she had felt when he said he must see her again, that he couldn't see a life without her in it. It was funny, but she thought that when she entered this house that all of the joy she had felt would be gone. Instead, it was a release. She wasn't frightened anymore, not of the future, not of what people would say and not even of Bullum! They were all nothing compared to the feeling of NEEDING to see him again. Jessy knew that in that moment she had come to realize that she would risk anything! Anything at all, her kids and even her life!

It was four days till Wednesday, four days until she saw him again, felt him again.

"How will I get through them?" she asked herself. "Four whole days without seeing his face." Jessy knew that she could gan along the butcher's anytime, on the pretext of asking if there was owt left, or owt due to come in, but that would be torture to her. So she would just have to wait! As she rocked herself back and forward she said, "Grin and bear it lass, grin and bear it! After all, it is a sweet pain!"

Shortly afterwards Ray and Freddy burst in the door shouting, "SURPRISE, WE'RE HOME!" Jessy stood up and looked at them, she was truly happy to see them BOTH, the way they stood together in the doorway, arms around each other's shoulders, made her smile. Jessy tried to put everything else out of her mind as she asked, "Well what are yer both doing here then? I thought that you had gone to see yer Da, our Freddy and I didn't expect you back for a good while, our Ray. Not with them lasses hanging about yer. Did none of them take yer fancy or summit?"

Ray smiled and walked over to Jessy, put his arms around her and pretended to dance with her, just really swaying on the spot.

"Why would I be interested in any other woman, when I've got the best of the bunch here?" he made her twirl round as he said it.

"Aw, stop it, our Ray, all this palaver. Let go, and let me go and put the kettle on."

Ray did as he was told, only after he had twirled Jessy another few times, both he and Freddy laughed as she staggered dizzy to the kitchen. Ray remarked jokingly to Freddy, but loud enough for his Ma to hear, "Having a bit too much suits me Mam, doesn't it, our Freddy? She looks real well on the drink. Don't yer think Freddy?"

Jessy had heard every word. She didn't reply, she knew it wasn't the drink that was making her look and feel well.

Freddy nodded at Ray, but he too knew that it wasn't the drink affecting his Mam.

Ray turned to Freddy after he had his cuppa, and after Freddy had wolfed down some of the cold bread and butter pudding. "Why don't yer make yer way up? I just want to have a natter with me Ma for a while."

As Freddy left the room, Jessy turned to Ray. "If yer want to have a talk, our Ray, yer better come through to the kitchen. I'll have to make up something for HIM to eat when he gets home."

Ray followed her through, she was a bit anxious. Did Ray know something? Had he guessed?

"Why are yer still with him, Mam?" Ray asked. "How can yer still do for him after what he's put yer through?"

Jessy gave a rueful smile, "Yer don't know how many times I've asked meself that very question, our Ray," she sighed. "What's me choices? Oh I know that yer gonna say that our Ruthie would help out, and yer right, she probably would. But is that fair on her and Ralphy? To have a whole family move in on them, and bring all the trouble that yer Da could cause to their door?" She turned to Ray and ushered him back to the front room saying, "Naw, I couldn't do that to them. They've done enough over the years, and they've got their own problems. They don't need anybody else's!" She sat down, Ray had his back to her, he put a shovel of coal on the fire, and poked it into flames.

"But how can yer bear it? When I'm away I keep remembering what he's done in the past, what he's capable of. I'm never sure if yer alright, or what I'm gonna find when I come home." He knelt down beside her, "Are yer sure, Ma? Are yer sure yer ganna be alright?"

Jessy looked at this lad of hers, she saw the worry on his face and in his eyes. She'd missed his face. As she lifted her hand to his cheek she thought, he's got enough on his plate to worry about, without having me in his head annaull. "Don't worry lad," she said gently. "Things are a lot better now. He leaves us alone most of the time and when he looks as if he's had a bellyful, we all know how to keep out of his way now. Besides that, he's getting older yer know, he's slowing down all the time. He can't even take his drink like he used to. Why, nowadays we don't see him awake much, it's taking him longer and longer to sleep it off. She patted his cheek, "So don't worry about us, we've got the measure of him," and she kissed him on the forehead.

Ray knew the conversation was at an end. He wanted to believe her, but he knew his Da, and he knew that if he wanted to do her harm that he would find a way. He mighten't even do it himself, he could afford to pay for others to do his dirty work. The only hope that Ray clung to was that his Da's greed outweighed his temper. As long as that was the case, his Ma and the others would be safe enough. He stood and said, "I'm away up then, Ma. It's been a long day." He saw the look of disappointment on her face. "Why don't you gan up as well and leave HIM his grub, let him fend for himself. I thought that I could get up early, and you and me could go for a walk, just the two of us, spend the morning together and then pick the lasses up from Ruthie's. How would yer like that?"

"Aye, good idea, lad. I'd like that a lot," Jessy felt excited at spending some time alone with him. She did as he asked and they went up the stairs together, he hugged her tight at the top, and whispered into her hair(wig), "I love yer, Ma, nigh night."

"I know, lad," she replied as he closed the bedroom door.

Freddy pretended to be asleep, he'd been thinking about what to do with his newfound knowledge. It was no good saying owt to his Da, well not at the moment anyway, nothing had happened. Anyway that would only hurt his Ma. Freddy didn't want that to happen, not just because he loved her in his own way, but also because he knew that if anything happened to her, his life would change for the worse. After all, she still looks after us! he thought. And anyway, thought Freddy, If our

Ray ever found out that I'd done owt at all that hurt his Ma, then he would lose him. That is if Ray didn't kill him!

Freddy went to sleep having decided to hang onto what he knew for a while, the last thought he had was, mebbie Georgie was the one to see, mebbie he would pay him to keep his mouth shut? We'll see!

Wilmy had been dozing in the chair, she too had had a long day. She woke suddenly, she hadn't been dreaming, that's not what woke her. It was the feeling of DREAD that was surging through her. Rarely had she felt it this strong. It filled her with so much despair that she had to sit for a while to come to terms with the strength of it. Over the years she'd learnt to heed these warnings, as she called them. To prepare herself, and regarded the phrase "forewarned is forearmed" as entirely true. She rose, and walked wearily to the bedroom where her youngest lass, Aggy was sleeping. She'd arrived earlier in the day, after a good hiding from her man. It was the same old story. He'd been on the "Pop" spent all of his pay and then knocked her about cause there was nowt to eat when he got home. Aggy was a good girl, thought Wilmy, better than most of her other bairns, and she wasn't stupid either. Wilmy had decided to let her stay, she'd even had it in her mind that she would keep her with her permanently, to help out.

"I'm not getting any younger," she said to herself, "and I've been thinking about having help for a while now, so you'll do the trick lass." She turned, "But I don't know what we'll do with the babby when it comes, We'll talk about that when yer feeling a bit better though. Then we'll deal with it when we have to!" In the meantime, she thought, rest! He'll not bother yer, I'll get the lads to see to him alright.

It wasn't the lass then! Wilmy knew this for sure. She knew that that wasn't what the warning was about. She sat awake for a while, the feeling still strong within her. When eventually she dozed it was a fitful rest, waves of dread still reaching her through her subconscious, giving her information that she couldn't yet grasp. She woke tired, but sure that the warnings would give her the information she needed to cope, if she would listen and give them a bit more time. All she felt at the moment was the abject certainty that there was to be CHANGE. Wilmy was on her guard and WAITING.

CHAPTER ELEVEN

Ray had been gone three weeks now. The time Jessy had spent with him alone on the morning of their walk was one of the nicest times of her life. They hadn't talked about anything in particular, just wandered and enjoyed each other's company. She knew he missed Durham, he kept remarking on the Castle and the Cathedral, the views over the river, the countryside around it. At one point she had said that he sounded like he was talking as if he'd never seen it afore. He had smiled and said that he was seeing it with fresh eyes.

When they got back, he went to collect the lasses while she made a bit to eat. Bullum was long gone, he'd never even seen Ray, and it was unlikely he would, cause he probably wouldn't be back before he had to go. He was getting the ten o'clock train that night. Jessy's stomach turned when she thought of him going away again. "But we've got the rest of the day yet," she said, "and we'll all make the best of it."

Ruthie and Ralphy had come along to see him off as well as one of the lasses from last night. He had hugged and kissed everyone, told the lass that she could write to him, then took her arm and walked along the platform until they were away from the others. The train had been a few minutes late, she was grateful for the extra time, but on edge as it prolonged her agony of seeing him go. The train came into view in the distance, he hugged her tight. She couldn't talk, it was pointless anyway. What could she say to him? "Be careful lad."

She knew that it wasn't in his hands. Instead she held on, using every second to feel him near her. When he peeled her away from him she could see that his face was wet. He pulled his hanky out of his pocket and blew his nose, and sneakily wiped his face. He was about to say, "Tah rah" when he saw Georgie hurrying along the platform towards him. He had his hand outstretched already to him as he got near. They shook and then Georgie pulled him into him and patted him on the back saying, "Good luck, lad."

Ray said, "Thanks and same to you," and as he turned to quickly hug Jessy again added, "Thanks for coming."

Then he was on the train, leaning out of the carriage window waving as it pulled away. Jessy heard him shout, "Look after yerself, Mam, remember go steady." He was looking at her, she knew what he meant and nodded. "Tar rah, Tah rah." He was waving and shouting to them all now. As the train put on speed he turned to give one last special wave to his Ma. He saw Georgie take her elbow, she looked up at him and he bent his head towards her, as if to say something! Ray's hand froze in mid air. He knew…. In that instant he KNEW. He'd felt that something wasn't quite right with her, not in a bad way, but different. Now he knew. His feelings of worry over her were lightened by a glimmer of hope. He closed the window and put his face against the cool of the glass, he was almost crying with relief when he said to himself, "Aw, I'm so pleased for yer, Ma. Please, God, let it be true!"

Jessy knew that his going would have been much worse if Georgie hadn't turned up, she was so pleased to see him that some of her sorrow was drowned out by excitement. She could see that there was a genuine affection between him and Ray and this made her happy. As this family group were leaving the station, Jessy turned to check that they were all there. She was totally surprised to see that Freddy had been crying. She had expected it from the lasses and Ruthie, but this was unusual for Freddy, to get upset over something other than food and money. As Jessy watched him bow his head to hide his face, she took Jean's hand and instead of talking Hetty's too, she put her arm around Freddy's shoulder. She felt him lean in to her, slightly, as she said, "Best be getting back, it's late."

Georgie shook Ralphy's hand, patted the lasses on the head, accepted a hug and a peck from Ruthie, and turned to Jessy lastly. "I'll say goodbye then. And don't worry if yer can help it, he's not daft, he'll know how to keep out of trouble. I'll be seeing yer?" The last part was directed at Jessy in question form, she looked at him and said, "Yes, I'll be seeing yer!"

As Georgie was walking away he thought, I wish that Freddy wouldn't stare all the time, it makes yer feel uncomfortable. Bye, he's a funny lad that one, hard to take to, real hard.

This would be the fifth time that she had met Georgie. In the first week after Ray going she had only been able to see him once. Freddy hadn't been able to stay in with the lasses, he said that his Da was running him ragged with messages. It was the second week when she knew she'd have to rope Ruthie in on her secret. Jessy knew that she couldn't go another full week without seeing him. It had made her physically ill, the waiting and the watching of the clock, remembering him and how he made her feel, then the doubts that he'd change his mind, it was all too much to bear. So she'd told everything to Ruthie, who didn't seem the least bit surprised. Ruthie was only too happy to have the girls stay with her. Sometimes, Jessy thought, I think she's as keen for me to see him as I am meself!

Jessy would have been right, Ruthie had gone beyond being happy for Jessy. She was now planning in her head ways that Jessy and Georgie could have a future together. She loved seeing her sister this happy, and she vowed that come hell or high water she'd do everything in her power to make sure it continued.

Jessy was getting ready, Ruthie kept bringing her new frocks and blouses along to wear, but she couldn't always wear them. They were a bit too dressy she didn't want to arouse Bullum's suspicion anymore than it already was. He'd already commented on how often she was at Ruthie's, saying, "Yer can live on less fucking money if yer eating along there that often." Ruthie always put the lasses to bed before Jessy left the house, but they never asked about Jessy anyway. When they were at Ruthie's they were spoiled rotten and between her and Ralphy, the lasses always had someone to entertain them.

Tonight she was wearing the grey dress that she had worn for Ray's "par tea." Jessy thought of it as her lucky dress, it was the dress she wore when both of the men she most loved had been around her! She combed her wig, she looked in the mirror at her own hair. Ruthie had told her to keep cutting it, to keep it short. It helped the wig stay on. She said that if it got too long it would stretch it, and then it would never go back. Jessy had followed orders but she often wished that it had been a bit bigger, cause even now it was a very snug fit, and she often got a bit of a headache when she first put it on, until she got used to it. Ruthie had told her that it should fit like that, and that she should bear it. After all, what's a bit of pain compared to looking good?" Jessy smiled, that was Ruthie all over! But she didn't have to wear the bloody thing all the time, did she?

She was getting ready in Ruthie and Ralphy's room. They had a full-length mirror. She stood and looked at herself in her slip. Now that she had got a brassiere she felt better in her clothes, not so straight up and down. She was thin, but she still had a waist. She tried to look at herself as she thought that Georgie might look at her. She imagined herself standing like this in front of him, the now familiar warm feeling came flooding through her. She walked over to the mirror, put her face up close to it and said harshly to her own reflection, "Now stop all that, yer haven't got time for messing about." She was turning away when she noticed her hair, it was from the side that she'd caught a glimpse of it. "It's growing in? She looked closer, it was short, but it was definitely growing back, even at the front. Whether or not it was the constant cutting or just time, Jessy could see that it was coming back. And not like it used to be, it looked thicker somehow. She picked the wig up again and spoke to it, "It's early days, but yer never know. I mightn't need you one day," she stroked it and said, "But for now we'll stay best of friends," and she squeezed it on her head.

She'd left a few minutes early, she couldn't wait any longer. She said to herself that she would walk slowly, but she still got there before he had arrived. She stood with her back against the big tree that was their meeting place. They had decided to meet here rather than the cottage as had been their first plan, because the nights were light and the cottage was too secluded. Anyone seeing a woman walking along there by herself would know that there was something going on. So they decided to meet here and then go for a walk, as if they had bumped into each other casual-like. After all, nothing could be more natural than the lad of the woman that Jessy cleaned for walking with her on their way home. Nobody knew that she wasn't going along to Molly's twice a week as usual. As it got dark, they had on their last meeting, made their way to the cottage. When they were together it was as if any risk was worth it, just to be alone together for a few minutes. Jessy hoped that they could go there again tonight. She wanted to feel him kiss her again, she wanted it more than anything.

Jessy was starting to panic, he was over half an hour late. He'd never been late before, he was usually there waiting for her. She heard the Cathedral bells chime another quarter of an hour. What could have happened, she thought, to make him this late? Mebbie Molly was playing up. He'd said that she'd started asking questions about why he was going out so early to do the 'blackout checks'. Jessy knew it couldn't be that, she knew that when he put his mind to something he would do it! She closed her eyes and leaned against the big tree, it was very quiet. She had seen nobody since she had arrived. She closed her eyes. "Please let him come, God, please. I'll do anything yer want, I'll even start going to church. I'll make the bairns go annaull, I'll stop swearing, I'll be a better person, I'll...OH PLEASE JUST LET HIM COME."

She heard the bells ring twice more. She was sitting now, with her back against the big tree. Something was dying inside her, she felt her stomach tighten, it was as if she was shriveling up inside. When she stood she actually felt smaller and thinner. "And OLD and dry," she whispered sadly to herself. "Aw well, it wasn't to be! He's probably come to his senses, seen it and you for what it really was, 'just a bit of fun'. Aye, that's all it was." She took in the deepest of breaths, then let it out on a long sigh. She wasn't crying, she couldn't. Before she started for home, she waited another few minutes, looking towards both ends of the dirt path that led to the tree. Jessy still had some hope left.

He wasn't at either end of the path, nor was he ahead or behind her as she walked home. But she kept looking up and behind, hoping!

When Ruthie turned round as she heard the door open, she froze. The look on Jessy's face shocked her. She rushed over from the sink and put her wet arms around her. Jessy was stiff, Ruthie tried to pull her into her, but there was no give in her. Jessy's voice was calm as she said, "I'm alright, don't fuss. I'll just sit and get warmed for a few minutes then I'll make me way home. Don't worry, yer can keep the lasses till the morrow." Ruthie was about to say something, but Jessy hadn't noticed, she continued on in a matter of fact way. "I wouldn't wake them now anyway, that's if they're asleep yet. Is that where Ralphy is now? Getting them off with another story?"

"Naw he's in the shop, working. The bairns have been asleep for ages now. Will yer tell us what's happened, our Jessy? I've never seen yer like this, yer know this...this..." Ruthie was at a loss to find the words. Jessy interrupted her thoughts.

"What, yer mean 'whipped?' Beat? Broken?" Jessy swallowed, and continued in a strange calm voice. "Oh I think yer have, our Ruthie, think on. The only difference this time is that I deserve it, for being so stupid. Yer want to know what happened? Yer really want to know? NOWT!"

Ruthie's face must have shown her confusion. Jessy smacked her lips in an impatient "tut" at Ruthie.

"Yer see, in order for owt to have happened, he would have had to have been there," she looked at Ruthie. "Now yer've got it. Ge..." she wouldn't say his name, not ever again! "He didn't come! Do yer not get it? I've been jilted, stood up. and whatever else yer fancy magazines want to call it. HE DIDN'T COME! HE CAME TO HIS BLOODY SENSES!"

Jessy had gradually got louder. The sarcastic tone and the way that she had spoke, Ruthie knew was just hurt. But unless she kept her voice down, the lasses would be up, and then Ralphy would want to know what was going on, then Jessy would leave without talking to her. She didn't want that!

Ruthie looked Jessy in the eye, and said sharply, "Lower yer voice, our Jessy. This is my home and I won't have yer coming in and talking to me that way, and waking the bairns up!" She took a deep breath and hurried on, "Don't get on yer high horse with me, cause I want yer to stay and talk. Do yer think I want to see yer like this? Yer not crying, but I know yer hurting real bad, our Jessy." She spoke softer now, "Please sit back down, stay and have a cuppa with us. I promise if yer don't want to talk, we won't! But don't go off home like this...PLEASE."

Jessy wearily sat down. Ruthie started to unbutton her coat saying casually, "Best take this off though, else yer won't feel the benefit." Jessy took over from her, stood and took it off.

"There, that's better," said Ruthie. She felt as if she was talking to a bairn. There was a glazed empty look on Jessy's face. She sat just looking straight ahead into the fire.

She was still sitting and staring when Ruthie brought her cup of tea. She was surprised to hear her speak.

"Isn't it funny when yer think that something that gives so much pleasure and comfort, can give so much hurt and pain annaull"

It took a couple of seconds for Ruthie to realize that she was talking about the fire. She decided to ignore it.

"Yer don't know what's happened, Jessy, he mightn't have been able to come. Why, anything could have happened. His Ma or Da might be poorly. He might have got the days mixed up and thought it was last night or even the morrow. Yer just don't know."

She still said nothing.

Ruthie tried again, "He could even have come down with something himself. Why, God forbid, he could even have had one of his fits. Cause I'll tell yer something, our Jessy, there must be something wrong, I cannot see him leaving yer just standing, not even sending a message with somebody." She looked at Jessy and grasped one of her hands and shook it a little. "Something must definitly have happened, it must have."

Some of what Ruthie said got through to Jessy, because it did make sense.

"How will we know," she looked at Ruthie, "and what if yer wrong? What if he just got sick of me, and if I start to think what yer've said could be the case, and then I get me hopes built up again, what happens then if yer wrong?"

"That could be the case," said Ruthie, "but I don't think it is, lass, I really don't. Why he's been like dog with a bone since the first time he met yer. Why would he change all of a sudden?"

There was a loud banging in the distance, it was coming from the shop. Ruthie stood saying; "I'll not be a minute, lass. I'll just go and get the daft sod who's at the door sorted. Fancy banging away at this time of night. I don't know what the hell they think they're up to. They'll have the whole street awake.

She dashed through the shop hallway muttering, "We're a bloody undertaker's, not a cobbler's! Why they'll even have those two old buggers awake, and they're deaf as posts." She was referring to Ralphy's Mam and Dad. They lived next door on the other side. His Da was alright, a bit miserable, but she supposed he had to be. His Ma was a real grump. She hoped he didn't wake her. She couldn't complain. They didn't see much of them really, well Ruthie didn't.

The banging had stopped, she could hear voices. Probably somebody with an emergency. Yer'd think they could wait till tomorrow when it was this late. Eeh, don't people die at an inconvenient time.

Ruthie was on her way back through to Jessy when she stopped and strained to listen. She'd thought she'd recognized the voice. She waited until it spoke again. Yes she was right! It was him, it was Georgie.

"What a bloody nerve," she was talking to herself again as she retraced her steps back along the hallway. "Banging on the door like that after what he'd done. Well he won't be upsetting her again, and that's a fact! I'll give that Mister a piece of my mind I will!

She almost bumped into them, she was walking so quickly. Ralphy was bringing Georgie through when Ruthie appeared in front of them. She was just about to tell Ralphy he was a silly bugger and that Georgie could go and sling his hook when she looked at Georgie's face. He was grey, and he looked tired. All she could think to say was, "What's happened? Is it your Mam or yer Dad?" Georgie looked quizzically at her, and replied calmly; "Naw they're both fine, it's nowt to do with them." Then he hesitated, "Why it is really I suppose, but not the way you're thinking."

Ralphy took Ruthie's arm, firm enough to hurt her a little, and pulled her aside. Then said in a low voice, "Is Jessy through the back?" Ruthie nodded. At this he turned to Georgie, "She's through there, lad. You gan on through, we'll be a while yet,"

"Over my bloody dead body!" Ruthie pulled her arm away from him. "I'm not having her any more upset than she is." She turned back to Ralphy, "As for you, yer soft sod, do yer know what he's done? He left her standing for hours, like a tattie, not even bothering to try to get a message to her, and too much of a coward to turn up and tell her face to face that it was over. So no, he doesn't get to see My sister."

Ralphy had walked roud her so that he could look at her when he spoke, he held her arms and was saying, "Ssshhh. Ssshhhh. Shush Ruthie." She finally calmed enough to look at him, instead of looking daggers at Georgie.

"There's things yer don't know lass, things Georgie has to tell Jessy." Ralphy saw the look of alarm on Ruthie's face, but he didn't expect the next outburst!

"Oh I bet there bloody well is! Don't tell me! YER MARRIED!" she carried on without pause, "That's it isn't it? Yer've got a bloody wife somewhere in France or some other bloody place? Well yer hear about this happening but yer nev..."

"SHUT UP! THAT'S ENOUGH." It was Ralphy.

Ruthie was halted mid-sentence, she nearly burst into tears. Why, her Ralphy had never spoken to her like that.

Ralphy looked at Georgie, who had been standing with his his face lowered, not wanting to witness any trouble that he was causing between them. "Do as I said, lad, gan on through and take yer time. We'll be through in a minute but we'll gan in the kitchen. You have the front room to yerselves."

Jessy was sitting with her back to him when he entered the room, she didn't know he was there. He saw how her shoulders were slumped, how she was fidgeting with her fingers, turning her hands over then back. It was something she did when she was nervous or upset.

He closed his eyes, and prayed. Please, God, help me to tell her. He wanted to walk up behind her, put his hands on her shoulders and kiss her head. But he knew that he would probably scare her. Instead he called her name from the doorway.

She didn't have to turn, she knew who it was, and she was filled with relief and thought, oh he must care still, he wouldn't have come here if he didn't, but that doesn't excuse what he did, what he's put me through! I'll not let him have it all his own way, but these thoughts were no sooner formed than he was in front of her, lifting her up, holding her to him. She held back for what could have only been seconds, then she couldn't resist him. She melted into him, she smelt his smell, felt his arms. She didn't care. The only thing that existed in that moment was her and Georgie.

They clung to each other, he still held her as he guided her through to the front room and when they sat, they were still holding each other.

Jessy had her head in his neck, they were on the couch. Georgie was stroking her back saying, "There, there, it's alright. Ssshhhh it's alright."

Jessy pulled away from him to look at him. She sensed there was something more. She too had the same thought as Ruthie and asked, "Is there something wrong at home? I mean with yer Mam or Dad?"

Georgie shook his head saying, "No, they're alright, well physically they're fine. They are a bit upset at the moment, that's why I couldn't get ter see yer. I had to stay with me Mam till she calmed down a bit. It took a lot longer than I thought that's all."

Jessy felt guilty. Georgie's Mam must have found out

about them seeing each other, she thought, oh, God, I wish I hadn't made her that promise, but when I made it to her, I DID intend to keep it!

"Why if yer were my lad I'd feel the same as her. So yer can't blame her for that!"

He looked at Jessy, could she know? Her next words made everything clear.

"After all, there is the age difference, and then there's Bullum and me having the bairns. Well yer can't blame her for thinking what she's thinking!"

He looked at her and smiled, she was chattering away, sorting things out in her head. He knew that she was aware that there was something else, he also knew that she didn't want to hear it.

She caught him looking at her and stopped in mid-sentence. She took a deep breath, then asked, "Is it over Georgie? Have yer Mam and Dad and the rest of them won?"

He took her face in his hands, and kissed her gently on the lips. Jessy thought it felt like a goodbye kiss. She kept her eyes closed so that the tears would not come out. She could feel him looking at her, but when he spoke he took her by surprise.

"I've been called back up."

"What do yer mean? Yer can't. Why, yer injured, they can't do that, can they?" Jessy was confused, she had never dreamed this would happen. He must have got it wrong, somebody had made a mistake.

"They can and they have. They've declared me fit for duty. I had me last medical today, and they told me straight away."

"Naw, they must have got it wrong. Yer've done your bit! They wouldn't do this, surely?" Jessy was saying words, but thinking, GOD, NO! PLEASE, GOD, NO.

He could see the fear in her face, the same as he's seen in

his Ma and Da's. He recognized the same wishful thinking, the same things that he'd said to himself that very morning when they had first told him. He'd had an idea that this might happen after his last medical two months ago. But he'd put it out of his mind until today. Now all his fears had come back to haunt him. God knows I don't want to go back to the DEATH-FILLED TRENCHES. They had told him that he probably wouldn't be on the front line again. But Georgie had seen it happen before, men had come back after an injury and within hours said they felt as if they had never been away. It had made no difference to them, nor would it to him. He knew this to be true, he'd seen it with his own eyes. Now he had to watch somebody else taking on the hurt that this fucking carnage brought with it. His Ma and Da were going to have their hearts ripped apart with worry again, and this lass, who had gone through so much, had yet more pain to bear. Oh, Georgie was frightened, but it was nothing compared to having to watch the one's he loved cope with this!

"It'll be alright, lass," he said gently. She was rocking herself back and forth with her arms wrapped tight around her. "We can write to each other now, and I'll write as often as I can. Yer can wait for mail from me and Ray now. Just think how busy yer'll be writing to both of us." He was trying to make light of it, trying to make her look forward to something. "And I know it won't last for long now, why it can't. If they're desperate enough to call up fellas like me, it must be a last shove. He paused, "And when it's all over, and I come back, we'll sort out a way to be together. Not just for a few hours neither. FOR GOOD!"

Jessy stopped rocking. She looked up at him with a tear-stained face. Oh I love this man, she thought, with all my heart, cause even now he's not thinking about himself. She smiled and leant back into him, he couldn't see the tears cascading down her cheeks as she let him tell of their future together, how it would be. He was telling her where they would all live, how she would leave Bullum and they would move away and start a new life. He said that he would look forward to the day when he knew that nobody could hurt her ever again, either her or the bairns. He even assured her that his Ma would come round, once the war was over and she saw how happy he was. He felt Jessy shudder.

"I know what yer thinking, but yer wrong. Me Ma's not half as stubborn as she makes out, she just needs a bit of time to get used to the idea." He hugged her tighter to him, then leant his chin down until it touched the top of her head. She could feel his lips move when he spoke.

"In fact, why don't we go and tell her our plans now? That should give her enough time, while I'm away, to get used to yer. She does like yer yer know! Anyway she'll need a bit of company and so will you, so yer can both help each other. Why, it won't be long till yer comparing me letters." He whispered, "But mind, there'll be some bits in there just for you, so don't read them all out to her!"

Jessy hadn't had to think about her reply, but she wasn't going to let him go to his Ma's and tell her anything more than she already knew. She was overwhelmed that he would push his feelings aside in this way, to make her feel better. Even putting her before his Ma!

"I'll have to wash me face but I'll pop to the lavvy first. I won't be long. I cannot go anywhere looking like this!" She needed to think by herself for a few minutes.

She was almost out the back door when he called gently, "Hurry back, lass."

It was cold and dark and quiet. Just what she needed.

She knew she had to go along with him with his idea of their future. Jessy knew it would never happen. The chances of Bullum letting her go were nil, where would he find such cheap labour anywhere else? Georgie didn't understand Bullum, the depth of his nastiness, his anger and temper, how he would use anybody who got in his firing line. Naw, she couldn't let him tell anybody what his plans were, not for anyone's sake. When the war was over she would tell him the truth of the matter. Till then, let sleeping dog's lie. She breathed in the cold sharp air in the yard, took a few seconds to get the story straight then went in the house.

"I've been thinking, Georgie, we should wait til this is all over afore we tell anybody." She put her hand on his mouth to stop him from talking. "I really think that yer Ma and Da's got enough on their plate right now without making matters worse for them. And it is like you say, I'll use the time to work on yer Mam, yer know, get her to like me a bit more. Then she'll be far more accepting of the idea of us getting together." She saw that he hadn't completely fallen for it. "In the meantime, we can still make plans together, it might be nice to make our own plans without anyone else interfering. It'll be our secret." He was silent, thinking! "What do yer think Georgie? can we do it this way? Please."

She seemed a lot better after having been out the back, he'd hoped the idea of making plans for their future would help her cope. He meant every word of it, he just wouldn't have mentioned them so quick, had it not been for this coming up. He mulled everything over that she'd said. She was right in one way, there was no point in making any trouble when he was going away, but he had so wanted her to know how he felt about her, and although he knew that she was right, he wanted to tell everybody so that there was no going back! It came into his head at that very moment, WHAT IF I DON'T COME BACK? Where will that leave her?

He looked at her, put his arm aroud her and said, "Whatever you want, Jessy, whatever you think is best, I'll go along with. As long as it makes YOU happy." He made a mental note to make some sort of provision for her, he probably didn't have time to do it afore he went, but he would see about it on his very first leave.

"Well let's leave it at that then Georgie for the time being, eeh? I could do with a drink, and I don't mean a cup of tea this time. How about you?" She stood in the middle of the room, looking vaguely around. "I wonder if our Ruthie's got any."

"I wonder if our Ruthie's got any WHAT?" Ruthie and Ralphy were standing in the doorway, they had been away for a long time. It had taken Ruthie some time to stop crying. Ralphy had never seen her this upset, she just kept saying, "AW no! Just when she'd got a bit of happiness. Just when she was happy. Aw, Ralphy, she was so happy." All Ralphy could do was pat her back softly and say, "Aye, lass. Aye."

"I was wondering if yer had owt in ter drink, Ruthie? Yer know a proper drink? I could do with one!"

It was Ralphy who spoke up. "Wait here, I've got something I was keeping for a special occasion. This is as good a time as any, it'll do as well for shock as anything," and he disappeared and returned seconds later with a bottle of whisky. Ruthie looked at him in amazement. He replied to the look, "From a very grateful client, and God bless her!" He handed the bottle to Ruthie saying, "You can do the honours, and make mine a large one. Will yer have one with me Georgie?" Georgie nodded saying, "But not a large one for me. I might still have a bit of talking to do when I get home. They're probably still upset at my house!"

Jessy and Ruthie went through to the kitchen. Ruthie was uncorking the bottle with her teeth. On the way, she picked up a cup from the sink and poured a glug of it out. "Get that down yer straight away, I'll get the glasses." Jessy swallowed it in one, it burnt her throat, but she didn't care. Ruthie passed her the glasses and she started filling them. She heard Ralphy say, "When do yer leave on Saturday then?"

She dropped the bottle onto the glasses. Ruthie was quick, she picked it up straight away.

SATURDAY? Today was WEDNESDAY! Jessy flopped into the kitchen chair, put her arms on the table and then her head into them and sobbed.

Georgie had heard her, he stood to go to her. Ralphy put his hand on his arm. "Now's not the time for you, lad" he spoke quietly and firmly. "There'll be times when yer can help her and times when yer can't, this is one of the times yer can't. She can't cry in front of you like she can in front of Ruthie. Let Ruthie manage it this time, eeh?" Georgie nodded and sat back down. "I'll go and get that drink!" said Ralphy.

When Jessy and Ruthie came through to the parlour, Ralphy had had more than one drink, he was nodding in the chair. Georgie was sitting staring at the fire, whisky still in his hand. Ralphy juddered awake when he heard Ruthie say, "Yer'll have to excuse him, he's had a real long day. He was up most of the night annaull." She had poured a small whisky for her and Jessy. She now turned to her husband who was just about to drop off again, "I'd like to make a toast, so have you got a drop left in your glass, Ralphy?" She gave him a nudge with her foot, "Come on, stand up for the toast. Ralphy sleepily stood, he was swaying with sleep and whisky. Ruthie stood next to him to steady him, she noticed his glass had nothing in it. She poured from her glass into his. Ralphy, who had been watching this, immediately drank the small transferred amount. Ruthie slapped at his arm, but she was too late. "Will yer wait till I say the toast, yer drunken get?" She linked him lovingly and transferred from her glass to his once more. This time she kept her hand on his arm.

"To the end of the war and a new future." Ruthie raised her glass and they all followed suit. Georgie looked at Jessy as he repeated, "A NEW FUTURE." Jessy merely mumbled, "To the end of the war," and drank the whisky.

Ralphy drank and then dropped into the chair and was asleep almost immediately. Georgie smiled and turned to Jessy, "I think it's time that I was going. Can I have a word with yer on the way out?"

"No need for that, lad, we'll be out yer way in no time." At this, Ruthie pulled at Ralphy's arm. He slid slowly from the chair to the floor. "Come on then, our Ralphy, let's away to bed," then as if she was talking to a child, "Come on then, yer can do it, that's a good lad." He slowly got to his feet, Ruthie put his arm around her shoulders and was almost carrying him through the door when she turned with him and said to Georgie, "I'll say 'cheerio' then, lad and I'm sorry about the way I went for yer, before I knew what was happening. Be safe and come back to me sister, please." She stood a few seconds looking at him and turned saying, "Take care of yerself then, and Ralphy wishes yer the best annaull, See yer." It was with a full and heavy heart that she climbed the stairs that night.

Jessy walked him to the back door. He stood holding her in the darkened room, looking out into the blackness. It was late and it was silent. They were both thinking the same thing: that this peace would soon end, this feeling of contentment was to be short-lived. Georgie turned to Jessy and looked at her in profile. To Georgie she was perfect. The way she held her head, the strength of her stance as she stood at that open doorway, looking out on a world that was at best unpredictable. A world where she had suffered and felt so much pain! And yet she was unaffected by bitterness, she didn't want to be pitied. SHE WAS JUST JESSY!

"I meant what I said, Jessy, about us having a future together, planning a future together." He hesitated, he was waiting for her to speak. He broke the silence when he could stand it no longer. "Talk to me, Jessy. Tell me that's what'll happen, that we have something to look forward to together, cause I don't know if I can get through this without YOU! I love yer Jessy, yer must know that I do. I want a life with YOU. Please say that yer feel the same about me!"

She turned to face him, she could see the truth and honesty in his eyes. How could she tell him how she felt? He was so sure, sure that if yer wanted something bad enough that it would happen. She knew that it wasn't always like that, but she couldn't tell him that. Naw, she wouldn't spoil his dreams, he would need them!

"Georgie, I will love you till the day I die, and if there is another place after that, then I'll love yer there annaull." She had been serious as she said this, she lightened the mood with her next sentence. "And when yer come back we'll go to Timbucktoo if yer want to." She kissed him on the nose and smiled. The relief flooded his face. She was happy for him.

They had arranged to meet the next night at the cottage, and the night after, his last night, at Ruthie's.

The meeting at the cottage was short. He explained to

Jessy that he couldn't be out too long as he told his Ma that he would be home. Jessy knew that he was trying to share his time between them, and she undertood that his Ma would want to be with him. But she couldn't help feeling put out. She wanted him here with her, holding and kissing her, like he was now. She pushed herself into him a little more. He'd already said that he "should be going" once, and she'd kissed him and put her tongue in his mouth. She was learning fast. She heard him groan, he started kissing her harder. She responded, pushing her open mouth further into his. She opened his jacket and put her arms around him over his shirt. She could feel the heat from him. One of his hands was undoing her coat, then he had his hand inside. He was rubbing her back then he moved his hand to the front. She was surprised at the feeling she got when he started to rub her breast. She felt as if she would melt into him, it was wonderful. His strong fingers were on her body, he was rubbing his thumb back and forth over her nipple. He was grinding himself into her again, she liked it when he did that! He had her up against the wall, he stopped kissing her and looked at her as he pulled away from her a little. He took her coat off, and hung it on the hook, then he did the same with his jacket. As he turned back to her she could see the bulge in his trousers. She took his arms and put them around her again, then she moved into him. She was in control now, his eyes were glazed, she was kissing him. She ran her hand down his back, then around to the front of him. She brought it to the bulge and felt it. He groaned loudly now, put his hand over hers and pushed it up and down. When she was doing it by herself he parted her legs with his knee. He was there, on the spot where it was most pleasurable. It didn't matter that he was rubbing her over her knickers, it still felt so good. He was pushing further with his hand between her legs, feeling her inside. "Yes Georgie. YES. Just there. Oh, Georgie, Georgie." She was saying his name when he suddenly stopped! He pulled away from her, turned his back to her and took in huge gasps of air.

"I'm sorry, Jessy, I didn't mean for all that to happen, well not here, not like this. I don't want yer to think that I would meet yer here to just go at yer like that. I just got a bit carried away tonight." He turned back to her. She was still dazed, he could see the look in her eyes of wanting him physically. He blushed as he saw her look down at him. He smiled at her, "You're a game one, Jessy, yer surprised me." He watched as her face took on a look of shame. He said quickly, "Don't get me wrong, I love yer for it. I'm just surprised that's all. I thought that it would take us a hell of a lot longer to get to where we are now. But I'm pleased that it didn't!" He took her chin in his fingers and lifted her face to his, and from very close he said, "I am going to kiss you now, Jessy, a gentle loving kiss. I don't want you to kiss me back, cause when yer do, I lose all control and who knows where we could end up?" He kissed her softly, she didn't kiss him back. She didn't open her mouth, but the kiss was still wonderful, he was kissing her gently and with love. He stopped and looked at her, "I want to be with you, Jessy, and I get the feeling that you want to be with me as well." She gave the slightest nod with her head, but her eyes had told him all he needed to know. "But not here. I don't want you remembering us in this place when I go away, I want something better for you, Jessy"

Jessy tried to speak, but it came out in a croak, her throat was so dry. She swallowed and tried again.

"It doesn't matter. It really doesn't matter where it is, where it happens. I don't care. I've never felt like this before, so yer can bet yer bottom doller that I'll remember it." She was taken aback when he burst out laughing.

"What yer laughing at?" She was smiling herself now, but she still didn't understand what had made him laugh. She tried again, "What is it, Georgie? Go on tell us? What yer laughing at?"

He'd stopped now, for fear of hurting her feelings. As he looked at her looking at him he brought her close to him again, "Well if yer still feel the same way tomorrow night, then I'll consider it." He was joking with her.

We'll see who's joking now, thought Jessy. She reached down and touched him, she left her hand on him. He swallowed hard and closed his eyes, she rubbed gently. It was having the desired effect. She took her hand away and was purposefully casual as she said, "Well, we'll have to see what tomorrow night brings won't we?"

He smiled down at her, "I think you're enjoying your new-found power, Jessy, yer've become a real tease. Be careful I don't call yer bluff."

He heard her giggle like a girl. When she smiles, he thought, she is lovely. He sighed and let go of her to reach for their coats.

They parted company just before the cut then Georgie turned back to make his way home. She saw her curtains move as she reached the gate. That'll be the lasses looking out for us, she said to herself, as far as they're concerned, I'm still doing a bit of cleaning on a night. She closed the gate. I'll go to bed with them tonight. I'm tired, I can cuddle into them. I didn't get much sleep last night, let's hope that tonight is a bit better. She didn't expect that she would get much more because although the shock had worn off a bit, the sadness was still raw in her about him going. She decided that she would put her mind to thinking about tonight, and she would see him again tomorrow night. "Aye, I'll do what Ruthie says, and get a bit of happiness where I can, cause she's right. Afore yer know it it's passed yer by!" She was trying her old trick of making her head fool her heart. It had worked in the past for her, especially in situations that she couldn't change, But that had been when there was only her involved!

"Stop fussing, our Ruthie. I'll probably end up in the old cottage, and that's none too clean. So this is a real waste of good clothes." She stopped and giggled, and thought of the previous night. "Well it's a waste of good top clothes anyway!" Both her and Ruthie had a giggle then.

Ruthie had dressed her from top to bottom. She stood back to look at the results of her efforts. Jessy was wearing Ruthie's best black coat, it had a fur collar, that framed her face against the blackness of the wig. Black patent leather shoes and a black and cream hat completed the outfit. The shoes had been a bit big but Jessy had stuffed the toes with newspaper, she was that determined to wear them. Underneath was the lucky grey dress, and underneath that was all of Ruthie's best underwear. Cream silk French panties, with matching top and a cream slip, edged with lace. The only thing that didn't match was the suspender belt, it was white, but it doesn't look too bad, well yer don't see much of it. In the main, Ruthie was satisfied with the outcome. Jessy was more than happy, she felt like a Queen. Even down to the stockings, silk with just one click in them and that was at the very top. She'd never worn silk stockings before. Oh they feel lovely against yer skin, she thought as she had gently rolled them up her legs. Now looking at herself in Ruthie's mirror she was glad that Ruthie had made her put on these lovely clothes. Not only did she look different, but she felt better too. She turned to her sister to thank her, but Ruthie put her hand up to wave her away. Jessy could see that she was 'full,' so instead she just smiled, and continued to look at herself in the mirror.

"Don't go getting all soft on me, our Jessy, cause I can't take it at the moment." Ruthie cleared her throat, "Anyway don't go forgetting that I'm just lending yer this lot, that is, except the knickers and the top, yer may as well have them, they don't fit me anymore now anyway." The latter part of the statement had been spoke in what Ruthie called her "business voice," now she went and stood behind Jessy and straightened her hat. "Yer look wonderful, our Jessy. Yer really do. He'll be proud of you."

"Eeh, well, it just goes to show, 'clothes do maketh the man.'" At this Jessy turned and hugged Ruthie, and whispered, "Having the best sister in the world helps as well!"

They'd left, Ralphy had kept the lasses out of the way. After all, if they saw their Mam, they would certainly know that she wasn't going cleaning. Not that Hetty would say anything to anyone, she was older now and was a good lass. Knew how to keep a secret she did, especially where her Ma was concerned. But the little un, well she was too young to be trusted not to say owt, not that they saw much of Bullum lately, well not if her and Ralphy had their way. But it wouldn't be Bullum they would talk to, it would be Freddy, and Ruthie didn't trust that lad a bit. Naw, he's a tale carrier him alright, best he knows nowt of what's going on!

"Stop yer worrying, and come over here beside me for a

cuddle." Ralphy had put the newspaper down, he had been reading bits from it to her, but she hadn't heard what he was saying. Ruthie remembered the look on Georgie's face when he had seen Jessy in all her 'finery.' It was the way that Ralphy was looking at her now. She rose and walked over to his open arms. "We've been lucky haven't we, Ralphy?" She nestled up against him, her last thought before Ralphy's lips found hers was, I'll have me work cut out when HE goes the morrow, I will that!

They left by the back door and followed the back paths through the edge of The Estate. It was dark and they knew that nobody would be around at this time of night. It was about quarter to nine when the cottage came into sight, they had not seen another living soul. The only folks out would be those on the way to the pub, and they had avoided the main pub routes. So they walked hand in hand in the darkness. Georgie kept on walking as they approached the cottage.

"We're here, Georgie, where yer going?"

"I thought that we'd go somewhere different tonight, somewhere special, as it is a special night."

He held her hand and kept on walking. Jessy was disappointed, she'd wanted to be alone with him. After all, she thought, we don't have much time to be together.

He sensed the reluctance in her. He stopped and turned to her.

"I want to take yer somewhere where I can show yer off to the world, where we'll feel like a proper couple instead of hiding away from everybody. Don't worry where we're going, yer won't know anybody! So don't ask any more questions or yer'll ruin the surprise."

He was excited, Jessy could tell by his voice. She'd have

been just as happy spending a bit of time alone with him, but she knew that this is what he wanted. She walked on with him.

They were in Durham now, the Cathedral bells had chimed nine o'clock. They'd just crossed the bridge over the river Wear and were in Elvet, the oldest part of Durham. It looked different in the dark, the Castle and Cathedral on the hill were only just visible, and it seemed quiet and a bit ghostly. Then one of the many pub doors opened and the sound of piano music and singing met them. They were standing at the crossroads, in the center of the small city. To the left was the road to the prison, to the right the market place and just ahead was the Royal County Hotel. The poshest hotel, it was said, in the whole of the north east. He took her hand and crossed, heading towards the huge front doors.

"We're not ganning in there are we, Georgie?" She'd pulled her hand away from him and stood still till he answered her.

"We are that, lass. We're gonna go in there and have a drink and a chat. Now don't go getting that look, yer as good as anybody else. Yer certainly look as good as anybody else tonight!" he looked into her eyes. "This is how you deserve to be treated, Jessy, this is how I think of yer. I want you to remember that" He kissed her on the lips and then waited for her reply.

"Well in that case we'd better be away in." She pushed the nerves and the fear down into her, linked him and started walking.

Oh, it was beautiful. The seats were all dark red leather, with buttons all over them. There were couches against the walls in the same colour, and the carpet was red and gold swirls. He led her to a table in a corner. She sat in one of the chairs and sunk into the softness of it. They had no sooner sat than a waiter came over with a tray. There was nothing on it, but he still carried it as if it was a trophy. Georgie ordered a sherry and a whisky. "Sweet or dry?" asked the waiter, looking at Jessy. "Sweet" was Georgie's reply. She looked around. It was fairly full, full of posh people, women in expensive clothes with lovely hairstyles and men in expensive black suits. But they weren't looking at them as if they were odd, they weren't even looking at Jessy's face. The waiter hadn't even raised an eye when he came to serve them. Yer would think that he would have, thought Jessy, what with them both having funny faces. He was coming back with their drinks. He placed them on the table in front of them, taking them from the silver tray one at a time, then placing a jug of water next to Georgie's drink, he placed a slip of paper on the table next to them and asked, "May I take your coat, Madam?" He turned then to Georgie, "Yours too, Sir?"

She took of her hat first and then followed Georgie's example with her coat, folding it around itself and laying it on the waiter's outstretched arm. She was surprised to see that under his top coat Georgie had on a black suit with a dicky bow tie. He looks lovely, he knows how to wear it annaull' she felt a surge of pride for him. He looks as good as anybody in here! She was glad she'd worn the grey dress, she felt comfortable in it and she knew that it had probably been a 'good un'. She smiled as she thought of where it had probably come from, but this posh lot aren't to know that are they?

Across the room a fella had started to play the piano, and she looked over. It wasn't the type of music that was played in houses, it was what Georgie told her was sort of classical. He was playing on a white piano in the corner of the room. She didn't think much of the music, it could have been a bit livelier, but she had to admit to herself that it was a smashing place. This thought was only made more certain when she visited the lavvy. Georgie had pointed out where it was. She walked hesitantly through the door and was amazed. It's an inside one! She looked around her. There was mirrors all along one wall and a couch and a table opposite. Furniture in the bloody lavvy? Well I never. Someone came in and walked past her to one of two doors on the other wall. She followed and opened the spare door. Why I'll be buggered. She closed the door after her and stood looking. It was like something out of one of Ruthie's magazines. She pulled the chain and the toilet flushed, after only one gentle pull. On the wall was a shelf. She felt the paper on it, it was soft. Never in the bloody world! Why, that's too good for yer bum, what a waste, and a war on annaull' Nevertheless, Jessy took a couple of extra sheets, folded them gently and put them in her hand bag, as a reminder, she told herself. There was a sink in the cubicle too. She could hardly wait to wash her hands with the sweet-smelling soap. It felt and smelled so good that she was tempted to put that in her bag as well. Better not, they might miss it. They might come in and check after I've gone. That would put the cat among the pidgeons. As she came out, the other lass was plumping her hair at the mirror. Jessy waited till she had gone and did the same. "Eeh, wait till I tell our Ruthie about this," she said to herself as she was leaving.

Georgie watched her walk towards him, she had taken to it like a fish to water. He was thinking that she had a natural elegance about her and that she didn't look out of place here. Jessy sat down and couldn't get the words out quick enough to describe the ladies lavvy. She was whispering, so that, as she said later, nobody would know that she wasn't used to that kind of lavvy. The waiter interrupted her conversation by collecting the glasses. Georgie ordered the same again.

"Eeh, this must be costing you a fortune, yer needn't have done this, yer know. I would have been happy enough just being with yer." Jessy was telling the truth, but it made her feel important to think that this was the type of place that he had wanted to bring her to.

"It doesn't matter, lass, as long as yer enjoying it. It's worth every penny to me just to see your face when yer came back from the ladies. Anyway it's not over yet, there's still plenty of time!"

With the mention of time he saw Jessy's face cloud over. He reached for one of her hands. They were under her hand bag on her knee. He'd noticed her hiding them there as soon as she had taken her gloves off. She put them back beneath as soon as she had taken a sip of her drink.

"I don't just mean plenty of time tonight, Jessy," he was looking intently at her. "I mean that we will soon have all the time in the world, cause not me Mam or anyone will part us when this is all over! Do yer hear me, Jessy? NOT ANYONE!"

"Aye I hear yer, so did half the room," Jessy tried to make light of it. She would live one day at a time. That's the only way she knew. But as she nodded in agreement to him, she felt a kernel of hope within her, deep inside.

They had had three drinks now, and there was three bits of paper sitting on the table when Georgie said he would have to go to the lavvy. Jessy picked one up to look, she wasn't good yet with numbers, especially when they were mixed in with writing like this was. As she studied them it got clearer, then she nearly shouted, "Bloody Hell" out loud. She looked again... "Nine and bloody eleven, for two drinks? Why they must have made a mistake, surely?" And there's three of them. She couldn't work out how much the total came to, but she knew it was enough to feed a family on for a fortnight. She was chomping at the bit by the time Georgie came back and couldn't wait to tell him about the mistake that they had made with the charges.

Georgie watched, amused, as she pointed out the prices on the paper. She did it so no one would see, but Jessy's idea of being casual left a lot to be desired. She was insisting that they had made a mistake, and that he should mebbie have a word on the quiet with the waiter fella. He felt the love for her swell up in him, he hadn't realized until now that she could be this funny, and yet attractive at the same time. She was a different person alright when yer took her away from all that hardship and let her be herself!

She pushed his knee with her own. "Whats making yer smile like that, Georgie? Did yer not hear what I was telling yer about the prices of these drinks?"

He leaned forward, "AYE, I did Jessy and I don't care!" She looked taken aback. "Don't worry, I can afford it. I might even have another, what about you? It's not often these days that yer can get a good bit of whisky, and I'm really enjoying it." He was teasing her slightly when he said, "How's your drink? Would you like another?"

She knew what he was doing, there was a feeling between them that had happened so naturally, and so fast that it amazed Jessy. She had never felt this comfortable and relaxed with anybody.

"I know what yer up to, yer know," she was returning his humour. "Yer know that I wouldn't know a good drink from a bad un." He widened his eyes in an innocent pose. "But as far as having another one goes, I'll say no," she whispered under her breath loud enough for him to hear. "Not at these bloody prices!" and sat back in her chair as she said, "But you please yerself, I've still got nearly a full one anyway."

He'd turned to catch the waiter's eye when he heard her say, "Georgie, I know what I would like."

He turned, she was serious now. He gently said, "Anything yer want, Jessy, yer can have.""

Jessy swallowed hard and took a deep breath. "I want to spend some time alone with you. It's very nice here, Georgie, but I don't want our last few hours to be spent sharing it with these "nobbs."" Her eyes were full, he knew that she felt the same as him. "Please let's go somewhere quiet, where we can be by ourselves. I really don't care where it is, just as long as we're alone."

He stood and picked up the slips of paper. "I'll go find the waiter and get our coats." He paused, "If yer sure that's what yer want."

She nodded and said, "I'll just pay a last visit to the 'you know where' for one last look. I don't want to sit here by meself anyway"

He was waiting in the hall for her. He had their coats over his arm. She went to put hers on and was halted by his words.

"There's no need," he took her arm. "We're not going far." He was leading her along the corridor. She was a bit disappointed. Where was he taking her now? He stopped outside a door and took a key out of his pocket and opened it. He practically pulled her through the door and then closed it. She was still silent.

"I hope yer not upset, Jessy, this was supposed to be a surprise for yer. But I didn't know how to tell yer without ycr thinking that I'd taken yer for granted. So I thought I would wait and see how the night went!"

The room was wonderful, but Jessy couldn't take it all in. She was surprised alright, but she didn't really know how she felt. Her first thought was, it must have cost him a bleeding fortune, then, what about Ruthie? She'll be worried sick. She looked at Georgie, he was standing looking at her waiting for her response.

"Is it ours all night, Georgie?" he nodded. She smiled and put her arms out to him and said, "GOOD." Ruthie would just have to worry this one time."

He laid the coats on the massive bed, she felt really awkward. It was as if he'd read her mind. He came and put his arms aroud her and she laid her head on his shoulder.

"We don't have to do anything, Jessy, we can just be together and cuddle and talk. I wanted to make yer remember this night, so I'll do anything yer want."

He was such a good kind man, and the thought of not having him in her life in a matter of hours left her desolated. She was so moved by his kindness that she burst into tears. He held her tighter and started to gently rock her in his arms. His own heart was breaking, listening to her sob, but he knew that he had to let her get it out of her system. He stood and held her until her body was still, then he lifted her face to look at her. She didn't want him to see her and buried her head in his neck. He persevered and lifted her face again, took his handkerchief from his pocket and wiped her eyes. "It's alright, Jessy. Ssshhh. It's alright. I know, I know lass. I know what's hurting yer, it's hurting me annaull

He kissed her forehead, then her eyes, soft gentle kisses around her face, ending up at her lips. He had only wanted to comfort her, but she was responding to him, kissing him back and then they were holding each other tight, feeling the excitement grow. He led her to the bed, still holding her. Jessy's last sensible thought before sinking into total passion was, thank God Ruthie made me wear the good underwear!

They made love most of the night, Jessy was a diligent pupil. Georgie showed her things and did things to her that she had never imagined, and with his help, she returned the favour. Jessy had never supposed that she could feel this way about a man. He was so gentle and yet so passionate. Even in love making he seemed to care more about her feelings than his, waiting for her to catch him up. She smiled as she remembered That had only been the first time, though, after that it was the other way round.

It was four thirty in the morning, and Georgie had drifted off to sleep. He was still holding her. Jessy was tired but she didn't want to sleep. She knew that if she did, it would be morning when she woke, The morning of the day Georgie went away!

She watched him sleep, felt his breath on her forehead, smelt the closeness of him. When she closed her eyes it was in an effort to capture and keep these memories, but sleep crept up and took over.

They were both woken by the knock on the bedroom door. Jessy heard it first and woke Georgie. "Georgie, Georgie, there's somebody at the door." She shook him and then he woke with a start. The knock came again, Jessy was frightened. What if Bullum's come? What if something's happened to the bairns? Before anything else came into her head, Georgie held her and said, "It's only breakfast. It must be seven o'clock. I ordered it for seven." He pulled his trousers and vest on and opened the door. A waiter wheeled in a table with silver dishes on it. Jessy wanted to hide under the blankets, but she just pulled them up to her chin. The waiter left without looking at her.

"What must he think of us, Georgie? I mean, we'll be the talk of the place."

"Aw Jessy, there's a war on lass. Things have changed, people are more accepting now. Everybody knows that yer have to get yer happiness when yer can. Naw, don't look like that, lass. Why we've done nowt wrong. Certainly no more than most of them in the bar with yer last night were doing." He walked over to her in the bed. "I bet none of them feel what we feel for each other." She looked at him and simply said with a smile, "They couldn't!"

Georgie had taken the jug from the undershelf of the trolley. He filled the dish in the corner with the hot water and turned and asked; "Do yer want to wash or eat first?"

"I need to go to the lavvy, Georgie, first of all, and then I think I'll have a wash afore, if that's alright with you?"

"You go to the lavvy then." She was pulling on her slip and dress. They were both still wrapped together, she had taken them off as one. Georgie was fascinated as she pulled them both on together and then just stuck her unstockinged feet into her shoes. He laughed when he said, "Why yer put them on nearly as quick as yer took them off." Jessy smiled shyly, "Eeh, be quiet, Georgie."

The night before he had shown her where the lavvy was, it was only just at the end of the corridor, but she had asked him to make sure the way was clear and that there was nobody using it before she would venture out. He did the same again without her asking, and she ran along the corridor before anybody could see her and before they could get to the lavvy before her. There was water in the bathroom but it was cold, so she wasn't in long. She popped her head out of the door, good, nobody there and she could see Georgie's head poking out of the room door looking for her. He was smiling as she ran towards him.

"You have the hot water, Jessy. I'll use the bathroom and give yer a bit of peace so that yer can get cleaned up and dressed properly."

"Why, don't be too long cause I'll have to be getting back. They'll be worried sick." As soon as she said it the wave of sadness hit her. "Aw, Georgie, why do yer have to go?"

He came away from the door and back to her, and took her in his arms. "It's not as bad as yer think, lass, there's no rush. I told Ralphy about me plans and this place, so they won't be worried."

She snuggled into him, "Why yer crafty dirty git!" She was teasing him.

He looked down at her, "I am that, especially when I want yer this much!"

He pushed himself against her to show what he meant. Then he was unbuttoning her dress and pulling it over her head. He made love to her again.

❧

She had stripped off and given herself a good body wash. There was still some clean water left in the jug.

Georgie was at the lavvy so Jessy pulled off her wig. It was such a relief to have the air on her head. She'd had it on all night, but the tightnesss hadn't bothered her until now. "It's cause yer had other things on yer mind, me girl," she told herself. She dipped her hand into the jug and scooped water onto her head, it felt good. She rubbed and scratched the water into her scalp, then took the scented soap and washed her face with what was left. She was having trouble finding the towel. She had soap in her eyes when Georgie knocked at the door.

"Don't come in, not yet. I'll not be a minute," Jessy wiped her face on the nearest thing, a blanket from the bed. She was panic stricken. My God, I'm naked. It hadn't occurred to her that he had only recently seen her naked, so she rushed to pull on her knickers and top. She was pulling her slip over her head when he knocked again saying, "Hurry up, lass, I'm out here in me vest." She ran to the door and unlatched it.

"I thought yer were ganna leave me out there all day and eat all the food yers..." He had stopped. He was looking at her, the smile frozen on her face. It suddenly dawned on her, she put her hands up to her head. She couldn't let him see her like this. She bent her head forward and tried to cover it with her arms and hands. She cried out, "Aw, naw NAW NAW NAW!" Then she sank to the floor with her head still buried. She was in a tight ball when he sat down beside her. He went to put his arms around her but she pulled away. She was sobbing hard, and in between sobs saying, "Don't look! Don't look at me! Go away," she started rocking herself repeating, "Go away, please go away."

Georgie's heart was breaking for her, to see her hurt like this. He put his arms around her again, firmly this time. She tried to pull away, but instead of letting her go he pulled her in tight to him. He was sitting on the floor with a leg on either side of her. When he wouldn't let go, she had buried herself tighter in to him, all the while trying to hide her head and face.

"Jessy, listen to me. Take yer hands away. I want to see yer." He had no effect on her. He continued in a firmer tone. "Did yer hear us, lass? Listen to me, Jessy, I want to see yer. I mean all of yer. You don't need a bloody wig to make me love yer. I already do." She was a little calmer now. "Come on, Jessy, let's face it, if either one of us was only interested in looks, then we would never have got together. None of us is an oil painting.

But do yer know after the first time I met yer, it didn't matter, cause yer are beautiful to me. YER REALLY ARE!"

He knew she was listening. "Oh I don't know how to describe it," he paused. "It's like, yer know, when you first saw me?" She nodded into his chest. "Well yer must have noticed me face, the scars and how it pulled, yer must have noticed it at first?" She nodded again. "But I don't feel that yer see them now. I don't feel that when yer look at me yer seeing me scars, at least I hope yer not!" She shook her head this time. He went on, "Well it's like that for me. When I look at you, I don't see yer in a wig, I don't see your scars. I JUST SEE JESSY."

He waited, after a couple of minutes she said, "I want to, but I don't think I can, Georgie." She took a deep shuddering sigh. "I really don't think I can."

He kissed the top of her damp hair, then stroked it. "Alright, lass, alright. You don't have to do anything yer don't want to." He leaned back to get up, sat on his haunches and said, "Come on, let me help yer up, then I promise I'll turn away while yer put yer hair back on."

He helped her to her feet. As he let go of her to turn away, she lowered one of her arms from her head and grabbed his hand. He turned back as she lowered the other arm, her face was still tucked into her chest, and she slowly lifted it to him. She had her eyes tight shut, but the tears were still running down her cheeks.

He had to be careful, he wouldn't lie to her. He took a few seconds to look at her, he smiled, there was no need to lie!

"Aw, lass. Aw, Jessy." He put his head next to hers, "Yer don't look any different! I swear I don't know what yer making all this fuss about. Yer really don't look any different." He touched her hair, it was soft and fine. "Why yer own hair's nearly the

same colour as the wig anyway. I don't care if yer never wear it
again, yer own hairs fine as far as I'm concerned!"

She'd opened her eyes. He was still looking at her, he was
telling the truth, he wasn't repulsed. She could still see the love
in him for her.

After he'd wiped her face with his handkerchief he led her
towards the breakfast trolley. Jessy lifted the lids on the now
cold plates. Her eyes widened, there was all kinds. There was
real bacon and eggs, porridge, bread and jam with real butter.
Then she saw the fruit. Two apples and one ORANGE! How
had they gotten a hold of oranges? She was pointing it all out
to Georgie, going from one plate to another. She was smiling
now, he was smiling with her. As he watched her the phrase a
sight for sore eyes came into his head because when Jessy was
happy and smiling, Georgie didn't see her scars on her face.
Georgie saw Jessy's SOUL in her face!

They ate the food. It didn't matter that it was cold. Jessy
thought it all tasted delicious. She'd never eaten like this
before, she was enjoying every mouthful. She even finished off
what Georgie left saying, "It's a shame to waste it. I really hate
waste." He was enjoying watching her eat. They talked about
the food then about the Hotel and the history behind it. Jessy
was very impressed when Georgie told her that it was where
Kings and Queens used to stay. That in years gone by it was
a coaching house on the main road from Scotland to England
and the last stop before the Scottish borders. The one thing
that neither of them wanted to talk about was him going!

They got ready and Georgie paid the bill and they left.
They walked slowly along the riverbank together, going

through the woods to get home. It was the long way round but Jessy had said it would be quieter, less chance of them being seen. Georgie didn't mind who saw him, but he had to think of Jessy. What kind of life would she have after he had gone if folk found out about them? So he would wait.

They got to the big tree and stopped. Had it only been three nights ago that she had stood here breaking her heart? So much had happened since then. Georgie stood with his back against the tree. He pulled her to him, she had her back to him with his arms around her. He laid his head against hers. His face was against her wig. It wasn't as soft as her own hair, he smiled when he remembered her at breakfast, no wig, no makeup, in her slip laughing and eating everything in sight. That's how he would think of her, how he would remember her.

They didn't speak for a while. It was the Cathedral striking eleven o'clock that prompted Jessy to ask, "What time are yer leaving?" It had been at the back of her mind for some time.

"My train's at half past eight, so there's no rush. I did say I would go for a drink with me Da this afternoon, yer know, just us two. But there's no rush!" He turned her to him, "Are yer coming to the station to see me off Jessy?" He knew the answer before she replied.

"I can't, Georgie," she looked down at her feet. She knew that if she looked at him she would break down. "I cannot do it!" She'd said it softly but he'd heard her. She continued in a stronger voice. "I just want to say 'cheerio' to yer ordinary like, yer know as if I was gonna see yer tomorrow or the next day, yer know, like when yer were teaching us to read." It was hard for her to talk, so she stopped. She knew Georgie would understand.

"Aye, well that's probably the best way of doing it anyway," he spoke with a false cheeriness. "It's not as if I'm gonna be a way long, not this time. The war's about over now. Everybody says so. No I'll be back in no time." He watched her nod her head, she sighed and said, "Aye, that's right, the war's about over."

"Yer have to believe, Jessy," he had noticed the defeat in her voice. "Yer HAVE TO BELIEVE that we've got a future together. I promise you that we will end up together, that I'll come back for yer." He turned her and hugged her tight to him, "AS GOD IS MY WITNESS, JESSY, I SWEAR I WILL COME BACK FOR YOU!" He had said it with such conviction that she DID believe him, and for the first time in her life, Jessy thought that she might have a future.

At the bottom of the cut they parted saying, "Cheerio," then "Cheerio" back. They couldn't touch each other now, it was too public. Georgie said under his breath, "I'll write as often as I can, but don't worry if yer don't get one straightaway. It takes a bit of time for the first lot to start coming through."

All Jessy could say was, "Aye, alright." She wanted him to go now. She couldn't bear this much longer. If he didn't go soon she might fall to the ground and beg him not to leave her. He said "cheerio" again. She replied. He was turning to leave when she said, "I LOVE YOU, GEORGIE, AND I KNOW YER'LL COME BACK." She turned and rushed up her own path. She needed to be alone before she went for the bairns from Ruthie's.

"Is that you, yer cunt?"

Bullum was home! He'd heard her close the door. She leaned against it now, and wiped her face on her sleeve. She took a deep breath and went on through.

"Oh, so yer've deemed to come fucking home have yer?" He looked at her in Ruthie's coat. "Well yer can't tell me yer've been fucking cleaning in that rig out." He waited for a reply. She couldn't think. All that she kept thinking was, why now? God, why now?

"I haven't had a bite to eat for fucking days, and yer come waltzing in here dressed up to the nines," He was watching her.

She had to think quickly. "It's our Ruthie's coat if yer must know. I borrowed it cause I was trying for a job at the Hall." She was pleased with herself. "And as for having nowt to eat, I leave yer something every time I go out. It's not my fault that yer never in to eat what I make when it's hot."

He was taken aback, but it didn't stop him. "Well, did yer get the fucking job then?" He didn't wait for her to reply. "I don't know how yer'd fit it in, yer've got that fucking many. Yer must be rolling in it. I'll have to mebbie stop giving yer as much for the 'other'. Cause that's been mighty fucking scarce lately annaull."

She was standing at the kitchen door, looking at him lying on the couch. He'd got bigger, he was fatter than ever. She was tired, so tired. "Yer can please yerself. I don't care anymore. In fact, keep all yer bloody money, I'd rather beg than let yer near me again. I'll get by!"

He was lying on his back so when he laughed it came out in a phlem-filled gurgle. She was wary of him when he was like this. She knew he had something up his sleeve.

He spoke through clenched teeth now. He was almost spitting the words out at her.

"Do yer know what they do to a 'Conchi' round here?"

Jessy didn't know what he was on about, she knew that a 'Conchi' was a conscientious objector, but she didn't understand what that had to do with her.

"Oh think on it, before yer gan running to that posh fucking sister of yours, ask yerself, yer stupid twat, why that so-called fucking husband of hers is not doing his bit?"

She laughed, "Why yer've come a cropper with that one, cause Ralphy tried to join up and they wouldn't have him. Cause of medical reasons."

He laughed again. "Oh really? Well that might be the truth," he started to raise himself. "But it might fucking not be annaull! And don't forget when yer thought of as a 'Conchi' not many stop to ask if it's the truth. Remember the Allisons, along Langley Terrace? Yer know, where the lad was caught in the house fire?"

He'd stopped talking and was watching her, he could see she was beginning to understand. He didn't want to push her too far, just in case she called his bluff. After all she was a good worker and she was cheap at that. Lately she wasn't even that bad to look at, so he needed to keep her here, but he needed her back under his thumb. He wouldn't allow her to think she had the upper hand. Cause come hell or high water she never would have!

He pushed himself up from the couch and reached for his crutches. She didn't flinch, she didn't care.

"I'm away out now to get summit." He was looking at her standing in the doorway, he grinned. "I'll be back late on tonight, make sure yer here. It's me night to gan upstairs!" He threw some coins at her feet, put on his coat and hobbled out.

She didn't cry, she was too empty. She sat in the silence. After a while she was able to think of Georgie, thinking of him gave her comfort. That's the thing, she thought, that's what Georgie doesn't understand, he doesn't know how evil Bullum can be. How he'll do anything to get what he wants. Why he even surprised me tonight at how far he'd go! She rose to go and get the bairns and looked in the shaving mirror as she passed. She spoke to herself, "Oh aye, he's won again lass, for the time being anyway. But don't you let him break yer. Naw don't you let him." She turned her face to the ceiling, clenched her hands and raised them to the sky and shouted at the top of her voice, "YOU'll NEVER TOUCH MY SOUL, BULLUM. NEVER, DO YER HEAR ME? NEVER!"

The lasses were home, they were playing with the Radiogram that Freddy had brought home a few days ago. Freddy was out, as usual, running around after Bullum she supposed. "Gan steady with that, you two, if yer break it there'll be hell to pay with our Freddy."

Hetty pulled Jean's hand away from the knob. "I'll do it, yer can't tune it in just turning it like that."

Jessy watched them together. Hetty was growing up fast, she was going to be a bonny lass. She had a way about her that was older than her years. She'd looked after Jean from the beginning, she was patient and kind with her. She had often relieved some of the burden from Jessy, and Jessy loved her for it. She made a mental note to take more notice of them, give them a bit more of her time now, and Freddy annaull. She realized she didn't know what Freddy got up to, and often didn't know where he was at or what he was doing, other than he was with Bullum. Jessy chastised herself mentally. They're ALL yer bairns, yer should have NO favourites.

Hetty had found a music station, she and Jean were swaying and pretending to dance. Jessy looked down at her hands. She didn't want to look at the clock anymore. It had said it was ten to eight. He would be at the station now with his Ma and Da. She imagined the scene, the platform would be packed, everybody seeing somebody off. His Ma would probably cry, and he would hold her and tell her not to worry. When the train pulled in he would shake his Da's hand, then they would hug briefly. She wished she was there, just to see him one last time. To see his look of concern when she got upset, to feel his arms around her, to tell her once again that he would come back! That everything would be alright.

The clock had hardly moved, it wasn't yet five to. It was still too late, she couldn't get there even if she wanted to! Anyway it was a time for his Ma and Da. They deserved to be alone with him. She knew it must be breaking Molly's heart to send him away again. She must have thought that she had him back for good, then this! Jessy thought about Ray. Naw, it was best this way, give them some time alone with him. Anyway, after the trick that Bullum pulled today, it's best that nobody knows about us, Georgie, not yet anyway.

It was over a mile and a half to the station, and it was nearly eight o'clock. Too late. She rose from the settle beside the fire, and went to get her handbag. She'd forgotten until now about the fruit that she'd brought back from the hotel. She took out the two apples, then the orange that she had wrapped in the soft paper from the lavvy. There was something else in there, wrapped in the other piece of paper. She took it out and unfolded it. Soap? He'd wrapped the soap up for her. She told him that she loved the smell of it, and he'd gone and wrapped it up for her. Jessy lifted it to her face, the smell brought back the memories of their night. She looked at the clock.

"Hetty, I'm popping out for an hour. Can yer look after things here do yer think?" She was already in her coat, she rushed through to the kitchen and halved one of the apples then gave it to them. "Don't go out. Don't go near the fire. I've built it up so it'll be alright till I get back, and don't answer the door to anybody, do yer hear?" Hetty nodded. Jessy held up the orange to them, their eyes widened. "If yer good and yer do as I say, I'll share it atween yer when I get home." She picked up her bag, put the tissue and the soap in it and was at the doorway when she stopped to ask, "Are yer sure yer'll be alright you's two?" Jean was too interested in the apple to answer. Hetty looked up and said with confidence, "Why aye, Man, I'm not a bairn anymore yer know," and turned back to the radiogram.

She wasn't even halfway there when she heard the Cathedral strike quarter past. She was walking quickly, but she didn't dare run, people would notice too much. She had decided to go along by the river, it was a bit longer but she could run a bit when she was down that way because it was out of the way of the main paths. It was just ahead of her now. She built up her speed ready to break into a run as soon as she was round the corner and out of sight of the houses. Jessy knew that she could make it if she ran most of the way. She could see the Castle and Cathedral ahead of her, getting closer, the station bank was to the left of them. She put on an extra spurt, the stitch in her side didn't even slow her down. It was going over on her ankle that brought her to tears, she twisted it and had to stop for a minute. It hurt like buggary for a few seconds. She put her foot on the ground and the pain shot through her calf. "Walk it off, lass. Walk it off," she told herself. It was pure determination that made her continue.

When the Cathedral bells struck half past, she wasn't even at the bottom of the station bank. Too late and she stopped, breathed air into her lungs and burst into tears. "Aw God, I just wanted to look at him again, ter see him one last time." She was leaning against the bottom of the station wall, sobbing. She reached into her handbag for the soft paper to wipe her face. It smelled of the soap. She looked up and sighed. She noticed that there was no train on or leaving the station. She tried to think. No, definitely not, she would have heard it if it had been in and was pulling out. Why, bugger a hell, lass, yer would have seen it never mind heard it!

He was still there. She hurried up the bank, the train was late. She'd ran up the station steps, and she saw him straight away, even among all the crowds of people. He was holding his Ma and speaking gently to her. His Da stood close to them and kept his head down. He hadn't seen her. She stepped back down one and then two of the steps. She bumped into somebody coming up them, apologized and turned and walked down another three. She could just see over the top step. She knew he couldn't see her, she didn't want to spoil it for Molly. She'd got what she wanted, she could see him!

He was on the train leaning out of the window. Molly was holding his hand and had to start to walk with the train when it started moving. She had to let go after only a few steps. His Da came up behind her and held her to him. It was gaining speed now, he was still waving. Jessy walked up the steps to keep him in sight, he was waving, his arm stopped in mid air. He leaned further out. He was squinting looking back at the platform, towards the end of the train. She raised her hand involuntarily and whispered, "Cheerio." He saw her just before the platform disappeared, he waved frantically. His Ma and Da thought he was still waving to them. Jessy left before they could turn and see her.

"Where've YOU been?" Jessy didn't like the tone of Freddys voice. She ignored him while she took off and hung up her coat. He persisted.

"Me Da wouldn't be none too happy ter know that yer've been out AGAIN."

Jessy guessed that Bullum had been moaning about her to Freddy. Nevertheless, something in the sly way that Freddy spoke to her made her wary.

"I forgot that I had an hours cleaning to do. I can't remember what day it is lately. I told Hetty I would only be an hour, and that's all I've been. So stop yer mitherin!"

She looked at Hetty, who nodded and said, "Aye, that's right, I must have forgot," she looked at Freddy, "When I said I didn't know where me Ma was, I meant that I didn't know where she was cleaning at, I knew she was out cleaning somewhere!"

Freddy still didn't look satisfied. "Oh is that right?" he said sarcastically. "I thought that yer might have gone to see Georgie off." He was waiting for a response from her. "After all, it is today that he gans, isn't it?" He was still waiting, "He is the one who did yer a favour and taught yer to read?"

Jessy turned on her heels and clouted him so hard across his head that he fell over.

"Now you listen to me, yer little shit. I'm yer Mother and you'll watch yer tongue when yer speak to me. What's more, I don't and never will have to explain myself to you! But I'll tell yer this, if Molly and her son choose, out of the kindness of their hearts, to bother to teach me something that will help me miss me son a bit less while he's away fighting for the likes of you, then it's nowt to do with you!" She took a deep breath. "It might serve you better if yer'd bothered to learn a bit of reading and writing then you'd be able to keep in touch with yer brother annaull. But instead of that yer'd rather 'suck hole' up to yer Da, and use whatever brains that yer have to listen to gossip." He was shocked she took the inititive. She went over to him and put her face close to his and looked straight at him. "Yer a greedy fat sly pig. Yer can be all those things when yer out, but when you come into this house yer better be bloody different. Do yer hear me?" She waited, "I SAID DO YER HEAR ME?"

"I hear yer," he mumbled.

"Well make sure yer don't forget, cause next time yer'll not see food for a month. Right?"

She was done. The lasses were speechless, she turned and picked up the coal bucket to fill it. She heard Freddy mumble. "WHAT did yer say?"

He looked at her sullenly, but he had a slight smile when he said, "I said I won't forget!"

She turned to get the coal and changed her mind. She went over and put it down at Freddy's feet. "Yer can fill that for your cheek, and yer can get used to filling it annaull. It might take a bit of that fat of yer if yer grafted a bit more."

He picked it up. She said to his back, "Bring enough for later, you'll be sleeping down here tonight. The bairns will be in your bed. Yer Da wants his own bed the night." She sat down wearily.

They were both listening to the news, her and Freddy, when Bullum came home. He was early. The lasses were in bed fast asleep. As she looked at him she noticed he only had the one crutch. He walked from behind the chair over to the couch. Jessy looked down because he was walking differently. He had TWO FEET! He ignored her completely, it was his usual way, and approached Freddy. "Well then, what do yer fucking think of that then?" He banged his new foot with his crutch, it made a dull solid sound. "Yer Da can wear the fucking trousers again, properly though this time, not with one fucking leg pinned fucking up."

"Eeh, it's grand that, Da." Freddy had gotten up and was walking around him. "How does it work?"

"What do yer mean 'how does it fucking work?'" He caught Freddy around the head with his fist. It was only a glancing blow but Jessy felt sorry for the lad.

"What did yer have to go and hit him for? He was only asking a question. How the hell is he supposed to know how a peg leg works?"

"Are yer all fucking stupid? What do yer mean 'work'? It's strapped on, that's all, it doesn't do nowt! For fuck's sake it's a boot on the end of a bit of fucking wood." He turned his back and walked towards the bottom of the stairs. He was talking to himself. "Stupid twats! 'How does it work?'" he was mimicking them, "Pair of stupid cunts!"

He turned to Jessy, "Bring me dinner up. I'll have it afterwards."

CHAPTER TWELVE

Georgie had arranged to have his letters sent to Ruthie's. Jessy went along every two days, not only to collect her mail but also to be able to write back to him. She was able to take her time and not have anybody looking over her shoulder. By "anybody" she meant Freddy, he had been different since the night she had given him a clout. He never back chatted her, but if possible, he was more sulky than ever. He made Jessy feel uncomfortable, he seemed to be watching everything she did. He even popped in Ruthie's more often now than he had ever done. She felt he was up to something, but couldn't put her finger on it.

She wouldn't think of him now, cause today was a good day. She had a letter from Ray and a letter from Georgie. She sat at Ruthie's table, first smoothing out one, then the other.

"I think yer have to open them to read them yer know." Jessy smiled at Ruthie and replied, "I will in a minute. Give us a bit of time, you're worse than me. Yer'd think they were bloody well addressed to you the way yer go on." She was only joking, and Ruthie knew it. Jessy had brought Ray's letter along to open with her, and she often read out bits of Georgie's. Not the nice bits though, thought Jessy.

Ruthie put the cups of tea on the table and sat waiting. Jessy watched her as she fiddled with the cup, then started sighing and blowing air out of her mouth. She could tell she was getting agitated. Jessy wondered how long she could make her wait before she said something. She kept a straight face but inside she was laughing when she said, "I might wait till I get home, yer know it's more private." She had made it sound like an innocent remark. She widened her eyes with a look of innocence when Ruthie said, "Yer having me on! Yer are, aren't yer? Yer bloody well having me on. Why I've never known owt as cruel."

"Aye, yer have a point." Ruthie could see that she was toying with her now, she smiled and snatched one of the letters from her hand. Jessy was chasing Ruthie round the kitchen table laughing when she got the feeling. It was a wave of sickness, she stopped and hung on to the back of one of the chairs. Ruthie thought she was still joking, and that it was a ruse to catch her. "I'm not falling for that one our Jessy, if yer want this back," she waved the letter in the air. "Yer have to promise to read it straightaway," she was waiting for a reply. Jessy looked up at her. "Aw lass, lass what is it?" She knew Jessy wasn't having her on, she'd seen it in her face. She helped Jessy to sit. She was holding her hand over her mouth, through her fingers. Ruthie heard her mumble, Jessy repeated the mumble, this time Ruthie understood. She ran to fetch a dish, brought it and put it under Jessy's face. They sat like this for a few minutes then Jessy pushed the dish away. "It's passed," she looked at Ruthie's worried face. "It's alright, lass, I'm feeling alright now. Don't worry yerself, it's nothing." Ruthie was shaking her head, "Nothing, my arse, it halted yer in yer tracks! Yer should go and see the doctor. I don't mean that bloody Wilmy neither I mean a proper doctor, so that yer can get it sorted. Will yer go, Jessy?"

"No need lass, I'm alright."

"If yer want, I'll gan with yer." Ruthie was waiting hopefully. She was taken aback by Jessy's next statement.

"Ruthie, I THINK I MUST BE PREGNANT!"

Ruthie sat down heavily in the chair next to Jessy. She was agog. "Are yer sure? How far on are yer? When's it due? Are yer pleased? What are yer gonna do?"

"WHOA WHOA. It's just occurred to me now!" Jessy was surprised herself, at how she hadn't noticed it before now. She'd had the signs, no periods, but she'd never been regular anyway, not since she'd been burnt, so that didn't help. But now that she thought of it, there had been other signs. She was hungry all the time, often got real bad heartburn, then there was this sickness. She had it a few times before, but it was never on a morning, so she hadn't related it to morning sickness. No hers was on an afternoon and sometimes an evening, but there again when she remembered back, she had had night sickness with Ray. "Oh, yer silly sod, Jessy," she said it out loud.

"What yer ganna do Jessy?" Ruthie looked horrified.

"Well what can I do? I'm pregnant and there's no getting away from it." Ruthie was looking at her strangely. The penny dropped.

Jessy reached over and took Ruthie's hands. "Yes. Yer right in what yer thinking. IT'S GEORGIE'S!"

"Are yer sure? I mean can yer know for certain? Aw, bugger it, what I really mean is do yer know when that fat bastard was last at yer? Or have yer put a stop to that?"

Jessy thought before she replied, how could she best explain this to Ruthie?

"All I can tell yer, Ruthie, at this minute, with all me body and soul I feel that this bairn is Georgie's. But in answer to yer question, yes I know when Bullum has been at me. Believe me, yer don't forget things like that." Jessy had her arms round her belly now. She was struggling to come to terms with what had dawned on her, never mind explaining her feelings to Ruthie.

"This calls for a fresh cup of tea. I'd put something stronger in if yer weren't the way yer are, but I'm gonna have a drop meself anyway." She put the kettle on. She had her back to Jessy, she was worried. Worried about both Bullum and Georgie's reaction. She knew that Jessy hadn't thought about all the consequences that this could bring. Her thoughts were interrupted.

"Anyway, Bullum always shoves us off afore he comes, that's been happening for years. He says he doesn't want any more mouths to feed. As if he feeds the ones he's got now!" She was waiting for Ruthie to say something. When she didn't, Jessy went on. "I know what yer thinking, accidents can happen and all that, but all I can tell yer is how I feel, and honestly, Ruthie, I'd put money on it that this is Georgie's kid!" Jessy was still waiting for her to say something, she was getting nervous now, this wasn't like Ruthie. She normally just said what she felt and to hell with what folks thought. "Say something, Ruthie, talk to us. I'm frightened enough without you gannin silent on us."

"Are yer sure yer want me to say what I think, our Jessy? Cause at the moment I'm petrified for yer and your carrying on as if this sort of thing is quite normal. I mean, have yer actually thought about the situation that yer in? Have yer thought about what yer gonna tell people, not just Bullum and Georgie, but the lads and the bairns. To say nothing of Georgie's Ma and Da?"

Ruthie let Jessy sit silent for a few minutes. "Anyway, how far on are yer? Yer can't be that far gone cause there's not a picking on yer and yer not showing." She took a deep breath, "Have yer thought about going to see Wilmy? She could make the problem go away!" Every bone in Ruthie's body was crying out "NO." She hated the idea of anybody getting rid of a bairn, let alone her own sister. But she loved Jessy more, and for the life of her, she couldn't think of a way through this mess that she'd got herself into.

Jessy was taken aback, then filled with a deep sadness. "Aw, Ruthie, yer can't be serious after all yer've said about women who do that! Surely yer don't mean it?" She held her belly tighter. "I couldn't Ruthie, I just couldn't. Even if I thought it was Bullum's, I couldn't do that. It's just not in us, Ruthie, yer know that."

"Aye, well yer might have no option." Ruthie was pacing the room, she was talking to Jessy like Jessy had never heard before. She wasn't shouting or anything, but she was speaking loud and clear. "You're telling me that yer sure that this is Georgie's bairn. Aye, well fair enough, but from what yer've told me, won't Bullum get the same idea? THAT IT'S NOT HIS? Even if yer right and it is Georgie's, have yer thought how yer gonna tell him? Have yer thought whether or not he'll believe it's his? Whether or not he'll want it?" She looked at the fear on Jessy's face and nearly softened, then thought better of it. She should be frightened. If she's frightened she might stop being so bloody daft and get some sense into her head. "This is not a film, Jessy. It's not a story like what yer read to us from the magazines. Yer've got to decide what yer gonna do. And whatever it is yer've got to get yer story straight. Dead straight. Cause if any of this comes out to Bullum," she took a deep intake of breath, "he'll kill yer!"

She knew that Ruthie was right, but she didn't want to hear it. For a few minutes she'd been happy, over the moon in fact, with the thought of having Georgie's bairn. All that had happened wasn't just a dream. Here was the proof. She had something of him to keep, to hold on to. She thought of the letters that she had received from him. He was always loving in them, and he talked about their future together. At first she hadn't thought much about it, pushing it to the back of her mind, telling herself it probably wouldn't happen. But over the fifteen weeks that he'd been away, with every letter that he sent she started to believe him a bit more. There was a chance that they could have a future together. What she hadn't realized until now was how much she had planned that future in her head. When she thought about it, she had, down to the fact that they would move away, with the lasses of course. Ray would probably get married and live near them, and visit all the time with his wife and family, when he had them. Freddy wouldn't visit so often, it would be too far for him to come. But when he did, he would be a changed lad, not sullen and sly anymore because he would be taking his lead from Georgie, not Bullum. Aye, he would change! Jessy was lost in the dream.

Ruthie put her hand gently on her shoulder and set the cup down in front of her. "I'm sorry if I upset yer, lass, but we've got to get our heads together on this." Jessy looked lost. Ruthie lightened her voice, "Don't worry, lass, we'll sort it out. Remember there's nowt WE can't sort out as long as we're together." Jessy gave her a weak smile.

"I cannot go to Wilmy, though, no matter what yer say. Why I'd rather Georgie didn't know anything about it and pretend that it's Bullum's afore I'd do that!"

"Could yer hurt him like that?" Ruthie waited for a reply, Jessy looked confused. "I mean, could yer let him think that yer got pregnant after he went away?"

Jessy thought for a minute, her heart was heavy. All the joy that she'd felt at first was melting away, and was replaced by a sense of dread at the mess that she was in. "Well, what else can I do Ruthie?" She put her head in her hands then looked up as the idea hit her. "I could say nowt! I mean say nowt to Georgie, till he comes home that is. Then I could explain everything to him." She was babbling now, grasping at straws, her head was jammed with notions, but none of them seemed right.

"Think lass! THINK." Ruthie was ahead of her. "Do yer not think that his Mam will know soon enough, that she'll tell him in her letters. Imagine how he'll feel if he finds out that yer pregnant, thinking that it's Bullum's and that you didn't tell him. Why yer'll not see him for dust. And rightly so. He'll feel that yer betrayed him, if not for "doing it" with Bullum, but for the fact that yer kept it a secret from him." She paused to think. "Are yer sure yer want to keep it, Jessy?" Ruthie saw the look on Jessy's face. "I had to ask, lass, but now that we know the situation, how's this sound to yer?" Ruthie sat at the table and took Jessy's hand. "This is what I think yer should do! First of all, yer need to tell Bullum that yer pregnant. Yer know, act as if yer fed up, annoyed and that it's his fault. Once that's done, write to Georgie and tell him annaull. But don't say what yer told me, yer know, about Bullum coming out afore he spurts. Just tell him that yer know that it's his bairn." Ruthie was watching Jessy to make sure she was taking all this in. "That way, depending on how he feels about it all, yer'll get to explain it all to him when he comes back, if yer want to that is? Yer'll have to ask him not to tell his Ma and Da though, say that yer don't want to cause trouble afore he gets back, and that if Bullum found out, yer life wouldn't be worth tuppence. That's the bloody truth, yer'll not be lying to him about that!" Ruthie took a long deep breath.

"Yer mean let everybody think that I'm just pregnant again, to Bullum?" Jessy was starting to understand.

"Aye, that's it lass. Yer just up the stick again. As far as anybody else is concerned it's Bullum's."

"But it'll be like lying to him, and anyway if I tell him that I'm gonna let everbody think that it's Bullum's he's mebbie gonna think that it could be annaull! Aw, Ruthie, I don't think that I can fix this."

"Yer can, lass." She held Jessy's hand tighter now. "Yer have to tell him that Bullum gets drunk and can't remember what he's doing. It's not far from the truth anyroad!"

"What if he doesn't want me when he finds out? What if he doesn't want us?" she touched her stomach.

"Well that's the risk yer'll have to take, but from what yer've told me about him, I don't think that will be the case. And if it is, then at least yer've still got the bairn and Bullum's none the wiser." She was waiting for some response. "But I'll tell yer this, lass, if yer detrmined to keep this babby and yer think that there is a future for yer with Georgie, then yer gonna have to fight for it! Which means, in this case, biding yer time and for once in yer life using that fat bastard so it works for you." She was holding and pulling Jessy's hand. "Come on, lass. ARE YER UP FOR IT?"

Jessy lifted her head, then lifted her cup. She looked up at Ruthie with a set chin and tears in her eyes.

"I am that, Ruthie. BY GOD, I AM. CHEERS!"

They sat and went over the plan another twice. Then Jessy read the letters to Ruthie.

The next night when Bullum came in, late and drunk as usual, Jessy had him a hot meal ready.

"What's the fucking occasion? Lost yer job or summit?

Why yer needn't think that a fucking bit of stew will get more money out of me!" He sat down to eat.

Jessy's heart was in her mouth. She'd told the lasses earlier about them ganing to have a baby brother or sister then sent them up to bed. They seemed happy enough, well, Jean more so than Hetty.

"As a matter of fact I have got summit to tell yer," she was standing near the kitchen door, her hands were in the front pinny pocket, she didn't want him to notice how nervous she was. He was looking and waiting. "I'm a bit l..." Freddy came in. Bullum looked up and asked straight away, "Did yer get it?" Freddy nodded and handed him some money. Bullum threw some change back at him, turned to Jessy and said, "Give the lad a fucking bite to eat then, instead of standing there like a fanny in a fit" Freddy smiled and sat down next to his Dad.

Jessy nearly threw the food at Freddy, she didn't like that he smirked when his Dad talked to her in this way. She was annoyed now. She stood well back, "As I was bloody well saying, I'm late again, yer know what that means." She waited, nothing."I'm bleeding pregnant again. I thought you were taking care of that side of things, being careful and the like. Well it didn't bloody work, did it?"

There was silence until the plate smashed off the side of the wall near her head, splattering her with stew.

"Well, yer needn't think that yer'll get any fucking more money of ME! Naw, yer getting no more out of me, that's a fact." He started eating again. It was Freddy's plate he'd thrown, not his own. Jessy nearly smiled, she turned away as he said through his mouthfuls of food, "Why, find some more fucking work, or ask that fucking barren sister of yours if she wants it. Either way it'll make no fucking difference to fucking me!"

"Freddy, there's some more stew in the pan. Get yer own,

and clear this mess up, cause I won't be doing it. I'm ganning to bed. I'll not stay and be spoken to like that by yer Father in front of me bairn."

Bullum looked up, smiled and then chuckled. He looked at Freddy then said to Jessy. "GOOD, fucking riddance. Piss off. Yer enough to turn me fucking dinner off, yer ugly cunt." Freddy was smiling, Bullum had had the desired effect. He was showing Freddy how to treat women!

Jessy slid the bolt through the lock, she was safe. It had gone well. "That's one step done. I'll write to Georgie tomorrow night and get the rest over with." She was whispering to herself, trying to calm her stomach, it was important that she keep healthy. She really wanted this bairn. "Please God, let him want it as well!"

It had been three weeks since she had written to Georgie, she was worried to death. She hadn't heard from him at all, she had never waited this long for a letter from him. Only in the beginning, but he had warned her about that. Every time she went to Ruthie's, Ruthie would look at her and shake her head then make up some excuse as to why he hadn't written. At first she'd hung on to these excuses, but now she was trying to accept that it was not going to happen. She was not going to have a future, she was not going to move away from Bullum and she had even started to think that she was probably not having Georgie's baby, but Bullum's.

She took the letter out of her coat pocket, it was from Ray. Every time she seemed to be at rock bottom, her Ray was always there. Aw, I miss him, and God willing, he comes home safe. Me life will still be grand, as long as he's in it. She was thinking aloud, "Aye, everything will be much better when

Ray gets back." What had been happening in her life had made her less conscious of his absence, now it all came flooding back, the desperate feeling of wanting to see his face, see him smile and call her Ma. She turned her face to the ceiling, "It'll be alright, God, I've still got my Ray!"

It was October, 1944 and Jessy had started to show, she was over five months gone now. She was on her way to Ruthie's, she'd had another letter from Ray. She would read it out to Ruthie and let her hear the good news for herself. The lasses were with her, they never missed an opportunity to go and see their Uncle Ralphy and Auntie Ruthie. It was now almost seven weeks since she'd written to Georgie. She knew that he was alright, Molly had told her so when she'd bumped into her in the street. So Jessy knew that he was still writing to his Ma and that his mail was getting through. Although her heart was broken, she carried on. She wasn't even angry at him. Ruthie had told her to treat it like a lovely experience, and when she thought about it, it was! Today was one of her better days. The news she had received from Ray had her all excited and she was feeling fine too. As she walked, there was a cold winter sun, but it was bright, and she was wrapped up in yet another winter coat from Ruthie. She smiled as she thought, the cold weather certainly had kept her kitted out. Ruthie and Ralphy were always busy at this time of year.

Ruthie was at the back door waiting for them. "Get yerselves in here side the fire, girls. I've left some odds and ends of make-up out in the parlour for yer to play with, and I'll bring yer summit to eat in a minute. Go on, give yer Mam and me a bit of time to talk," she ushered them through. "Let us get in first," said Jessy, "what's yer hurry?" Ruthie smiled and held up the letter from Georgie.

"How can yer be so calm, Jessy? Go on then open it!" Ruthie was sitting at the table with Jessy, she hadn't even bothered to make a cup of tea.

Jessy's hands were steady, she felt calm. "Yer know what it's gonna say don't yer, our Ruthie?"

"You can't know that for certain, Jessy, at least he's wrote back to yer. Anyway he might have just got yer letter, like I've said before, and be writing straight back."

Jessy sighed and looked at her. "So why didn't he write and ask how I was? Ask why I'd stopped writing to him? Worry about what had happened to me?" She turned the letter over in her hands. "Naw, he's doing the right thing and at least writing back to let me know his feelings. Don't look so disappointed, lass. Why yer taking it harder than I am!" She squeezed Ruthie'shand.

"Do yer mind if we don't open it now, Ruthie. I've just got a letter from our Ray and I don't want to spoil the day. Why don't I read that out to yer instead?"

"Aye. I bloody do mind. You mightn't want to hear what he says, but I bloody well do. If only to hate him when he gets back. Cause if what is in that letter is what yer think it is, I will bloody hate him. Who does he bloody think he bloody is? It takes two to tango, and he was bloody well keen enough when he was using me and Ralphy to lie for him!" She took a deep breath. "And that goes for you annaull Jessy, there's not only you involved in this, yer know. Why, I don't know how yer can think that yer can push us out now when..."

Jessy put her hand up to quieten her. "Alright, Alright. Don't go on. I don't know if I've ever heard anybody use 'bloody' as much. If yer stop I'll read the letter to yer. Alright?"

She nodded. Jessy opened it and smoothed it out onto the kitchen table. She sighed deeply and began.

"My dearest Jessy,

Please forgive me. I was dreadfully shocked by your news. So shocked that I didn't know what to think. At first, like a coward, I could only think of all the problems this would bring. I was not just thinking of me, Jessy, you must believe that, my dearest. Despite my certainty to you in the past, I have always known that for us to be together would be difficult. I am ashamed to say that when I first heard about our baby, I felt it had been made impossible. I was so very wrong, my darling. These weeks of not being able to write to you, I couldn't until I had sorted out what I needed to do, have almost driven me mad. I realize that in all of this despair I need you more than ever, and that I will for the rest of my life. You are the only thing that has kept me sane.

So forgive me please, Jessy. When this is over (and on a brighter note, it should be soon, the Yanks are making a hell of a difference) we will go away. I have sat these last days working out my money. I think we should be alright. We will start a new life together, the three of us and the girls, and any of the rest of your brood that wants to come along. I wish I was there with you to see how you look. I sometimes wonder how big your 'bump' is. I know exactly how far on you are, I count the days.

Write to me soon, please. I miss your letters. I miss you, everything about you. I think about our night together all the time. How loving and open you were. Better stop thinking about that side of things or things will start to happen. See, you still have the same effect upon me as ever, my love.

Stay safe and healthy, Jessy, and stay away from Him. It won't be long now, my love.

Yours forever, Georgie.

PS. I have just heard that all leave has been cancelled. I know it is bad news in a way, but it must mean that we are making a final push. With any luck I'll be home to see the birth of my child.

Cheerio again. Xxxxxx"

He had underlined "cheerio" several times. Jessy kept looking at the letter, words were jumping out at her. "OUR BABY." "MY CHILD." She looked up at Ruthie, tears were pouring down both of their faces. Ruthie jumped up, she grabbed at Jessy's hands and pulled her up with her. Then like some six year old she was skipping round the table and singing at the top of her voice. "I TOLD YER. I TOLD YER. DIDN'T I TELL YER ALL THE TIME? I DID, I TOLD YER. OH I TOLD YER ALL THE TIME." Jessy was skipping with her, the lasses came to the kitchen door, faces made up badly, now everyone was laughing, they were all skipping round the table. After a few minutes Jessy sat, the others were still playing. She picked up the letter and kissed it, folded it back up and shoved it in her pinny pocket. She patted it thinking, It's as if he'd seen me dreams, she felt full of love for him, and she felt loved.

"What a day." Ruthie was out of breath, she gave Jessy a smacker of a kiss on the head and dropped into a seat. Now that the excitement was over, the girls had gone back to playing with the make-up.

"It's not over yet lass," said Jessy. "I've still got our Rays letter to read yer, and there's more good news."

Ray was coming home on leave. His regiment was being transferred, he didn't know if he would get home in time for Christmas, but if not, he said it would be a few days after. She wished Georgie could have got leave, not just for her sake, but for the sake of Molly too. Jessy knew what it was like to be constantly worrying about them.

The house was quiet, the bairns, even Freddy were in bed fast asleep. She wouldn't be long in going up herself, she was tired, it had been a helluva good day but a tiring one as well. She patted her belly and said, "Goodnight, Georgie's bairn." Jessy felt content, she liked it when they were all in the house, safe and sound. She was pleased that Freddy hadn't waited up for Bullum coming in. He'd had too many late nights recently. "Mebbie that's what makes him the way he is," she said to herself. "He's moody and sulky one minute and then as nice as ninepence the next. Aw, he'll probably grow out of it!" She couldn't keep her mind on one thing or the other. Best get off. She paused at the doorway. I'll read his letter one last time afore I go up. Her pinny was on the hook on the back of the door. She put her hand in the pocket of it and pulled out the letter. She had opened it before she realized it was Ray's letter. She folded it back up and went back to the pinny. Her heart sank like a stone, she had Ray's letter in one hand, the other hand was feeling around in the pocket of the pinny. She took it down off the hook and turned the pocket inside out.

STILL NOTHING!

Jessy ran to her coat, turned its pockets too. Still nothing!

"Sit down and think lass," she spoke forcibly to herself. "Think where yer had it last" She could remember taking it to and from her pinny at Ruthie's to read it, she'd read it over and over. But she knew she had put it back, or she thought she had. I wouldn't have put it in me coat, not when me pinny has a pcket in it. She was almost in tears with panic. She looked in the pinny and the coat again, she looked around the house, in case it had dropped out. She couldn't let Bullum find it. The thought filled her with fear. She continued her search, even going out to the coalhouse and the lavvy. Aw, why did I bring it back with us? she thought, I never do. I always leave his letters along Ruthie's. Yer stupid cow, Jessy, that's what yer are, a silly stupid cow.

She checked and double checked, she had to make sure. When she was certain it was nowhere to be found, she sat down and cried. She was still crying as she mounted the stairs. She only slept fitfully that night, and the only reason that she dozed off towards dawn was the thought that she must have left it at Ruthie's.

CHAPTER THIRTEEN

Hetty was back from Gloria's, she hadn't stayed long. The doctor had her on the same tablets that he'd given her Ma, and she was sleeping. The lasses were coping alright at the moment, but she would pop back along in the morning.

Jean had opened a tin of soup and was heating it for their Ma. Hetty didn't like giving her tablets on an empty stomach. She couldn't remember the last time that her Ma had eaten, she had managed to get a cup of sweet tea down her once or twice but that was all.

"Are you gonna take it up or shall I?" Jean had the tray in her hands.

"I'll take it if yer like, you've done enough today." Hetty was looking around her, whilst she'd been out Jean had cleared everything away. "Yer can get yerself away home if ycr like, take some of that food that is left. It'll do for your lot's dinner." She turned to go up the stairs, Jean touched her arm.

"It's alright, I'm staying with you the night. I made the arrangements earlier so they're not expecting me back anyway What about your lot? Will yer have to nip home to see to them?"

"No, I'm the same. I told them to fend for themselves tonight." Jean turned to go. Hetty said, "Thanks, our Jean," and started up the stairs. She had only got to the second stair when she heard voices. Jean turned and looked at her. "She must be awake." Hetty replied, "She must be!" Hetty lingered on the second step. "Why don't yer come up and see her while she's awake, she might like that?" Jean nodded and walked up behind Hetty.

Jean was about to ask, "Who's she talking to?" when the voices stopped. Instead she turned to Hetty when they got to the top of the stairs and said, "It didn't sound like me Ma, did it?"

"What do yer expect, Jeany? She's full of tablets and groggy as hell. She's not gonna sound the same is she?"

All the same, Hetty hesitated at the door handle. She pulled back and instead of opening it, she knocked.

Jean looked at her, but said nothing. There was no answer. Hetty turned the knob and opened the door slowly. She looked in. She was still sleeping. They both went in. Hetty put the tray down and Jean pulled the bedclothes up over her Ma.

"She must have been dreaming or talking in her sleep or something." Jean nodded.

Hetty lifted Jessy up the bed a little. "Wake up, Ma. We've brought yer some soup and yer tablets."

Jessy stirred and opened her eyes. "Please let me sleep, lass. Just let me sleep." Hetty smiled at her and said, "Aye, alright. As soon as yer've had a bite to eat. Look, Junie's made yer some hot soup." She lifted the bowl, took the spoon and held it to Jessy's lips. Her eyes opened and she repeated her request, "Please let us sleep, lass." The tears were running down her face as she said "It's important!"

Hetty gave in, she took one of the tablets and held it out to Jessy. She took it and Hetty held the glass for her to drink and swallow. Jessy turned her head and looked at her bairns, "Yer good lasses." She was drifting off again, "Yer always have been."

WATCHING

They closed the door softly as they left the room; It was dark on the stairs. It must be about seven o'clock, thought Hetty. Why wasn't it dark in the room?

It was December the 26th, 1944. Boxing Day. It had been a quiet Christmas, not only because Ray hadn't made it back yet, but Jessy's mother had died the week afore. Jessy went to the funeral with Ruthie and the bairns. Although she was sad she felt no real sense of loss. It was a long time since she'd had owt to do with her Ma. No, in the main, she'd gone along to support Ruthie, and to show her respects. Her Da had shed a tear or two, crocodile tears, thought Jessy cause he didn't give her Ma the lickings of a dog when she was alive. He'd soon buggered off to the pub with the rest of the fellas after she was put in the ground!

Ruthie was different, she was hurting real bad. Jessy had been along most nights for the past week, and she was here again tonight. She knew that if Ray did get home and she wasn't there, he would know where she was. At the moment, though, Ruthie needed her more.

The lasses and Freddy were sitting playing with the couple of things that they had got for Christmas, mainly from Ruthie and Ralphy. Freddy had been around a lot more lately. When she asked, "Why yer not with yer Da so much these days?" he had replied, "There's not much to do this time of year and anyway our Ray would want us to look after yer when yer the way yer are!" Jessy knew she should be pleased at his new-found consideration for her, but although she tried to think well of him, she felt uncomfortable when he was around. A wave of guilt washed over her, as she watched him now. He was reading with Hetty from the book she had got for Christmas, he was helping her with the words. He's GOOD! she thought, he catches on quick, he'd been reading with the lasses a good bit lately, doing their homework with them. At first it had been Hetty helping him with his words, but now it was the other way round. Well mebbie that crack around the head I gave him made him think?

"Has our Ray got home yet?" Ruthie had come down the stairs. Since her Ma had died, Ralphy had made her sleep, if she could, for a couple of hours of an afternoon. He said it was the only way that he could get her to stop her crying. Jessy looked at her now and knew that there hadn't been much sleeping done, she probably just went upstairs to please Ralphy. No, she could see from her face that she had been crying again.

"No, not yet lass, but yer know what he said in his letter, "Expect him when he arrives," besides that I don't know if the trains will have been running yesterday, what with it being Christmas and that."

Jessy followed Ruthie through to the kitchen. Thinking of Ray's letter had reminded her of the one from Georgie she'd lost. It hadn't been anywhere to be found. She double-checked everywhere and her and Ruthie had gone through Ruthie's place with a fine tooth comb. No. it was definitely lost. It's a shame. Cause it was a lovely letter annaull'. She mentioned it to Ruthie again as she put the cups out.

"Stop fretting over one bleeding letter, our Jessy. If it's lost, it's lost. Yer've got plenty more where that came from. I'll tell yer this, yer fretting more over that letter than yer are yer own mother dying!"

Jessy decided not to rise to the bait. Instead she said calmly, "I was only wondering where it could have got to. I mean, I was more worried that Bullum would find it than I was about losing it!" This was only a half truth, she considered all of Georgie's letters a bit of him and she hated not having them all.

"Ruthie came up behind her and cuddled into her back. "I'm sorry, I don't know why I said that. I know it's different for you with me Ma than it was for me." She swallowed hard.

"It's like I really miss her Jessy, and I don't know why. It wasn't that I saw her that often even."

"Yer saw a lot more of her than I did, yer probably saw a lot more of her than me bloody Da did. Especially these last few years, he was always along the pub. Our Freddys told us a few times how he'd borrowed more money from Bullum to feed his 'boozy nights'." Jessy stopped she was trying to find a way of explaining how she felt to Ruthie. It wasn't the first time that Ruthie had asked her why she wasn't more upset. Jessy wanted to make her know her feelings, without spoiling the memories that Ruthie had of their Ma.

"It's just that once I got married I didn't see much of her, Ruthie, and she never visited me neither. Aye, alright it would have been difficult with Bullum, I know, but mebbie cause she didn't make the effort then neither did I. So let's leave it at that shall we? It's mebbie 'six of one and half a dozen of the other' to blame. Eh?"

"Aye alright, I'll say no more about it." She bit down on her lip and then blurted out, "Aw, it's such a shame though, yer were both so much like each other. She was a 'grafter' annaull our Jessy, and she didn't have a much better life than you."

Ruthie was crying again. Rather than keep letting her get upset like this, Jessy hugged her to her saying, "Now don't go getting yerself all snotty again. It's not as if I didn't feel anything for her, after all she was me mother. And yes, in a way I DO miss her, but just not like you do."

This seemed to do the trick. Ruthie wiped her eyes and sniffed a couple of times before asking, "So yer've got no idea when the prodigal son will be back then?"

"None, just that it could be anytime. Yer know what he said in his last letter, so we'll just have to wait."

"What do yer think he'll say when he sees yer the way yer are?" Ruthie looked down at Jessy's now swollen stomach.

"I don't know really. I'm hoping that he's alright about it. I cannot tell him about Georgie yet can I? I mean I can hardly keep the bairn a secret from him but he doesn't have to know all the ins and outs yet."

"I wouldn't worry, yer know our Ray, he'll forgive you anything. Yer can do no wrong in his eyes." Ruthie started to fill up again so Jessy changed the subject.

As they both talked about how short meat was to get and how hard it was to make a proper meal, Jessy thought, things have changed a bit between Ruthie and me, and not only cause of me Ma dying! There's more to it than that, it's as if she gets a bit, she struggled to find the word, not angry when she sees me, not jealous, more envious? Aye, that's it, I feel she's envious! She smiled to herself, yer must be mad! What has Ruthie got to be envious about you for? She was stroking her belly as they were chatting, and she saw Ruthie look down at her hand and imitate her, stroking her own stomach unconsciously. Yer fool, Jessy, she thought, it must be like torture to her. Seeing yer get bigger, seeing how easy it is for yer and having to talk about it all the time with yer.

Jean had come running through, "Is there owt to eat? We're all hungry?"

"How about some condensed milk on bread? Will that do yer?" Ruthie walked over to the pantry.

Jean looked back through to the other room, Jessy saw Freddy nod his head, "Aye, thanks, Auntie Ruthie." She stood waiting.

"Yer'd better do more than one slice if yer've got it to

spare, cause that greedy sod who's sent her to ask will eat all of that one."

Freddy had heard her, he looked down at the book as his face went red. Why did his Mam always have to show him up, always going on at him? He wanted to cry, instead he got angry.

Jessy carried two plates through, one with a slice of bread, halved for the girls. The other whole one for Freddy. "Here, yer greedy get, shovel that down yer face. And don't eat the lasses' as well as yours." She turned to go and was talking to Ruthie on the way back, "I don't know where he puts it, he cannot be hungry. It's just greed with him, plain and simple greed! Yer wouldn't believe me if I told yer what he'd put away tonight afore we came along. Why, there's no filling him man!"

Freddy pushed past her at a run, and went out the back door. He slammed it hard after him.

Jessy flew to the door to tell him to, "Get his fat arse back here," but Ruthie stopped her before she could open it.

"Leave him, lass, he's hurt about what yer said about him, that's all. He's only took it out on the door and nowt else. What harm has he done?"

Jessy felt guilty. "Aye, well if he doesn't like the truth, then he should change, shouldn't he!" She felt bad, after all, he had been trying lately. She had to give him that.

"I know but yer do go on at him a bit sometimes, our Jessy, I sometimes think that yer forget that yer've got TWO lads and two lasses,"

"Eeh, our Ruthie, how can yer say that? Why, I've always treated them all the same. If anything our Freddy has shown he has wanted more over the years and he's generally got it. Naw, I'll not have it said that I've ever treat him any different to any of the others"

Ruthie smiled, she knew that Jessy hadn't noticed her

contradiction. "EVEN RAY?" Ruthie's question brought Jessy's head up sharply.

"Now that's not fair, Ruthie, our Ray's away at war, he deserves to be spoilt a bit when he comes home." She stopped to think, "I might save a few treats out of the rations, for when he's here, I'll grant yer that, but that's only because I know that he's not getting owt to eat when he's away."

"Aye, alright Jessy. Don't get on yer high horse, I was only saying that mebbie he feels a bit left out, that's all."

Jessy shrugged her shoulders, but her voice had softened when she said, "I know what yer saying, lass, and I'll bear it in mind."

Jessy sat up til late that night, she hoped Ray was going to arrive before Bullum came home. She looked at the clock. There's no chance of that happening now, she thought, and decided to go up. Freddy was still sitting listening to the radiogram. "Are yer gonna make yer way up, our Freddy, or are yer gonna sit there all night listening to that bloody thing? I wouldn't care if there was ever any good news on it, and even when there is, yer don't know whether to believe it or not!" She was trying to make conversation with him, some of the stuff that Ruthie had said had made her think a bit. Freddy was having none of it, he looked up at her with sullen eyes.

"I'll be up in a bit." He saw the look on her face and added, "I'm not doing anybody any harm am I?"

She was too tired to argue with him, and when she thought about it, he wasn't doing any harm.

"Well not too long then." He nodded. "Nigh night then, Son."

"Aye, nigh night."

As she mounted the stairs Jessy wished she could like this lad of hers a bit more. She knew that she would always love him, but liking was a different matter. Mebbie what Ruthie had said had a bit of truth in it. Eeh, but it's hard, he always seems to be up to something, planning something. Like now, he was a huffy little get, alright, and none too forgiving, but he'd even surprised her when he'd not spoken a word to her since coming home, until now. Well no use worrying, she told herself, he'll come round in his own time.

She was on her way out, it was still early but she was gonna try and get a bit of meat so she had to make an early start cause there had been nowhere open for the last couple of days, what with it being Christmas. It would have been alright if he'd got here sooner, but they'd ate all that was in now, and anyway it wouldn't have kept. It was the 27th of December, 1944.

She opened the front door, and he was there. Her heart lifted when she saw him. He looked older, more grown up. She put her arms out to him and saw his face change from a smile to a look of anger.

"He couldn't bloody well leave yer alone, could he? The dirty bastard," he was looking at her belly. "Why didn't yer tell us? How far gone are yer?" He was firing questions at her, she'd briefly forgotten that he didn't know of her condition. He was mad, real angry. She put her hand on his chest to stop him when he tried to push past her asking, "Is he in there now, the lazy fat git?"

"Wait Ray, please wait. Don't go causing any trouble, for my sake, son. Yer'll only make matters worse. Please don't spoil this for us, Ray, I've been looking forward to seeing yer so much. Don't go causing any trouble. PLEASE?"

He stopped and held her, she could feel his heart hammering against his chest. "Aw Ma, couldn't yer just keep out of his way? What are yer gonna do? Yer too old for all this palaver now. It could be dangerous for yer."

Jessy smiled at him, and thought, this is gonna be harder than I thought, to tell him that the bairn was Georgie's. Well either way, he's not gonna be happy, he may as well be angry about the truth as a lie. She'd made her mind up to tell him, and she would, but not yet, not like this when everybody was around. No, I'll tell him later when we have a bit of time together, then I'll be able to explain everything a bit better.

"Watch what yer saying, our Ray. I'm not over the hill yet yer know, and anyway I'm only having a bairn. Yer forget that I've done it afore once or twice. As far as it being dangerous, well I can tell yer now, I've never felt this well in a long time, and I'm as strong as a horse. So stop all yer worrying. There's women older than me having bairns, and yer don't have to look far around to see that that's the truth." She paused, she wanted to calm him down, stop him from messing everything up afore she got a chance to sort it out.

"Why, Hetty Soames has just had another, and she's a good seven years older than me. I'm still in me forties yer know, not me nineties!"

She was joking with him, trying to make him smile. It didn't work, but he looked more resigned to her being pregnant when he said, "I know, but Hetty Soames isn't my Ma, and she hasn't had the kind of life that you have."

She took his hands, and looked at him seriously. "I'm fine, our Ray, honest I am. In fact I'm a bit excited, yer know how I love bairns, and having this one is the icing on the cake to me. So stop all yer worrying and please don't go making things worse than they are. Eeh?"

He didn't understand her, but he smiled and nodded. "Where yer off to at this time of the day anyway?"

"I was off to the shops to get a bit of something. Yer can walk with us if yer like, or are yer too tired?" Jessy hoped he would say yes. Bullum was still asleep on the couch and she didn't want him to start when Ray was in this mood. He was never pleasant when he first woke up, and she knew it wouldn't take much for Ray to lose his temper with him when he was in this frame of mind. I'd better get him told bloody quick, she thought, or else there'll be no living with any of them!

"Aye, I'll do that. I'll just say hello to the others, and put me top coat on. It's bloody freezing out here."

She turned to go back in with him. "Gan steady lad, try not to wake HIM. We'll go straight through to the scullery, and I'll make yer a nice cup of tea and a bite. But we better not be long, or I'll get nowt."

Freddy had heard them, he had been standing at the door. He was listening to see if his Ma would tell Ray what he already knew. Tell him that she was intending to run off with Georgie, that she had made plans that didn't include me or Ray. Freddy listened closer from the back of the door. He remembered something, something at the back of his mind. The letter had said something about Ray, something about him visiting them! But NOT me. He'd never so much as been mentioned. He was fifteen now, and regarded himself as a man, but at that moment, when the realization hit him, he could have broke down and wept. So that was it, that's why she was treating him like this. She's gonna piss off and leave us. He swallowed hard and thought, Why, We'll see about that.

Jessy watched in amazement as Freddy stood hugging Ray. It was unusual for him to show his feelings like this, but she had to admit that it was a heart warming thing to see. Ray looked happy enough with it, and she knew he was only ribbing Freddy when he said, "Steady on, lad, if yer grip any tighter yer'll take the wind out of us." Both of them sat down together at the table while Jessy got a bit of bread and marge ready. When she brought it over Ray told her to sit down and that he and Freddy would bring her a cup of tea for a change. Freddy smiled at her saying, "Aye, you sit down, Ma."

She watched them both talking together, neither of them mentioning the obvious state of their Mam to the other. It was as if both of them were wary of the other one's thoughts on the matter. The lasses woke up and came down the stairs quietly, they both came through to the scullery and were overjoyed to see Ray. He listened while Hetty told him about school and how she was getting on. Jean was on his knee from the moment she saw him, snuggling into him for warmth. Both lasses still had their nightclothes on and as Hetty went to make another cup of tea, Jessy noticed that she had grown. From the side she had a good little bust on her. She'd always been a bonny lass, but she looked more like a young woman now. As Jessy watched her chatting away with Ray she thought, I'll have to see if our Ruthie's got any old nighties, that one's a bit threadbare and thin. No sooner had Jessy thought this when she noticed Hetty's nipples pushing through the thin cotton cloth. "I'll do that, our Hetty, you gan and get a cardi to put on. Yer look frozen." She skipped out of the room, breasts jiggling as she went, saying, "Alright but don't let our Freddy eat me stotty cake.

Ray smiled at his Ma, stroked Jean's hair and said, "They're growing up aren't they Ma? Yer'll soon have lads knocking on the door for that one," he inclined his head towards the door that Hetty had just gone through. "She's a good lass though, and our Freddy here'll look after them in that respect. Won't yer Freddy?" Freddy nodded with enthusiasm. "Oh aye, yer can trust us to take care of that. I won't let any 'no gooders' near them. Yer can bank on that." Freddy looked pleased that he'd been chosen by Ray to complete this task. Jessy smiled at him and ruffled his wiry hair as she passed. He didn't smile back at her.

Ray was putting on his overcoat, Freddy went and got himself a scarf. Jessy was already dressed in coat, scarf and gloves. "Where yer off to at this time of the morning, our Freddy?" she asked as she opened the back door.

"I'm ganning with you two. Our Ray says that yer ganning along the shops." He started to comb his fingers through his hair.

"Not looking like that yer not, me lad, why yer haven't even had a wash yet. Anyway I'd rather yer stayed here with the lasses, in case Bullum wakes up in one of his moods. You seem to be able to suss out his moods better than most, so just keep the lasses out of his way."

Ray turned to him and saw the look of disappointment on his face. "We'll not be long. When I come back, how about you and me do something? You think about it and let us know, we'll even gan to the pictures if yer want. How about that?"

Freddy watched them walk away. She's left me out again, he thought. He turned away as Bullum woke.

They walked slowly together. There was a few people up and about now, and all of them that knew him stopped and had a word with Ray. Jessy was edgy, she wanted to get on her way afore there was nowt left, but it seemed the walk took forever. Ray sensed her mood and asked, "What's the matter Ma? Are yer alright?" more than once. She nodded each time. Who was she to spoil his day? She watched him smile and joke on with the lasses that he bumped into. Aye, well he is a handsome bugger, and even if he hadn't been, those lasses would have still made a beeline for him. Cause there was a real shortage of men these days. She smiled at him as he took her hand and linked it through his arm. She had decided to have a talk to him on the way back. They could mebbie call in Ruthie's for a warm cuppa, it was bitter out here. Ruthie would be pleased to see him and Jessy knew that she would feel better telling him the truth with Ruthie backing her up. But best get a bit of food first though.

She called at the grocer's first to get what she could with the rations that were left. The lass behind the counter couldn't take her eyes off Ray. Jessy got the impression that he thought it was funny, but she knew he was enjoying it annaull. She nearly dragged him out, the lass wouldn't stop talking. As she turned the corner the queue outside the butcher's was a mile long. She passed the front door to walk to the back and noticed that the doors weren't yet open. She and Ray continued walking, there was a buzz of noise behind them. "They're wondering why it isn't open yet," said Jessy to Ray. "It is unusual though. Yer can normally set the market clock by Bill Gregg's opening times." Ray nodded. They both turned again at the noise behind them, some people were leaving the queue. They watched as the lass from the grocery store, the one that had been giving Ray the eye, made her way up the queue of people, saying something to them every now and again. She had seen Ray, and was heading towards him, he took a few steps towards her. Jessy stood stock still. She knew. Before she heard the words SHE KNEW. But she didn't lose consciousness until she heard the words. "AYE, KILLED IN ACTION. SUCH A SHAME!"

CHAPTER FOURTEEN

Wilmy had had a helluva night. Aggy was sleeping now. She was lucky, thought Wilmy. The lass had lost the bairn but she was young enough to have more. She fell into the chair and stretched out her swollen legs. She thought about the previous hours. It was odd to carry until nearly eight months then to get a stillborn, but the lass hadn't felt the baby at all the last week or so. Just as well it came out, if it had stayed, it might have poisoned the lass' blood annaull. Wilmy sighed with tiredness and nodded off.

There was loud banging. She was groggy, the banging went on, it wouldn't let her sleep. "Whoever it is, fuck off, gan and get somebody else. WE'RE CLOSED!"

"Wilmy, Wilmy, come to the door. Wilmy, it's me, Ray. Open up."

She pushed herself up onto her aching legs, she wouldn't have opened the door to anybody else.

"Whoa, lad, hold on," she shouted as she unbolted the front door. The look of desperation on him brought her awake.

"Yer have to come. Me Ma's in labour and it's too soon. She's in a real bad way, yer have to come NOW!"

He'd pushed past her, took her coat of the hook by the door and was holding it out for her. Wilmy took it and walked past him to the bedroom door. "Is Bullum in the house, Ray, does he know?" She had opened the bedroom door and saw that Aggy was still sleeping, the gin should keep her out for a while.

"He went out straight away when we brought me Ma back," Ray answered her question.

"Well that's just as well, cause if he knew that I was tending yer Ma in his house there'd be hell to pay. Are yer sure he's not there?"

"NO. Now come on, Wilmy, and he won't be back either, not for a good long time anyway. He said as much, he's not bothered about the bairn! Howay man, I'm really frightened for me Mam."

He was pushing her forward along the path. She was trying to walk faster but she couldn't keep up with him, so he had to keep doubling back to tell her the story of what had happened. Wilmy had known that Jessy was pregnant again, she'd thought she was bloody stupid for letting herself be caught, but that was by the by now. She didn't know how far along she was, but she couldn't be as far on as their Aggy, it didn't bode well.

When they had carried Jessy home she was still unconscious, one of the women had noticed that her water had broken, otherwise Ray had thought that she'd only had a fainting fit. She opened her eyes when they laid her on the bed, then closed them again as the tears rolled onto the pillow. She kept them closed when Ray took her hand and said he was going for the doctor. She had gripped his fingers and said, "No. Wilmy."

He didn't want to leave her, the lasses were here but they were too young. "Freddy, Freddy come here!" He was shouting from the top of the stairs. Hetty came to the bottom of the

stairs. "He's gone! He went out when me Da did, our Ray."
Jean followed her up the stairs. Ray turned to Hetty.

"I have to go out for a bit, but I'll be back as quick as I
can. I have to gan for Wilmy," the lasses still weren't dressed.
He couldn't wait for them even to put their coats and boots
on, he knew that he would be quicker. "I'll not be long, just
sit with her. If she stirs, Hetty you gan and get her from next
door!" as he left the room he shouted, "Get yerselves dressed
while I'm away."

Freddy was still angry when they brought his Mam home.
As they carried her up the stairs he smiled to himself and
thought, that'll spoil yer time together right enough.

Bullum was already pulling his braces up over his dirty
shirt. He saw Freddy smile as they carried Jessy up the stairs.
He knew that he had a cohort when he shouted up the stairs,
"Can she not fucking do anything fucking properly? Can a
man not get a bit of fucking peace in this house?" He turned
to Freddy, "Fetch me big coat, I'm away out of this fucking
mess. Yer can come if yer like?" Whilst Freddy was fetching
for him, Bullum stood and let the men who had brought his
wife home leave before he shouted up the stairs in anger, "If she
fucking dies, tell that fucking snotty sister of hers to bury her
free of charge cause I'm not fucking paying for it! So don't even
bother to come for us, and yer can tell her from me it won't
make a blind bit of fucking difference to the housekeeping she
gets, she's getting no fucking more." Ray was boiling inside, he
wanted to kill him. He took three steps out onto the landing
and said to Bullum standing at the bottom, "Get out. GET
OUT AND LEAVE HER ALONE, OR SO HELP ME I'LL
SWING FOR YER!"

Bullum could see that he meant it. As Ray disappeared back into the bedroom he shouted, "I'm going and I won't be back till all this is fucking finished." Although he'd had the last word, he'd got no satisfaction from it. Bullum was a wise enough coward to know when to let go, but he'd get even with Ray if it was the last thing he'd do. He left slamming the door. Freddy stuffed something into his pocket and followed him. Hetty and Jean were sitting on the floor hugging each other, rocking gently together.

Wilmy had been tending to Jessy for nigh on four hours now. She was bleeding heavy, but still no sign of the bairn. Jessy was having the contractions right enough, but for some reason the lass didn't seem interested in pushing this one out. Her sister, Ruthie, had come down after hearing the news and was sitting next to Jessy, who was drifting in and out of consciousness now. "She's that tired that I don't think she has owt left to push with." Wilmy was talking to Ruthie from between Jessy's legs. Ruthie knew it wasn't just the tiredness that had sapped Jessy's strength. She tried to wake her saying, "Come on, Jessy, come on. Try. Yer can do this. Come on, lass. Please, Jessy, try for me," then she lowered her voice and whispered in her ear, "Try for Georgie."

Jessy opened her eyes as another contraction came. She raised her legs higher and bore down with all her might. Wilmy thought the tears running down her face were from the pain, Ruthie knew different.

"That's helped a bit," said Wilmy looking inside Jessy. "If she can give us another few of them we might be alright."

"I don't know if she'd got owt left, Wilmy." Ruthie had turned herself to look at Wilmy.

"Why, she's ganna have to, lass. I'll tell yer that cause if she doesn't help me here not only will this baby not come out alive, but I'm worried about Jessy as well now!"

Ruthie walked to the bottom of the bed in order to speak quietly to Wilmy.

"What do yer mean? She's gonna be alright isn't she? I mean, for God's sake, she's had four already." There was panic in her voice and she looked at Wilmy for help.

"Aye, but for some reason, this time's different. Look here," Wilmy nodded at the dark blood seeping through the old towels and bits of sheet on the bed. "Looks to me as if the afterbirth is coming away afore the bairn, and I don't like the look of all this blood neither." Wilmy bit her bottom lip in frustration, folded her arms over her chest and looked straight at Ruthie as she said, "What the hell's going on? Cause I'll tell yer now, she wasn't trying at first, and I can't believe that she would carry the bairn for as long as she has and then not want it to be born. Naw, yer right in what yer said, she's had four already. So she bloody well knew what she was letting herself in for. So what's gannin on?"

Ruthie was upset, she put her head down and mumbled, "Nothing."

"Nothing, my arse, now lass yer either tell me now what's got her like this, so we can find a way of fixing it, or I can't be responsible for the outcome." Wilmy took a hold of the sobbing Ruthie and shook her slightly. "Don't you go quitting on me annaull, that's all I need. Come on, pull yerself round, lass." She was talking in a softer voice now. She nodded at Jessy on the bed who was just starting another contraction. "We need to concentrate on her now."

Jessy pulled herself up, Ruthie rushed to support her back. Wilmy was back at her station between Jessy's legs. As Jessy pushed there was more blood. Wilmy rubbed her hand in the wetness of it and slowly put her hand inside of Jessy. She felt the head, she felt around for the cord, then she pushed further and gently inched around the baby, feeling its little legs to make sure that they were free.

"Why, there's nowt stopping it, apart from herself," she was talking to Ruthie and looking at Jessy as she wiped her bloody hand on a bit of sheet. "Meself, I think that SHE MIGHT HAVE LEFT IT TOO LATE. If she'd pushed like this afore now we might have got somewhere. As it is she's tired now and the bairn's not doing too well neither. I don't know what's got into her, I can understand her not wanting another bairn to that lazy fat bastard, but if that was the case, why the hell didn't she come to see us sooner, like when she first knew?" Wilmy had been partly talking to herself, so at first she didn't quite hear what Ruthie said.

"What's that? Can yer talk a bit louder, I'm down this end yer know," she was busy cleaning Jessy up a bit so she could see things a bit clearer.

"I said, it's not Bullum's bairn." As soon as she said it she turned to Jessy who had not spoken a word since she asked for Wilmy when she was brought home. "I'm sorry, lass, but I'm that worried about yer." Jessy closed her eyes and squeezed her hand.

Wilmy walked round to the top of the bed whilst Jessy was resting briefly. "Are yer telling me that this that's happening is down to another fella?"

Ruthie nodded, she wasn't expecting what happened next. Wilmy raised her hands in the air and started laughing. She was jigging on the spot now, looking up at the ceiling saying, "Bloody good for her, bloody good." She calmed a bit and asked, "Whose is it?"

"Georgie Gregg, the butcher's lad." As soon as Ruthie had said it, her subconscious corrected her. The late butcher's lad.

"Oh so the rumours had been true." Wilmy had said it so matter of factly as if it were an everyday occurance. Well it's not a bloody everyday occurance for MY sister, thought Ruthie.

"What rumours would that be then, Wilmy? The rumours that yer hear when yer listening to the gossip from all the slags that come to see yer for God knows what? Or the rumours that yer hear from one of yer, is it sixteen or seventeen kids, when they've got nowt else to do?"

Wilmy had to leave her reply, Jessy was starting again. She was getting weaker, this one she hadn't seemed to push at all. It wasn't going well!

There was knock on the bedroom door. Ruthie answered it but kept the door only slightly ajar behind her. Ray asked if there was any news, he looked terrible. He must be worried to death, thought Ruthie.

"No, not yet lad," she couldn't hide the worry in her voice.

"Is she gonna be alright, Ruthie?" his voice sounded desperate. "The lasses are upset and I was wondering whether I could take Jean along to Ralphy? Hetty says she won't go but the little one seems to be suffering!"

"Aye, do that lad, and tell Ralphy I'll be back as soon as I can," she laid her hand on his arm as he turned to go. "Don't worry, lad, she's a lot stronger than she looks, she'll get through this."

Ray couldn't speak, his throat was full and his eyes had filled up. He nodded and she watched him go down. Halfway down the stairs he turned and said, "I'll turn the radiogram on for Hetty, but can yer just check on her in about ten minutes?"

"Aye, alright, now get yerself away and try not to worry. As I said, yer Ma's a strong un."

As she closed the door she wished she felt more confident about what she'd told him. She took a deep breath and went back to the bed.

Freddy was standing in the doorway of the Hare and Hounds. He was out of the cold and his Da had bought him a ginger beer. He could see everything that was going on. It's nearly like being in the pub standing here, he thought. He could see Bullum with an ugly looking woman, he saw him buy her a drink. She was laughing a lot, so was his Da. Funny that he'd never seen his Da laugh much. He looked different! Freddy fingered the scrunched up letter in his pocket. It mightn't be so bad, he thought. Me Da bought us some chips earlier and then a pie a bit later, and now the ginger beer. There he was having a good time and laughing, which is more than his Ma did except when she was with her sister. Naw, come to think of it I never see her laugh much, not when I'm around anyway. A great feeling of sadness washed over Freddy as he stood, he didn't know what he was feeling. To him it was just a bit of a pain in his belly but it made him think. It made him take the letter from his pocket, open it and look at it again, looking for some part of it that included him. Some words that mentioned his name. He scrunched it up and rammed it hard back into his pocket. He felt the anger starting, it was better than standing crying. His anger was directed at Jessy, she was going to leave him and run off with Georgie. She'll take the others but not me! He struggled to keep the tears in, made fists in his pockets, then said in his head, "NO, YER BLOODY WON'T, MA."

It was over! Ruthie put some coal on the fire downstairs, Hetty looked frozen. She realized she was shivering herself. She looked at the lass watching her, waiting for the news.

"Yer Ma's gonna be fine, hinny." Hetty ran to her and cuddled into her. She sat, taking Hetty with her on her knee and held her close.

"But yer not gonna have a baby brother or sister." Ruthie now started to cry. They were hugging each other when Ruthie realized that she didn't even know whether it had been a boy or a girl. The tears came freely as she remembered the little form that Wilmy had held hung upside down in the corner of the room. She saw Wilmy holding it by its ankles and smacking its arse. There was no sound from it, it just hung limp. Jessy didn't know yet, she had passed out after the last contraction. Ruthie had been worried but Wilmy had told her to let her sleep, that there was enough time for her to find out about the bairn. She had sent Ruthie away while she cleaned Jessy up, but first she had checked that the bleeding had stopped and told Ruthie that Jessy would be weak for a while, but that she should pull through.

As soon as Ruthie left, Wilmy quickly loosely wrapped the dead bairn in a sheet. "I'll wrap it properly later," she said to herself. "It's this lass who needs me help now." She knew she had to get the rest of the afterbirth away from her, and make her feel a bit more comfortable. "Yer won't be able to cope with the pain of yer body as well as the pain in yer head, hinny, so I'll do me best for yer." She busied herself, and as she did, she talked to Jessy. It didn't matter to her that she couldn't hear, it was Wilmy's way of letting out some of her own feelings. Well that's two today, two that I've seen dead! Mind, in your case it's mebbie just as well. Cause with the father being dead annaull, if Bullum had ever found out the truth, he'd have probably killed you and the bairn." Wilmy looked at Jessy's face, she was still sleeping. "But yer can remember this if yer can hear us, lass, the bairn yer had inside yer was a fighter. Aye he was, right to the end. When I pulled him out he was alive, lass," she paused to think. "He must not have been able to breath by himself that's all."

She washed her hands in the now luke-warm water, she felt cold. She pulled the blankets up around Jessy and put her coat on and started clearing away again. She heard a noise on the stairs. She stood and listened, nothing! She was rolling the bloody sheets when she heard it again, a creak, then another. Wilmy's skin prickled. She tiptoed to the door, she opened it a crack, there was nobody there! She was about to close it when she saw the top of his head appear above the balustrade. She froze. She watched as he came up another stair, if he turned now he would see her. She forced her shaking hands to close the door gently. She stood with her back against it. All that was going through her mind was, OH MY GOD! OH MY GOD! OH MY GOD! She kept saying it over and over in her mind. She closed her eyes and breathed deeply. Pull yourself together. He's creeping up the stairs to catch yer here. She could feel his presence through the door. HIDE!

Freddy had come home. When he walked through the

parlour door, Hetty started crying again. Ruthie cuddled her tighter with one hand and beckoned Freddy to her with the other. "Come over here, our Freddy, I've got summit to tell yer."

Me Ma's not dead is she?" Ruthie's heart went out to him, he looked genuinely worried.

"Naw, lad, yer Ma's not dead, but she'll need a bit of looking after for a while." Ruthie was surprised at his next action, he went and turned the radiogram up. It had been fairly loud anyway, Ray must have put it up to let Hetty listen to the music, so that she wouldn't fret so much. But now it was LOUD.

"Well, that's alright then," he said in answer to Ruthie's reply. He kept glancing at the door to the lobby that led to the stairs. "Don't worry, yer can go and see yer Ma later, as soon as she's feeling a bit better." Ruthie was nearly shouting to make herself heard. "Freddy turn that down a bit and come over here. I need to tell yer something."

"Aye, in a minute. I just want to listen to this."

Wilmy ran and picked the bundle up and shoved it under her coat. She pushed herself against the wall behind the old wooden wardrobe in the corner. The bundle under her coat was making her bigger. She breathed in further and thought, Why the hell did I pick it up?

She held her breath as the door opened. She knew it had opened because she could hear the racket from downstairs, that's how she knew when it had closed again. There was silence for a few seconds. She had her eyes closed tight, she knew if he found her here he would kill her. He'd warned her many a time in the past, by word and deed, and she knew he was capable of it, especially when he'd had a drink. She could smell him in the room, the smell of stale beer and sweat. Wilmy had never been this frightened, part of her wanted to shout out for help, but most of her wanted to stay hidden.

Bullum looked around the room. Jessy was alone on the bed. He grinned then chuckled to himself. He looked at Jessy and said under his breath, "The fucking witch has gone then, has she?" he was talking to himself, Jessy was still asleep. "I know she's been. Aye, she'll have been alright. Shame, though, I would have liked to see her sort this one out." He threw the letter Freddy had given him down on the bed. "Oh aye, I would have liked to see her stand up to me in me home on this one, the fucking cunt." He ground the words out in a snarl from between clenched teeth. He took his one crutch and lifted the bedclothes with it. He prodded Jessy's flat belly, and fought the urge to bring it crashing down in her face. "Why, if she's not here ter bash the shit out, you'll have to do!" He put the crutch against the bed and leaned over Jessy. "Now who could blame us? Being married to a fucking dirty whore, if I lost me temper a bit!"

Ruthie patted Hetty on the rear as she sat on her knee saying, "Come on, up yer get, lass." She stood and walked over to the radiogram. She looked at Freddy, "Are yer gonna turn that bloody thing down or not?" He was sitting on the floor, cross-legged, rocking himself back and forth. Ruthie went to reach for the knob. He grabbed her hand roughly, looked at her and said threateningly, "I'll do it!" He watched his Auntie Ruthie pull her hand away and back off from him. He burst into tears and ran out. Ruthie's fear was overcome by her compassion for him, she forgot about the noise and followed him. He was standing outside near the coalhouse, breaking his heart. Ruthie went up and put her arms around him. He collapsed into her. "There, there lad," she was patting his back. "It's gonna be alright, don't worry it'll all be alright." He was talking, but his head was buried in her shoulder. She pulled away to hear better what he was saying.

"I didn't know he was dead, honest I didn't. Not till after me Da told us, after he knew. But I didn't know I swear I didn't." He swallowed and took a breath. "I wouldn't have said owt if I'd known. If I'd known he was dead, I mean." He was looking at Ruthie, willing her to understand, she looked confused. She took him by the shoulders and made him look at her as she said, "What is it Freddy? WHAT HAVE YER DONE?"

He wanted her to understand, not be angry with him. "I only gave him the letter cause she was gonna leave us. She was taking the rest but she was leaving me here." He was imploring her with his eyes.

"What letter? What letter are yer talking about?" Ruthie sounded serious now.

"The letter from that Georgie fella telling her about their life with the ba..."

Ruthe shook him before he finished. "Yer didn't give it to Bullum, DID YER?" She knew the answer before he nodded.

Jessy could feel the weight on her head, she tried to open her eyes but everything looked hazy. There was a dark shape in front of them, she closed them and tried again. It was a bit clearer now, she could make out a face. It was smiling down at her. No, not smiling, laughing. She could hear it, the face was getting clearer. She felt her stomach contract as she recognized him. Then she was wide awake with Bullum's hand over her mouth!

"Yer can hear me now, yer filthy cunt, can't yer? Well you listen to me now. All yer high and mighty act over the years and yer'll let owt atween yer fucking legs, but yer were fucking caught this time though weren't yer? How many fucking more have been in yer fanny? Aye, I wonder how long yer've been taking us for a fucking idiot." She could feel his spittle on her face, his hand over her face was pushing her further down into the thin mattress. She daren't move, she looked around the room. SHE WAS ALONE.

Jessy stopped wanting to struggle, she gave into him. He had reminded her of HIS death, and she didn't really care anymore about anything else. KILL ME. KILL ME IF YER WANT. She was saying it to Bullum with her eyes. I DON'T CARE ANYMORE.

Bullum felt her body relax, saw the fight go out of her and thought, no, no yer don't, yer not gonna fucking rob me of me revenge, yer dirty cunt. He took his hand off her mouth. He knew she wouldn't scream; if she did, he'd fixed it with Freddy so nobody would hear. He looked down at her lying in her stained slip, make-up smudged and no wig.

"Why, he deserves a fucking medal, I'll give him that. He must have had a stronger belly than most, cause look at yer! Yer a fucking mess, nowt but a mess of a whore. He's better off where he is than having to fucking sleep with that every fucking night. Naw, there's one that got off the hook. As for yer baby," He saw Jessy's eyes widen slightly.

"If that fucking witch has got it at her house, I'll find it. When I do, I'll kill the fucking both of them, make no bones about it. That cunt has pushed me too far this time. I bet she's fucking been in on this since the beginning hasn't she, the cunt?" He was inches from her face. He stared at her, looked into her eyes, could see that he was getting through to her, then he stood and said, "I think I'll away there now." He watched her, she tried not to show any emotion, even though her heart and head were thudding and her stomach churning. As he stood he looked at her again, then spat out, "Yer might be a ugly whore but yer lasses aren't." He smiled, coughed deep and spat on her. "I've been thinking for a while about Hetty. Now there's a fruit ripe for the picking alright!" He was watching her still, he saw a movement out of the corner of his eye at the same time that he saw Jessy's eyes look towards the door.

He threw his crutch through the open bedroom door. It hit Wilmy full in the middle of her back, she fell against the wall at the top of the stairs. The bundle dropped out of Wilmy's coat, it rolled out of the loose sheet onto the floor next to Wilmy's feet. She was winded, she bent slowly to pick the little soul up. She could see Bullum in front of her. She forgot the bairn as she saw him pick up his crutch, he was at the top of the stairs blocking her way down. She couldn't get past him. She put her hands around her head and crouched down, waiting for the blow to come.

Jessy pushed herself up into a sitting position. She was dizzy and weak, but she was desperate. As she tried to stand, she fell back on the bed. She could hear Bullum shouting and laughing, but the words were muffled, she thought she heard, "Well that's saved me a fucking job," and then he laughed again. Jessy thought he must have meant that Wilmy was still here. She pushed herself up again, she was able to stand this time. "I've got to help Wilmy," was the thought that pushed her on. She managed the few steps to the door and then held onto the frame. She watched him through the open door, laughing and pointing his crutch at something on the floor. She took another step and looked. She looked first at the thing on the floor and then to Wilmy. She clung tight to the landing rail as the realization hit her.

Bullum turned and saw her, "Come on. Come on then. Have a look at yer fancy man's bairn."

She was inching along the landing rail, fighting off the waves off unconsciousness. She saw Bullum raise his crutch, she heard him say, "But yer better be quick."

She shouted, "NOOOOOOO" and heard Wilmy scream. She threw herself in front of him and before she fell to her knees, she pushed with all her might. She saw his face stop smiling as he fell backwards.

Wilmy collected her thoughts almost immediately. She saw Jessy looking at the bairn, Wilmy knew it must be a shock. Jessy hadn't known it was dead. She quickly scooped it up in the sheet. With her other arm she tried to lift Jessy. "Get back into the bed, lass, and don't say a word. As far as anybody's concerned, HE FELL!" She didn't have time to mess about, she gripped Jessy's arm tightly saying, "Do yer understand?" She led her to the bed quickly, almost lifting her off her feet. It was only a few steps but she was hampered by carrying the bundle. She dropped Jessy on the bed, she lay there exhausted. Wilmy turned at the door as she was hurriedly leaving. "Remember, he fell!"

Hetty came to the back door to tell Ruthie that she'd heard noises and banging. Ruthie was still standing, staring at Freddy. "Aye, alright hinny, it's probably the drums in the music. Nowt to be bothered about. Get away in, lass or yer'll freeze." She turned to Freddy and said in a harsher tone, "You get in annaull, and turn that bloody noise OFF! Not down, mind you, but off. Do yer hear?" He nodded. "I'll be in in a minute. I just need to think a bit," she was talking to Hetty who was still protesting about the noises. "Take her in, Freddy, I'll be in to see ter you in a minute." When they'd gone she breathed the cold night air deep into her lungs.

"RUTHIE? RUTHIE, WHERE ARE YER?" It was Ray's voice and he sounded scared. She rushed into the house and he met her at the back door. "What's happened? Whats gone on?"

"What are yer on about, Ray?"

He grabbed her hand and dragged her along behind him. At the bottom of the stairs was Hetty and Freddy, she looked past them. Bullum was in a heap, twisted and wedged in the bottom of the stairwell. His huge body seemed to be jammed, his wooden leg was the only thing that looked straight. His other leg was twisted all about and one of his arms was behind his back. He wasn't moving!

"Take them through there." He nodded to the parlour door and gently moved Hetty and Freddy towards her. "While I gan and check on me Ma." He took the stairs two at a time. At the mention of his Ma, Ruthie suddenly came to her senses. "Oh, our Jessy, our Jessy." She was trying to scramble over Bullum's body to follow Ray up the stairs.

"Wait there, Ruthie, stay where yer are. Look after the

others." Ray had been sharp, she did as she was told and stood holding Hetty. The bairn was trembling. Or is it me? she thought.

Ray expected the worst when he walked into the room. The relief that came when he saw that his Ma was safe and sleeping made him say out loud, "THANK GOD!" He took her hand, Jessy pretended to open her eyes from her sleep. "It's alright, Ma, go back to sleep." Jessy closed her eyes again to keep him satisfied. She felt him leave.

Wilmy was standing at the end of the cut, she could see the front door from here. She'd only just missed Ray, she saw him coming along the path to the house as she had run out the front door, and nipped round the side when he opened the gate. Her head was in a spin, she didn't even know why she had avoided him, but something had happened that night to Wilmy that she wouldn't have believed. It was when she was scrambling over Bullum to get out. She had to stand on him, not that she minded, and she might have not been as careful as she could have been, and mebbie she did stand a bit too long on his rotten carcass. It was then that she felt a tiny movement and heard a slight sound. At first she thought she was imagining things. She put her hand inside her coat. Is it warm or is it me own body's warmth that I'm feeling? She took the bundle from inside her coat, and stepped down from Bullum on to the ground. The hand nearest her grabbed her leg. She nearly dropped the bairn. She turned and Bullum had his eyes open and as he tried to open his mouth to speak, blood oozed out. His hand fell to the floor and he closed his eyes. She heard the air escaping his lungs and at the same time another small sound. She looked down and the bairn was looking straight at her. Eyes wide open.

Ruthie was sitting with Jessy, Ray had gone for the Doctor and he'd sent Freddy with Hetty along to Ralphy's. Jessy was awake, she could hear Ruthie talking to her but she wasn't listening. She looked at the ceiling and prayed to die.

Wilmy had to know, she had to know if Bullum was still alive. Not only for her own sake but for the sake of Jessy too. She'd seen them all leave, all except Jessy's sister. Wilmy knew that she would be in the bedroom with Jessy. The bairn whimpered again, she knew she couldn't be long cause the bairn needed to be in the warmth. It needed to be fed. She pulled her coat collar up but left the top button open to give HIM air but keep him out the draught. There was someone standing on the other side of the cut in the shadows, watching her. She peered to try to make out who it was, the figure stepped forward. Wilmy was transfixed, she found herself loosening the sheets around the bairn's face. She hoisted him up out of her coat a little and turned him to face the figure in the shadows. Wilmy felt a tremor run through her from her toes up, her whole body was in the light of a full moon that also lit the stranger's face. She watched calmly and without fear as Georgie smiled and gave a slight nod of acknowledgement. Their eyes met, the bairn whimpered and she looked down at the wide eyes in the tiny face. The same eyes that she'd been looking into a few seconds ago! Wilmy knew he had gone even before she looked up. She was pulling her coat around her and the bairn, she was filled with a new sense of urgency.

"Aye, yer a miracle alright, but yer problems might not be over yet, me bonny lad." She started walking towards Jessy's house. "Nor mine neither, not if that bastard's still breathin." She hurried along the path clear in her mind what she had to do. The house was silent save for the voice of Jessy's sister upstairs. Wilmy looked down at Bullum's twisted ugly body, she prodded him with her foot, he didn't move. She still couldn't be certain. The last thing Wilmy wanted to do was to touch or put her face near his to see if HE was breathing. But she knew she had to be certain! She was crouching almost far enough to touch him when she heard the running footsteps. She hurriedly pushed herself up and touched Bullum's hand as she did so. IT WAS WARM. She headed quickly for the back door.

Freddy had taken Hetty to Ralphy but left straight away, saying he wanted to get back to his Ma. It was a LIE. Although Freddy was riddled with guilt, it wasn't that which was driving him. He had formed a plan in his head as he had hurriedly walked with Hetty. Freddy knew that the house would be empty except for his Ma and Ruthie, and they would be upstairs. It wouldn't take him long to do what he had to do!

When Ray had got to the Doctor's, he was out on another emergency. He waited twenty minutes. Then he got the address from the Doctor's wife of where the emergency was at. He decided to walk along to the house where the Doctor was; it wasn't for Bullum that he was doing it, but he was worried about his Ma. As he looked at the address on the scrap of paper he realized he would practically have to pass his house, would he have time to call in and check on his Ma one more time?

Ruthie felt the draught blowing up the stairs from the open front door. "I'll just go and pull the door to," she said to Jessy. She had to pass Bullum. He was wedged that tight that the only way past was over him. She put her toe on him tentatively and then skipped over him. She did the same coming back. HE GROANED.

As Ruthie turned and looked at Bullum she felt NO sympathy towards his predicament. Instead her head filled with total hate for him. She stepped one step back down the stairs, to look at him closer."Die you Bastard, just DIE!"

Ralphy wanted to be with Ruthie, he knew how she felt about Jessy. If anything happens to Jessy, Ruthie will be ter take away, he thought. Hetty had told him that they said her Ma was going to be alright. But Ralphy knew that they wouldn't tell the bairns owt else, so as not to worry them. He went next door to his Ma's and asked her to come and sit with the lasses. Then he put his coat on and headed for Ruthie.

Bullum knew he was in a bad way. The waves of pain that came over him were excruciating. He tried to see through the fog that was in front of his eyes. He knew he kept losing conciousness, but it was only when he tried to move, so this time he would stay still. He could'nt be sure that he would come out of the next blackout. He'd seen figures in front of him more than once, they were a blur, but he knew somebody was there. Each time they either disappeared or he passed out As he lay he tried to focus but the rolling mist in front of his eyes seemed to be getting deeper and darker. Bullum felt a sense of urgency, a sense of fear from something far greater than he, Bullum, had any control over. From the centre of the fog appeared a dark shape. It moved, he couldn't make out what it was, but he sensed it was watching him. He waited till the pain subsided a bit, then he timed himself, as best he could, before the painful waves came rushing in again. He timed it well, taking as much strength as he could from the lull, and waiting till the last moment. "Help me?"

The dark shape seemed to jump backwards. He watched as it came closer again. He waited, it moved. Something was pressing him down, pushing down on his head? The weight was getting heavier, it was harder to breath. He tried to move to get away from the pain, such pain! There was a sound like a clap of thunder in his ears then a lightening bolt of pain, white and hot surged through his head.

The foot pushing down on his head had Snapped his Neck!

Bullum had tried to cry out, but the broken ribs that had punctured his lungs would'nt allow any more air through, he'd used the last of it! He saw the fog billowing away, the blackness came fast, he watched until the very last bit of fog and light were gone. THEN BLACKNESS. THEN NOTHING.

Wilmy hurried along the road and tried to look normal. She had the bairn under her coat. She nodded to people she passed as if it were a normal day. Somebody or other tried to talk to her, but she kept on walking answering, "Got to rush, got to get back to our Aggy." She knew that she had to get the bairn to Aggy's breast soon, or not only would the bairn suffer, but all her plans would be out the window and all. She must have been out of the house over five hours now. She prayed that the lass hadn't woken and gone looking for her bairn. She walked a bit faster, her feet felt like raw lumps of meat.

Ralphy was sitting on the edge of the bed with Ruthie, she was snuggling into him. She looked over her shoulder and saw Jessy watching them. She pulled away sharply, wiped her eyes and said, "Let's hope the bastard's dead, eeh?"

There was no sign that Jessy had heard anything. She looked back at Ralphy. He was looking at her and then put his finger to his lips.

"Aw, don't worry, our Jessy doesn't care whether he lives or dies at the moment. I'd say for her sake he's best off DEAD, not just for her sake but for everybody's. He's evil through and through, why yer know yerself about what he's been saying about YOU! Naw, I hope and pray that he's dead, cause everybody's life will be better without him in it."

"Yer shouldn't talk like that, Ruthie," Ralphy answered, then he saw the look she gave him. She wasn't gonna go back on what she'd said! So Ralphy held his tongue and kept his feelings in check. "Well he didn't look too grand when I passed him on the stairs, and if I'm owt to go by, he's either already dead or on his way."

"Did yer not check, Ralphy, as yer passed him like?" Ruthie asked casually.

Ralphy hesitated before he answered.

"Naw, naw I didn't. If yer want the truth, I did'nt care, and I was in a hurry ter make sure you were alright. But if yer want us to check him now I will?"

"Naw, that's alright, lad, come and sit back down with us. Let the Doctor deal with it."

Ray was on his way back with the Doctor. He'd found him but he had to wait while he finished up what he was doing. He'd tried to hurry him along, not for the sake of his Da but because he wanted to get back to his Ma. What a 'leave' this is turning out to be! The house was in sight, the Doctor put an extra spurt on when Ray did. He's doing well, thought Ray, for his age!

Doctor Lynus, was a man in his early sixties, and was known for his strict beliefs. The only way Old Lynus stopped his lecturing was if he was paid to do so. Once that happened, when he had the money up front yer could drink yerself to death if yer wanted to. Or as he was so fond of saying after he'd put yer coppers in his pocket, "I'm not yer keeper, nor yer maker, and I'm pleased I'm not yer undertaker."

Freddy was looking at the bread and dripping that Ralphy's Mam had put in front of him. For once in his life he couldn't eat. The hate he felt for his Da surged up in his throat and made him taste the bile. He remembered how Bullum had laughed as they stood in the doorway of the pub after reading Georgie's letter, how he'd grabbed him by the face til it hurt. He smelt his breath as he told him that the butcher's lad was dead, how it had been the talk of the pub! Before he had let go of his face he'd come close and held a shilling in front of him saying, "Yer'd have got more if he'd lived, but take it anyway, cause yer job's not finished yet." He told him about the music on the gramaphone. When Freddy had said, "Yer won't hurt her, will yer?" he had turned on him, vicious-like, "Yer can't back down now, yer fucking sneaky yella bastard, just do as yer told or it'll be you who gets me temper." He'd stepped back then patted Freddy's head, "Yer are yer Father's son though!"

All the way home and since then, all Freddy could think was, I needn't have told him. Aw, God, I needn't have told him. HE was dead anyway!

He played around with the bread in front of him, pushing it this way and that on his plate. He was justifying his actions by blaming first Jessy, then Bullum. His hate stayed with Bullum, He remembered how he'd got the radiogram, that had been Bullum's doing. Aye, alright he didn't have to take it, and he didn't have to let his cronies beat the fella up so much, but what did he expect when he didn't pay up? Worse than that, Bullum had always bragged about how much money he had. Freddy felt the anger surge, that had been a lie annaull. When he'd managed to get into Bullum's bureau there was hardly five pounds in it! The money was in his pocket now, with a book he'd found saying who owed money. He'd keep that for the future! A new surge of anger engulfed him. FIVE FUCKING POUNDS! He was nearly as angry as he had been when he'd first forced the lock of the bureau with his pen knife. It took him a couple of minutes to accept that's all there was. He'd closed the lid, feeling utter frustration. He clenched his fists tightly, his body was stiff and tight with rage. He could do nothing other than scream in his head, he couldn't even allow himself to make a sound in case he was heard. Freddy stood over Bullum's twisted body seething with hate.

Then he was running hard along the path to get back to Ralphy's. He ran all the way, he had a stitch in his side and his chest was burning. He entered the yard and opened the door to the lavvy and sat and sobbed. Ralphy had seen him sitting as he passed him on the way along to Jessy's. Freddy had said that he'd changed his mind about ganning home, and that he'd just been sitting in the quiet, thinking. Ralphy swallowed his story, thinking the lad was upset. He had said kindly, "Well, get yersel in now, eh? Me Ma will make yer a bite to eat!"

Wilmy shoved a pan of milk on the dying embers of the fire. While it was warming she took a damp rag and hastily rubbed the bairn down. Now that she could see him properly she checked him over. "Aye, everything's in the right place, me lad." She wrapped him in a clean towel, and kissed the top of his head. "I've said it afore and I'll say it again. Yer a bloody miracle, yer are that." There was no sound from the bedroom. She poured the luke warm milk over a chunk of bread and sprinkled a bit of sugar on it, took off her coat quickly and threw it on the chair. Then she picked up the bowl and the bairn and went through to Aggy.

She shook the lass gently. It didn't take much to wake her, she must have been coming out of the sleep. "I thought yer gonna sleep the clock round lass and this fella's hungry." Wilmy had said it matter of factly. Aggy looked confused and groggy with sleep. She looked at the bairn Wilmy was holding out to her and automatically put her arms out. Aggy pushed the towel aside to see his face, then burst into tears saying, "I thought he was dead. I thought he'd died?" She was looking at Wilmy for answers. "Why, it was a close thing, lass. I thought he had meself at one time, what with him being so quiet, but he pulled through alright, once I'd got the snot outta his throat." Wilmy was pulling Aggy up in the bed ready to put the bairn to the breast. "But I thought I remembered seeing him dead?" Aggy was still anxious. "That'll have been either the pain or the gin, lass, yer were probably dreaming. Yer did have a rough old time of it yer know!"

Wilmy watched as Aggy bared her breast, she looked at Wilmy for help. Wilmy showed her how to hold her swollen nipple between her forefinger and thumb. She watched as Wilmy squeezed gently until a drop of breast milk fell onto the bairn's lips. He puckered and started sucking on air. "Now put him to the teet, lass, he's ready." Wilmy stood a couple of minutes as the bairn took the nipple and held on for dear life. "He's definitely ready for that! I'll say he is." Aggy was smiling up at her. "Aw, it feels lovely, and didn't he take it well, Wilmy." She stroked his head as he was feeding, then put her own head back and relaxed into the pillow.

"Well, I'll have to be on me way, lass. I'm needed elsewhere." Aggy looked frightened. "There's nowt to worry about, just change teets when he's emptied that one. By the looks of him that'll not take long." Wilmy was already in the kitchen before she'd finished the conversation. She put her coat back on and picked up the bundle that was lying in the open bottom drawer of the cabinet and shoved it under her coat. Wilmy wrapped her coat round the lump and craned her head round the bedroom door. "Be sure to have the bread and milk yerself. Yer'll need it to make more breast milk. I'll not be long, keep him warm next ter you till I get back then I'll build the fire up." She had opened the front door when she heard Aggy shout, "But how will I know when to change breasts?" Before she closed the door Wilmy shouted back, "Yer'll know!"

The doctor looked at Bullum wedged at the bottom of the stairs. He was standing in the lobby of the front door. He turned to Ray and said, "I'm sorry to tell you this, but he's dead!"

"But yer haven't even looked at him yet?" Ray said accusingly.

The doctor sighed with impatience, and approached Bullum. He lifted his free hand and felt his wrist, he crouched down wearily, groaning as he did so, and laid his head against the massive chest. The smell of stale sweat and stale beer was almost overpowering.

"Well, there's no getting away from it, he's dead!" He stood up, groaning again. "I take it he fell down the stairs drunk?"

The doctor tut tutted. "Well, I'd say he broke his neck, and looking at him, most other bones in his body too." He peered closer for a moment before turning away. "If he hadn't broken his neck he'd have probably died anyway. Looks to me like he's got a punctured lung." He paused and thought for a minute. "Can't have been dead long though, the blood in his mouth is still wet and there's very little sign of Rigor." He'd been talking to himself. He turned to Ray as Ralphy came down the stairs. Ruthie was only briefly in view at the top, then she went back to the bedroom.

"This is me Uncle Ralphy, Doctor," Ray nodded towards Ralphy as he came down the stairs. Ralphy stopped when he got to Bullum and stretched to step over him. The Doctor watched and waved his hand, "I wouldn't worry, he's past feeling anything." He turned to Ray saying, "No need for introductions. I know Ralph well, know his Father better," he spoke to Ralph now, "Is your father well? And how is your Mother doing these days?"

Ralphy told him his parents were well, explained Ruthie was the sister of the dead man's wife Then they went into the front room and exchanged pleasantries for the next couple of minutes.

Ruthie came into the room, she had run her fingers through her hair and straightened her dress. The Doctor's face brightened when he saw her. "We were just talking about you and your misfortune, my dear." He crossed the room and took her hands in his. "Are you alright in yourself?"

"Very well, thank you," Ruthie replied with a smile. The Doctor eventually let go of her hands, put his thumbs in his waistcoat pockets, puffed out his chest and whistled through his sparsely-furnished mouth, checked that his audience were paying full attention then said, "This is a bit tricky." He paused for effect. "Because the fella didn't die of natural causes there will have to be some involvement from the Coroner. You realize that of course?" He was looking at Ralphy who nodded. "It's just standard procedure, that's all." He turned to Ray now. "Your uncle can verify that, and he'll tell you what goes on. But I shouldn't worry, it looks like a straightforward case of Accidental Death to me. You'll have him in the ground in no time!" He rubbed his hands together and looking at Ruthie asked if there was any chance of a hot drink, explaining he'd had nothing since lunch.

"Why, aye," said Ruthie, "but afore yer have it can yer take a look at me sister? She's just lost a bairn today!"

Before the Doctor could reply Wilmy came into the room saying, "Well, at bloody last, Doctor Samual Lynus. Yer are still practicing then?" Wilmy wasn't really taking a risk, it was well known in the area that the Doctor came in his own good time. Anyway she knew Sam Lynus of old!

"Well, I am a busy man, especially in the winter. As well YOU know." He was on the defensive now, just where Wilmy wanted him. But his next question rankled her a bit.

"Perhaps you would like to tell me what all this has got to do with you? Because if I remember rightly, we've spoken of this in the past and I don't mind telli..."

Wilmy interrupted him. "Don't you go getting on yer high horse with me, DOCTOR," she stressed the word "doctor." "Yer've used us enough in the past when yer haven't had a midwife handy, so yer know that I'm capable." He was about to speak when she carried on, "I wouldn't be half so busy if yer were able to be found, but yer'd rather deal with the toffs than come down here and see to the likes of us. Aye, yer haven't changed, Sam, yer master's still money!"

His tone had changed now, he was seething underneath, but it wasn't worth getting into an argument with this one.

She knew him too well. Anyway it suited him having her down here, she was right, there was no money to be made on The Estate. "Don't go getting all upset, woman, I was merely asking you what your involvement in all this was?"

"With him at the bottom of the stairs, NONE. With the lass upstairs, this." She pulled the bundle from under her coat and thrust it at the Doctor. Ruthie turned away and hid her face in Ralphy's chest. Doctor Lynus unwrapped the bloody sheets carefully, until the bairn's face was visible.

"I took it away and cleaned it up straight away. The lass upstairs was too upset for us to just leave it lying about for her to see. She'd been through enough today." The doctor was nodding with fake sympathy.

"Well, under the circumstances, you probably did the right thing. Looking at it, it's not far from being full-term. That being the case, it's just as well you returned it for me to examine." He wrapped the sheets around the bairn.

"Just over seven and a half months," said Wilmy. "But aye, I agree with yer Doctor. It is a big-un for its age, and as for bringing it back, there was never any doubt about that. Why, I'd already made arrangements with this lass here for them to bury the little thing!" She looked intently at Ruthie.

"That's right, Doctor," said Ruthie sweetly. "Wilmy did us all a favour by taking it away for a while, and cleaning it up. God knows there was enough going on here without having to worry about our Jessy asking to see the bairn. I mean, surely it was best that she couldn't, with her being as upset as she is. Well not until she's come round a bit more anyway, and she's able to cope a bit better." Ruthie was looking at the Doctor wide-eyed. "I hope I didn't do the wrong thing?"

"The Doctor put his arm around Ruthie's shoulders. "Don't go upsetting yourself. There's no harm done. Why there's no need to mention it to the police even. We'll forget it ever happened. The fetus is back here now and we'll take it from there." He was patting Ruthie's shoulder. He turned to Wilmy, "I see no reason to make a song and dance about this, but you may wish to leave before I send for the local police, in case they start asking questions as to why you're here!"

"Aye, yer right, we wouldn't want them asking any questions would we SAM?" Wilmy was looking at him directly. "If that happened there's no telling what would come out in the wash! IS THERE?"

He coughed and cleared his throat and mumbled, "As you say, as you say."

Wilmy fastened her coat and turned to go. Ruthie said she'd show her out. At the same time the Doctor turned to an ashen-faced Ray and asked him to go and get the local policeman. The doctor then joined them in the doorway, but made his way up to check on Jessy. I still haven't been offered that cup of tea, he thought.

Ralphy stayed in the front room. He sat down, he hadn't known anything about the burial arrangements for the bairn, and he didn't think that Ruthie had either. He could hear Wilmy and Ruthie murmuring together. I hope they get their bloody story straight!

Fred Sykes was the local copper, he'd brought a young lad with him explaining that he was a trainee P.C. When he walked in, the Doctor stood and shook his hand. "Sorry to bring you away from the fire, Bill. It's straightforward enough." They were walking to the stairs as they were talking, the young P.C. following. "It's a straight forward case of Accidental Death." he pointed to Bullum. "He must have fell down the stairs drunk, you can still smell it on him. I don't suppose that would have helped." The doctor kicked Bullum's wooden leg, "I'd appreciate it if you could take this through to the other room when you have finished looking at the body. I've got the wife upstairs recovering from a stillbirth, and I'd rather she wasn't disturbed." He then went on to explain what Ray had told him had happened to his Ma, to the two policemen. Fred was sympathetic enough, but the lad started noting what he was saying in his notebook, he showed no concern!

"Seems simple enough." Fred Sykes was looking up and down the stairs, then at the way Bullum was lying. "He's jammed in tight enough alright." He turned to the Doctor. "What do yer reckon killed him? Was it a bang to the head?"

"I believe he has a broken neck. He would have died instantly, however the Coroner will have to verify it."

Fred Sykes knew that the Coroner wouldn't rock the boat. If Sam here said he died of a broken neck due to the fall, then that was good enough for him. The young P.C. was peering down at the body. "He's got a mark on his head, sir." Fred Sykes asked himself again why he had been landed with this toffee-nosed kid. They didn't need him, lord knows there's not enough men left for there to be any increase in crime! He was sharp when he answered. "Aye, well it's no wonder, he fell down the bloody stairs, lad."

Nevertheless, he turned to the gathered assembly and asked, "Did anybody see what happened?"

There was silence until Ruthie broke it. "Well, I didn't, cause I was arguing with our Freddy about the radiogram being on too loud, and our Jessy was still in bed. Naw, the first we knew about it was when our Ray here walked in the door and told us about it. That's right isn't it Ray?"

Ray nodded, "When I came in, he was like he is now. I went for the doctor as soon as I saw him."

Fred Sykes stood a moment, "So yer didn't go for the doctor straight away for yer Mam?"

Ray looked flustered. Ruthie interrupted, "We all thought it was better to get the bairns out of the way first. That's what our Ray was doing. He was taking the little un along to Ralphy here while we sorted everything out."

The young P.C. was writing everything down. He interrupted with, "When did you find out that your sister had...," he stopped to think, "had an accident?"

Ruthie looked at Fred, he nodded for her to answer. "Why straight away, one of the women that had been there when our Jessy collapsed, came and told us, then I came straight along."

"So when exactly did you go for the doctor?" It was the young P.C. asking again. He was looking at Ray.

"Why I've already told yer, man! As soon as I saw what had happened." Ray didn't like this kid, he was asking too many questions.

"So you didn't go for the Doctor to tend to your mother? Were you not concerned for her health?"

Ray was getting angry now. He didn't like the way this lad was talking to him. "Aye, I was worried about me Ma, but Wilmy was tending to her and our Jean was right upset. I thought it was the best thing to do to get her out of the house." As soon as he'd said it, he knew that he'd let the cat out of the bag about Wilmy. "She's only seven yer know, it was no place for her."

The young P.C. started to say something, but was interrupted by Fred Sykes, who was annoyed at the lad for asking these questions. After all, it made HIM look a fool. "I'll deal with it now, put yer notebook and pencil away a minute for God's sake." The lad looked taken aback and more than a bit put out, but he did as he was bid.

It was Fred Sykes who turned to the Doctor now. "Is this THE WILMY that we've all grown to know and love? What was she doing here?"

"Well as far as I can gather she was in the locality when it all happened, that is outside the shops. I believe she accompanied them home, as an act of kindness and to offer to help." He looked at Ray who nodded.

"Aye that might well be the case, but she's not qualified to do that kind of thing." He paused, "Mind you I'm not saying that she's not capable, we all know that she knows her stuff. But what..."

The doctor interrupted Fred again. "Might I have a quiet word with you, Fred, in private?"

Fred Sykes followed Sam Lynus through to the kitchen, the young P.C. tried to follow and was rebuffed when Fred turned to him saying, "I think the Doctor said private, lad!"

Doctor Lynus didn't give a fig about whether Wilmy got into trouble or not. He was more concerned with his own neck. But he did know that Wilmy wouldn't go down without a fight, even if that meant taking him along with her.

"I didn't want to say anything in front of the others, there's no point in making the situation worse than it is. I believe that the lass upstairs asked for Wilmy before she passed out. Now, you and I both know that there is no law against asking for a friend, and if that friend does their best to help in this situation then I should imagine that would be classed as only natural." Fred was agreeing with him so he went on. "I've checked the baby and the mother, and from my examination, if it hadn't been for Wilmy being..." he thought, "there at the time, then we might have had another body on our hands! As it is the wife will probably pull through, thanks to what Wilmy did!" Fred was still nodding along with him. He summed up, "As for the baby, then even if I'd been on the doorstep, there would have been no different outcome. It was stillborn!"

"So let me get this right, Sam, what you're saying is that the lass went into labour, her son and some friends helped her home, among which was Wilmy. She stayed with her and helped her, until the rest of the family could get to you. In the meantime the husband came home dead drunk, went to see his wife and fell down the stairs! Is that what yer saying?"

"Well I know no more about the husband than you do, Fred, but the rest of what you said is an accurate account.

Fred sighed, he didn't want anymore paperwork and trouble than he already had. He trusted what Sam said to be the truth. After all, he was the DOCTOR. "Truth be told, Sam, I thought it was as simple as that, but you know we have to ask questions." He turned to go back to the other room saying, "Well that's cleared that up for me alright," loud enough for everyone to hear.

When they got back to the front room Fred Sykes turned to Ralphy, "We'll be on our way now. Can I leave you to sort out removal of the body? Yer know the procedure alright don't yer?" He didn't wait for an answer. Ralphy's Dad's business had been trading too many years for Fred to be worried. He walked to the door with the young P.C. in tow. Then he turned and said softly, "I'm sorry for your loss, especially the bairn."

Doctor Lynus took pleasure in explaining to Ruthie, over a cup of tea, what happened next. She really is a lovely looking woman, he thought. She appeared to hang onto his every word, and with her smiling compliments, his self opinion soared to even greater heights. It was with some reluctance that he left her to go and check on Jessy again. He was rewarded with a smile when she followed him up the stairs with a cup of tea for her sister.

Bullum's body had been moved from the stairs, it took a bit of doing, but Ralphy and Ray had eventually managed to get him out. The Doctor had supervised, but did no lifting. Bullum's new wooden leg had been the sticking point, literally. It had snapped clean in half before they had managed to pry him out. The Doctor remarked that if he'd had one of the old fashioned ones, it would have snapped its strapping and probably come off in the fall! And that as it was, it was almost certain that the new leg had cost him his life. That and being DRUNK!

Ruthie waved him off from the front, graciously thanking him for all his help. The Doctor had hung on to her hands, advising her that she could call on him at anytime if she needed assistance or advice. She had gradually pulled her hands from within his, and dismissed him by saying that she had to get back to Jessy.

Ruthie closed the door and sank down to the floor behind it. "What a day!" she rubbed her eyes and prepared herself to go up and face Jessy.

Wilmy sat in the chair by the side of her own fire, she inhaled deeply, "What a bloody day!"

Ray had gone back the day after Bullum's accident, he hadn't asked for any further leave. Ruthie had told him that he was better of out of it. He'd wanted to stay with his Ma, but once again Ruthie had assured him that she would be alright and that he couldn't do anything for her at present. He felt as if there was something going on that he didn't know about, something concerning his Ma, but he didn't want to rock the boat and he too felt uncomfortable around the Police when they were asking questions. He sat with Jessy most of the afternoon before he went back. She hadn't spoken since it had happened. Ray knew it wasn't Bullum's death that was upsetting her, he presumed that it was the bairn that had made her this way. He held her hand and spoke gently to her, telling her that she already had four kids that needed her and loved her. One day she would be a grandmother. With Bullum gone she had a good life ahead of her and that he would ALWAYS COME BACK to look after her. When she cried silently, he wiped the tears from her face, when she closed her eyes to try to sleep he bent forward and laid his head on the bed next to her stomach. He'd dozed and woke to find her hand on his head stroking and fingering his hair. Ray had wanted to pick her up and wrap her in his arms to keep her safe, never to leave her again. When he looked at her face he also knew that he could be no, or very little help to her now. His final words to her were, "Don't worry, Ma, you've lost all yer gonna lose. I'll see yer soon. Promise." He bent and kissed her head. He whispered, "I know yer loved Georgie, Ma!" and left.

It was the day of Bullum's funeral, Ruthie and Ralphy had laid the bairn to rest the week before. The inquest had declared Bullum's death to be accidental and had released the body two days previous. Ralphy had collected it and was dealing with everything. Ruthie was spending as much time as she could with Jessy, she'd been down every day for nigh on a fortnight now, and although there wasn't a lot physically wrong with Jessy, or so the Doctor said to Ruthie, she was still so very worried about her. Jessy hadn't said a word since she'd heard about Georgie. She'd not spoken to anyone, not even the young P.C. who'd come back the day after the event to take a statement. He'd said that he would have to ascertain what had exactly happened from other sources, and that he would have to ask everybody concerned a few questions. Ruthie had a word with the Doctor, who said he would sort it all out, and he must have cause the snot-faced little get hadn't been back. Ruthie was warming some broth to take up to her. Jessy ate, she always ate what Ruthie gave her, but she wouldn't budge out of the bed. As Ruthie walked in, she noticed that the room was starting to smell. She'd made sure that the piss pot was emptied twice a day, and that she washed Jessy often and changed the threadbare sheets once a week. But the smell was still there.

"Why, I've got to say, our Jessy, this room stinks. How yer can lie there and not throw up with the smell amazes me!" She put the tray down on the floor and took the bowl and spoon ready to start the usual process of feeding Jessy. As she lifted the spoon, Jessy opened her mouth ready to accept. Ruthie whipped the spoon away, spilling some of its contents on the blankets, and banged the spoon and bowl back down on the tray.

"Oh, I've had me bloody fill of this, our Jessy. If yer well enough to eat, then yer well enough to bloody feed yerself. For Christ's sake, woman, how long is this gonna go on?" She started stripping the bed, Jessy clung to the sheet and pulled it up around her neck. Ruthie was in a frenzy. She'd kicked the tray to the side and was pulling the bedding off and throwing it behind her. Tears of anger and frustration were pouring down her face. She got to the sheet covering Jessy. "That'll do yer no bloody good, cause I'm gonna get yer out of this bed if it's the last bloody thing I do. Quit in yer own time, Jessy, not bloody well mine!"

She yanked at the sheet but Jessy was holding onto it tightly, she pulled again, still the same thing, Jessy pulled harder. "Well there's nowt wrong with yer bloody grip though is there?" She pulled as hard as she could! The sheet tore in half right across the middle, Ruthie dropped her end. Jessy looked and then started gathering the torn sheet to her, she had the two halves in her hand when she looked at Ruthie, who was staring at her, looking sorry and guilty, but also tired.

Jessy burst out laughing. No more, she ROARED with laughter. "Good tug of war, Ruthie," she said, smiling. Ruthie was wary at first, then when she looked at Jessy, she knew that she had her sister back!

Wilmy had heard of the outcome of the inquest. It was the talk of the street. She hadn't been back to see Jessy, she couldn't face her. Wilmy looked over to where Aggy and the bairn, David, were sitting. Aggy was feeding him again, they were both doing well especially the bairn who was thriving and getting stronger every day. She wished she could get some joy out of all of this, but she was riddled with guilt at what she'd done, even though she knew deep down that she had done it for Jessy! The visit from the young polliss hadn't helped, she'd sent him away with a flea in his ear, saying that she knew nothing of what had happened after she had left, and that she was only there in the first place to help a friend, something that anybody would have done. If he wanted to know owt else he should ask the Doctor. He hadn't wanted to go though, she'd had to tell him to piss off, leave her alone and then slammed the door on him before he had left. Wilmy knew that he would be back, she sensed it in him, he was young and keen and trying to prove himself. She knew what had to be done, she'd been thinking about it since the very day she brought the bairn home to Aggy.

Aggy changed breasts as Wilmy sat beside the fire watching her. He was a good bairn, thought Wilmy, he took his feeds well and was no real bother during the night. She looked at the little pink face suckling on the teet. Yer coming along alright, me lad, yer are that and yer've got all yer bits, but there's summit not just right with yer isn't there? The bairn's eyes that had been tight shut with contentment, opened wide. He shifted his gaze away from the breast and looked directly at Wilmy. She watched in amazement as he stared at her for several seconds. Yer imagining things, she told herself. How the hell could he be looking at yer when he's too young to see owt clearly yet? It was some time later as she was making the tea in the kitchen that she told herself, "If yer ganna do what yer ganna do, yer best get on with it, cause putting it off'll only make matters worse!"

Jimmy Corrigan, or James, as his Mother liked to call him, was finding it hard to settle into his new job. He had wanted to be a policeman for as long as he could remember, but when the war had come, he'd fully intended to join up. Neither he nor his family had ever suspected he was colour blind. He knew there were ways around this, if he'd really wanted to join up. But, he chose to stay and 'do his duty' in other ways less upsetting, less dangerous and more enjoyable ways.

Fred Sykes was the big stumbling block at the moment in what could have been a very nice way of life. It wasn't only that he was slow and wouldn't listen, but he treated him like a fool in front of people too. It was this attitude in part that had made young Jimmy determined to prove him wrong. In a way, Fred Sykes, with his slow steady ways would prove to be the greatest incentive that young Jimmy could have in his new-found career. In the meantime though, Jimmy was finding it difficult to get him to listen to him about anything. He'd been more than disappointed when he hadn't been able to speak of his findings at the recent Inquest into Bullum's death.

Fred Sykes was trying to be patient with the lad, but this was the fourth time in as many days that he'd come to him with some so called facts to the case. He decided to put a stop to it!

"Now look, lad, even if what yer saying is true, the Inquest is over. The case is closed. It's finished, right?" The lad looked down at his notes. Fred was starting to lose patience. "What makes you think that you know better than everybody else, better than people who've been doing their job for a sight longer than you? And I'm warning yer now if yer don't stop being a bother you'll cut yer own throat, yer will, cause whether yer believe it or not, yer gonna need these people in the future, yer gonna need their co-operation and help. This is a close-knit area. Aye, it's rough, but in the main, everybody helps everybody else. Yer know, 'honour among thieves' and all that. I'm telling yer if you go upsetting the applecart now, yer won't be long in the job." He paused and waited for some reply, and when none came he added angrily, "Not only will yer mess things up for yerself but you'll mess them up for me annaull. I won't allow that to happen, Jimmy! Do yer understand me? I SAID, DO YER UNDERSTAND?"

Jimmy mumbled "yes" swiftly, placed some papers on Fred's desk and left the room.

Jessy came down the stairs fully dressed. Ruthie had gone home to change. It had been Jessy who had insisted that she attend Bullum's funeral. Ruthie didn't understand, and said as much to Jessy. Jessy's reply of, "There's something I've got to do, Ruthie, and it's got to be done now and today at HIS funeral!" did nothing to ease her mind.

"Yer not gonna get yerself all upset again are yer, Jessy? Cause if that's the case I'll not be going, naw, not even to support yer. I don't even think you should go! But yer not gonna bloody well listen to me, I know that."

Jessy knew she was bluffing, that Ruthie would always be there for her. But she did her best to reassure her that she would not be getting upset. Ruthie didn't look totally convinced but she let it drop. She left with Hetty and Jean. Ralphy's Ma was going to keep an eye on them while Ralphy was doing the funeral.

Freddy looked shocked when his Ma come down the stairs. He'd been out on the 'money round' and he thought he would have some time to himself to count out what he'd got and look through his Da's book to see who else owed what.

"Go and get yerself washed and changed into yer Sunday best, our Freddy, and be quick." He looked at his Ma standing there in a black hat and coat. Before he could say owt she guessed his thoughts.

"Yes, yer right in what yer thinking. You're coming to the funeral with us. So gan on, get a move on."

He put his head down as he passed her, he couldn't look her in the face. He knew that she knew it was him who had given the letter to Bullum. He could have denied it, if she'd asked, but this was the first time he'd heard her speak since that night. Anyway, what was the point? Who else could have given him the letter?

Freddy sat next to Jessy with Ruthie on her other side. The vicar was droning on about this world and the next. Jessy heard very little. She was here for a purpose. The vicar eventually said, "Let us pray." This was what Jessy had been waiting for. She knelt without taking the prayer book that Ruthie offered and closed her eyes.

"Forgive me, God for what I've done. You've already taken so much away, and I know that I had something to do with it for lying to Georgie's Mam." She hesitated, trying to find the words. "But I'll tell yer what yer did was CRUEL, REAL CRUEL!" She felt the anger and the sadness well up in her, she tried to control it. "I want yer to know that I know what I did was wrong, that I broke yer commandments, but can this please be an end to it?" She swallowed and tried to moisten her throat. "I know that I still owe yer, for the murder of Bullum. And I wish I could tell yer that I'm sorry for what I did, cause I know that would sit better with yer. But if yer as all-seeing as they say yer are, you'd know I was lying! So I'll make a pact with yer!!! Do what yer want to me, send us to hell if yer like, take me life if yer want." She stopped to breath deeply. "But PLEASE, GOD, don't take it out on our Ray. Don't take me bairn away from us." She was struggling to keep from crying. "I can cope with anything, I know I can except THAT. I'll accept that I'll never see Georgie again, not even in the next life and I'll go to hell for killing Bullum if that's what yer want, but please just leave our Ray alone!" Ruthie and Freddy had stood to sing a hymn. Jessy gave one last plea

"PLEASE, GOD. I'll never ask for owt else. I promise."
"Amen"

It was over and done with, Bullum was buried. There'd been no tears, Jessy looked round as she left the churchyard. There were one or two people from the street that she recognized. Ruthie saw her looking. "No need to stay lass, to thank the likes of them for coming, they gan to anybody's funeral. It's not to pay their respects neither, like they would have yer believe. Naw, they're after a free meal. Well they'll be sadly disappointed this time won't they?" Ruthie took her arm and ushered her along. Freddy followed. Jessy slowed down and waited for him; when he was level with her, she took his hand in hers and carried on walking.

The lasses were pleased to see her when they got back to Ruthie's. Jessy thanked Ralphy's Ma for looking after them, then sat with one of them either side of her on the couch. Freddy stayed a while with them, then said he had to go. Before he left he kissed Jessy on the forehead saying, "Tah rah, Ma, I'll see yer along home. Don't worry about owt to eat, I'll get us something when I'm out."

Ruthie piped up with, "No need to bother. I'll make something for them all." He was waiting. Jessy knew what for. "I'm sure there'll be enough for yer if yer want to come back yerself, won't there, Ruthie?" Ruthie looked at Jessy when she asked the question and was about to say something when Freddy said cheerfully, "No need, I'll get summit while I'm out. But I'll get a few extras for us tomorrow then?" He was asking the question of Jessy. "Aye, that'll be a help, lad. Thanks." Then he was gone.

"What's got in to him?" asked Ruthie, taken aback by Freddy's change of attitude.

"I'm hoping he's sorry!" Jessy rose to give Ruthie a hand. "I'm hoping that taking him to church and seeing his Da buried might make him change his ways. Well, that and me taking more notice of him. I wish I'd listened to yer afore now on that one, Ruthie."

"Aye, well we'll see," said her sister as she poured the water into the pot. "I wouldn't go getting yer hopes up though."

There was a knock on Ruthie's back door. They both stopped what they were doing. "If that's some bugger expecting a cuppa and a bite to eat, cause of the funeral then they can think again." Ruthie stomped to the back door.

Jessy turned when she heard Ruthie say, "Come on in, Molly, she's just there."

Georgie's Mam stood in the doorway. She looked at Jessy and said gently, "Can I have a word wih you, lass?"

Jessy's heart went out to her, she'd lost so much weight and her face looked sunken and desperately sad. Jessy nodded. She didn't know what to do. Ruthie took hold of Molly's arm and led her to a chair saying, "Sit down, the kettle's just boiled."

As Molly sat so did Jessy. Ruthie poured the tea and handed the cups to them both. She left the room quietly and closed the door.

There was silence for a short while, then Molly took a deep breath and said, "I've just called to let yer know that we're moving. We're selling up and moving back to Darlington, where me family comes from. We both feel that we need to make a fresh start and..." Molly breathed deep again. "I want to be near me sister and brother. I just don't want to stay around here any more." Her voice had cracked, Jessy could see the tears in her eyes.

Jessy looked down at her hands in her lap, she didn't know what to say, she didn't even know if she could say anything, she was so full of pain. Molly took a sip of her tea and Jessy did the same. There was silence.

"I didn't know that yer had family over there. Georgie didn't ever say anything about his aunts and uncles or cousins." She could have bit her tongue off. Jessy looked away as Molly grabbed her hands.

"Aw, lass, that's one of the reasons I'm here," Molly was gripping Jessy's hands tight now, "tell us that I didn't stop yer. Tell us yer had a bit of time together. I used to get the feeling sometimes when he went out that he was seeing yer. Please tell us that yer had a bit of time together, that he had a bit of happiness. I cannot live with meself thinking that I'd spoiled his time that he had left!" Molly was crying openly now.

Jessy was desperate to comfort her, but she didn't know what or how much to tell her. She watched this woman, this mother try to pull herself together, try to stop crying and compose herself. She waited, now she was holding onto Molly's hands.

"Molly, if it helps yer to know, we had some time together. A few hours now and again." Jessy gave a wry smile. "Not as much as I would have liked, but some. When I made yer the promise, Molly, I meant it. I swear. But in the end I couldn't keep it." Jessy put both of Molly's hands together and held them tight. "I loved him, Molly, more than I can ever make yer know, there was nothing I could do about it!"

Molly took her hands from inside Jessy's, patting Jessy on the knee as she did so. She pulled a handkerchief from her coat, and wiped her eyes. She looked Jessy in the face as she said, "I'm glad, lass." She stood and as Jessy stood, she took her in her arms and said into her neck, "I'm sorry, Jessy, I was wrong." Molly put her handkerchief back in her pocket and headed for the door. Jessy followed. Molly turned back as she opened it to say, "We had a small service for him last week. I was going to send word to yer, but I'd heard yer were..." she struggled for the right word. "Indisposed. What with everything that was going on with yer." She hesitated before she said, ""I was sorry to hear about the bairn, yer've been through a lot, lass." She was waiting for a reply. Jessy couldn't speak, her throat had stopped working. She nodded and forced a croaky, "thanks." Molly kissed her on the cheek and whispered, "be brave, lass" and left.

Ruthie heard the door close. When she got to the kitchen, Jessy sat with her head on the table with her arms wrapped round it. She was sobbing uncontrolably. Ruthie stood next to her and lifted her arms and pulled her head into her belly. She stroked Jessy's head while she cried it out. The lasses came through to see what was the matter, but Ruthie sent them away. Jessy was calming a little when she lifted a tear-stained face to Ruthie and said, "This is the last time, Ruthie, the last time that I'll cry over Georgie, the last time that I'll think about Georgie. From now on I don't want to hear his name ever again." She put her head back to Ruthie's belly and was quiet now. "I can't, I can't think about him ever again. Not just for the hurt, Ruthie, but I made a deal with God and I've got to keep it!"

Ruthie didn't know what Jessy was going on about, she didn't ask, she just stroked her head until she calmed. It was enough for now.

From that day Jessy blocked her memories of Georgie from her mind. Oddly enough, nobody ever mentioned his name when she was around, not Ray nor Freddy and not Ruthie. There was always a part of her that felt a bit empty, but Jessy refused to ask the question as to why. She lived with the feeling until it became a natural part of her. She was as good as her word, she never thought about Georgie again.

UNTIL NOW.

Hetty and Jean sat downstairs listening to Jessy talk in her sleep. Jean asked, "Should I go and wake her?"

"Naw, leave her be. She can't sleep for much longer now anyway, the stuff the doctor gave her will be wearing off." Hetty had listened and it wasn't her Ma's normal ramblings, no it sounded to her as if she was having a conversation, answering and asking questions like. Hetty was in two minds to go up when Jean said the same as she was thinking. "She's talking more in her sleep than she does when she's awake, our Hetty." Hetty rose from the chair and had made up her mind to go up when there was a loud knock on the door!

CHAPTER FIFTEEN

The war had ended, and Ray had come home safe. The
Lord had kept his side of the pact with Jessy!
Wilmy was gone. She'd moved away with the bairn
and the lass. She'd got the note from her not long after Bullum
was put in the ground. Jessy remembered finding the note on
the floor of the lobby as she was going up to bed one night.
She supposed that Wilmy had left it for somebody to drop off.
Jessy sat down by the fire and read.

To my friend Jessy,
When you get this letter me and our Aggy will have took
the bairn and gone. We have to go cause our Aggy's fella is
a real badun. And he won't leave her in peace. It's time for
me to move on anyway, to have a more peaceful life meself.
Things have been getting too much for me these past few
years and the world is changing. I think yer should know
that the polliss had been back to me door twice now, it's the
young un that keeps coming. Don't worry, Jessy, I have told
him nowt. I owe yer one for saving us from Bullum's crutch
that day, so yer can count on me to take yer secret to the
grave. Afore I say "cheerio" to yer I want yer to know that
I'll miss yer. You have been a friend to me, and your lad,
Ray, like one of me own. In fact I think I feel more for you
and yer lad than I ever did me own. I shouldn't say it, but

it's true. Yer life will be a lot better now, lass, yer may not think it now, but at least yer'll not live in fear of yer life, or worse. from HIM. I've got to go now, Jessy, take care of yerself, lass. See Ya. WILMY.

Jessy folded the letter, took it upstairs with her and put it in the old tea caddy with the letters from Ray in her drawers. She felt sad and her heart felt heavy as she went to bed that night.

Jessy didn't know that Wilmy had pulled Freddy aside the same day. She wasn't gonna go and give that little bastard free reign. She'd called him into the house when she'd seen him come out of one of the houses in the cul de sac. Him and his cronies had come out all smiles. He'd turned to them and told them he'd see them later and reluctantly entered Wilmy's house. "Sit down, Freddy, can I get yer a cup of tea?"

Freddy puffed his chest out, and pulled down what looked like a new waistcoat over his rounded belly. "Aye, that will be very nice." he said in his posh business voice.

"Sit yerself down, lad, make yerself comfortable." She watched him sit, take a packet of tabs out of his coat pocket and light one. Wilmy approached him with the cup of tea, "Yer seem to be doing alright for yerself thse days, Freddy."

"Not bad. Aye canny. Just carrying on me Da's business that's all."

Wilmy was standing over him, he reached out to take the cup from her. Wilmy leaned over and poured it over his crotch. He jumped out of the chair screaming. Aggy came running in with the bairn. Freddy looked at her and shouted, "She's fucking MAD, she's just poured boiling tea over us." Wilmy turned to Aggy saying, "Gan back through with the bairn.

We've just had a little accident here, that's all," then turning to Freddy she said harshly, "Stop being such a cry baby, there was milk in it, and I cooled it with a bit of water annaull. Not such the big fella now are we?" Aggy smiled and left the room. Freddy was trying to hold his trousers away from his body. His face was blood red with rage when he turned to Wilmy and said, "You'll fucking pay for this yer will." Wilmy was angry now, he could see it in her face. He backed away from her, til there was no further to go. He was standing against the wall, she was real close, her face inches from him.

"I KNOW WHAT YER DID," she said it again, just as calmly, "do yer hear me? I KNOW WHAT YER DID." She turned away. Freddy's redness was replaced instantly with a grey colour. As she walked away she said casually, "And don't think yer can play the innocent with us, cause it won't wash." Freddy was sweating, still standing with his back against the wall. "I'll not keep yer long," she turned to face him, "I want nowt from yer, Freddy, so yer needn't worry about that, and it might ease yer mind to know that I'm leaving annaull." He still said nothing, but his shoulders had relaxed a bit. "No, I want nowt for meself, it's yer Ma I'm thinking about. So think on, Freddy, change yer ways, make that lass's life a bit more bearable, cause if I hear that you've caused her one bit of worry, and I will hear, yer know how much family I've got left round here! I'll not think twice about telling that young polliss some home truths, and who knows what he might find while he's looking into yer beating folks up for money. Aye he's keen that one, likely to blame yer for everything that goes on round here if he's given half the chance." She'd finished, he still said nothing. "Now get out! And think on, you're not the only one with spies. I'll be watching YOU, Freddy."

Freddy left, he was quivering inside with rage and frustration. She needn't have done that, she needn't have shamed us. Why now that me Da's dead I was gonna look after me Ma and the bairns anyway, and look after them I bloody well will. I AM A MAN NOW! Freddy walked home through the fields, he didn't want anyone to see the wet patch on his trousers. He kept saying to himself. I was gonna look after them anyway, I WAS. Cause that way me Ma will love ME!

He was almost home before the picture came into his head. The picture of Wilmy's lass and the bairn as they had ran into the room. He stopped walking, there was something at the back of his mind? A cold wind made the wet patch on his trousers even colder against him. He dismissed his thoughts and hurried home.

Jessy had a small widow's pension, money that was coming from Ray, and Freddy put some into the pot'. She'd never been so well off. She didn't have much to spare, but she could pay the rent and the bills and feed them all. In case of emergency she had the money that Freddy had gotten from Bullum's bureau. He had forced it open the day after Bullum's death, giving it to Ray for Jessy. Ray kept the Four pounds until Jessy was well. The peace of mind that this gave Jessy helped her a great deal.

Freddy had given up on the money lending business not long after the war ended. When the men came home there was no way that he could threaten the women and old uns anymore. He'd started doing odd jobs and ended up on a building site as a labourer. Everybody was amazed that he stuck it, cause it was hard dirty work, and bitterly cold in the winter. What they didn't know was that Freddy was never out much in the cold, and he didn't do that much work either! The Book that Freddy had hung onto had had stood him in good stead, especially with the Foreman of the building site, who was courting the daughter of the Builder. Freddy's job had appeared as if by magic when he had mentioned that the foreman's future Father in Law could mebbie pay him what was owed. With this first success at blackmail, Freddy had seen an easy future. Bullum's Book came in very handy over the years, not merely as a book of outstanding accounts, but as a means for Freddy to exert his need to control and feed his need for power. Although he never kept Jessy short of money, and as far as she knew he was working hard, his Ma never seemed to grow any more fond of him. He would boil inside sometimes, after watching the paltry amount of housekeeping that Ray would hand over to her. But looking at his Ma's face, yer'd think he'd given her the bloody world.

Ray had a job at the milk marketing board factory, and Hetty was working in a grocers in Durham. Jean was still at school and doing well, she'd passed her eleven plus, the first one in the family to have any kind of qualification. Jessy's life was good. In the main she was content with her lot. She never once let any light into that cold dark space in her stomach that she had closed off all those years ago.

It was 1950 and Freddys 21st birthday. He wanted a party. Jessy had said yes. After all, she thought, he works hard, he deserves to celebrate. Her and Ruthie had been baking for a couple of days now, ham and egg pie, sausage meat rolls, Madeira cake, egg custards, the lot. They stood back and looked at the assortment of food on the table in Ruthie's kitchen. "Why, that should do them," said Ruthie, "and that's without the stotty cakes yet!"

"Aye, we've done a grand job there, if I say so meself,"

replied Jessy, "I'll take what I can carry back with us now. Can you and Ralphy manage the rest when yer come or should I send one of the bairns to help?"

"Naw, we'll be fine. I won't be long anyway. I'll just have a bath and then I'll come along and help yer with the stotty cake sandwiches."

At the mention of the bath Jessy smiled and looked at Ruthie, "I could get in with yer again if yer want, give Ralphy summit to clean up again!"

They both started laughing. The joke was on Ralphy. He'd put a new-fangled INDOOR bath in for Ruthie a few weeks ago. It even had hot water to it, heated by the fire. The only problem was that it was so big that yer only got one bathful of water, then the water ran cold again. Jessy had come round to see it when it had first been put in. Ralphy proudly demonstrated his new purchase. It had pleased him to see how impressed Ruthie and Jessy had been, so when Ruthie said, "Get yerself away out then, our Ralphy, while me and our Jessy give it a try!" He'd laughed and left them alone to play. Jessy was surprised at the suggestion, but when she looked at Ruthie's face she knew that she was in a bloody mischevious mood and that she wouldn't take no for an answer. They both stripped down to their undergarments, the bath was still running. Ruthie felt it. "More cold." She turned the hot tap off and the cold tap on full. They both stood looking at each other. Ruthie felt it again. "Still more cold," she sighed with frustration.

Jessy asked, "Are yer going in in yer knickers?" Ruthie had removed her slip and bra. "Do yer want to?" had been Ruthie's reply as she felt the water again. This time she turned the tap off. She looked at Jessy and laughingly said, "Last one in's a lazy sod." She pulled her knickers down and kicked them off her feet, and jumped into the overly-full bath. Jessy stood for a second then she did the same. They were both laughing as she stepped in and flopped down into the lovely warm water. They swapped ends, washed each other's hair with Ruthie's scented soap, and were still carrying on like kids when they heard Ralphy outside the door. He hadn't been too happy, they'd made that much mess with the water that it was coming through the ceiling downstairs. He wasn't happy when he told them to, "Get out and get dressed" through the door.

He'd fixed it well enough, and he saw the funny side of it after a while, especially when he explained that he'd taken one of his Ma and Da's rooms to put the bath in, and that when the water came through, it was in his Ma and Da's bit of the house. His Da was sitting dozing in the chair at the time. When he woke up, he thought he had peed himself! They'd all laughed so much. Jean had asked nearly every night for a week for Jessy to tell her the story about the bath.

Jessy slipped her coat on and picked up the stacked plates that were wrapped in towels and tied with a knot for carrying. She was still giggling inside. Ruthie walked with her to the door, then touched her arm. "The worst of it all, our Jessy, was that there was no hot water left for Ralphy." They hugged each other and started laughing again. "He had to wait till the next day." Ruthie had the giggles, she only just got the words out. After a few seconds they calmed and broke apart. "See yer in a bit then," said Jessy. "Aye, see yer, yer never know, I might let Ralphy share me bath," she was still laughing. "Yer know, save on the hot water." Jessy turned back at the gate saying, "Aye, you do that lass, save a bit of water." Ruthie gave her a cheeky one-sided wink and waved.

Jessy never saw Ruthie alive again. Ruthie ran the bath,

not too full, slipped either getting in or out, banged her head on the cold metal side and drowned. Ralphy's Ma had found her son sitting on the floor banging the sides of the bath with his fists and head, screaming!

Ralphy's Ma and Da closed the business, just shut it down. Their time was spent looking after Ralphy, he never recovered. He blamed himself. In his mind he had bought the bath for Ruthie, therefore he had killed her! In his despair he would have killed himself to be with her, but Ralphy knew that it was a Mortal Sin and was petrified that he would never see her again.

Jessy visited him every week, she was the only one that he ever let in to see him. Jessy's own terrible grief was somehow pushed back into her when she looked at Ralphy. She couldn't think his name without quietly saying Ruthie's. If it was like this for her, how must it be for him? Ruthie and Ralphy, Ralphy and Ruthie. There couldn't be just ONE! Jessy knew that if they had been blessed with bairns Ralphy could mebbie have pulled himself through. Yer had to keep going for them. She thought of Hetty and Jean, how they too were hurtin. Aye, yer have to be strong for yer bairns, she thought, 'even when yer think yer can't go on. YER DO!

Even through all his pain, Ralphy knew that Jessy and the bairns would be hurtin annaull, He felt their hurt as well as his own but he couldn't bear to see the lasses! It reminded him too much of happy times. Ralphy knew that his Ruthie had been the mainstay in that family for a long time, often keeping their chins up when nobody else would have been able to. Aye, he knew they would feel her loss.

So Jessy and Ralphy would sit side by side quietly, never

saying very much. She would hold his hand and they would both remember the Light that had gone from their lives!

He died two years later without ever leaving the house again. HE WAS PLEASED TO GO!

CHAPTER SIXTEEN

The years passed. After Ruthie's death Jessy had coped better than anybody could have imagined. Aye, she was bad for the first few days, but once Ruthie was in the ground she seemed to come round. Ray had known her secret, and kept it with him his remaining years. At first he thought that she was just tired, that she needed to sleep or to be alone. She would look at the clock and go upstairs, the same time every night by herself, stay up for a couple of hours and then come back down. HAPPIER.

It took him a couple of weeks to understand that she was "visiting Ruthie." It was the same time that she would have put her coat on and gone along to see her, she would always be back around the same time annaull. Ray had chosen to sit with his Ma after Ruthie's death. It was on one of these occasions that he'd sat on the landing listening. He listened as his Ma laughed and joked, waited for a reply to her questions and answered the silent questions back. And so began a regime that was to last Jessy all her life. Over the years her family had become used to her nap time. At the beginning, when they had asked, "who the hell is she talking to?" Ray had always replied that she was talking in her sleep. That it was a comfort since Ruthie died, and he made light of it.

Jessy knew that Ray knew, but they only ever spoke of it once after Ralphy's death. Jessy had come down the stairs, made and handed a cup of tea to Ray and whispered, "Everything's alright now. Ruthie and Ralphy are back together!" He looked into her eyes that were filled with tears as she said, "He was so lonely." He stroked the cheek that was leaning in to him and said, "That's good, Ma." Jessy looked into Ray's eyes and knew he understood. He always had! Even from being a lad. For some reason when Jessy looked at Ray she had always known that she could GO ON.

For over twenty years Jessy spoke to Ruthie every day.

I am here again with you!

I, the Watcher now know and fully understand my purpose. As I look at Jessy on the bed, and feel all of her agonies, I know that she will soon be released and that I and the others who are now present will TAKE HER. We are all waiting for someone, just one more helper for Jessy. There's still things she needs to know before we can continue. The circle is not yet completed. BE PATIENT.

Hetty and Jean answered the door together. The old woman with the walking stick smiled and nodded first at one then the other. "You're Hetty and you're Jean. I'm right aren't I?"

Jean smiled and looked at the old woman. "Aye, that's right. How did yer know? Do yer know us from somewhere?"

Hetty was silent, she was looking at the face of the old woman. Jean turned to her, but before she could say anything, Hetty slowly said, "It's Wilmy isn't it?" Hetty knew, but Wilmy nodded.

"Well, are yer gonna let us in out of the cold, or are yer ganna stand there all night? I've sent the taxi away now, so yer'll have to let us in. I'm ganna pay me respects to yer Ma whether you like it or not."

Jean looked at Hetty as she took hold of Wilmy's arm to help her up the step.

"I can see you've not changed much," said Hetty. "Yer still as sharp as ever."

"Aye and I'm not past being able to give yer a clip around the ear still."

Hetty knew Wilmy was joking, but she turned to her and said, "Oh don't think I would put it past yer."

Once they were up the step, Wilmy brushed Hetty's hand away and walked with ease through to the living room. She looked around, "I take it she's upstairs? I'll away up. Yer can give us a hand if yer like!"

"Will yer not have a cup of tea while we tell her that yer here?" asked Jean. "She's sleeping, the Doctor gave her something."

"Naw, I'll be going straight up! She'll wake for me. But I'll mebbie have that cup of tea later." She turned to the stairs, "And I wouldn't mind a bite to eat if yer can manage it."

Hetty knew that there was no point in saying owt more, Wilmy would do as she said. She took hold of her arm again. When they got to the bottom of the stairs she noticed a faint light from the landing, but she turned the main light on anyway. She led Wilmy up the stairs. Halfway up, Wilmy turned to Jean who was behind and said, "Here, take this, it's only hindering us anyway," and passed the stick to her.

They stopped outside the door. It was silent. Hetty turned to Wilmy to ask her to wait til she went and woke her Ma. But Wilmy put her hand on the door handle, pushed it open and walked in. Jean rushed to put the light on.

Jessy was sitting up, wide awake. She was looking at the door, she put her arms out, Wilmy sat next to her and bent into Jessy's waiting arms. "Aw, Wilmy, I thought yer weren't coming," Jessy's voice broke and she was crying into Wilmy's shoulder. Hetty and Jean watched at the doorway as Wilmy shushed their Ma and patted her back. From between sobs Jessy said, "Yer will help us, Wilmy, won't yer? Yer will, eeh?"

"Why, lass why do yer think I'm here?" was Wilmy's reply. "I've never let yer down afore have I?"

Wilmy turned her head a little way towards Hetty and Jean. "Yer can leave us now, she'll be alright with me. I PROMISE yer." Hetty backed out, watching her Ma. As Jean went to close the door, Wilmy said, "Yer good lasses. Yer Ma's proud of yer both. I know she is."

Jessy looked at her girls, "Oh, I am that, Wilmy, I really am. I really love yer both annaull."

Hetty wanted to stay, to listen to them talk. Wilmy swiveled round in the chair, took a couple of steps and closed the door saying, "See yer in a bit."

As they were coming down the stairs, Jean turned to

Hetty, "Is that the Wilmy yer've told us about afore? The one that me Ma went to when me Da burnt her?"

"Aye, that's her. That's Wilmy!"

"But how old must she be? She looks as if she's in her bloody eighties."

Hetty paused to think, she was adding up in her head. "And the rest. Why, me Ma's gone seventy, and as far as I can remember, Wilmy was a good twenty years older than her."

Jean was wide-eyed as she said, "Never."

Hetty put the kettle on. Jean was buttering bread, ready to put a bit of ham on it for Wilmy.

"Do yer think we dare put the telly on for a bit?" Jean asked. Hetty had decided to use the best cups, with saucers. She laid them on a tray ready for the plate from Jean. "If yer want, it might cheer us up a bit, eeh?" She was relieved that they were talking about something normal. Yet Hetty felt uncomfortable for some reason.

"Aw, Wilmy, I'm that scared."

Jessy looked at Wilmy's face, she knew it was older and yet now that she looked at it close up, it looked, well, like it always had!

"I can't live without him, Wilmy, not without Ray." She brought her knees up, clutched her belly and rocked back and forth. "You know, don't yer? You know how special he was? Oh, Wilmy, I could have gone through anything, as long as I knew he was around." Jessy sank back on the bed, she was so very tired. "I can't live without him, Wilmy! I just can't." She shuddered looked down at her hands and said very quietly, "But I can't die neither, cause if I go to hell, I'll never see him again anyway." She turned to tell Wilmy about the pact. Before she could speak...

"There was no pact, lass, there was never any need for one." Jessy opened her mouth to explain. Wilmy stopped her by saying,"YOU never killed Bullum, Jessy. He was still alive after he went down the stairs."

"But how did..."

"Does it matter, lass? Does it really matter now?" Wilmy leaned forward and took Jessy's hand, she stroked the wrinkled scars. "You were never ganna go to hell, as you call it, Jessy, not you, lass. YER LIVED IT."

A dry harsh sob, was followed by a smile from Jessy. "Are yer sure, Wilmy, are yer really sure?" Wilmy smiled back and nodded. Jessy closed her eyes with the joy of relief. Her body felt lighter on the bed, her eyes didn't feel heavy anymore. Through her eyelids came a light, it was filling the whole of the darkness behind her closed eyes. Wilmy was still holding Jessy's hand as Jessy once again saw Bullum raise his crutch over Wilmy and the little bundle. She saw herself as she pushed Bullum, she saw him fall, she saw his eyes open, feet passing him. Then she saw Wilmy at the bottom of the stairs, with Bullum's hand around her leg. She looked through Wilmy's eyes at the bairn she was carrying as it opened its eyes! Jessy gasped at the realization then she understood immediately. She watched as Wilmy put the bairn to Aggy's breast, she saw Wilmy writing the letter to say goodbye. She clung tight to Wilmy's hand as the visions in her head moved on. She saw her son at different ages in his life, from a bairn to a Man. She felt the goodness of him, and the joy that he had in him, and was proud! She kept her eyes closed as she said, "Thank you, Wilmy. Thank you for saving him."

"Why, that's grand isn't it? There's Wilmy getting all the thanks again. There's a few more who wouldn't mind being thanked, yer know." The voice was jovial, Jessy knew it instantly. She opened her eyes to smile at Ruthie.

"Ruthie? I thought yer weren't coming to see us. I haven't seen yer for a few days now."

"I've been here all the time, Jessy." Ruthie was walking towards her. The light from the window was bright in Jessy's eyes, there were others there, other figures but Jessy couldn't make them out. A feeling of such happiness came over Jessy as Ruthie sat on the bed and touched her face. The light was warm on her face as Ruthie touched it, the pain she had felt left her completely, and the emptiness in her disappeared!

"I've missed yer Ruthie." Jessy was looking at every detail of Ruthie's bonny face.

"I din't know how, lass. Yer talked to us every day!" Ruthie was still the same, joking on with her sister.

"Aye, I know, but it never really seemed real. I liked to think it was, but a bit of us never really believed it."

"And now?"

Jessy breathed deep, took Ruthie's hand from her face and held it. "It must be real now, mustn't it? Cause I can feel yer now. I couldn't do that afore!"

Ruthie leaned towards her saying in a hushed voice. "It's as real as it gets, Jessy," then she cradled Jessy's head against her chest. They sat hugging each other until a man's voice gently said, "Hey leave some of that for me." Jessy watched Ralphy walk from the light over to Ruthie. Ruthie stood and took his offered hand. He looked at Ruthie with a face full of love, Jessy's heart was full. They stepped away from the bed still looking at each other.

Jessy turned to Wilmy, "Look, Wilmy, they're back together. Ralphy and Ruthie are together." As she said the words she KNEW.

JESSY KNEW SHE WAS DYING.

She wasn't frightened, she was just concerned about the others she was leaving behind. "What about me bairns, Wilmy, and what about Gloria and Ray's bairns? They'll need somebody now!" Wilmy nodded and passed Jessy a bit of scrunched up newspaper.

As the golden curl fell out onto the bed, Ray said, "And they'll always have somebody." She looked up and he was there. She didn't want to blink in case he went. She couldn't speak, she held out her arms wide beckoning him into them. When he did come and hold her tight, she smelt again the smell of him. Soap and tobacco. She breathed deep and held tight. She had her head nestled in the nape of his neck when he spoke. "The bairns aren't bairns anymore, Ma, they're grown up and married with families of their own. As for Gloria and my lasses, and me new grandbairn," he had spoken with pride, "they'll never be alone. We'll always be there to help if it's needed. In their own way they'll know, just like you did."

He took hold of her arms as he held her away from him, looked into her eyes. "It's time, Ma, yer've done your job here!" He gently pushed her back into the pillows, she closed her eyes. She took a deep breath and kept on breathing in.

Jessy could feel the air going through her body, touching and bringing to life her whole self. As if everything inside her was being washed, all the nasty dark places were being cleaned. She murmured, "I'm ready."

She felt the kiss, gentle and loving on her lips, at the same time that she felt the last knot in her belly open like petals on a flower. She kept her eyes closed as she heard him say, "Remember this?" The smell of scented soap came to her. She smiled and without opening her eyes said, "Oh, YES GEORGIE, I REMEMBER!"

Jessy could feel him lying next to her, feel his breath on the side of her face. She turned her head, lifted her hand and touched him. She stroked his face. It was smooth, no scars, no eye pulled down. "Let me see your eyes Jessy." His voice was still the same, still loving and gentle. Jessy had no fear of how she looked to him. She knew it was going to be alright. His eyes were inches from her own. When she opened them, she saw her hand on his face, it wasn't twisted anymore. Jessy looked into his eyes and saw what he was seeing. The young Jessy, the carefree girl she would have been without scars and wrinkles. Her eyes never left Georgie's as he brought his lips nearer, "I told yer I would always come back Jessy."

Jessy turned to look back, she was on the other side of the window now. She saw the old Jessy lying peaceful on the bed. Still smiling. Georgie put his arm around her waist. "Don't be sad, Jessy, there's a new world waiting for us, one where you'll be happy. You deserve to be happy, Jessy." Jessy turned her back on the room and faced forward. Ahead of her was Ralphy and Ruthie walking hand in hand, and there was her Ray with Wilmy on his arm. Up ahead of all of them was another figure, it was in the distance. Jessy strained to see it, as she watched, it was swallowed up by light, a light that kept getting brighter. The figure reappeared, it seemed to keep changing shape. Sometimes it looked like a young lad skipping ahead of them, the next moment it was a fully-grown man. He turned back as if to wait, smiled and waved. She returned the wonderful smile she had been given before recognizing the giver. She leaned into Georgie and started walking. Ruthie turned back and shouted, "Oh by the way, I had a word with Saint Peter and he says that yer don't need the wig, our Jessy." Her and Ralphy were laughing as she turned to Georgie.

"Don't worry, Georgie. I AM HAPPY."

Jean and Hetty had both fallen asleep. It had been a long day for them. The tea was stone cold and the sandwich was curling up. Hetty woke first and shook Jean. She's out for the count, thought Hetty as she shook her again. "Wake up, our Jean, yer've been asleep ages. The house felt different to Hetty. She would have let Jean sleep on, but she didn't feel like going upstairs to her Ma and Wilmy by herself.

Jean was groggy as she said, "Eeh, sorry our Hetty, I must have dropped off. Did yer manage to have a nap yerself?"

"Why I closed me eyes a couple of times that's all. We'd better go up and see what's gannin on. Wilmy's been up there a good while now."

It was quiet, the bedroom light was still on as they opened the door. But the chair where Wilmy was sitting was empty.

"Where's she gone?" asked Jean, looking around the empty room and pointing to the chair.

"She must have left. Mebbie she didn't want to wake us."

"So much for you not having a nap then, our Hetty," said Jean smiling.

Hetty wasn't smiling, she was looking down at her Mam on the bed. She knew before she touched her that she was dead.

Jean saw her face and gasped as she realized what Hetty knew. "Aw, NO. NO, OUR HETTY."

Hetty ran to hold her little sister. She folded her in her arms and let her cry. When Jean had calmed a bit, she looked past Hetty's shoulder and through broken sobs asked, "What's that on the bed?"

Hetty turned, walked over to the bed and picked up a bit of newspaper, underneath it was a lock of hair. She picked the orange curl up and put it in her palm. She remembered.

Hetty remembered how Wilmy had had to shave Ray's head when they were little. She remembered the balaclava' he'd worn, she saw his young battered face and knew.

"It's our Ray's," she spoke to Jean calmly, she was feeling calmer. "Wilmy probably brought it for her."

"But why would sh…"

"I think it means she's with our Ray." Hetty had walked back to Jean with the curl still on her palm. Jean looked at it. "It's bonny, isn't it Hetty?" Jean touched the curl in Hetty's hand.

Hetty replied with pride saying, "Oh aye, he always had bonny hair, our Ray," then she pushed her sadness away as she gently wrapped it in the paper.

"Go to the phone box and ring for the Doctor. I'll see to things here." Her head was in a spin and her heart was breaking as she remembered. "Oh yer better gan and get our Freddy annaull!"

"Are yer sure, our Hetty, yer don't mind being here by yerself?" Jean was concerned, she felt a bit uneasy herself.

"I'll be fine, now gan on, and be quick."

When Jean had left, Hetty sat in the chair Wilmy had been in. She looked around the room. One of her Ma's drawers was open. Hetty looked at her Ma. "What were yer looking for, Ma?"

She looked at the contented smile on Jessy's face and noticed a small bar of soap on the pillow next to her. She walked round the bed, bent to pick it up from the pillow. It was lying in a hollow, that's how she hadn't noticed it at first. The dent in the pillow was head-shaped. Hetty looked at her Ma, her face was turned towards the dented pillow. She picked the soap up, walked over to the open drawer, took out the open tea caddy and dropped it in. Hetty sat next to Jessy and took her hand. "Did he come and see yer, Ma?" She sighed for her own loss, put her head down on her Ma's hand. "I think yer happy now, Ma! I really think yer are!" then she cried.

Doctor David McFarlan sat watching the phone on the desk. He had on his top coat and his bag was by his side. He had sat like this for almost thirty minutes. He knew the exact moment that Jessy had died. HE FELT IT! He picked the phone up on the first ring. Jean confirmed what he had known. He stood holding his bag, breathed deeply and said to the darkened empty room, "If this is the GIFT, Gran, THEN I DON'T WANT IT!"

Wilmy continued walking and smiled. "Yer will one day, me bonny lad, one day soon yer will!"

EPILOGUE

Jimmy Corrigan had been moved to the new Police Headquarters at Aykley Heads in Durham. He was the new Chief Inspector. He stood looking out the window of his new office. He had had a very successful career. At forty nine he was one of the youngest Chief Inspectors in the country.

It was very late. He'd stayed back to get all his files sorted out, and settle into his new place. He was amazed at what he had collected over the years, how many hand-written notes he had taken. Not for official use, but for his own purposes. That's one of the reasons Jimmy had got on. He was thorough! That and the fact that Jimmy needed to be right. He would go to almost any lengths to prove a point. It had been Jimmy who had showed, by his own number of arrests, the importance of using informants. Squeelers, as they were called, had been a vital part of Jimmy's success. Even in the beginning, when he'd had to pay for information from his own pocket, he'd known in the long run it would pay out. At first it had only been one or two he used, but now he had a network of them out there. There wasn't much that went on in Durham that Jimmy Corrigan didn't know about! So why was he feeling like this? "This should be one of the best days of yer life, Jimmy me lad," he spoke out loud to an empty space, in the hope that the sound of his own voice would lighten the feeling of remorse that had come over him.

His thoughts went back once again to Ray Stevens, the

fella that Jimmy had persecuted for many a year had died today. He was the same age as me, thought Jimmy, and if truth be told, under different circumstances I could have probably liked him. He walked back to his desk and sat in the chair. Waves of guilt washed over him, he leant forward, put his elbows on the desk and rested his head on his hands. He remembered.

Freddy Stevens had been his very first squeeler. It had all come about not long after the Bullum Case. Jimmy remembered he hadn't been able to let go of the feeling that something more had happened in that house than they had been led to believe. Even after Fred Sykes had told him to leave well alone, he still continued visiting the family, "just to clear a few things up," was his explanation. When he got nowhere with any of the others, he turned his attentions to Freddy. He had pandered to Freddy's overblown ego and sense of self-importance, and more especially to his blatant greed.

It was Freddy who had told him of the whereabouts of everybody that night. He had left unanswered questions in Jimmy's mind. After the Coroner's findings there was NO case to answer, but that hadn't stopped him wondering. He realized now that he had taken it a bit too personal, he'd listened to Freddy over the years, not that he ever said anything specific, but now that Jimmy looked back, it was him that had definitly led him to believe that it was the lad, Ray, who had been responsible for the death. Since then he had given the lad hell. Freddy, his own brother, had shopped him at every opportunity. It was Jimmy who had reported Ray for claiming Social Security when he was out of work and doing jobs on the side. It was Freddy who had told him that his brother was selling copper piping to the scrap man from the same building site that he, Freddy, had just got him a job at. It hadn't stopped there either. Over the years Jimmy had questioned Ray's wife for 'weighing in' scrap, sent his own men round with the bailiff to evict the family from their home, and latterly tormented what was already a tortured mind about the accidental death of a bairn.

Jimmy didn't like Freddy, but he had used him! Until recently, that is. Over the years Freddy had provided Jimmy with information about many a scam that was going on in Durham. He always seemed to have his finger in some sort of pie. Even if some of his information had often been vague and unsubstantiated, there was always a kernal of truth in it! In his younger days this hadn't bothered Jimmy. He'd cut the cloth to make the coat! But times had moved on, and neither Freddy nor Jimmy saw much of each other now. Freddy was successful in his own right and Jimmy had avoided Freddy purposefully over the last few years. They'd both had bigger fish to fry.

Jimmy lifted his head and sighed, he couldn't shake off this feeling that was hanging over him. He tried to qualify his actions by picking up and reading again the dog-eared notes that lay on his desk from the Bullum case.

To this day he felt there was something wrong with the Coroner's findings. "How can death be instantaneous when HE was heard by the sister in law moaning after the so-called fall?" Jimmy was talking out loud, he did this when he needed to sort things out in his head. As he looked through the notes again, he re-lived his first week on the force "There had been a canny few who could have done it, they all had the time." He sat in his chair and turned on the desk lamp.

"And according to this, they all had motive as well, cause according to the talk at the time, this fella, Bullum, was a right cruel bastard. Aye, family's family after all!" He started jotting things down, it was like a puzzle to him.

"There was the sister in law. She admitted she was alone with the wife in the house for a while. Then there was the wife herself, how ill had she really been? The Doctor at the time wouldn't let him question her saying that she'd been through enough. Fred Sykes had agreed with him. But that still left the brother in law. According to Jimmy's notes, the brother in law came into the house when his wife was upstairs with her sister. Nobody saw what time he arrived, he would have had ample time to do something. Jimmy remembered the mark on Bullum's head. It had been brushed aside as a scuff from the fall but it didn't look like that to Jimmy.

He leafed through the notes again. "There was a woman called Wilmy, the Doctor had mentioned her. They'd all said that she'd gone afore the fall happened, but he'd never actually been able to make certain of that. He'd called on her a couple of times, and been sent away. She must have told Fred after that cause he was told to lay off her. Then she had moved out of the area anyway.

And of course there was Ray. Freddy had told him about the conversation that he'd had with Bullum, when he'd threatened to "swing for him." This had been confirmed by one of the fellas who'd helped him home with his Ma after she had passed out. Freddy told Jimmy of the bad feeling between Ray and Bullum of the beatings over the years, and how Ray had behaved when he found out that his Ma was pregnant again.

Jimmy stood up and walked back to the window. He knew there was still something he was missing. It had occurred to him over the years that Freddy could be setting the lad, Ray up. After all, what kind of brother would shop his own kin? But Freddy's alibi for the time of Bullum's death was the only one out of the whole of the family's that was iron cast. He had been sent away to the sister in law's just after the fall. Before that he was outside with his aunt and sister!

Jimmy shoved his hands into his trouser pockets and clenched his fists. He didn't like this feeling inside him, it stopped him from concentrating. There was something at the back of his mind, on the end of his tongue, but the more he concentrated, the further away it got.

"Yer a bleeding idiot, Jimmy Corrigan!" he shouted now to himself. "Doubting yerself. Yer know who killed Bullum. Yer know it was Ray! Why man, it's like that fucker Freddy said. HE had to pass the house to go for the Doctor. He would have had plenty of time to stop off and call in."

Jimmy took the old notes from his desk, scrunched them up in his hand and then threw them into the bin. He turned off the light and walked to the door. "Why yer had no proof then, and yer've definitely got none now, now that he's in the ground." He stood for a moment, letting the full moon light the room. "But I still say it was Ray! Aye, that's who I would have still fingered for it. RAY."

HE WOULD HAVE BEEN WRONG!

I am finished. I have done what I said I would do when we were first introduced: I HAVE stopped someone I love from hurting anymore! There will be still more trouble, and problems ahead for Jessy's family, but the role of Soul Watcher is no longer mine. It will be for others to try to guide Bullum's restless spirit away from those that remain. To protect them from HIS darkness that will affect and influence them all. But in order for that to happen, the whole story must be told! There is still much to tell!

For those of you who still disbelieve then think of this, we are often referred to as Guardian Angels. And one day you WILL believe in them! Trust Me!

My time is up, the Cathedral bells of my home, MY DURHAM are ringing.

My final word will be to the writer of this book.

THANK YOU.

Thomas.

AUTHOR BIO

J. A. Pettitt was born in 1955 to a proud but poor family in the North East of England. Leaving school with no qualifications the only option was to progress education through Evening Classes and over the years Economics, Marketing, and Law become chosen subjects. The avid reader of books from childhood never forgot the pleasure they had given. Particularly fond of the classics, this first novel uses that well founded knowledge in a down to earth way to achieve a book that should be an inspriration to readers everywhere.

ENDNOTES

[1] Smugly Happy
[2] Child
[3] A Toilet, usually outside
[4] As well or also
[5] A kitchen or work area
[6] Anything
[7] Nothing
[8] Large, flat bread buns
[9] Small bench around a fire used for sitting
[10] Prostitute